Love, War, and the Mess In Between

Love, War, and the Mess In Between

KIRI JANE ERB

Foreword by Andy Steiger

RESOURCE *Publications* · Eugene, Oregon

LOVE, WAR, AND THE MESS IN BETWEEN

Resource Publications
An Imprint of Wipf and Stock Publishers
199 W. 8th Ave., Suite 3
Eugene, OR 97401

www.wipfandstock.com

PAPERBACK ISBN: 979-8-3852-2812-6
HARDCOVER ISBN: 979-8-3852-2813-3
EBOOK ISBN: 979-8-3852-2814-0

VERSION NUMBER 12/29/25

In Memory of
Simon Richard Michael Morley
Forever Woven Into Our Lives

"What the world expects of Christians, is that Christians should speak out loud and clear ... and confront the blood-stained face that history has taken on today."

ALBERT CAMUS, "THE UNBELIEVER AND CHRISTIANS," 71.

Contents

Foreword

The human heart was built for story. Not all of us can recite Newton's Laws, do calculus, or explain how the stock market works. In fact, you'd be hard pressed to find any one piece of knowledge that's universal, except perhaps stories—Goldilocks and the Three Bears, Romeo and Juliet, Frodo's journey to Mount Doom. Stories are timeless. Different cultures around the world have their own versions, but the truth remains that something about stories resonate in the human heart. We cherish them. We remember them. We remake them over and over again in our novels and films and songs.

As a Christian, I believe the reason that stories move us so deeply is because they find their source in our Creator—the God who imagined the sun and moon and then made them so. The God of Christianity is a God who, in part, defines himself by his creativity. It follows that if we are made in his image, then our imaginations are neither silly indulgences to be tolerated or wild beasts to be tamed. In fact, Christianity itself is a story—the story of humanity's relationship with God, which finds its fulfillment in Jesus. When Jesus lived on the earth, he didn't teach his followers with dry lectures or lists of dos and don'ts. He told stories about farmers, or lost treasure, or wayward sons—all tales with truth at heart that tell us something deeply profound about who we are, what kind of world we live in, and the God who came to save it.

Story, like metaphor, has the ability to reach the depths of the human heart, even the hardest of hearts, like nothing else can. Yes, stories can be fun and entertaining, but the good ones are those that help us to see the world more clearly and live in it more fully.

The book you hold in your hand has the same mission: to tell a story that not only delights and entertains you but also startles you awake to the truth of the Christian worldview. All of the themes we love most in our stories are included: struggle and redemption, sacrifice and love, longing and hope. Amidst it all is an exploration of truth. When our wonder at the beauty of the gospel grows dim, may stories like this one, flowing from a redeemed imagination, cast a light all the brighter—allowing us to see afresh the true story that is behind every story.

Dr. Andy Steiger
President and Founder, Apologetics Canada

Acknowledgments

First and foremost, I wish to thank my family, especially my husband, Josh. We have had some incredibly busy seasons given all the responsibilities we hold, and yet he has not failed to encourage me in my dream to see this book become a reality. He has stepped into so many roles when I have not been able. Thank you for all your love and sacrifice. I could not think of a more incredible life partner with whom to share the adventure of life.

I am also abundantly thankfully to my three children, Caleb, Lydia, and Zoe, who have shown me endless patience and love throughout the writing of this book. I am so proud of the young people you are becoming. May you also follow the dreams that God has set in your hearts. I will always be your loudest cheerleader.

My mother, Valerie Jane Morley. I am so incredibly thankful for how you have believed in me in every season, even those in which I have put dreams and talents on ice. Your value for education has had an incredible impact on my life, and I am truly so proud to call you my mum.

Thank you also to Jennie and Peter Murray. They have literally moved countries to help support my family. I can never repay you, but I hope that you know there will be no end to my gratefulness. Thank you both for believing in this project and the mission of Jesus in the world. You both pour out your lives so selflessly. I am in awe.

Thank you also to the village that has rallied around our children during this time. I think especially of Sydni Cankovic, for all the times you have loved on Zoe as your own. The Smit family, for your endless support. The Middletons, who we love dearly, and the Galloway family, for inviting our girls on so many incredible adventures! These last years have been so much richer for you all being in them and supporting us as a family.

I must also recognize my dear friend, Maria Enns, forever the first person to get an early draft of this project. It was incredibly raw, and yet you still encouraged me. Thank you! The book-themed baby shower when I had Zoe so many years ago is also one of my most treasured memories.

Thank you also to our church families present and past: Northgate Church and Crossroads Church. Thank you also to the Phil and Jennie Gaglardi Academy for cheering me on!

A special note of thanks also to Soul Edge Ministries and Apologetics Canada. What a joy it is to run alongside like-minded men and women who feel like family. Thank you, Andy, Nancy, and team, for your encouragement and for sowing into this project so selflessly.

I am also very grateful to my editors, Michael Martin and Joy Tansky, who have both engaged with different elements of this book. Michael showed excellent attention to detail and helped move the project forward at an important time. I am also deeply grateful to Joy Tansky for her sharp eye as this project neared completion. I don't know if I could have done it without you! I will forever be thankful for your willingness to give your time, energy, and expertise. You are truly brilliant.

To all who offered their time, knowledge, and kindness along the way—your presence has made this work possible. This includes Dr. Michael Burdett whom I credit for making me a better scholar and Dr. Stephen Backhouse for his encouragement.

I especially want to thank those who have read or reviewed different parts of this book. This has included: Dr. Max Baker-Hytch (Oxford University), Dr. Andy Steiger (Apologetics Canada), Dr. Logan Gates (Toronto University), Dr. Michael Butler (astrophysicist), Dr. Joel Hampkins (O'Hara Professor of Logic, University of Notre Dame), and PhD(c) Steve Kim. Also, Matthew Kinnemore, Pete Murray, Rachel Braun, and Loraine Baluyut. Please note that any and all errors are entirely my own.

Thank you also to the excellent scholarship of those I have mentioned in the book. These include the incredible Dr. Kate Kirkpatrick, whose reading of Sartre and his relationship with theology has deeply informed my approach in this book and my personal understanding. Also, Dr. Lexi Eikelboom, whose work on rhythm and theology has been particularly formative for my work. Likewise, thank you to Dr. Preston Hill, whose friendship is a joy. Preston, your vision, bravery, expertise, and dedication are changing the world. And last but not least, Dr. John Milbank. Your scholarship and leadership have impacted many, including me. It was an honour to study in the program you founded at the University of Nottingham.

I would also like to thank the whole team at the Oxford Center for Christian Apologetics (OCCA) for your support, including Rahil Patel, who has gone above and beyond. Thank you also to Dr. John Lennox, President of OCCA, for your kindness and friendship.

A special note of thanks to David Goa and the St. Macrina Centre. Each and every generous conversation deeply enriches both my thought and life.

A final thank you to the entire Wipf and Stock team, especially Matthew Wimer, for making this book possible.

I am truly humbled by the team that has supported this journey. I could not have made it alone.

Introduction

Partnering with Jesus to fold love and life into the world is a core idea in this book. In fact, it was written in and through this partnership. While I may not be an artist like many in my family—my mother is a landscape designer, my father was a graphic designer, and my sister, Jennie, is a very skilled industrial designer and artist—it was a creative act of worship. Worship with words, weaving threads of ideas together into an interlocking tapestry.

With a BA in politics and international relations, a master's in systematic and philosophical theology, a healthy appetite for historical fiction, and an existential itch, this was always going to be the book I was going to write. Thoroughly multidisciplinary and raw.

There were many moments when I wondered if completing this project was possible. However, I knew I had a message to share. And that message? Why Jesus is essential in a dead and dying world and why we ignore this at our peril.

It is not to be read as an essay but as a companion for thought. To inform or sharpen your response, to journey with, and to inspire further exploration of truth.

MY GOALS WERE TWOFOLD

A Bridge

This book is a gift to the thinking person who wants more to bite into and relishes the idea of a little "world-building" or fiction at the same time. Someone who knows some basic philosophy or theology but isn't quite ready to be set adrift, alone in a sea of academic texts. Or who is ready but wants to join the adventure and see how this unfolds.

It is my hope that this book may help propel others, either already passionate about Jesus or yet to discover him, further ahead in their thought so that they may feel more confident and better equipped in using their own gifts and talents to reach others. I have attempted to connect dots between big themes to offer something of a scaffold.

A quick note on form. It is my contention that theology makes most sense—and should be—embodied. After all, Jesus took on flesh. World War Two historical fiction enabled me to do this, whilst also weaving in atheist, agnostic, and Christian thinkers of that time, to enrich and pull out certain threads of philosophical and theological debate. However, this form also comes with certain restrictions, such as how much one can say within a dialogue. One cannot give an entirely linear presentation of all the facts. Likewise, to keep the book at a reasonable size, I have also had to cut or truncate certain topics, for example, Nietzsche's later interest in the crucified Christ. However, since more detailed engagements are available elsewhere, given the goal of bridge-building and making introductions, the benefits may outweigh the costs.

An Apologetic

I don't believe that apologetics often brings people to faith. But I value it because objections to faith can get lodged within us. It is hard to fully appreciate the Gospel or respond to it when there are big, often raw and honest questions standing in the way. For this reason, some common objections are shared by my characters. These were responded to, in part, as the story allowed. This book may also be seen as one big apologetic regarding the gift of God's life to the world.

If you do not like spoilers, perhaps read this next section later. However, for those of you ready to learn more, it may be helpful to know the basic outline of the three acts in terms of theological engagement.

Act One—The Anxiety

1) Through Peter's wrestle in Act One, my goal was to lay foundations and introduce readers to some key philosophical figures that will pop up again later in the book.

To prevent any misconceptions at this foundational level, it is worth pointing out that in Peter's initial conversation with Edwin, sin is not disregarded as insignificant. Instead, the argument is that while sin further disconnects us from relationship with God, others, and ourselves, shame is especially interesting in that it may reveal a more primary ontological disconnection between humanity and God (that in turn informs the "sin-nature"). This opens up the idea of existential anxiety and how it manifests in our lives. The aforementioned philosophical figures—including the atheist Jean-Paul Sartre—come in here. The isolation and alienation of human life sketched by Sartre is compared to the Christian perspective as shared by his friend, Gabriel Marcel, which identifies a similar starting place but genuine hope for love and connection. In a sense: a different mode of being in and through the gift of God's/Jesus's life.

While at first glance this debate may seem a little obscure, if Pope John Paul II (Karol Wojtyła) was to be believed, it was, and perhaps remains, "the central problem of our age."[1] After all, what we believe about human and communal life will impact how we choose to live and whether we become the living or (in a sense) the atomized, isolated, living dead.

At the end of Act One, in 1992, Peter is about to embark on a communal project that hopes to offer an alternative to capitalist consumption, promising to be an almost edenic way of life. There is some tension among its leaders about whether this community can be (eclectically) spiritually engaged or not; however, "God" is parked outside its gates.

Act 2—The Rubicon

This community in the Vosges Mountains takes on the name *Le Rubicon*. Lots happens here . . . and the honeymoon doesn't last long. During this time, Peter is looking for foundations to rebuild his life upon. This isn't as clean and clear cut as he would like it to be. Even his beloved mathematics seems to let him down.

Peter considers the structure of reality, whether this is actually conducive to human flourishing, and learns firsthand of the dangers of trying to enforce one's own ideas of heaven on earth.

1. Wojtyła, "Participation or Alienation?," 72.

Act 3—The In Between

This final act does not shy away from engaging the problem of evil head-on. This is the most theologically constructive section. It traces a path engaging concepts such as *privatio boni* and thinkers as diverse as Albert Camus (who is woven throughout the book), Jürgen Moltmann, and N. T. Wright. Given the format of the book, this engagement (like the rest) is not presented as a water-tight essay. However, it paints a picture of a world stuck in the mess in between: in the church age, an age where Jesus has resurrected and ascended, and yet we are still awaiting his return and the new heaven and earth. In this vein, this act builds on the foundations already established to suggest ways of thinking and living in this tension. There are no easy answers. Perhaps, as I argue, easy answers should be refused. However, that does not mean there is no hope. A hope that shines brighter in the darkness.

Having written my master's dissertation on the intersection of time, trauma, and theology, a note here is valuable. As someone who has experienced significant trauma, and having studied it on an academic level, I felt it remit for Alexi, one of my characters—who would also have walked through trauma—not to have questions and thoughts about it. While the field of trauma theology is still in its infancy, I find it remarkable how many of its core ideas further highlight the way in which the gospel is practically relevant to the experiences of human life.

Please note that I am not interested in asserting an unthoughtful victory narrative, to demand or expect recovery from those suffering. After all, as theologian Shelley Rambo insists, the hands of the resurrected Jesus still contain wounds.[2] However, as psychiatrist Judith Herman demonstrates in her landmark book, *Trauma and Recovery* (1995), looking at recovery for those with PTSD (post-traumatic stress disorder), individuals desire for the suffering to end, meaning that the concept of recovery (or healing) is meaningful.[3]

In *New Studies in Trauma and Theology*, series editors Cockayne, Harrower, and Hill develop the concept of "double witness," which argues that one must absolutely i) give witness to pain, but that it is also possible to ii) bear witness to the hope of Jesus. In this way, the depths of Holy Saturday—the liminal intermezzo of pain—might be met in a dignifying

---

2 Rambo, *Spirit and Trauma*, 57; Rambo, *Resurrecting Wounds*.

3 Herman, *Trauma and Recovery*.

way by the "dawn" of Holy Sunday—allowing one to move towards resurrection.[4] It is in this spirit that I have addressed this topic.

FINAL THOUGHTS

We all know the pain of searing loss. Of heartache. Of asking, How is it possible to live in a world where the absurd, the awful, and the irrational are possible? It is for these reasons that this book exists. Of course, getting rid of God would be easier. But what would that solve? All it does is impoverish our ability to consider the traction that the gospel has on human life. And, if I am honest, only the gospel does justice to both the pain and the path forward.

A BLESSING

May your heart and mind be encouraged as you trace the contours of this story.

God Bless,
Kiri Jane Erb

4 Cockayne, *Dawn of Sunday*, x, 7–8.

ACT ONE

The Anxiety

1

WW2

The Opera

GERMANY

Friday, August 14th, 1942. Bayreuth, Bavaria.

The Second World War wasn't all genocide, then, of course, a word yet to be birthed in the wake of so much death. By 1942, its dominion had already been building for three cavernous years, with a taproot running deep inside many more. Empty and dark, like a rotating storm cloud, it forced its way to new atmospheric heights, compounding to ingest life, hopes, and dreams at an insatiable speed. Erratically illuminating this cloud were flashing jolts of lightning, charged by rancid, plague-like concepts. This was the nerve center of the whole thing: a worldview parasitic upon the fertile ground of pain and hatred. But no, the Second World War was not all genocide; for some, it was punctuated with parties, pomp, and lavish operatics.

In Bayreuth the same year, like many times before, heavy theater curtains pulled back like an iris contracting to reveal the rich vignettes of nineteenth-century composer Richard Wagner's tragic opera. This was his epic three-day, four-opera Ring Cycle, *Der Ring des Nibelungen*, the height of excess and opulence. This opera was structured, not by chance, much like the Dionysia, an ancient Greek festival held in honor of the wild god whom even the Greeks would not claim, alleging that he was "from the East." His name was Dionysus. He was, for the Greeks, somewhat akin to Loki in Norse mythology: a violent trickster bringing bloodshed with a smile. He encapsulated reversal, revenge, and tragedy. Ensconced at the foot of the Athenian Acropolis, yearly this Greek festival would celebrate and, perhaps, appease Dionysus with competing performances in a bull-blood cleansed theater. But while sacrifices were made, could you ever really trust Dionysus to uphold his part of the bargain?

Ministering to the repressed uncertainty in the summer of 1942, just days before the slaughter of Allied forces at Dieppe, the upper echelon of the Third Reich gave themselves to this rich experience, hoping to be molded and attuned by it. Punchy, brass-heavy music rose as if to defeat gravity, riding upon a cavalry of dashing strings sent forth from a secret place deep beneath the stage. It intoxicated them like a vapor spilling out from the *Mystischer Abgrund*, the "Mystical Abyss" between the stage and the audience. Here, even the conductor seemed caught up in a trance, at times almost levitating above the curious Victorian-era dining room chair on stilts that clung tenaciously to where Wagner had positioned it more than half a century before.

In the late 1800s, Wagner had wanted his fully immersive theater to change the world, to see German culture reborn with Siegfriedian bravery, but even his genius could not have predicted its historical entanglement with that of the Third Reich.

Adolf Hitler first encountered Wagner's genius at just twelve years of age by watching *Lohengrin*. But it was later—in the 1920s, almost forty years after Wagner's death—when Hitler began visiting Wagner's family here in Bayreuth. Soon after, while in prison following his role in a failed coup attempt, it is thought that Hitler may have dictated *Mein Kampf* upon the stationary given to him by the dynasty heiress, Winifred Wagner.

Moving into the 1930s, akin to Paris, dizzied by its "Crazy Years"— thick with smoke, coffee, and the full fragrance of jazz dives spilling into the cobbled streets—Germany reached for comparably fleshy indulgences in an attempt to placate its wounded soul. However, even in its Weimar Republic incarnation, folly and distraction could not heal the pain and humiliation of the defeat of Germany in the Great War. Nor could it feed the hungry. Hitler cultivated this unrest, bristling with promises and charisma. Soon, his appearances began to upstage the famous actors at Bayreuth. Then, when Hitler's celebration of his 1933 rise to power as chancellor of Germany also coincided with the fiftieth anniversary of

Richard Wagner's death, the two became united, with the theme of that year's Bayreuth Festival becoming "Wagner and the New Germany."

The music congealed into a stirring, hearty meal, infused with the impassioned vocals of opera singers against stimulating, dark dramatic visuals. Greed and vengeance trigger it all, with a labyrinthian tale spun first around an accursed ring. This ring was forged by a greedy dwarf, Alberich, who had stolen magical Rhine gold from the Rhinemaidens. Alberich renounced love in order to gain the ring's power. However, when Wotan, King of the Gods, stole this ring from Alberich to pay a debt, the dwarf cursed it so that those who do not have it covet it, and those who do live in fear of being killed for it. From here, the threads of this epic tale unwind, daring to ask the question: which is greater, the power of love or the love of power?

Many young men think they know a lot about love, but having already lived the full arc of a passionate love through to its heart-wrenching end, one young Frenchman in the dimly lit theater, Matthias, knew more than most. His palms were sweating. So, too, was his brow, which he had wiped with his handkerchief so many times over the last few days that one might have thought he had caused his birthmark. The plan had all worked remarkably well, perhaps too well, leading him into the belly of the beast. Matthias's papers were authentic—he had to press for them, of course, calling in favors when this opportunity had arisen—but the Vichy Ministry of Culture, where he worked, had come through. The ministry was, after all, eager to reaffirm their alignment amid the complex dynamics of collaboration against considerable speculation and concern that the southern Free Zone of France may also be occupied soon. Since a representative had been asked for, how could the ministry say no? Sending him would be a fresh gesture of cultural diplomacy towards their occupiers, who remained eager to tell a story of their cultural revitalization of Paris.

Since Matthias, in his late twenties, was representing the ministry, they had even given him an impeccable uniform to wear. It included a crisp starched collar and kepi hat boldly emblazoned with a bright *tricolore* double-faced axe badge, the collaborationist *francisque*. He looked the part, but this made him feel even more like an imposter. Surely, the Nazi officers around him would still be able to sniff out his real intentions. Matthias had quickly learned that while they seemed to have a supernatural ability to pinpoint a threat in the unseen with the efficiency of a bomb disposal expert, they extracted it with all the delicacy of a butcher.

Time, it seemed, seeped differently through the confines of hours and days during the Ring Cycle. The adrenaline-inducing "Ride of the Valkyries" didn't do anything for his nerves. "*Pas maintenant!*" he kept telling himself, "Hold off!" As often as he failed to hold it together, his eyes dashed right to a certain SS senior leader, Oberführer Schulze, seated five rows in front of him. It had to be him, based on the silver, double-oak leaves on his collar, the bragging scar on his left cheek, and a nose that had been broken without affording any thought as to how it should have been reset. Suddenly, the back of the Frenchman's hand gained a sharp stabbing pain. It was her—his companion—digging her nails into his skin while somehow maintaining her docile look and decorum. He knew what she meant: "Stop! Control yourself."

The uncomfortable seats meant constant pressure, causing the Frenchman's hip bones to cut painfully into his buttocks. Moving just spread the pain. Yet, the rest of the audience seemed enamored. Like all of Europe he had, at least, already heard of the magnificent heldentenor, Max Lorenz. A giant of a man, Lorenz—half-dressed in leather with weapons and shield—took a leonine pounce upon the stage. He owned each note, rolling his *r*'s with zeal and skillfully opening his throat with spectacular ease. Truly resplendent, the tenor embodied Siegfried, a mythic role whose genesis harks back centuries deep within Nordic and Germanic folklore. Now, Siegfried had been forever reset in this: Wagner's all-encompassing vision feast for the heart and spirit, a total work of art he called *Gesamtkunstwerk*, hoping to resurrect the art of Greek tragedy with all its amoral human contortions of trials and passion. Siegfried's Wagnerian reincarnation cemented him as the heroic idol in the hearts of the German people.

And yet, even Lorenz, "Hitler's Siegfried," was not safe. Hitler's word, it seemed, was as fickle as that of the scheming Greek god Dionysus. You see, Lorenz also knew a lot about love. Soon enough, in the spring of 1943, his wife and his mother-in-law, both Jewesses, would be home alone when the SS burst in to take them away. While they narrowly escaped by calling desperately for aid from a bedroom phone, that was outrageously close for Lorenz.[1]

1. The SS were ordered to leave after the sister of Hermann Göring was called. After this, Göring stated in a letter, dated March 21st, 1943, that Lorenz and his family were now under his personal protection. See the documentary by Schulz and Wischmann,

Matthias could have told Lorenz that no one was safe, for his wife had not been so lucky. When he closed his eyes, all he could see was his attempt to run to her, as if through treacle, always too late. He found her body in the Grand Bassin Rond, a fountain that, in times of peace, would be home to toy boats and smiles, flanked by the majesty of the Louvre. But just as the Louvre had been emptied of its greatest treasures, so too, daily life had been impoverished, seemingly emptied of all the spirit that made men humane.

She was found face-down, floating. Matthias jumped right in. The water? Inconsequential, were it not for being her grave. Before he embraced her cold body, the wind had been pushing her along by inflating her skirt like a sail. Everyone, for fear, had left her there, afraid that they, too, would be accused of being part of *La Résistance*. But Matthias? He cradled her, rocking her, her lips blue and lifeless. How long do you hold your beloved? Whatever the answer, it would never have been enough.

Matthias sat uncomfortably in his uniform, struggling to swallow down the foul-tasting spittle—having absorbed the abhorrent residue leaching from his painful memories. Restraining himself, surrounded by the enemy and dressed like a traitor, he felt forcibly folded into history, slowly suffocating there. Some might say that France, too, had been forced into the straitjacket of history. You see, France officially folded her hand and collaborated with the Nazis back in 1940. But, despite France being impaled by the lightning-fast Blitzkrieg culminating in Dunkirk and cultural humiliation, like Charles de Gaulle—the French voice of leadership on the radio from London—Matthias knew they could do more. And he wasn't alone.

Matthias had restrained himself as best he could. Waiting. Recoiling. What were a few more moments after so long? As the climax began—*The Twilight of the Gods*—a captivating duet gripped the audience, and the Oberführer left his seat without company. Matthias couldn't lose this chance. He coughed into his moist handkerchief and took to his feet. As he began to rise, the woman beside him rose also, leaning over as if whispering something sweet but instead issued a demand: "Let me lead." She followed it up with a smile for others to see, framed by her curls. He didn't want to cause a scene. His eyes darted in thought, recalculating. Whether she liked it or not, he'd need to escort her partway.

§

Max Lorenz, especially minutes 36-38.

She was dressed in the German style of the season, the sheer ends of her dress, catching the currents of air behind her, billowed with grace. She knew she could execute the mission better than Matthias. The moment the door closed on the auditorium, the sound was muffled, but it still held power: a hegemonic, dominating presence. The orchestra shifted also, into playing a different refrain, more jagged and dissonant. It seemed to abet her to look, subtly, into adjoining rooms as if she too was weaving through a forested epic complete with Greco-Roman allusion, dragons, inhabitants of Valhalla with winged helmets. Her soul flickered with pride and promise as if anointed, perhaps, by Brünnhilde, the powerful princess Valkyrie.

When at last she found the Oberführer, she could also feel the eyes of others upon them. This forced her to approach for what felt like an eternity, as if simply enjoying the impassioned throes of the music. It lapped over them: the inbound rub consoling her heart that this would all be worth it, while its retreat left wounds naked and raw. Finally, she followed him into a distant room as the timpani and cymbals rang out, mercifully masking her heartbeat.

It was dark. Too dark. Then? Confusion. In an instant, her hand jolted from hovering just above her side to behind her back. He held it there painfully. A thin crack of light shone deep into the room. It found the silver imperial eagle with the swastika and wreath in its talons atop the skull and crossbones on the Oberführer's peaked cap. She wouldn't be foolish enough to scream.

"Good," he said, without loosening his grip. But just as he did, she broke out of the lock by forcing her elbows out towards him with all her might. She gained a breadth of distance large enough to grab his revolver. Somehow, she placed it on the Oberführer's temple. The muzzle of the gun, crude and uncannily simple, bore just a hint of warmth. It disconcerted her how, in this frozen state, she could feel the suppleness of his skin beneath it. In this new position, the slice of light fell upon them afresh. In it, he could see the small hollow at the base of her neck rise and fall in pace with her racing heart.

As if this had all been nothing, he closed the door with his right hand. "Put that thing down," he said condescendingly, refusing even to raise his voice.

"Excuse me?" she replied.

He flicked on a light, revealing a distinguished and decadent room. "You do have some fight in you. I hope you forgive me for thinking otherwise."

She could now see him properly. Animated and close; so close she could see in detail how exactly the scar on his cheek had healed over. She lowered the gun slowly. After watching him for days she had wondered what this moment would be like. "Tilapia," she said, finally offering the code word.

"Yes. I know who you are. Who else would have been burning a hole in my neck for days straight? It was good that you came without that liability. He's going to get you killed." She didn't know how to respond. He continued, "Can I have that back, Fräulein?"

"Yes," she said, embarrassed when she fumbled it slightly. "So you know—"

"Yes," he said firmly, breaking her off.

"And you—?"

"Yes, of course, Violet," he added with a smile as he readjusted his lapel. Her name sounded different in his mouth. A chill ran down her spine. The Oberführer continued, "I wouldn't have lived this long if I didn't know everything about you—and everything else that matters— would I?"

Violet wasn't sure whether this made her feel safe or much, much more vulnerable. She also realized that the Oberführer hadn't tried to fight, having chosen to play instead. Clearly, her apprehending the gun was merely an amusement to him.

Her eyes couldn't help but dart between the familiar red, white, and black swastika. She sought, quickly, to steal what understanding she could. At some point the Oberführer had turned to help the *Résistance*. But no one could tell her why. Everything about him was crisp and meticulous, an air of having it all together. There was nothing to arouse suspicion. After a few long moments, he said firmly, "I am sorry to disappoint you, but I have no use for you," his vivid blue eyes seeming to revert to a steel-gray stare. He turned to go.

"No. No!" Violet said, before realizing that she had raised her voice. She immediately regretted this knee-jerk reaction.

"No?!" He turned back in an instant, infuriated. "Your little group of academics in Paris think that I should risk my life, and everything that depends on me, to let you play *Résistant*?"

"But they said that if we met you here, you would—"

"What? Gamble on a girl and her sweaty friend?"

"Then why did you approve the paperwork? We may not have—"

He cut her off again with his arrogance: "You've not even killed a man, have you?"

"Let me finish!" she protested, raising her hand to his face to speak directly, eye to eye. He was not accustomed to this directness from a woman, nor many men, given their fear of him. "No. I have not killed a man," she said, "but men have killed many members of my family, and that means I, we, would do anything."

"Compose yourself," the Oberführer replied. "You're not the only one who has lost family. It doesn't mean you are . . . capable."

The time that he took to choose that specific word angered her. She had never been anything but capable. That's why it stung that she wasn't around when they came for her husband at the museum. And now? Now she felt stripped down in his eyes to nothing more than a little girl! "Anything I need to learn, I will. And Matthias? He has information. In his position, he can pull strings—strings that are on his desk every day. They trust him. Why can't you?"

"Paris is a hotbed for your kind. I can't risk it. You'll all hang, or worse. Before the week is up, one of you will crack and jeopardize us all."

"It doesn't have to be Paris. I am tough! I can go anywhere – even lead airmen over the mountains."

"Are you?"

She replied sternly, "Look. You underestimate me, but they would too. I grew up as the only daughter with six brothers. We spent our childhood living in the mountains, living off the land, and learning them as they etched into the fibers of our hearts. The Vosges are—"

"The Vosges Mountains, you say?" Schultz's posture suddenly changed. His eyes somehow softened from a steel-gray to vibrant blue. He leaned in, "I may have use of you. But you wait. Do nothing differently until you hear from me. Nothing. Walk the same way, talk the same way. Or we will kill you ourselves." Violet listened, swallowing in agreement. He tapped her chest, distinctly, above her heart three times, slowly as he thought. "You take everything unto death. It is that simple." She nodded, scared to breathe lest her chest rise and push back, even in the slightest way, against his fingers.

"Here," Oberführer Schultz said, "you might need this." He passed her a cigarette box with a false bottom in it and a pill—unequivocally cyanide. "Oh, and one other thing: wear less makeup. The *Führer* dislikes it, and you're already too pretty to go unnoticed. You have to blend in. Be plain—as plain as you can. Don't make me regret trusting you, Violet."

The Oberführer slipped out, leaving the young Frenchwoman shell-shocked. Disorientated in relief, she foolishly didn't leave enough time before slipping out of the door. It closed again much sooner than expected. The Oberführer turned instantly. Even worse, there was an immediate reckoning. She locked eyes with an army captain right across the hallway. It figured; the place was crawling with them. While the Oberführer couldn't openly scold her, Violet braced for the utter disappointment that she would feel from his eyes.

That would have been her lot had it not been for a voice that cut through the tension. "It's embarrassing!" Matthias said in his best German, rushing over and grabbing her by the arm. His grasp snapped Violet back into her usual clarity. She immediately clued into what he was doing. Playing the concerned brother, he scorned under his breath, "He's not good enough for you," but of course, loud enough to make the captain laugh. Suspicion dissolved into amusement.

"But I—" Violet played the young woman, head over heels in love, very convincingly. Matthias reached for her hand and, with an equally well-played embarrassed look, pulled her into a quiet space as if to reprimand her.

Maybe he is good for something, the Oberführer thought with a smirk as he strode off to the beat of the rousing chorus. Matthias just saved her life. The Oberführer was thankful: he didn't have the appetite to kill her today.

2

Alexi

Breadcrumbs

AMSTERDAM

Tuesday, February 2nd, 2016.

The wind whips right through me because my bones are hollow, the marrow sucked out along with my hope which is dead. I can feel them now, the people, that is, for these were their streets. So many died of famine and cold in the Dutch Hunger Winter before the Allies arrived, despite resorting to a diet of bark, nettles, and tulip bulbs. "How apt: an austere February in Amsterdam is where it ends," I said to myself. The last glimmers of promise unwound from my heart like the Christmas lights that were being peeled away from the old bakery window and dropped unceremoniously into a dirty white bucket. I wrung my hands from the cold, not because it helped but because it was habit.

The first time I was here, I was lying to myself. I'd willfully surrendered my reason to clothe it in a mirage. *My father is kind, gracious . . . everything that my mother is not*, I thought. *He's the secret other that made me, me.* But was I lying about him or myself? So desperate to justify my worth against the drone of abuse from my mother—that my mind had made my own—that I'd followed breadcrumbs.

A sickeningly happy couple came to my flat on what had, to that point, been a typically bland Tuesday evening. They smiled, presenting some half-completed paperwork and a small box of jewelry, all apparently stashed together beneath the floorboards of my childhood house. It was endearing that they cared, but the jewelry couldn't have been worth anything for if it was, my mother would have pawned it long ago. But the paperwork? That caught my eye immediately. It had my name on it and, more importantly, a complete name and address from 1993 in the column labeled "Father." Apparently, my mother never sent it to the government. Typical. But to this, I grabbed hold and didn't let go. *At least her obituary was good for something*, I'd told myself, chilled by my own honesty, for it had led them to me.

I was thankful that the couple found it while stripping that house down to its bones. Someone needed to tear it apart. Images of it still haunt me daily, like that hole in the plaster where I was almost hit in the head by a Nokia when my mother's boyfriend couldn't get the stupid infrared to work. Everyone turned and laughed, and my face flushed with blood. I froze. As soon as I remembered how, I ran for the darkness beneath my bed, silently sobbing into my unbrushed hair. I was seven, or close enough.

Oh, and that front door that would never lock! It flew open in every storm. Or, more accurately, it was complicit, flung open by some new stranger who brought their storm into our lives. I wished it locked, and locked forever. I wish it had kept the storms out. But the thought of the house being stripped back made me think that I might also rebuild. Being given his address offered a vein of hope where there hadn't been any.

To be clear, I don't regret leaving that seaside, or rather, mud-side town—Victorians knew as much about prime holiday spots as they initially did about cholera. No, I regret that I fell so deeply into a fantasy. I sold everything worth anything quickly online. I was ripped off, but, at the time, I figured that at least it got me onto my first flight. It sounds stupid now, painfully naïve. At twenty, I should have known better.

The breadcrumbs eventually led me here, to Amsterdam, as they did him. My father's name? It was, or is, Peter. And why did he come here? Because, apparently, the only traction he could get in a world slipping between his fingers came from whichever square foot his old school friend, Edwin, stood upon. It turns out we are too alike. I thought needed him, but now I wonder if the weight of me would have crushed him.

3

Peter

Anxiety

Wednesday, November 4th, 1992.

A tall, gangly man in a long woolen overcoat and shined leather shoes ran at Peter, nimbly changing course. He darted with grace around the other pedestrians as they went about their business in the market square. The warmth of the embrace took Peter by surprise, his old school fellow affectionately crushing his spine. It also quite effectively—and wholly unceremoniously—lifted him several inches from the cobbled pavement.

Peter looked weary. "How have you been?" asked Edwin, radiating with sincere gratitude as he looked down upon Peter's—actually quite respectable—six-foot frame. Peter hunched over slightly to avoid engaging the world head-on. "If I'm honest, things have been better," he replied, exhaling into the crisp morning air. This mist poised reverently, hanging, collected for a beat before blooming forth.

With deep concern, Edwin drew Peter into the narrow streets and canals that encircled this district of Amsterdam. "Come, let us find somewhere to catch up," he said. Edwin courteously warned Peter not to walk upon the cycle paths, but it transpired that he was already too late: he'd just escaped a collision earlier that morning. It was a metaphor for life at the moment. The French-Algerian philosopher Albert Camus had written that "at any street corner, the feeling of absurdity can strike any man in the face."[2] It just so happened that this absurdity can also come equipped with silly little bells, spokes, and speed. And that, for some reason, he was being disproportionately targeted.

Peter caught a glimpse of his woeful attempt at a clean-shaven face and prematurely graying mousey-brown hair in the glass door of a Dutch family bakery. It shocked him: this troubled man, almost unrecognizable to himself. This bakery had gratuitously effused into the streets the homely scent of cinnamon for decades. Fitting, given that the spice had been exchanged here as far back as the seventeenth century, and yet also ironic given how far from home this Sri Lankan spice was. It had once been traded for a princely sum during a seafaring age, just like the wildly inflated tulip so synonymous with Amsterdam but first acquired from the Ottoman Empire.

The coffee shop, far removed from the archaic realities of musket-and-pike colonialism, sold comfort in the form of buns and hot drinks. They did so on dainty crockery abreast traditional tablecloths and, of course, *stroopwafels* served best when the syrup melts, warmed over drinks. "You look so happy!" Peter told Edwin as they settled. Sitting slightly back from the table because of the sheer length of his legs, Edwin took his time to lean in, softly replying, "I am Peter. I truly am."

Peter couldn't quite understand how his awkward friend seemed to live in such a different reality from the one that had drained all life from him. Peter sat observing, searching Edwin's face for any hint of inconsistency.

Edwin sported a neat black but graying goatee, a red (immaculately pressed) shirt under his jacket, and thin historic glasses glued on one side—for, on principle, he wasn't going to discard them. And yet, most captivating and confusing were the expressions of joy resonating from Edwin's face. Edwin explained normal life as if full of glory. Entranced, Peter hardly caught a word but watched him closely, curious, oscillating between cynicism and being inspired. Time danced past more smoothly than it had in years; ordinarily feeling utterly stuck and desynchronized from the rest of the world. Peter at once knew he had made the right choice to come. Blaise Pascal insightfully wrote that "all men's miseries derive from not being able to sit in a quiet room alone,"[3] but Peter had done enough of that . . . and never was he truly alone.

2. Camus, *Myth of Sisyphus*, 9.
3. Summary of Pascal, *Pensées*, 66–72. Especially section 139.

Just then, an insidious thought forced its way in, threatening to send Peter headlong into a debilitating spiral of fear—the all-too-familiar kind. Mercifully, he felt oddly present enough to ebb back, tearing himself from its clutches. He released himself into the peaceful stream of Edwin's thought. Perhaps it was a grace that Edwin had? The grace of being able to anchor his friend and stop him from falling headlong into the abyss?

After finishing their tea and *stroopwafels*, Peter cut Edwin off in mid-flow: "What is your secret, Edwin? Like, what makes you so alive? I mean, you've just shared about the pain of trying for kids and all the other ups and downs, and yet you look so . . . unshaken."

Pausing for a second, struck by the impossible challenge of capturing the essence of his joy in words, Edwin simply answered, "Follow me. I want to show you something." Leaving a generous handful of change on the table, Edwin led Peter out of the door and across a street or two back towards the central canal, the *Grimburgwal*. "This is one of my favorite places to come and think, Peter. Water almost encircles this part of town," said Edwin, thoughtfully giving space for Peter to take in everything that he was seeing and sensing. "There are three main canals here that radiate outwards," Edwin said, gesturing eccentrically to illustrate his point. "You could consider them to be like stretch marks, each canal marking an expansion of the city as it pushed past its containment to grow forth with new vision."

"Oh, I get you," said Peter.

"When you ask me about what makes me feel so alive, you must remember all the stuff from school—all the pranks and stuff, the ways the boys treated me?" Edwin asked.

"Well, yes," said Peter, the memories already simmering away in Peter's mind. "I still can't believe they did all that. I tried to help."

"I know. And you did," Edwin paused. "After we left school, life still wasn't easy. I didn't just stumble upon joy."

"What changed?" asked Peter, eager to hear.

"What changed everything," Edwin began, "was an encounter with a living, loving God."

Peter didn't mean to scoff, but he did.

Driven by compassion for his friend, Edwin planted his flag clearly: "Love is directional. God's love orientates outward—just like the canals, Peter—to others. To us. It's not sentimentality. It truly means something: it's the gift of God's self, his life, affirming all that is good, true and beautiful. Love *is* God's identity. Since we are made in his image, love is essential to the existence we're made to experience: thriving when we know God's love and share it. It changes everything."

Peter stood overlooking the canal, confused at how a fairytale could so dramatically affect the life in front of him. If it were anyone else saying this, he'd dismiss it in an instant. Really, he didn't want anything to do with God. God, he thought, was not real, and yet God had also done too much to spite him. While smart enough to know this was a contradiction, he also knew that deep down he was angry at God; so angry he wanted to step away from anything spiritual. In fact, he already had. He'd made an art out of it, which was easier than you'd think. Given that people knew he was a teacher specializing in mathematics, Peter just rehearsed the words: "Like the philosopher and mathematician, Lord Bertrand Russell, I prefer the austere, cool clarity of reason."[4] It generally did the trick to shut the conversation down, especially since speaking about philosophy was almost as perturbing as dialoguing about religion. But Edwin? He deserved a little more—it was only fair: he *had* asked Edwin for honesty.

"I know that sounds far-fetched, especially when it seemed like there wasn't a drop of life in our chapel services at school," said Edwin.

"The only thing alive in those were our stomachs!" Peter joked, vividly remembering the grumbles and mumbles of hungry growing boys that would fill the stagnant silences, sparking competition that involved experimentation with some truly frightful concoctions!

"Right, hey!" Edwin retorted. "Honestly, after school, I entered a decade of mental torture. Sure, I had the grades to forge my way in the world, but it felt like the world didn't want me—it only wanted what I could offer it. I was *this* close," Edwin said with weight in his words, slowly lifting his pinched fingers in front of his eyes. Two women in weighty wool jackets hurried past them on the bridge, trying not to interrupt.

"I've been there too," Peter whispered out of pain, echoing his dear friend's heart. "How on earth did you come out of that? Because it's not like the world changes. It's hostile; people only want you for what you can do rather than who you are. They just use you."

Edwin could sense the freshness of the pain poisoning Peter's heart. "Honestly, it's got more to do with the concerns of this world, this sordid state of affairs, losing its traction in my heart."

"How?"

---

4. Russell, *History of Western Philosophy*, 383.

"By being replaced by something much more beautiful and power-ful, a different mode of life." As Edwin said this, he lifted his eyes towards a boat being lulled in the gentle swell of the water caused by the wind lapping the surface with the speed and agility of a lazy skimming rock.

"Just give it to me, Edwin." Peter pleaded.

"Why don't we talk about what's going on with you first?" said Edwin gently, eager to give Peter an opportunity to share.

"I can't without polluting this place with four-letter words." Chang-ing tact, Peter continued in as much jest as he could summon, "Let's just say teaching over-privileged kids calculus while they are otherwise intent on being slaves to pheromones is the least of my problems."

"You know, I'll always listen," Edwin said, hunching over with his arm on the bridge railing so that he could speak to Peter, eye-to-eye. But seeing that Peter was resistant to give anything more, Edwin continued, "That comment on slavery is pretty insightful."

"It is?" Peter scoffed.

Edwin smiled, knowing that Peter would know the answer to his question: "Who's traditionally thought to have written the first book of the Bible?"

"Hmmm . . . Moses?" Peter answered tentatively.

"Mother Agnes would be happy that you got that one." Peter's mouth twitched up slightly with the patina-tinged joy of nostalgia. Edwin con-tinued, "Moses or not, the first audience of Genesis was the Israelites— that nation that Moses led out of Egypt who had been . . .?"

"Slaves?"

"Right."

"Wasn't Pharaoh afraid of how many there were?" Peter interjected. The details were coming back a little.

"Exactly! There was clearly a disconnect somewhere about who they were and what they were capable of. So, what do you think Genesis is saying?"

"I haven't the foggiest . . . 'Be good!'?" Peter attempted.

Edwin helped him out: "Slavery had robbed them of the full knowl-edge of their history and destiny. As part of restoring this, a good and ethical law will be shared. But before that, Genesis communicates the foundations of their history and with it, the bedrock of their identity. This was vital, because despite being set free from Pharaoh and the towering Egyptian gods, seemingly now at liberty to chart their own trajectory, the Israelites were *not* yet free. Not really. They were not yet living in the fullness of what God had created them for," Edwin exclaimed.

"Oh? So, it's about how to be free?" Peter asked, processing.

"And more importantly, what's holding them back. Though it's worth pointing out that the idea that people *should* be free was almost unthinkable at the time in the ancient Near East."

"Really? Why?"

"Because many people were enslaved by others and, beyond that, humans were thought to have been made to be the slaves of the gods. Genesis is radical because it doesn't just deny that but significantly raises the bar. Humans are made in the image of God! Part of the beauty and genius of Genesis is that goes even further, to reveal a deeper problem: the real content of their slavery—our slavery. Why? To free them into flourishing as who they were made to be, the sons and daughters of God!"

"And the real content of their slavery was?" Peter asked.

"Chains on the inside, not just on the outside," Edwin offered, causing Peter's gaze to seize upon the bike locks along the bridge. "If they couldn't live in their freedom, how could they be expected to usher that in for the rest of humanity?"

"A great job they did of that!" Peter said, sarcastically. He didn't remember much, but he remembered the Bible being brutally honest about these failures.

"There's a difference between being aware of chains and taking them off," Edwin said, drawing Peter's attention to a student not far from them who was wrestling with his bike lock. The light relief was welcome. Edwin continued, "The ideas of slavery and freedom are central to understanding how radical the gospel really is. I don't know about you, Peter, but the two messages I got from school were that, one: I'm a sinner; and two, it was mostly about living forever in some distant heaven—"

"—and not perishing in hell?" Peter added.

"Right. Then I better follow Jesus!" Edwin continued.

"That's pretty much what I got, too," Peter agreed.

"But here's the thing," Edwin offered, "there's truth there, but to reduce it all down as if that's the whole story doesn't do it justice. We're missing so much of the depth of the good news: what it actually means to be a people who are set free."

"Then, what does it mean?" Peter challenged.

Edwin offered, "Think about it this way: do you remember the stained-glass window in chapel?"

"Jesus leaving the ninety-nine sheep to look for the one that had escaped?"

"Right. What sort of predicament do you think the escapee sheep could have gotten itself into?"

"Knowing those things, probably upside down, stuck in a ditch somewhere," Peter said.

"With brambles wrapped all around it."

"—sounds about right."

"Well, a good shepherd deals with the sin and the shame—the brambles keeping the sheep captive—but the whole time he's doing it because of the value and worth he sees in the sheep. I used to think that God was so sin-obsessed. Instead, he's us-obsessed—he cares; he wants to free us."

"Interesting," Peter said skeptically, his eyes darting as he thought. "And the living forever part? Isn't that just a copy of all the old legends: a thirst for immortality?"

"Like a Greco-Roman legend?" Edwin clarified.

"Right, just a spiritual trope for self-obsessed humans."

"What if we had it wrong, Peter? Humanity has always been curious about what is beyond or after, which makes sense if eternity is in the heart of man.[5] But what if it's less about living forever and more about whether we are free to really live now? Are we the truly living or the living dead?"

"Like zombies?"

"Something like that! This is where freedom and slavery come in. Freedom is the ability to flourish into the fullness of who we truly are. Slavery, on the other hand, means to be caught, frozen, as death invades life; stuck in self-defeating, dehumanizing patterns or modes of existence."

"Freedom and slavery; I get it. But you're actually saying this dynamic's central to the gospel?"

"What it practically means," Edwin answered. With an air of mystery, Edwin gently continued, "You still love history, right?"

"Right," Peter said with a nod, just as a narrow boat chugged its way under the bridge, its roof packed full of foliage, practically a floating jungle.

5. Eccl 3:11.

"Well," Edwin continued, "at the time of the New Testament, the Greek word for 'good news' was *euangelion*. Before Christians used the term, it was used when a herald read aloud a declaration after a battle like: 'Good News, this or that king has broken the siege.'[6] You know," Edwin elaborated, "how armies of kings or emperors would starve people out, encircling them and—"

"Throw in diseased animal carcasses?" Peter offered, struck by the memory of them building a trebuchet together from balsa wood in year seven. He hadn't thought about that in a while.

"Exactly."

"So, Christians reused the word?"

"They were making a point," Edwin explained. "Through his death and resurrection, Jesus, the truly righteous king, has broken the siege over both the world and our lives. So that we might live and dream again, not just survive another day. That's really what Jesus declared when, in Nazareth, he unrolls the scroll of Isaiah in Luke 4. Like a manifesto for his kingly mission, he declares that he is going to free the prisoners, release the captives, heal, and invite us into the Year of Jubilee: a joyous, deeply relational peace!"[7]

"So, you don't just mean a physical freedom?" Peter inquired.

"Right. He breaks the full depth of the siege that impacts our lives."

"That's interesting," said Peter. "Because whatever he did or didn't do, life still feels like a cruel joke."

"I understand," said Edwin, "I felt exactly the same."

"If God is love, why does it hurt so much?" Peter grimaced.

"Because it wasn't meant to be like this. You know, Peter, I thought that Christians were just meant to pretend that everything was okay, just kind of grin and carry on—"

"—slap a verse on it—"

"—But what I missed was that the Bible starts by staring this problem right in the face. Just three chapters in, we see this titanic 'fall' that affects the whole fabric of reality, ripping it at the seams. This changes everything. The rest of the Bible is pointing to how Jesus deals with it!"

"Hmm," Peter said, right before challenging Edwin, "but if it's not all about heaven and hell, what's Jesus saving us from?" He needed clarity.

---

6. Regarding the historical context for the word *euangelion*, see, for example, Evans, "Mark's Incipit and the Priene Calendar Inscription," 69–81. Also, Wright, "What Is the Gospel?"

7. For the term "manifesto" in this context, see Wright, *Simply Jesus*, 67–86.

"The siege in which we find ourselves after the fall. Our reality is ruptured; distorted by death, darkness, and disconnection.[8] But it doesn't stop there, Peter. Like the Israelites, the problem isn't just external; it's also internal: the shock of this rupture reaches our deepest internal places."

"But how?" Peter struggled to get his mind around it.

"What if God isn't simply loving, but he *is* love? Self-giving love. What if God isn't this big opposing presence that judgingly lords over us but is instead the personal, self-giving foundation for our lives? Our being. Then, the narrative of the fall in Genesis three becomes about falling away from the fullness of relationship with God, and with it our nourished, flourishing selves."

"And so?"

"Honestly, Peter, trying to live on without the one who is Life feels like death."

"*That* I can agree with," Peter admitted.

Edwin added, "Losing the full vibrancy of this essential connection disrupts all our other relationships: those with others, creation, and even ourselves."

"Ourselves?" Peter asked.

"One hundred percent." Edwin continued. "It's as if the rug—the 'Ground of Being'—is pulled out from under us.[9] Disconnection from the one who is Life lays us bare to an existential anxiety that we were never meant to know."

"Existential anxiety?" said Peter, despairingly. He tipped his head up, involuntarily, while his hands broke away from the railing. Embarrassed, Peter tried to brush it off as a joke: "Of course you would say that!"

Seeing this, Edwin returned to familiar territory: "What if those brambles—the patterns of sin that keep us stuck—don't indicate how good or bad we are? *We're made well, Peter!* Instead, they're a symptom— a painful symptom—of something else."

"Of a bramble-infested, messed up world?" Peter offered, trying to follow.

---

8. This lucid summary, "death, darkness, and disconnection," follows Glen Scrivener's articulation. See Scrivener, "What Christians Believe." Also see: https://321.speaklife.org.uk/course/321

9. This term, "the Ground of Being," is used by Paul Tillich. See Tillich, *Courage to Be*; Tillich, *Systematic Theology, vol. 1*, especially part II. While complete separation is impossible, Tillich speaks of the aforementioned disconnection as estrangement.

"It absolutely says something about the structure and state of the world, but," Edwin continued, "it's also about us: our condition and vulnerabilities. What if, being stuck in these dehumanizing patterns, this slavery to sin—even when it hurts ourselves and others—reveals how far down this rupture in reality goes: affecting the very foundations of our being?"

"What would that mean?" Peter demanded, seeking clarity.

"We start blaming ourselves for the lack we feel of secure, reliable love. Then, we turn in upon ourselves with self-hatred."

"Loathing," Peter whispered—just barely. "So, sin's a symptom?" he added, more audibly.

Edwin trod carefully around his friend's heart: "In a certain sense, yes! I'm not justifying it. But I think it also shows that we're struggling to cope. Like the person who almost kills the rescue swimmer who's come to save them."

"You got that from lifesaving in Scouts!"

"Guilty!"

The honesty required when talking of self-hatred scared Peter. Attempting to compensate for his sudden flush of emotions, Peter recalled, "The drowning person can climb on top of you, so you're meant to knock them out, right?"

"That's what I remember!" Edwin replied. "In the same way, sin's not always rational: it's an attempt at survival, but it's also entirely self-defeating."

Peter countered, parroting what he'd heard in school, "But surely we also have choice and responsibility?"

"Of course! Sin can become incredibly calculated and intentional. But I wonder if that's not secondary. We tend to do what's helped us get the desired result or relief before, so why not keep doing these things?"

"I've not thought about that before," Peter admitted while rotating the idea, looking for vulnerabilities.

"What do you do with a symptom?" Edwin asked Peter.

"You can treat it but should also look for the root cause, right?" he offered.

"Exactly," Edwin said. "In the same way, God's not into external behavior modification or making us prove that we're good enough somehow. Instead, he wants an honest relationship with his sons and daughters. And it's through this honest relationship that any freeing, holistic transformation happens. Flourishing."

Peter was in two minds. He'd heard this Christian "sons and daughters" language before. It sounded jarring; sickly sweet. But Edwin also talked about hard, real stuff. Peter wasn't sure how it all fit together. *If* it fit together. "So then, what *is* the root cause of sin?" Peter pushed. How he hated saying that word!

"The human heart, Peter. After the shock of the fall, the affections of the human heart now curve back in upon themselves."

"Like recoiling in pain?"

"That resonates with me. Though this may be a chicken-or-egg problem. Regardless, there's a Latin phrase I think you'll appreciate, developed by the Protestant reformer, Martin Luther, building ideas engaged by Saint Augustine in the early fifth century. It's *homo incurvatus in se*, meaning humankind curved in upon themselves."[10]

"Like a boomerang?"

"I've often thought about heart affections like the flight path of an arrow, but a boomerang could work too. Essentially, since love is directional—"

"—like the canals?" Peter offered.

"Exactly. Love first extends beyond ourselves. Since we are made in the image of God to share and give love we still try, instinctively knowing it to be good. But then the conviction to love others—the arrow—slows in the space between us and them, until it returns in desperation, curving back towards ourselves. Whatever work the arrow accomplished during this flight—of performing to elicit or capture praise and affection from others—it is never enough. We were not made to live on the fickle gifts of the finite world alone but to know the secure love of the infinite one. So, whatever spoils we can scrape close, the heart goes hungry, a hunger that underlies the enslaving, self-justifying attitudes of 'I must' and 'I need.' I've always appreciated what Alexsander Solzhenitsyn wrote: 'The belly is an ungrateful wretch, it never remembers past favors, it always wants more tomorrow.'[11] In the same way, without being fully satiated by the love of God, I think that the heart becomes just as ungrateful and deceitful as the stomach. Conflicted: both idealistic and heinous, but, yes, deceitful. St. Augustine captured this well, confessing, 'I became to myself a region of destitution.'"[12]

---

10. Jer 17:9. See Luther, *Lectures on Romans*, 291, 346, 426, 513, 540; Augustine, *Confessions*, II.iii(6)-II.x(18). Also, Tillich, *Systematic Theology*.

11. Solzhenitsyn, *One Day*, 127.

12. Augustine, *Confessions*, II.x(18).

Just then, a large, off-white seagull jumped down beside them. Peter had felt the wind batted against him before he saw its wings. It had found a small breadcrust. It claimed it before leaving again as quickly as it had swooped in.

"The hunger's real," Peter joked, surprising himself with its undercurrent of honesty.

Edwin laughed before slicing right back to the heart level: "Peter, we start to do things we said we'd never do. We start to treat even the people we love as a means to an end." Edwin stopped, seeing the glint of tears starting to build in Peter's eyes, betraying his tight lips.

Peter knew that Edwin had noticed. Peter pounded the metal railing three times with a closed fist, angry at himself. He knew Edwin *was* trying to help; the problem was he didn't know what he needed or what to ask.

"We can stop if you want, Peter," Edwin offered gently.

"Sorry. No. I," He stuttered before taking a deep breath. "It gives me hope to see you like this." *Besides, what else can we talk about?* Peter reasoned. *My story? No thank you.*

"We can—" Edwin started.

Peter interrupted, "Edwin, we both know you're awful at small talk! Besides, you've always read me like a book. Maybe I'll finally understand myself!"

"Oh, Peter. I'm still a mystery to myself."

"Just tell me what helped you," Peter protested, eager to pass the spotlight back.

Edwin recalibrated for a second. "What helped was a diagnosis that made sense of my internal world." He paused. "You know what?" Edwin then continued, drawing Peter in, "I've found there to be something more primary and revealing about the reality in which we find ourselves, than my struggle with sin."

"What?"

"Shame," Edwin offered vulnerably.

"But isn't shame just feeling guilt about sin? How can it be more revealing?" Peter said dismissively.

"Ah, but there's a distinction: while sin is substantial—where we've not rightly upheld someone's worth, shame—a graceless judgment about ourselves—needn't be. It can also be the result of smoke and mirrors: completely unfounded."

"Like Adam and Eve being ashamed of being naked?" Peter pulled from somewhere foggy in his mind.

"That's really interesting, isn't it? They were created perfectly and the Fall doesn't seem to affect our bodies directly; only our perception of them. God even asks them who it was who told them they were naked."

"So, why's it more revealing?" Peter asked, intrigued.

"Unfounded shame helps us see beyond the complicated dynamics of sin and guilt to reveal how deep the rupture in reality goes and how it affects us."

"Really? How?" Peter probed further.

"By perceiving something to be missing, some lack we blame ourselves for as if we're meant to be self-contained and all we ever needed. Shame sets us up for that moment of awareness: that glimpse of reality—beyond distraction—where we're shocked, chilled to the bone, to find emptiness and lack. That's what I meant by existential anxiety—this shock and its effects."

"Like the moment you realize there's really only two choices: to crumble or commit?" Peter offered, recalling the confluence of life and death so strongly that he almost tasted blood.

"Right. It provokes fear. Life feels on a knife edge: as if there is nothing and no one to pull you through."

"But you . . .?" Peter restarted, confused. "You're saying it's normal—that we can all feel this—but there's still a God out there?"

"Yes. This is exactly the reality—the frozen, cold, chilling siege—that Jesus releases us from," Edwin affirmed.

"Surely that's cognitive dissonance: hanging onto your hypothesis regardless of new evidence to the contrary?" Peter provoked, eager to see his reaction and study him for any cracks in confidence.

"There's nothing new about this evidence, or the good news," Edwin said, refusing the urge to become defensive. "I find the fall hypothesis compelling precisely because it doesn't disregard but engages with the evidence not just out in the world, but, as I said, also from the deepest part of myself."

God, Peter reasoned, was either who Edwin said he was for both of them or not at all. It couldn't be true for one of them and not the other. It scared Peter; he knew Edwin's poker tells, and none of them alerted him to a lie. Edwin really believed this stuff.

Edwin connected back, "I find that passage you mentioned, where Adam and Eve first feel shame, incredibly insightful."

"Really?"

Edwin continued, "It's fascinating: a physical reaction provoked by an internal change. As if, by discovering the aching depth of their disconnection from God—the Life of the world and their spiritual foundation—they now also unjustly judge themselves as lacking or not good enough and needing to hide."

"There's something to that: the fear of being exposed, spilling over to the outside!" Peter admitted.

"Now, consider what happens next. Do they only hide from each other?"

"They also hide from God," Peter said, just as a bike sped past, ringing its bell.

"Right. Shame disconnects on social and spiritual levels, causing us to put up barriers."

"It isolates," Peter said, instantly aggrieved that again he'd given more away than he'd planned to.

"So true," Edwin said softly. "I found isolation not to be a safe, padded cell, where I was insulated from the world: protected. Instead, the deeper I went, the more it forced a confrontation with the raw reality of existence. Peter, I felt like a man coming to terms with a gaping cannonball-sized hole in my abdomen. Turning inwards upon myself and finding this emptiness threw me further into a spiral of anxiety."

"I'm so sorry, Eddy," Peter said. "If I had known . . ."

"Thank you, Peter. I walked through the shadow of death, but praise God, I made it to the other side. But when I was in it, that siege of sin and shame felt insurmountable. I did everything . . . everything deeply human to try to backfill the nothingness that gnawed at me. I tried to gather for myself a secure foundation of love, of life and being, that I could stand upon, secure. Peter, everything was an empty promise." In his mind, Edwin could see the deceitful wrappers of these promises fading under a hot desert sun as he ran desperately towards an oasis mirage.

Peter interrupted, impatient to know: "How Edwin? How did this Jesus stuff actually help you?" His voice cracked under the weight of his vulnerability.

Together, they looked back out upon the water. Edwin gently rubbed Peter's back. The trees lining the side of the canal bent in unison as a fresh gust of wind relieved them of their most golden leaves. They swung down to perch upon the tension of the water. Peter deserved more than a neatly packaged soundbite or trite answer. Edwin replied, "Peter, whatever freedom you see in me wasn't about positive thinking or pulling myself up via some metaphysical bootstraps. Life is not something you can have or earn abstractly, like a thing," Edwin shared.

"Then what is it?"

"It's a who. What's the opposite of disconnection?"

"Reconnection?"

"Exactly. Like the rings of the canals or a fountain of living water, God really is a committed community of self-giving love that radiates outwards. This delighting-in and upholding each person—Father, Son, and Holy Spirit—is so deeply connecting that God can be called one. We're made to share in this nourishing love. It's what we were designed for and *who* we flourish in."

Peter looked at Edwin, urging him to continue as he filtered it all through his experiences.

Edwin obliged: "This analogy of water is woven all through the Bible," he said, "from Genesis to Revelation, peppering the scripture."

"Seasoning them," Peter added with a flickering cheeky smile he'd enlisted to ward off the raw edge of his emotions.

Edwin appreciated the lightness but responded, with the supple heart-bound duty of a confession that only a true friend is worthy of, "In a really dark moment, I felt impressed to open a Bible. It was one of those small black school ones, the only one I had. This is where it fell. It spoke right to me." Edwin continued tenderly, "It was about water, written by the prophet Jeremiah. Peter, it couldn't have made more sense to my life or the reason for my slavery: the mode of life that was killing me." Now burnt deep into his memory, Edwin shared Jeremiah 2:13: "'My people have committed two sins: they have forsaken me, the spring of living water, and have dug their own cisterns, broken cisterns that cannot hold water.'" He paused; "It surprised me."

"In what way?" Peter asked.

"I expected something vindictive or condemning. Instead, I felt relief, as if I had finally encountered a truth strong enough to free; a truth I'd heard of but never encountered. I realized that the whole time when we'd been living beside religion, I had never even tried to know God, and so—what else could I have done? To survive, I'd desperately dug my own cisterns to try to keep hold of any trace of life I could find."

"Sorry, what's a cistern?" asked Peter.

"If you think of a well, you wouldn't be far off, except they're dug to collect and store the rainwater in hot desert climates."

"Got it," said Peter. "Sorry, do go on."

"What stood out to me was that in 'forsaking,'—having nothing to do with God in any real sense—I was ultimately alone. You must be familiar with that freezing fear of being exposed and unknown in this raging world. I could feel the blisters on my heart from where I'd labored to forge my own way through life—hoping to secure my own foundation."

"Digging your own cisterns," Peter offered, following.

"Exactly. You can think of them like strategies complete with pseudo-identities crafted to try to get love and acknowledgement from other people. No matter how hard I tried, any affirmation or acknowledgment and love that I captured just seemed to seep out of the cracks of my heart, the broken cisterns. It made things worse." Each remark bubbled up inside of Edwin as if he couldn't help but offer up his holy confession.

"Worse?" Peter asked.

"The more successful my façade was at gaining praise, the more my real self, inside, felt ignored and ashamed. The gap between the two just got bigger. Peter, the cisterns were empty: like pointless, futile, empty wells, no matter how many I dug."

"So, what did you do?" asked Peter, wincing as if bracing for some cutting news.

"In all honesty, it was more about what I *couldn't* do," Edwin answered cryptically. "If I could have kept saving myself, I probably would have. I'd keep performing—churning out another breakthrough, basically a machine. For a while, it seemed to work just fine, but it wasn't sustainable. All they did was mask what was really happening to my soul as it wasted away. Rather than securing myself, I'd lost myself; cantilevered too far. I'd sacrificed my life and humanity but even that wasn't enough. It was utterly exhausting, like living on a treadmill."

"Like Indiana Jones running on a falling bridge," Peter threw in, recalling with fondness one of the last movies they'd watched together secretly in the boarding school attic: kings lounging among the bats.

"Oh, Peter, I miss those days of you jumping 'round the dorm room in your stripey pajamas to avoid the lava—" Edwin said.

"—and poison socks—"

Edwin smiled softly, "Too bad the beds only had three springs in them!"

"Those were some damn good antics," Peter said, fondly amused that Edwin had remembered his homemade PJs from Nana. Her care packages during that first year of school had meant the world.

Realizing the urgency, Edwin reorientated back to the matters of his heart: "After everything I'd built finally collapsed, I saw all the way down to the ruptured moorings—the chilling nothingness left in the absence of God. All I felt was darkness, death, and disconnection. I could still make out the beauty and fingerprints of a wonder-filled world, but it felt like none of it was for me: I'd never reach joy and peace. The ruptures between them and I seemed impossible to overcome, too cavernous and treacherous." Edwin's heart began to swell: "But he broke the siege, Peter! He made a way when there was no way. He found me where I was, a crumpled shell of a man, and he resurrected me."

"Thank you," Peter said, reversing roles: now the one to rub Edwin's back.

"Peter, freedom and peace didn't come from carving a better mold for water to seep into—it wasn't about changing myself or my identity so that people could praise me. That just forced me into clothes that I didn't want to wear, to do things I didn't want to do. The secret, Peter, is Jesus sharing his Life; getting into the direct path of this spring, or fountain, of living water."

"Proximity to God?" Peter only just held back his knee-jerk reaction—*So then, where the heck is he?* But he had no appetite to fight with his oldest friend. Not yet, not during their first day back together. But he wouldn't let him off the hook later—that is, neither Edwin nor God.

Edwin replied, "Right! It was about closeness. I can't tell you what a relief it was not to have to change or re-market myself to be someone else," said Edwin.

"All the while, I wanted to be more like you," Peter admitted, turning towards him.

"And I, you, Peter," Edwin said, hand strongly placed with assurance upon his shoulder.

They stopped for a minute, reacquainted with the gentle lap of the water against the brick canal sides. Peter *could* see a new confidence. All his memories of Edwin harbored this fragile but lovable gem who was rejected by the world. Before, he stuck out like a sore thumb: perpetually uncomfortable. He was still utterly unique but now somehow to relax into who he really was, the home in his heart meaning that he was "at home" anywhere.

"I get that: changing and compromising yourself to please others," Peter said to break the silence. "If you had only seen me a few months ago, pandering to make life comfortable for an over-privileged cat."

"I thought you were allergic?!" Edwin chuckled.

"Exactly! I'm an utterly tragic case. I thought I was in love—not with the cat! With—" Peter cut himself short. Despair swept back in through his cracks, catching his naturally playful spirit off-guard, attempting to stifle the seed of hope and reestablish its claim. Peter tried desperately to gather himself. He squeezed the metal railing tighter. Almost saying her name had brought it all too close. It had put him on edge. "Honestly Edwin, part of me wants to believe, but I don't know what part that is. Is it because we're made for this or because of school indoctrinating us? Or maybe it inoculated me? Heck, I don't know. Part of me wants absolutely nothing to do with him." As he spoke these words, his anger whipped up like the white caps on waves. He became more and more afraid; afraid of lashing out at his most dear friend. Hurting himself was one thing, but he'd never forgive himself for hurting Edwin. "Thank you for sharing, Edwin. I just need some time," he said, tears colonizing his eyes.

"Whatever you need, Peter. I won't be offended."

"Just don't count on converting your heathen friend!" Peter smirked, half-serious, turning away as the first drops fell.

"How about you come to dinner tonight? Edith's quite the chef," Edwin suggested. Still turned, Peter accepted, eager to think, maybe sketch, and, most pressingly, breathe. Much of what Edwin had said made sense, but his world just seemed so shot through with pain, and he was bleeding out.

4

WW2

The Fuselage Floor

LONDON

Thursday, September 30th, 1943. 161 Squadron, RAF
Tempsford, Bedfordshire.

How surreal that Henry's door to the future would be the circular hole
cut in a Halifax's fuselage floor. Ironic, almost funny even, given that he
had spent much of "his war" so far looking at aerial photographs, but not
one of those times had he imagined that he would be recruited and his
life, in part, put in the hands of men following one of his maps. That's not
to say that Henry was, by trade, a map maker. Really, he was a graphic
designer who had one small role in a series of isolated actions that finally
evolved into target maps of secret locations. Being "far too bohemian," as
one man had put it, to join the forces, his skills had been put to use in the
top-secret operation "Hillside" in an old home—Hughenden Manor.[13]
This house was fitting in its role to help fight against an antisemitic fascist movement, given that it was famously owned by Benjamin Disraeli,
an Italian-born Conservative who served as Britain's first Jewish Prime
Minister under Queen Victoria. Disraeli had thought of himself as part

---

13. "Operation Hillside" exhibit by the National Trust at Hughenden Manor, High
Wycombe, UK.

of "that sacred and romantic people from whom I derive my blood and name."[14]

"No cushy Lysander drop-off?" the 161 Squadron pilot and navigator joked, looking gallant in their sheepskin flight jackets as they had left the outbuilding on Gibraltar Farm for their modified Handley Page Halifax. Lit by the moon, they were clearly cooking up another insult before Henry saw their eyes dart. They pulled themselves together quickly. "Breaking you in easy, hey?" one said, with both admiration and dread.

He should have been used to it—but it still stung. Having two regular arms but only one hand (the result of a tragic childhood accident) seemed to have the same effect as carrying a loaded gun—only worse as people pitied you. "It's what the mission requires," Henry replied, almost holding back. "Besides, you're the ones stuck taking these B flights." And with that, they smiled beneath their dark and strong mustaches. Perhaps they would remember this "Joe" among the others.

As it turns out, the very thing that disqualified him from the regular armed forces was the perfect cover for the SOE (Special Operations Executive), or so he was told. Henry also liked to think it both made his right hand more talented and allowed his quick wit to fly beneath the radar.

Churchill ordered the creation of the SOE, with the directive to "set Europe ablaze" through espionage, sabotage, and reconnaissance.[15] This was despite Air Vice-Marshal Arthur Harris's initial insistence that RAF airplanes and pilots were needed elsewhere and were not going to "carry ragamuffins to distant spots."[16]

As it happens, Churchill's father, Lord Randolph Churchill, had locked horns with fellow conservative Disraeli on many occasions in the House of Commons. This heritage of the battle with words no doubt left a mark on the young Winston, who worked hard to take control of his stammer. In doing so, he developed his epoch-shaping power of speech that roused the nation against the odds.

In the same way, Henry, hurtling through the cold, dark night with just thin metal between him and the sky of continental Europe, was determined not to let the thinly veiled doubts of others defeat him from the inside out. He could feel a strength inside of him, invisible to others

14. Hawkins, *Early Novels*, viii.

15. Winston Churchill's directive was given to Hugh Dalton on Monday, July 22nd, 1940, at a war cabinet meeting. See Dalton, *War Diary*, 62.

16. Correll, "Moon Squadrons."

but just as real as anything made of flesh—and perhaps even more so, being incorruptible by bullets and shrapnel. He detested help, which he considered babying. Instead, he overcompensated, helping and leading whenever he could.

After months of training in the SOE, in just a few moments, Henry would be guaranteed his first glimpse of the French countryside, firmly in the European Theatre. Oh, what he would give for Mrs. Askell—a mother-like figure at Hughenden, who arrived like clockwork to find him hunched over the maps—to bring him some good sturdy tea and gossip! His face creased as he smiled at the year he'd spent there. He dearly missed his own nieces and nephews but took to giving little Sophie and Archie piggyback rides under the expansive oak trees. They probably felt sorry for him, expecting this one-handed "uncle" of theirs to die somewhere in the war—which he had no intention of doing.

The pilot held a modified cockpit map, cut into a long strip with just fifty miles or so buffer on each side of the route. Henry had never seen this before. Anything was good as a distraction – the wait was dire. It was made worse by blackout curtains and the nauseating smell of lacquer recently sprayed onto the aircraft. He suddenly made the decision he had been long weighing up over the English Channel: he was going to need to rush to carefully transfer a small section of microfilm into a carefully calculated new location. Why? Everything had been ready, more than ready. They had put the microfilm in a specially crafted watch pin and, in turn, placed that within a hollowed-out matchstick. He could breathe. *It was all still there.* But his mind had started ticking, nagging: *It wasn't the best place for it.*

He decided his best bet was to borrow thin pincers from the flight crew. The crew didn't even notice, entirely focused, so different from the reckless banter and bravado they displayed before they left, sharing stories of missions and friends—those times they'd cheated death on harrowing bombing missions.

One story had been beaming about last July when, for the first time, they ingeniously used thin, falling aluminum pieces to confound the German radar (code name: "Window"). The result? One apocalyptically large fireball with sun-like intensity around the once proud city of Hamburg. The navigator then joked that, as rumor had it, the local populations thought that if you put the "window" aluminum in vinegar you might reveal a secret message from the Allies. While this was unlikely to be true, releasing carefully worded letter bombs from the sky became an essential part of psychological warfare. Little did the navigator and pilot know, but in '45 one of these men would be involved in the satisfyingly named Operation Cornflakes. This would include "sprinkling" anti-Nazi propaganda into the German postal service, *Deutsche Reichspost*. After dropping eight "special" mailbags onto a mail train at Linz, bound for Austria, they would be dutifully collected with the rest and delivered, ready for the breakfast table—hence the name. But one man, only *one* of these brave men, would live long enough to be part of it.

Propaganda like "Cornflakes" was one thing; firestorms consuming a city were another. He couldn't help but see the parallels in how Coventry was targeted by the *Luftwaffe* in the Blitz. Everyone had heard about Hamburg in the theaters, but it was another thing to know someone had been there. Now it felt more real. It made him realize that the sandbags they had been practicing combat on were now going to be real people, and the targets had names. Of course he knew that, but now it was sinking in. Could he even do what he was meant to do?

Stuck waiting in the fuselage, Henry wondered afresh if one of the maps he had worked on had played a role in it somehow. There had been some maps with an awful lot of magenta on them, meaning targets. Why? Because magenta was the color that showed up best under the amber light inside the bombers: the light that enabled as much night vision of the countryside below as possible. The idea of aiding so much death and destruction was nauseating. But what other options had there been? Henry and his friends had reasoned that by doing their job well and creating accurate target maps then, perhaps, civilian casualties might be reduced—munitions factories wouldn't be confused for hospitals. Henry's mind was spinning; threads of guilt and justification tangled, tightening in his mind, slowly slicing into his soul like a cheese wire. *Enough*, he thought. *Now isn't the time.* If he were doing this—and he *had* committed—he was going to do this right.

While the crew seemed focused, Henry struggled to trust them; not that trusting others came naturally to him. Right before they had talked to him on the runway, the pilot and navigator had agreed with an enthused optimism that this SOE sortie would be incredibly uneventful, as if, perhaps, to spite the all-too-present Nazi threat.

Henry controlled what he could. He took the pincers and returned to something familiar, detailed, precise, lest his mind become snagged, transfixed even, by the magnitude of his own mission.

The Halifax wasn't quite as drafty as the Whitley in which they had trained, but it was still cold enough to merit getting back inside his sleeping bag. He wedged a small silver locket between the mounds of his legs. When he had left Hughenden, little Sophie had asked her mother's permission to give him the locket, which had once belonged to Disraeli's wife, but that was more than Henry had done—he didn't ask permission to bring it because he knew the answer would be no. He started the job of putting the microfilm, already inside the watch-pin, inside the hollow locket-pin itself. A superior position, he thought. In a pinch, the value of the locket might divert from its clandestine use, whereas caring about a box of matches too much would arouse suspicion. That was the theory, at least. For, no matter what the experts said, they all knew that agents were hiding important secrets in matchsticks. He'd tried telling them, but they hadn't listened. For better or worse, he alone was now in charge of executing this short string of missions, and that depended on whether he lived or died. So, he had decided that—overcompensating as normal—he was going to change the location of the microfilm, and he wasn't going to tell anyone. The bumps and jolts only served to strengthen his resolve to get this done quickly—and well. His sigh hidden beneath the constant sounds, he stretched out for stability in his sleeping bag with his feet on one side of the fuselage and his back pushing on the other, a spare bag acting as filler.

The watch-pin was almost in. But, by the spite of fate, it suddenly disappeared from his grasp. The airplane had hit a particularly bad spot of turbulence. His instinct was to look up. *Who saw?* Who was judging him? His next was to immediately locate it. He felt so utterly foolish. Couldn't he have done this later in the *Résistance* hideout when he wasn't moving at a ridiculous speed? Blood started to rush into his ears. The noise had been oppressive, but now his ears were ringing and he felt sick. He'd failed already. *Where, where is it?* He was panicking but tried not to make a scene. It felt like an age.

It was, it turns out, under the indent of his elbow, still on his sleeping bag. *At least gravity is predictable.* He grabbed it and, as quickly as he could, placed the watch-pin inside of the hollow locket-pin. Done. He then put the locket in a pocket right against his body where he could feel it. He looked around. No one had noticed, the other agent trying his best to read. Henry started to breathe again.

Ordinarily, General Charles de Gaulle liked to keep the SOE agents quite separate from his Free French forces, and yet this occasion differed due to the idiosyncrasies of one vital cell out in the east of France in the Vosges Mountains. These mountains separate the Lorraine Plateau from the plain of Alsace. This border region, which had often been given and taken in war between France and Germany, was now effectively annexed and earmarked for German settlement. Given the history of this highly contested land, many young men in Alsace-Lorraine had already been forcibly conscripted into the German army as *malgré-nous*, meaning "against our will." Some of those that Henry expected to meet had escaped this fate by hunkering down in remote farm buildings, gathering with diverse and—if not like-minded then, at the very least, like-hearted—others to resist. Now that Hitler's non-aggression pact with the USSR had been broken, there were also Communists among them.

Henry carried with him a photo from training, which they would promptly burn. It was of him and Vincent, as they knew him. The *Résistance* cell had argued that they would only trust another agent who had known their beloved Vincent—who had died just months before in Lyon at the hands of "The Butcher," no less. He had proven himself loyal to the end. Henry carried a message and orders from de Gaulle himself to re-secure their essential allegiance.

After this, there was going to be the issue of promptly getting to Paris to meet with Ophélie. This *nom de guerre*, Ophélie as in Ophelia, was not lost on him. It was ironic: an agent who embodied the very opposite of her cover, Shakespeare's Ophelia of feminine fragility. In underestimating her, she was privy to much of the Reich's information passing both desks and lips. Henry was promised that a *Résistant*, or two, would guide him over the Vosges and smuggle him into Paris. There were so many details out of his control. Depending upon others was not his strong suit, as the trainers had reminded him.

Before too long, Henry's cozy RAF-issue sleeping bag was forced to spill its warmth into the cabin—like the warmth escaping the chest cavity of the Scottish stag that they stalked and gutted in training. He had been used to getting oxblood-colored ink upon his hands, but that had been a completely new experience: looking down and seeing real red blood.

The dispatcher prepared Henry and the other agent, a wireless operator, to jump. Theoretically, they would make a team, though they would hardly see each other, security being of the utmost importance. This was thoroughly understandable when these wireless operators, or "pianists," lasted an average six weeks in the field. The German radio direction-finders had become so efficient that it didn't take any longer than twenty or thirty minutes to triangulate their position and track down the operator. Like most things, it was better not to think about.

Desperate to get his point across, the dispatcher shouted, "You've got a short window. If you get it wrong, we can't change it—they'd have to wait for another broadcast from London." He turned to the pianist: "We'll make sure you have a Welbike sent down in case you need it. It'll parachute down a couple of hundred meters away from you. God be with you both! For Victory!" he shouted over the noise of the four engines. At least the engine roar helped usher adrenalin to take over—the hot air balloons at Ringway in Manchester were far worse because the silence made the drops more eerie, giving too much space for a pensive mind. But the real thing was imminent—their mass hurtling through the dark night towards the drop-off point.

On the outside, everyone was physically ready, down to hats tied tight under chin. *A Lysander landing would be great right now*, Henry thought. Unless one jumped through perfectly upright and rigid, one's face would meet with the metal around the aperture: "ringing the bell," they called it. While this was more of an issue in the Whitley, their trainers had drummed it into them that they needed to jump forward enough to ensure the parachute pack also cleared the hole: too far and you would earn a collision but too close and the resulting catch of the chute would also propel one painfully forward. Just right was the ticket. Henry was tensing his body as his mind rehearsed the moment, neurons firing.

The countryside really did look the way Henry had drawn it. White for water, as the moonlight reflected back at them, dark areas of dense forest. There was no 3, 2, 1. The officers were poised to leap as soon as the dispatcher's arm fell.

That was . . . Now!

Clear.

Freefall.

He made it! He was out!

The chute opened automatically.

They were low. Almost too low. It would be fast.

Everything paused. Silence. Surreal. No noise. Nothing. Cocooned inside of his slice of fate; indignantly impervious to the vicissitudes of earthbound conflict. If only it had lasted. The fresh air made short work of wicking away the officer's fears as it clawed away the beads of sweat. Though new ones spawned, gloating, teasing.

Henry's mind circled, insulating itself from the evening's frigid cold. Nevertheless, his thoughts nudged darker—there was that awful business of agents being lured to their deaths when wireless radio agents had been forced to set traps, sending them parachuting into enemy hands. These were often new agents like him, finished before they had even begun. That's why they now used unique coding errors in transmissions to help verify that the message was not coerced. That was but a small comfort.

In the moonlight, Henry could just make out his "pianist" leaving behind him, followed by the long C-type containers dropped by the other planes and that devilishly wonderful Excelsior Welbike. *I hope he gets it.* The C-types brought supplies to sweeten up their meetings: a new clandestine radio set and explosive charges, including Nobel 808, a new plastic explosive. Others were packed with "limpets," charges with magnets designed to stick to trains and the like, all cushioned with horse-hair discs.

Thoughts of inadequacy nicked his heart as gears snapped into place. Shadows: his shadow had declared and given away his position in a training exercise near Loch Nevis, Scotland. At least he wouldn't have to worry about that at night. You only have one life in the field. If it hadn't been for one instructor, he might not have passed training at all, not that he could tell another living soul now. Self-doubt gave the Nazis the upper hand—so it couldn't be tolerated. Lives counted on the impeccable execution of each aspect of the mission.

Parachute bellowing open and hung in history, Henry was far away from the king's protection or the force of Churchill's stirring speeches. He was never more aware that, in this particular instant, he was not in control; that was until he set foot upon solid ground. Then, when finally in the field, he would have to remind himself, as he had been instructed many times, that Queensberry Rules of gentlemanly combat would not win the war.

Suspense? Ungodly. Yet only seconds.

Then time snapped back. He could already hear the Shepherds barking, jumping, pulling battle-hardened Nazi soldiers in anticipation of catching his scent as if they were cursing him, taunting him, eager. He could now see the small reception party turning off the small four-volt pocket torches they had used to help guide the planes.

"Forti Nihil Difficile." For the strong, nothing is difficult, Henry recalled as fast as the wind could snatch away the words, bracing to land.

This conviction had sunk deeply into his heart, having seen it each day as he reported for work, carved above the fireplace at Hughenden.

Then? Knees on the ground, his legs absorbed the impact. Then? He'd fallen forward. He was there. He was okay, he thought. *Yes, I'm okay.*

No sooner had his hands and knees hit the frost-singed ground than someone had started collecting his parachute. That threw him off— he was going to do that. There were more people than he had expected. Of course, because they had to be fast. Despite his adrenaline, he froze for a moment. Then? A touch. A female *Résistant* grabbed his shoulder. He could just make out her face. "You can do this," Violet spoke into him, having done many new things herself recently.

5

Alexi

Ragdoll & Rage

AMSTERDAM

Wednesday, September 2nd, 2015.

The Dutch youth hostel would be cold and impersonal were it not for being nauseously warmed by the decades of memories forced into the second-hand furniture foam like souring milk spills. This was the first time Alexi had left the UK, and everything felt overwhelming.

She had tried to get comfortable on her metal bunk bed. The blankets were blue felt, with edges covered over with an inch or so of a silkier material a grandmother had labored over. They had a wartime utility about them, only giving way slightly as Alexi tried to nestle herself in. She forced them up around her back and sides before grabbing hold of her faux leather journal. Inside it, the creased note goaded her with white noise. It was written in biro with hash angular strokes by a woman who wanted to see the back of her: the mean middle-aged lady who she had found living at Peter's old address in Egham. The note was torn from a notepad advertising in a neat, controlled, monotone black font "Harold S. Pearson," a dentist from Virginia Water near London. Yet it contained the first wisps of real adventure. "Professor Edwin Lukkien," the horrid lady wrote while her forgettable, rotund husband sat watching from the kitchen, distanced by the light blue carpeted hallway striped by recent Hoover marks. This was probably more interesting than that poor man's lukewarm lunch and melting Vienetta. The lady was taciturn and brisk. "If anyone knows where Peter is, he would," she spat right before she stopped her beloved ragdoll cat from leaving the house. *It was probably trying to escape.* The professor, she had said, could be found teaching at the University of Amsterdam—that is, he could have been in the early nineties.

The whole memory irritated Alexi like a serrated knife trying to catch a hold of skin. She couldn't charm that old bat. She almost didn't even get the note. When she'd first arrived, the woman said she had no idea who she was talking about. But instinctively, Alexi knew that something was off. Alexi had crept around the side of the house—cutting her hand on the fence in the process—only to hear the lady moaning to her husband, "She looks just like him." The subsequent long and obnoxious doorbell ring, which followed quickly on the heels of several hard knocks, was received just as well as you could imagine. "You lied to me! I heard every word you said!" Alexi stood impetuous, with tears in her angered eyes. "Don't you understand? You know him. You know something!" The lady had just stared; used to chairing very morally upright neighborhood-watch meetings, not being caught in deception. She tried to close the door. Alexi placed her foot in it. "I don't have anywhere else to go," Alexi finally admitted, foolishly showing her cards. Only then had the woman written down Edwin's name. And that had brought Alexi here.

As if to spite the memory, Alexi slammed the journal shut upon the note and grabbed a thickly woven woolen cardigan that, mercifully, someone else had left. She ran down towards the tight back stairway where paint sloughed off the ceiling like dead skin to reveal a water-stained turquoise plaster beneath. Upon reaching the kitchen, Alexi was thankful for having had at least the forethought to pack her decent pair of socks, but she still had to tip-toe across the freezing tile floor. The dirty white appliances had seen better days, as had the cupboards whose plywood doors barely remained on their hinges. Pushing aside more empty plastic bags than actual supplies, Alexi was pained to discover that aside from a collection of disparate coffee samples that previous visitors had left, British tea was something in short supply. There was a collection of small white bags dusted in a ubiquitous brown powder, shoved in the back corner. She sighed. *Good enough.* Milk was another hurdle; the fridge full of plastic jugs with names scribbled on top. Despite the effort, most were long abandoned.

Alexi crawled back onto the bed, thankful for not having to meet anyone. She only pretended to be an extrovert. Making the best of it, Alexi flicked back her long blond hair and pulled her journal toward her. The slow spin of the tea was comforting to a point. Its warmth helped ease her anxiety. She watched as the milk from her cup began to form small clumps.

Despite not having readied herself for the day, her opalescent eyes were just as spirited as ever. When she turned them towards the pages, she couldn't help but be caught afresh in the contours of her imagination. "Smart" was the last thing that had been spoken over her. And yet ideas—interesting, multidimensional, engaging ideas—had long been Alexi's cozy place. She played with them like a cat plays with a mouse. Here, she was in control—not fate, nor pain, nor anyone else—only she pulled the punches for a change. The problem was, however, that ideas didn't necessarily equate to truth or answers. Her mind was just whirling on the obvious with an insufferable intensity: What was her father like? Did she really look just like him? Could Edwin really help? Would he? What if when she found Peter he was surrounded by an adoring family and "dad of the year" kindergarten crafts?

With a jolt, she suddenly snapped back into her body, sending small taupe splatters over her page. "*What am I doing?*" she said to herself. She was here, and no matter how much more comfortable waiting and thinking was, her answers were just outside. Alexi grabbed her Aztec-pattern bag (a Glastonbury market stall find) from the locker with the same care afforded to her chipped nail polish: none. Alexi cursed as the fraying plaster from the fleshy heel of her hand caught on the lock, gouging the wound from the fence deeper still. She didn't have time for pain.

6

Alexi

Disarming

AMSTERDAM

Wednesday, September 2nd, 2015.

Alexi's heart skipped a beat in the eternity in which the door swung open. Then there she was: a lady with elegant short hair and red glasses in a white apron smeared with oil paint. Immediately, she noticed Alexi's distress. She looked around. "Are you okay?" she asked, peering down the alley in case there was anyone pursuing her. "I'm okay, I'm—It's not . . ." Alexi had rehearsed this in her mind over and over, but she was expecting the professor, not this lady.

"You're not okay!" Edith said, pointing out Alexi's bleeding shin.

"Oh, it, uh . . ." Alexi felt foolish. She always had words.

"And your hand!" Edith immediately peeled off her apron and wrapped her arms around Alexi's shoulders, shepherding her into the house. "Let's sort you out."

Alexi knew that the scuffed pedal—from the bike she borrowed from the garbage area behind the hostel—had met with her shin. She knew that she had been bleeding. Again, she didn't have time for pain. Yet now she felt both wounds. It was weird. What spell was this lady crafting? It was disarming her.

Right away, she noticed a room off to the side. A bedroom. It was clean and immaculate, just waiting for an occupant. How did people come to live this way? Her bedroom growing up was textured with dirt and debris; nothing crisp or coordinated.

While the house was skinny, the entry soon opened into a respectable kitchen and dining room with light beaming through a skylight, bouncing off the clean white walls. Edith got Alexi to sit on a bar stool and brought over Band-Aids and cotton swabs to clean her up.

Alexi was trying to take it all in. The place was not extravagant, but everything was weighty with intentionality. The mugs were handmade from speckled clay. The sink? Clean, aside from a couple of plates and knives from this morning's toast. Plants were everywhere, thriving, from small succulents, multiplying and fleshy, to spider plants spilling over in abundance, hanging from the ceiling.

While Edith had given Alexi a quiet second to reorientate before even tending to her wound, before she knew it, it was all done. *Already?* Alexi thought. Just a reserved "thank you" came out. It should have been embarrassing, but it was kind of nice for someone to care.

"Can I get you breakfast?" The disarming continued.

7

____

Peter

Jerk Chicken

AMSTERDAM

Wednesday, November 4th, 1992.

In a similarly disheveled fashion, twenty or so years before, Peter had arrived in the early evening with a cheap bottle of wine. Chilled from his time by the canals, his emotions felt warmed the moment an aromatic wall met him—the spices in jerk chicken. Edith looked just the same, just with a face slightly more taut and wearing a weaker glasses prescription.

"You remembered!" Peter shouted, lighting up.

Embraced by his dear friends, they drew him into the warm glow behind them. Directed right to the couch, Edwin exclaimed, "How could I have forgotten? Though I'm sure it will pale in comparison to Nana's cooking."

Peter smiled a deep smile, one that all those small muscles hadn't felt in a while. Peter had now thought about Nana for the second time that day. It felt like an age since he had truly thought of her, yet as his childhood nanny, she had so deeply formed the first six years of his life that she still impacted him every day. While Peter's parents had been out at diplomatic events and back and forth from Cairo, Nana was his one stability. Part of the Windrush generation, Nana was the one good thing that his parents had ever done for him, the worst being their decision to separate them by sending him away to boarding school. Too small, perhaps, to be surrounded by cavernous cloisters, gothic towers, and all that "Rule, Britannia!" patriotism.

8

Alexi

The Ache

AMSTERDAM

Wednesday, September 2nd, 2015.

"What is your name?" Edith asked.

Alexi replied but then got right to the point.

"Peter? Peter Cummings?" Edith exclaimed, "Of course we know Peter!"

Alexi hadn't realized anyone else was in the house, but as soon as Edith called him, Edwin emerged from the top floor and down a black metal circular staircase. He'd shot into action, ripping himself from a project the moment Edith had said someone was here about Peter.

Edwin was gracious but wasn't expecting a twenty-year-old girl; instead, an investigator or even Peter himself, perhaps. But that might be too much to hope for after all this time. He lived with a constant ache for his friend.

It didn't seem like two decades since Peter had last shown up at their door. It was the same day that Peter had tried to grapple with Edwin's perspective on reality, which Peter had found paradoxically both too foreign and too familiar. Edwin could vividly remember the warmth between them and—attached like an aroma to the memories—the conversation.

9

Peter

Condemned Like Tantalus

AMSTERDAM

Wednesday, November 4th, 1992.

Cradling a glass of wine in one hand and a starter of fresh sourdough in the other, Peter and Edwin followed Edith into her studio—a space she'd recently reclaimed from Edwin's overflow study. Here, she'd been working on her paintings inspired by their last trip to Calcutta. The vibrant interplay of color and shape marked the collision of faith and real life in a way that confused yet intrigued Peter. He was surprised to learn that Edith had felt drawn to India as a young woman to explore Buddhism and Hinduism and yet had somehow come back a Christian.

Edith's paintings juxtaposed the clamor of life against empty space. It provoked in Peter a question he'd been mulling on over the afternoon. "I've been thinking about what you said about the anxiety caused by looking down and finding a cannonball-sized hole. That emptiness. What do you think causes it?"

Edwin replied, "I think it connects to that rupture—that disconnection from God—the fall away from being as we fell away from God's being. Remember Luther's term, *homo incurvatus in se*?"—humankind curved in upon themselves? That hole in the heart, that black hole, isn't just a feeling of nothingness, but it's also the insatiable." Edwin reminded him, "Like a broken cistern, the human heart finds itself aching, hungry, and this hunger incites sin and violence."

"Right," Peter said. He felt the hunger but had decided he didn't want to swallow Edwin's conclusions whole. Edwin encouraged Peter that he might be surprised how this all related to the works of philosophers as different as Søren Kierkegaard and Martin Heidegger. "Of course you'd suggest philosophy," Peter jibed.

"It's not that bad!" Edwin said.

"Of course, his favorite is Kierkegaard," Edith said.

Edwin didn't need any further permission. He leaned over immediately to grab his cane—the crooked end of which he used to swiftly scoop his top hat off the shelf and onto his head. "Kierkegaard," he explained, immediately adopting his mannerisms, "wrote during the Golden Age of Denmark, the cradle of the bourgeois aesthete." He continued, "Kierkegaard was a quirky, oft-caricatured, and newsworthy philosopher who wrote under eccentric pseudonyms."

"That's a mouthful," Peter joked. "Say that later in the evening!"

"And?" Edith added leadingly to Edwin.

"Well," Edwin obliged, "Kierkegaard had a strong proclivity for striding decisively around his beloved Copenhagen, wielding his cane theatrically as he made his point," Edwin said as he, too, waved his cane up in the air. He got so into character that, in pushing Peter to move in a certain direction, like Kierkegaard did his conversational partners, he became a danger to Edith's easel and almost made Peter spill his wine. "Sorry, good sir," he said, before removing the hat and, with it, his caricature as if *this* was what made him a liability. Peter just laughed. That was his friend, sure enough.

"You bring out the goofy side in him," Edith smiled. Peter could see that he would make the best dad one day. He dearly hoped that for them.

Edwin pulled himself together to explain how "Kierkegaard often took a critical and sarcastic tone but usually did so for good reason. He called the church out from its nationalistic hiding place to look more Christlike. He also wrote powerfully about the human condition, especially anxiety."

"Now I see," said Peter.

"Due to the fall," Edwin explained, "Kierkegaard also thought that humans find themselves at a distance from God, our finitude alienated from his eternal nature. Like what we were talking about earlier." Edwin recited purposefully, "Looking 'down into the yawning abyss . . .

anxiety is the dizziness of freedom,' for freedom 'looks down into its own possibility.'"[17]

"A radical freedom?" Peter said, trying his best. As a mathematician, philosophy felt like a foreign language to him.

"A shocking freedom. Now, Kierkegaard suggests a solution: 'When the sailor is out on the ocean . . . when the waves are born and die, he does not stare down into the waves because they are changing. He looked up to the stars because they are faithful . . . by the eternal [God] one can conquer the future because the eternal is the ground of the future.'"[18] Edwin explained, "If Kierkegaard is correct, then in understanding that we can choose to allow God to break in and ground our lives, anxiety can actually become a force for good: our tutor. It can help us realize the desperation of our condition, revealing the importance of responding to the call to surrender—to take seriously Jesus' call invitation to die to oneself—so that one might truly live. Rather than struggle and strive, this invitation is to rest 'transparently in the power that establishes' our lives."[19]

"What does that mean?" Peter asked, happy to look foolish in front of Edith.

"That this posture of rest is a restoration through reconnection. We can stop being the god in our lives by letting go of (or sacrificing) the attempt to save ourselves. Making this powerful and somewhat paradoxical decision allows God to actually be God for us, freeing us to know the transformative joy of being his sons and daughters—upheld and free to flourish."

"Now you've really got him going," Edith laughed in the warm glow as the wine made her cheeks rosy.

"Oh, he's my responsibility again?" Peter jibed back.

Despite his teasing, since Peter seemed uncharacteristically receptive, Edwin couldn't help but dig a little deeper to contrast Kierkegaard's position with that of the controversial but ever-so-important twentieth-century German philosopher Martin Heidegger. A little cheeky, but he felt the takeaway was worth it. "For Heidegger," Edwin explained, "the solution is different. He thought that humans—*Dasein*, those who have found themselves thrown into this world—should take stock of death all-the-more resolutely. With this posture of being-towards-death, *Dasein*

---

17. Kierkegaard, *Concept of Anxiety*, 75.

18. Kierkegaard, *Eighteen Upbuilding Discourses*, 19.

19. Kierkegaard, *Sickness unto Death*, 41.

can 'conquer' the possible distortion of angst into 'cowardliness' with the conviction to turn and craft oneself. This becomes a "passionate, anxious freedom toward death."[20]

"So, rest transparently in the power that establishes you or create yourself all the more passionately?" Peter asked.

"Something like that!" Edwin affirmed.

"Some great choices!" Peter laughed.

"Have you met Sartre yet?" Edith inquired as she spun the wine in her glass while her palate remained transfixed by the salty residue of olives. She was thinking that Peter should also know something about the famous French existentialist philosopher if he was really going to Paris soon. Besides, it connected directly to the topics they'd engaged. [21]

"Me? No. I've heard his name a couple of times. But honestly, I've got no idea," Peter admitted.

Edith explained, "Sartre published his important work, *Being and Nothingness* (*L'Être et le néant*), in 1943, but it was only after the Second World War that his ideas really reached the masses."

Edwin needed no further excuse to grab his copy on the shelf that quite fortuitously hadn't yet made its way with many others to their banishment in his actual study upstairs.

"Those masses," Edith explained, "turned up for his speech, *Existentialism is a Humanism*, to a sold-out, fanatical audience where he explained his existentialism as nothing else than 'an attempt to draw all of the conclusions inferred by a consistently atheistic point of view.'"[22]

"An atheist? Then why do you—?" Peter started.

"—want to tell you about him?" Edith guessed correctly, as it turned out. "I don't believe that theology should be an isolated discipline," she replied. "If it really relates to life, especially human flourishing, as I think it does, then it should have something both distinctive and relevant to say in larger conversations. I think it goes the other way too. Sartre, for example, is not irrelevant to theology. Instead, he's fascinating because his work offers a vivid account of how fallenness might be experienced by the human person."[23]

"For example?" Peter pressed.

---

20. Heidegger, *Being and Time*, 245.

21. For an in-depth academic study of the connection between theology and Sartre, see Kirkpatrick, *Sartre and Theology*.

22. Sartre, *Existentialism is a Humanism*, 53.

23. See, Kirkpatrick, *Sartre and Theology*, 115.

Edith answered, "For one thing, he didn't think that humans just experience anxiety but that they *are* anxiety."[24]

"Well, that's just fantastic news," Peter said sarcastically.

"Now, I wouldn't go that far," Edith shared, "but Sartre's not afraid to peel back the skin of normality and reveal what I—we—think relates to the shocking ungrounding of our fallen being, ripped from its moorings." She paused, graciously turning to Edwin, "How would you explain this?"

"Well, let's connect it back," Edwin said, holding onto Sartre's brick of a book. "No one writes or thinks in a vacuum. Sartre read Kierkegaard's *The Concept of Anxiety* after being mobilized for the French forces in 1939.[25] The following year, after the German *Wehrmacht* swept through the continent, Sartre read Heidegger's *Being and Time (Sein und Zeit)* as a prisoner of war. Ultimately, he argued in his War Diaries that the phenomenon he thought they both tried to describe was 'one and the same thing: freedom as the apparition of nothingness in the world.'"[26]

"An apparition? Like a ghost?"

"It's an interesting way to put it, right? Almost as if our discovery of ungroundedness, or nothingness, haunts us."

"How would that work?" Peter probed. There was something about everything being stripped down to the foundations that he could relate to.

Edwin continued, "For Sartre, the shocking absence of self might be likened to the absence of a friend you expected to meet. Sartre can claim that *we are* anxiety, by defining anxiety not as a psychological phenomenon but instead as part of the structure of reality as humans experience it. Anxiety looks like human freedom becoming conscious of itself as its own nothingness. As a result, he thinks we're struck with the enormous task of creating and establishing ourselves. Which is why he famously said we're 'condemned to be free.'"[27]

"That sounds like digging those cisterns," Peter suggested.

"Right. It captures all too well the all-consuming drive behind the slavery I've known," Edwin argued. "It's for that reason I find Sartre quite bleak. Aside from striving for authenticity in our self-creation, he offers no alternate mode of being. This is it. *But,* you see, to a newly liberated

---

24. This existential anxiety is also translated as anguish. Sartre, *Being and Nothingness*, 67.

25. Sartre, *War Diaries*, 131–32.

26. Sartre, *War Diaries*, 132.

27. Sartre, *Being and Nothingness*, 462.

French audience who had endured years of German occupation during World War Two, the identification of humanity with freedom (even if anxiety came along with it) was particularly inspiring."

"Why?" Peter asked.

"Because this continent was ravaged. Many found themselves needing to rebuild from the ground up, and Sartre spoke with confidence about the sheer magnitude of the potential of the individual. So, while Sartre argued that humans find themselves irrevocably stuck in the liminal space between being and nothingness (*le néant*), he also asserted that they alone were empowered and responsible for what happened next: what life they would build."[28] Having rejected any concept of a fixed essence, an omen or God to guide us from the outset, existentialism demands we create our own meaning and thus set our own agenda."

The smell from the kitchen was amazing; it would be ready soon but not quite yet. While Edith had just picked up her drink again, she quickly changed her mind. Finding a spare couple of inches to place the glass down on the sideboard between jars of water and stacks of pastels, she seized hold of a fresh canvas. She ripped off the clear plastic, adopted her preferred position on her wheeled painting stool, and squeezed Mars Black acrylic paint onto a palette.

There was something refreshing about passion. Taking a broad brush, Edith immediately launched into making strong satisfying marks, perfectly navigating the tension between precision and fluidity. Her skill and vision entranced Peter. A monochrome scene quickly emerged, starting with a central couple. As she teased it into being, Edith explained, "Ideas don't—and shouldn't—exist by themselves. You need to know about the humans behind them." She made another bold overture of pigment before continuing, "While you'd have been hard-pressed to call Sartre handsome, he had a striking and memorable appearance."

"So, the man's Sartre?" Peter asked.

"Right," she said as Edwin stood back, observing with a growing smile.

Edith postured Sartre's figure sitting at a bistro table. "Despite his wandering left eye beneath thick glasses and scruffy attire," Edith continued, "his charisma and intensity were unquestionable. He dedicated the same feverish concentration to everything, whether his studies or piano playing—even when, as Simone de Beauvoir confessed, he had no talent

---

28. Central to this freedom, for Sartre, is the human ability to choose to negate, reject, and thereby navigate the world.

for music. He was *the* philosopher of freedom." Then Edith started working on the figure with him. "De Beauvoir," Edith explained, "was notable in her own right; elegant, chic, and no academic underdog. She wrote novels that peered into the lived human experience and became an icon of second-wave feminism. You've probably heard of her book *The Second Sex*?" Peter nodded, so Edith continued, "They shared a mutual respect. After the war, both their work and lifestyle captured the imagination of Paris, yes, but also the world."

"Edith's more than my equal," Edwin confessed, never failing to be in awe with the speed at which she could masterfully bring a scene to life.

Blushing just slightly, Edith continued, "While Sartre and de Beauvoir studied philosophy in Paris in the 1920s, it was an introduction in the '30s that changed everything. This story is almost canonical now in the annals of philosophy. De Beauvoir's version explained that their friend and fellow philosopher, Raymond Aron, had just returned from studying in Berlin in 1932. It was he who made the introduction over apricot cocktails at Bec De Gaz on the Rue Montparnasse." Edith prompted Edwin.

Edwin launched in as Aron while Edith added new black lines, effortlessly suggesting the drinks before them. "'You see, my dear fellow, if you are a phenomenologist, you can talk about this cocktail and make philosophy out of it!'"[29]

"A phenomenologist?" Peter asked.

Edwin jumped in, "Phenomenology was born at that monumental tipping point: the dawn of the twentieth century. It was also an important time for the history of mathematics, right?"

"I know a little," Peter said, happy to boast that he'd actually come prepared with a book about that in his bag. He hoped to read it in Paris. "So, what's important about this school of thought?" Peter asked. *Wow, I haven't said that in a while*, he realized.

"Great question. It's more of a method. Edmund Husserl pioneered this rigorous qualitative method of studying how phenomena (*zu die Sachen selbst*) present themselves to human consciousness by first suspending the biases and conclusions—including God or no God—that we already have. Through the phenomenological method, Husserl was hoping to correct the excessive focus on objective, quantitative scientific

---

29. Beauvoir, *Prime of Life*, 135.

methods that he thought had caused, as the title of his book attests: *The Crisis in European Sciences*."

Peter teased him, "There's something wrong with numbers and stats?"

Edwin laughed, "To his credit, modern man since the Scientific Revolution had been obsessed with the quantitative approach and what it had seemed to have achieved. But Husserl thought, for good reason if you ask me, that it neglected to value the subjective 'lifeworld' (*Lebenswelt*)—the everyday foundation of human experience—with devastating results: cultivating a worldview that led to profound alienation and a loss of existential meaning."

"Basically, it made us feel pretty awful?" Peter asked.

"I think so," Edwin replied. "Since our worldview sets what we prioritize, there was, at best, little space—sacred or otherwise—afforded to our inner worlds."

"And at worst?" Peter asked.

Edwin replied, "Humanity undercut itself by intentionally hollowing out the unseen elements of life, including the spiritual."

Peter touched back, "So, Sartre liked phenomenology?"

"Absolutely," Edwin replied. "By introducing him, Aron had given him fresh tools to directly explore and think about the experience of embodied existence."

Having listened closely while developing her scene, Edith jumped in: "Including how we find our minds and affections directed or comported." It felt fitting, just then, to make more bold, directional lines on the canvas. These became the boulevards, either side of the corner café adding the depth of perspective.

"Now," Edwin continued, "Heidegger connects here because if Edmund Husserl is considered the father of this method, then Heidegger might be considered the rebellious 'son' reworking both phenomenology's questions and answers."

"You said Sartre read him when a POW, right?" Edwin nodded back at Peter. Peter continued, "So, Sartre uses this method?"

"He's certainly inspired by it," Edwin answered. "He claims to have used phenomenological analysis in *Being and Nothingness*. For example, in helping him divide reality into two parts: the being-in-itself of objects and the human being-for-itself of consciousness."

"Objects and humans? That seems straightforward enough," Peter quipped.

"I agree," Edwin said. "But what's most interesting is how he distinguishes their different types of being by the dynamics at work, which involves the directionality of minds and affections. He finds this worthy of attention because he becomes—rightly, I think—concerned about how we tend to treat ourselves and others as objects. He says something in here," Edwin said, cracking it open where he had a note tab. "'Each human reality is at the same time a direct project to metamorphose its own *for-itself* into an *in-itself-for-itself*.'"[30]

"In English?" Edith prompted Edwin.

"Basically, we attempt to change ourselves to be acceptable as an object of worship. Yet in doing so, 'man loses himself as man in order that God may be born.'[31] Sartre even says, 'all my projects translate' and reflect this, 'in a thousand and one ways.'"[32]

Edith explained nonchalantly as she leaned in to add a little fine detail, "Of course, he means our self-election as god in our lives, even if it's painful and tragic."

"Oh wow," Peter reacted. "Get rid of one God and billions spring up, like when Hercules cut a head off from the monstrous Hydra—"

"Not only growing back but multiplying," Edwin replied with glee. As boys, they'd bonded by reading Greek myths, so it felt fitting to speak this language while reconnecting. It really was this or Elvish.

Edwin wanted to show Peter why this all mattered. "What Sartre was getting at wasn't lost on someone like the philosopher, playwright, and novelist Gabriel Marcel. Fifteen years Sartre's senior, Marcel had come to faith in Jesus when already in his forties with an established career."

"This will be Marcel," Edith slid in, drawing Peter's attention to a figure she'd just sketched in—shorter, with a round face and pronounced mustache—standing beside Sartre and de Beauvoir's bistro table.

Edwin continued, "They knew each other well, watching each other's plays. In that decadent Parisian decade, the 1930s, they made a habit of teasing each other at Marcel's Friday night gatherings while heaping food onto their plates. Basically, they weren't afraid to joust. While divergent on whether God is a logical contradiction or the real hope of humanity,

30. Sartre, *Being and Nothingness*, 636.
31. Sartre, *Being and Nothingness*, 636.
32. Sartre, *Being and Nothingness*, 620.

Marcel acknowledged that Sartre's philosophy resonated widely with people because it was 'not without truth.'"[33]

"Like?" Peter jumped in.

"Marcel also highlighted the 'irresistible urge' Sartre identified as the human attempt, 'continually renewed and inevitably doomed to failure, at the divinization of himself.'[34] Of course, this is exactly what we'd expect given the fall narrative in Genesis three. Marcel said that it 'lends a disquieting semblance of the tempter's promise: *eritis sicit dii*.'"[35]

Edith translated, fully turning round this time, paintbrush poised in the air, "That's where Eve is told that if they eat—partake in the fruit of the tree of the knowledge of good and evil—then they will be *like* God, knowing both good and evil."[36] Edith added, "Like God, but not *really* God. Isn't that interesting?" Peter agreed, inciting Edith to muse, "I often wonder if it's the being *like* a god unto ourselves that sets up for this living death. That's what God warned eating the fruit would bring. If so, this makes his warning of death not a vindictive punishment but a prophetic warning of what being severed from the one who is Love and Life, would honestly be like. It's honesty, not cruelty."

"How would that work?" Peter asked, recalling that Edwin had said something similar by the canals.

She responded with another question: "Well, what defines a god?"

"I don't know; I guess that they're worshiped?" Peter replied.

"And what happens if we occupy the position of a self-elected god in our hearts? Since we're not actually God, are we owed worship?" Edith pressed.

"No . . . So, I guess we start throwing our toys out of the pram?" Peter joked.

"Right. And, perhaps, try all the more desperately to get it. This is where Sartre's *Being and Nothingness* describes *homo incurvatus in se* so well," Edith explained. "Distanced from a satisfying experience of love, life really hurts! Project after project, pointless, painful. Why does it hurt? We were made to know we are loved," Edith replied. "Now magnify that. Billions of hurting people, hurting each other every day as they try to navigate life away from the one who is Life, screaming 'Love me!' with

---

33. Marcel, *Existentialism*, 84.

34. Marcel, *Existentialism*, 84.

35. Marcel, *Existentialism*, 84.

36. Gen 3:5.

their lives. I tend to think that's why the one tree is called the tree of the knowledge of good and evil, not just the tree of death."

"Why?" Peter interjected before she could get to it.

"Soon after this, the fall narrative, the Hebrew word for 'know' is used to describe the intimacy of Adam and Eve knowing each other and having a son. It evokes an intimacy; a living-through, close knowledge, not a head knowledge. It makes sense to me that as humanity entered into a new, fallen mode of reality, we start to know—to intimately live through—the realities of both good and evil, the highs and lows, love, lack and loss, all driven by the shocking discovery of nothingness at our core: existential anxiety."

"That *is* really interesting," Peter encouraged. But he quickly changed his tune: "But do you think it's reasonable to say that eating some magic fruit can change reality?"

Edith welcomed the interruption, resting her brushes on an absorbent towel. "I think the narrative makes more sense when we appreciate some of the logic that even goes unspoken in the secular world today."

"Like what?" Peter pressed, intrigued.

"Like smelly water," she teased.

"What?"

"Perfume. Think about the adverts you see all the time. How do you separate one brand of overpriced, smelly water from another?"

"Marketing, I guess," Peter replied.

"And what's that based on?"

"Well, they say sex sells," Peter suggested.

"True! Marketing suggests that this physical smelly water is better than another because by buying and using it, it might offer you something far more valuable—you will be more alluring to the opposite sex," Edith said.

"I agree, but what's that got to do with the Genesis stuff?" Peter asked.

"Every day, we're surrounded by marketing trying to sell tangible things, physical, as if they are able to give us something invisible. While I'm convinced most of this is snake oil, the logic behind it taps into something true: that physical things may take on deeper significance."

"Which is why it works?"

"Right. An obvious example is a sentimental significance, but even deeper than that, things may take on a spiritual significance. Whether the Genesis story is literally true, or simply communicating truth, I think the fruit presents to humanity a spiritually significant choice that will impact the whole of life."

"That's so interesting," Peter encouraged. "I'm sorry, I interrupted what you were saying before about knowing and nothingness."

"All I was going to add," Edith said, "was that Sartre *only* seems to understand life—and indeed love—in this fallen, amputated mode of existence."

"And by mode, you mean a way of living?"

"Right," Edith replied.

Allowing Edith to return to the canvas, Edwin explained, "It's the way we try to save ourselves; the attempt to secure for ourselves real life." He had been ready with his thumb wedged between the pages of *Being and Nothingness*, ready to illustrate this with the perfect quote: "As the vain attempt to found one's own being, each of us declaring with our lives: 'I am the project of the recovery of my being.'"[37] Edwin continued, "I relate to the desperation Sartre shares when he said, 'I want to stretch out my hand and grab hold of this [my] being . . . like the dinner of Tantalus; I want to found it by my very freedom.'"[38]

Edwin continued, "So, for Sartre, even the lover's goal is not altruistic, but to 'possess a freedom; to capture a 'consciousness.'"[39] This is what he means when he says that one becomes god—worshiped by another. This isn't an incidental point for him but shockingly central: 'To be man means to reach towards being God. Or if you prefer, man fundamentally is the desire to be God.'[40] Knowing this project is in vain and will never satisfy us, Sartre calls humans a 'useless passion.'"[41]

"That's overt for an atheist!" Peter admitted. "But, Edwin, if I'm honest, I forget the myth of Tantalus."

"Really? That's one of my favorites," Edwin said. "Tantalus was the prideful king who thought he could gruesomely test the gods! But they saw right through it. So? They condemned him to the underworld. What else, right? Anyhow, now he could not seize for himself what he desired, because—"

37. Sartre, *Being and Nothingness*, 386.

38. Sartre, *Being and Nothingness*, 386.

39. Sartre, *Being and Nothingness*, 389.

40. Sartre, *Being and Nothingness*, 587.

41. Sartre, *Being and Nothingness*, 636.

"Now I remember!" Peter jumped in. "He stood in a pool of water beneath a fruit tree. When he attempted to gasp fruit, the branches lifted out of reach."

"And when he bent down to drink the water," Edwin added, "it receded. It's where the word tantalize comes from."

Edith couldn't help but turn and lend her voice: "Like Tantalus, the full recovery of our being, by our own effort, seems out of reach. So, this ache—this existential anxiety—corners us into being those self-hating demigods, never feeling enough in the aftermath of this tragic self-election and perpetual reshaping."

"Well," Edwin concurred, "we're made to receive a knowledge of our worth through relationship with God (echoed in relationship with others)—not perform to earn it. The rhythms of life were meant to center around lovingly receiving and giving gifts freely, forming healthy relationships. Instead, we find ourselves erratically stealing praise, desperate to outperform others. Our world is not at peace. What is it that Mother Teresa said?" Edwin prompted Edith, who, he explained, had volunteered at her mission in India.

"The quote you're probably thinking of is 'The poverty in the West is a different kind of poverty—it is not only a poverty of loneliness but also of spirituality. There's a hunger for love, as there is a hunger for God.'"[42]

"That's the one," said Edwin.

Edith added, "She also said, 'The hunger for love is much more difficult to remove than the hunger for bread.'[43] And she would know; the nuns feed so many people every day."

This all gave Peter much to think about. No matter how much we want to reach out, to love, we really do seem hopelessly curved in upon ourselves, even more so as we recoil in pain. To lighten the mood, he shuffled towards the kitchen, joking, "This self-hating demigod needs a little more sustenance!"

Edith stayed back to quickly add a couple last details and clean her brushes. But Edwin followed, tasked with checking on the status of dinner.

"It smells amazing!" Peter complimented, helping himself to a little more sourdough to tide him over.

"All, Edith!" Edwin replied. "I better not wreck it!"

42. Teresa, *Simple Path*, 79.

43. Desmond, "Interview with Mother Teresa."

Without thinking, Edwin had brought Sartre's *Being and Nothingness* with him. He put it down on the kitchen island to get the serving utensils and heat pads out. The book really was a brick!

"How can someone write so much on the topic of nothingness?" Peter asked Edwin, tongue in cheek. "Seriously though, all that, and he doesn't even give an answer?"

"His goal was to understand and describe the human condition—the mammoth responsibility of freedom—not to provide an 'answer' per se. But I would counter that our freedom, as I'd define it, actually gives us a choice to live in a different mode of being."

Peter challenged him, "So you'd say there *is* an answer?"

"There's no getting away from ourselves. So, for Sartre we're stuck *as* anxiety. Since this informs all our projects, we find ourselves as the being who folds nothingness into the world." Edwin let that sink in for a second before continuing. "Likewise, good news is not founded on an escape from ourselves or this world, as some have assumed. Nevertheless, it's precisely because of this interface with our lived reality that it gives real hope! A hope that rests on being reconnected with God and resurrected to new life. Edwin paused. He could talk about philosophy and theology all day, but something else felt much more important: he was terribly worried that Peter was going to isolate himself after arriving in Paris. Seeing an opening to discuss relationships, he had to take it. Edwin continued, "We can be free from the enslaving project of the recovery of being because, through Jesus, God shares his being. Peter, this changes everything: it empowers us to live in a new mode where existential anxiety no longer determines the form of our lives or communities."

This seemed to have some logic to it, but was it true? Peter didn't have the energy to store his hope in lies. Peter asked, "You're saying that Sartre only sees humankind as fallen but not the potential?"

"Exactly. Essentially, Sartre fails to see the power of healthy community. Marcel thought Sartre was stuck on this plane of *eros* and lust, 'unable to see any robust form of love or interpersonal connection beyond the use and abuse of others.'[44] Edwin explained, "This is because, by defining freedom as autonomy, he rejects—" Edwin paused to silence the oven alarm.

44. Marcel, *Mystery of Being II*, 10.

After a second of near chaos—oven mitts going everywhere and a small billow of smoke that he clearly didn't want Edith to know about—Peter teased, "Are you going to make me beg?"

"Sorry, Peter," Edwin laughed as he placed the two pans—the roasted jerk chicken and plantains—on the counter pads; "Sartre rejects grace!"

"Of course he does; he was an atheist!" Peter said, as Edwin slid back onto the bar stool next to him.

"Ah, grace defined more widely: as a free gift, given from other humans as well as God," Edwin clarified.

"Okay," Peter said, tentatively. "And that matters because . . .?"

"Because this rejection is not a peripheral thing," Edwin replied. "In fact, Marcel argued that Sartre's 'central intuition' was an explicit refusal grace,[45] claiming that grace had 'never been denied with such audacity.'[46] Now," Edwin explained, "Sartre actually foreclosed himself against grace the moment he committed himself to defining freedom as autonomous action." Edwin tapped on the cover of *Being and Nothingness*, "He wrote in here that 'Freedom is precisely the nothingness which is made-to-be at the heart of man and which forces human-reality to make itself . . . nothing comes to it either from the outside or from which it can receive or accept.'[47]

Edith entered the kitchen—book under her arm—while she dried her damp hands. Right before Peter could reply, Edith interjected, "It's even more than that," she said with zest, having kept abreast of the conversation while cleaning her brushes. "Sartre vilifies gifts—basically anything uncontrolled or not self-initiated—as creating a dynamic of destructive enslavement to others. That's why in his play *No Exit*, he wrote, 'Hell is other people.'[48] He thought that even the gaze of others objectifies." Right before checking on the chicken and sides left on the stove—suspicious given that she'd detected a slight burning smell—she tossed Edwin his Marcel book, narrowly missing his wine glass. "Here, sounds like you'll want this."

Peter laughed, Edwin too. They were hilarious together. He loved that Edwin had found someone who not only put up with but encouraged his nerdiness!

"'*No Exit*,' that sounds so direct, so final," Peter noted.

45. Marcel, *Homo Viator*, 183.
46. Marcel, *Homo Viator*, 166.
47. Sartre, *Being and Nothingness*, 462–63.
48. Sartre, *No Exit*, 47.

"Right?" Edwin agreed, "Very different to breaking the siege: making a way when there was no way."

Peter asked, "So, hope rests on defining freedom differently? How?"

Edwin replied, "What if freedom doesn't mean autonomy, but to be unrestrained in a different way: the siege being broken so that one can flourish, to make full use of our gifts and talents?" What if Marcel was right and Sartre had it upside down, and this rejection of interpersonal love on the altar of autocratic freedom is instead what keeps us enslaved? Doesn't his vilification of gift-giving set humanity up for a worldview that starves us?"

"That's a lot of what-ifs," Peter teased.

Edith turned back toward them, having placed down a sauce-covered spoon approvingly and removing the pan from the heat. She explained, "Flourishing depends on being open to give and receive gifts, starting with the gift of Jesus' life. This changes us. It needs to. You see this dynamic first on the cross: Jesus gave his life freely. It wasn't taken. The gift of his life poured out—*kenosis*—interrupts the way the world has turned inwards. He re-establishes this pattern of giving, of love!"

"You know," Edith continued, "in Genesis, God said that we'd die, but he didn't say we'd stay dead. The rest of the Bible is about God's plan to resurrect people and communities. But we can't avoid death; that's where Jesus making a way when there was no way comes in. We're invited to die to this old mode of life, being our own self-hating demigods—the living dead—manipulative and parasitic upon the life and affections of others. By joining in Jesus in his death we can also be resurrected, to live rooted—grounded—in the one who is Life. This grace is the gift of Life himself. Hence why Jesus calls us to follow him by retracing his paradoxical pattern: lose your life and you will find it!"[49]

"That sort of makes sense, but isn't God just controlling?" Peter said, verbalizing some fear that had clung to him for God knows how long.

Edith replied, "I've actually found the evidence to go the other way. He's not forcing us into this relationship. In fact, I think, more often than not, we're frustrated that God seems hidden."

"Right!" Peter exclaimed, instantly pivoting. "If he's loving, why isn't he more obvious?"

"Great question," Edith shared, "I think there's a tension here. Even in the fallen world, signs point to God woven all throughout creation:

---

49. Matt 16:25; Mark 8:35; Luke 9:24.

the starry heavens above and the moral law within, as Kant put it. But God also needs to maintain some distance so that his presence is not overbearing, and we can freely choose relationship."

"Huh," Peter replied. He'd never considered any positive. He'd mull on this one.

Edith underscored, "Forcing a relationship would not be his nature, for that wouldn't be love. Marcel actually explained our relationship with God as 'one freedom to another—a relation of the same type as that which succeeds in binding lovers.'[50] We flourish when turned toward God and each other."

"Oriented outward, like the canals?" Peter asked, turning to Edwin.

"I think so!" Edwin replied. "We also can't offer the world something that we don't have. So, we're either the being who—through our actions, projects, and lives—folds nothingness into the world or the being who has known the pain of this lack but is also dignified with the remarkable opportunity to fold love and life into the world. Peter, I think there's a natural delight that comes through being receptive and participating in this pattern."[51]

"Just think of how central the relational dynamics of giving and receiving are to our healthy development," Edith suggested. "This informs our vital attachments as we grow." Of course, Peter thought of Nana. Edith then shared Marcel's example of a small child who gives you 'three bedraggled dandelions.'[52] Edith recounted how, "You would expect them to study your face, awaiting you to admire them—for your 'recognition of the value of its gift.'"[53] Edith asserted, "There *is* a vulnerability in relationship, absolutely, but this open posture also makes possible this joy-filled response of delight. Which, interestingly enough, is what the Hebrew word for Eden means."

"Delight? Huh," Peter echoed.

"Are you sure you didn't want this?" Edwin joked admiringly, offering her back his Marcel book.

---

50. Marcel, *Metaphysical Journal*, 58.

51. The word 'participation' is drawn from the Greek *koinōnia*, meaning fellowship. See for example, 1 Cor 10:16.

52. Marcel, *Existentialism*, 102.

53. Marcel, *Existentialism*, 102.

Edith responded cheekily, "He also talks about gift-giving resulting in an 'accretion'—a gradual reinforcing—of being, right?"[54] She knew she was correct.

"She doesn't need it," Peter affirmed.

"Evidently not," Edwin said. "Me, on the other hand..." He turned comically to a well-loved page to summarize, "For Marcel it's clear, Sartre is left with 'an atrophied world where we fail to recognize ourselves,' whereas being 'open to the other' makes one 'more accessible to oneself.'[55] Essentially, Sartre masterfully describes our fallen tragedy but is blind to its redemption."

"So, the fate of humanity hangs on whether we're up for accepting gifts?" Peter asked.

"First the gift of his Life," Edwin clarified graciously, "And then gifts between each other. Healthy community is priceless."

"Then it's a good job you didn't reject my cheap wine!" Peter joked.

Edwin chuckled, "Which brings us full circle to Kierkegaard."

"Don't even think about it," Edith teased, having seen his eyes dart toward his top hat.

Jovially, Edwin continued, "Kierkegaard thought that, in the context of our fallen, anxiety-inducing, dizzying freedom, 'eternity's demand upon man is to be a self'! For Kierkegaard, this can only be achieved through relationship to the eternal one, God."[56]

"And that demand means?" Peter asked.

"God is urging humanity to consider how we live, encouraging us to establish the fullness of our humanity in him. The alternative seems to look like enslavement, where in becoming gods that others might find acceptable, we are complicit in our atrophy into objects: idols. This demand suggests, nay screams, that we have real choice."

"Speaking of choice," Edith asked Peter, "do you want to plate up?"

Over the rest of the evening, they ate good food, drank good drinks, reminisced, and made good (and sometimes bad) jokes. Conflicted, Peter pushed back and back again when things of life and faith became too close and personal. But that made it a holy evening—for it engaged an authentic wrestle that entered the unseen sanctuary of the soul.

---

54. Marcel, *Existentialism*, 102.

55. Marcel, *Mystery of Being II*, 10.

56. Kierkegaard, *Sickness unto Death*, 57.

If only they had known that it was the last time that they would see Peter. Not knowing what had happened to him prolonged the freshness of their grief.

10

Alexi
Cross-legged

AMSTERDAM

Wednesday, September 2nd, 2015.

"You're Peter's daughter?" Edwin asked, voice cracking, with a tear already half the way down his cheek. He placed his hand on hers, both shaking.

"I mean, I have this," Alexi said, taking back her hand to clumsily find the paperwork in her bag. "But I never met him, or—"

"It's okay. It's okay, honey," Edith said.

They barely looked at it, knowing it to be true; sincerity in her eyes.

"Can I hug you?" Edwin asked before they embraced.

Alexi had arrived with no idea of what to expect. What had she stumbled upon? Such love but also so much pain. What did that mean about him? Or herself?

Before she knew it, she was sitting cross-legged under a woven blanket, looking at photos. In one, Peter was in a school's formal naval uniform, hair swept over. He was handsome and kind-looking. There was another of Peter sailing. And another with him at a fireside as a Boy Scout surrounded by four other young boys, one of them Edwin. Each of them had worn long white shorts with drawstrings drawn too tight, and, despite it being black and white, one of them was clearly a freckly, red-headed boy with a delightfully old-looking camera around his neck.

It was a while before the glorious foretaste of joy passed and a lump set up in everyone's throat. They hadn't seen him for at least a year or two before Alexi had been born. And no one else that they knew had either. Edwin had, after all, been his best friend.

"Look, the postmark has the date, Edwin!" Edith said, having found one of the postcards that she was looking for. "Peter was here in 1992, right before going to Paris. He wanted to find peace for his soul. He was the most remarkable man, Alexi. The world just didn't always see that."

Peace? What did that mean? Alexi thought. *How would the clamor of Paris help with that?*

"There's a couple more postcards. I'm sure of it," Edith said, pouring over scrapbooks and photo albums to look for them.

11

Peter

Nana & Cairo

FRANCE

Thursday, November 5th, 1992.

Peter's train ride from Amsterdam to Paris was painful. He had promised them that he'd try to find healthy community but had no idea what this would look like or whether he'd follow through. Nothing in him wanted to leave the safety of Edwin and Edith's house. It was the only place he felt truly known. But he needed to test and think. Besides, Peter knew he was a people pleaser—if he stayed, he would have just shoved down all his doubts, pain, and fear, never affording them the space to be dealt with. Sure, Edith and Edwin would have encouraged him to do just the opposite, but he wouldn't have listened.

Why was that always what he did? It's like he enjoyed drinking poison, making life so much harder for himself. Besides, he had promised himself before going that he wouldn't agree with the Christian stuff. He was a mathematician. He liked the clear, cool, and calm. Surely, that's what his heart needed when it was so tumultuous, not leaning into all this about love and emotions.

So then why did he have one of those black school Bibles in his bag, taunting him? That was entirely a function of his fear of disappointing people. Interrupting the hugs and tears right before Peter had walked to the train station, Edwin had given this to Peter as a gift. He said he was sorry that it was a school one, but that didn't make any difference. He was open to listening to Edwin, but the Bible? He'd never understood a word of it anyway—this impossible-to-get-into book. Edwin, to his credit, looked him right in the eyes and said, "I know you, Peter. Don't just take it because you are afraid to disappoint me."

"No," Peter had answered, "not at all. I want it." That was a blatant lie, but it came out so naturally from his lips.

As the world whisked by outside of the train window, he searched his heart. He already knew the root where this fear of disappointment came from. While he'd long forgotten what her face looked like—and he hated himself for it—he remembered the feel of Nana's last gentle kiss upon his forehead. He saw her delicate golden cross swing and lean forward towards him and noticed the rich color of her skin. Nana did not want to give him over to the sort of life she foresaw for him at the school. He was just a baby, just turned six, but his parents wanted him there. How painfully ironic that while he couldn't remember the details of Nana's face, he had their faces of disappointment etched so deeply. They were diplomats who didn't have time for a child, and while Nana was clearly the best thing for him there was no prestige in having him home or at a normal school: he needed to attend the best. Their disappointment? When he called them crying; they didn't want to hear of his sorrows, only his success. Soon, they just stopped answering. Then, they stopped coming to the awards evenings at the school because the one time they dressed up they found nothing to celebrate. Perhaps this child of theirs, they must have thought, was un-shapeable. They didn't even care to tell him when Nana had passed away—the reason her packages had so abruptly stopped the second year. Disappointment: that was their last verdict. Their verdict right before they, too, left this world, dying in a car accident in Cairo.

Besides Edwin, who was also just a young boy trying to figure out his way in a confusing world, there was no one who truly cared. No one who would walk him through this all. A teacher dressed him in black, took him to the funeral, and then made sure he was back for Latin. A stiff upper lip was expected; he knew that.

At least math had a right and wrong answer, and he could please people by giving it to them. Sure, he wasn't going to be Einstein, but he made sure he did as well as he could. And one day he would be a good math teacher. He *was* a good math teacher. But the fear still gnawed at him: who was he going to disappoint next?

Clearly, he had to take the Bible from Edwin even if he had no intention to read it. But it didn't mean he was unfeeling; he felt all too much as he passed it over, instead grabbing hold of his book on the history of mathematics. Mathematics was safe: a conversation with a diversity of opinions at higher levels like any discipline, but it was ultimately all about decoding this masterful world that scaffolded all the rest of reality. At least, that's the lens through which he'd come to see the world.

However, even that comforting worldview was somewhat under threat. Given his university study, of course, Peter had heard of scholars like the Lord Bertrand Russell and the great German mathematician David Hilbert. Though, before starting to read this book, he'd never fully appreciated the chaos in the field at the turn of the twentieth century. Funny, that life goes on and we hardly know anything about it. It was all such a big deal for these geniuses back then. It reaffirmed Peter's worry about whether anything really mattered at all and if there were really any secure foundations.

12

Alexi

A More Noxious Neurosis

FRANCE

Friday, September 4th, 2015.

Alexi feared that the love she felt was just secondhand. What would happen when the novelty and euphoria wore off? If she stayed, they'd get to know her, and she wasn't going to open her heart to them if they were just going to reject her. Besides, she had to leave Amsterdam, more determined than ever to find Peter. What had happened to him so that he never went back? And why did they love him so much when that horrid lady in London, just like her mother, wanted to see the back of him?

Sitting on the train, Alexi watched a mother and daughter carrying grocery bags take their seat. Funny, Alexi thought: while her own mother was deadly afraid of being left alone, if she was honest, she was afraid of being known. Wasn't naming meant to absolve that curse of some of its power? Even that didn't work for her. Her mother, she had long perceived, had filled their house with all sorts of people, doing who knows what, while for all of that, she was lonely. Being known was much harder than addressing being alone. *Trust me to have a more noxious neurosis,* Alexi thought.

But is that true? Alexi asked herself. *How can I fear something I don't think is possible? Maybe it's like being afraid of the dark or ghosts?* If being known is an impossible thing, Alexi reasoned, rather than let all those parasitic and abusive people into her life like her mother did, she'd rather be lonely.

And yet lonely hurt. Sure, turning on a bubbly, carefree persona meant she could attract people like moths to a flame. Though, somehow, she was the one always getting burnt. Was it even worth it? It was worse when guys would just call her "the blond." And what? Pursue her because of her hair color? Lonely hurt. It hurt so bad, especially when others looked like they enjoyed each other—like the gaggle of friends gathered at the back of the train. *Could they not see that they were one step away from being used and abused?* Alexi bit her lip and wiped a solitary tear.

To brush past the emotions, she shoved her hand into her bag and pulled out the two postcards that Edith and Edwin had given her. What did she actually know?

The first postcard was touristy and sent from Paris. Peter seemed hopeful in it but didn't say much. The most important part was the address. Edwin said that when looking for Peter, he'd visited there. He'd apparently spent all his leave for years on end, overturning every rock he could think of, but the trail had run cold so close to where it had begun. But Alexi didn't trust other people. As with the lady in London, sometimes, if you pressed a little further, you could get the information you needed. So, Alexi was on her way there.

The second postcard, from almost exactly six months later, looked ratty. Perhaps the result of being held so many times as Edwin sought insight? It looked homemade, with a hand-drawn painting on the front—a fox cub and almost a crest-like image with the words "Le Rubicon" on it. That really didn't give her much to go on: apparently, *Le Rubicon* was the name of a river Julius Caesar crossed before leading his army into Rome. The whole painting felt like a puzzle. If only the other side could have been more helpful. Peter told them to tune into some radio broadcasts that he'd been a part of but mostly congratulated them on their "wonderful news." Edith explained to Alexi that this was about them finding out that they were having a child—Lili—who, this weekend, was away at a retreat. Alexi found this all endearing, but it hardly helped.

The third postcard? They didn't have it. Edwin wasn't sure if they got it back from the inspector. Yes, when Edwin couldn't go any further, they'd hired someone to try to find him. But this was years ago. They assured Alexi that the inspector hadn't found anything of much worth. Peter just seemed to have disappeared.

13

WW2

Whispers & Whimpers

FRANCE

Thursday, September 30th, 1943. Vosges Mountains.

"Duck!" Violet said, arriving at the threshold of an old farm building in a wild, sequestered spot. Henry did so but was immediately met by the muzzle of a guard's gun.

"That's how we welcome him?" Violet snapped.

"Got to teach him who's in charge," the *Résistant* said as he reluctantly lowered his gun to let him through.

The Blitz-ravaged streets of London, whose previous glory would live impervious in Henry's childhood memories, all seemed a million miles away, as did mapmaking in Hughenden and the rugged Scottish Highlands, relentlessly blasted by the storms coming from the Atlantic. His mind flashed between them all as if to try to find an equivalent. But there wasn't any.

Other members of the *Résistance* soon came in with dirty hands and knees, having buried all extraneous debris. "Why didn't we get the bike?" a particularly aggressive man demanded, asking the main officer while tugging on the lapel of Henry's freshly distressed "costume" as if to test the integrity of English handiwork along with the man's heart.

"*Ce n'est pas mes oignons*," Henry said, breaking his grip with a smirk just half-lit by the lamp.

The man laughed. *None of his business?* "Where does he think that accent's from?" he questioned maliciously.

Henry immediately felt foolish, and fear gripped his stomach.

"It's *Provençal*," Violet said almost instantly, "from the South." That was a blatant lie, but she wasn't going to let him demoralize this green man right from the start. Besides, since that man had been causing them all trouble recently, she figured the others might turn a blind eye. It was worrying though. *Was he ready?* This was real life: there wasn't any trial run.

Moments later, others appeared. *How many were living, or at least gathering in here?* Henry thought. Their chests rose to draw in air, faces red and sweaty, speckled with muddy water. While Violet had taken Henry directly, they, it turned out, had been the bait, misdirecting the Nazi efforts. They'd crossed a wide network of streams, not once but five times in order to have the shepherds lose the scent trail. Henry was trying to decide on how best to thank them—as opposed to a ridiculous straight-up "*merci*," but it seemed that, given their stifled sounds of frustration, he had already disappointed them. Why? The Brits had brought explosives and one motorbike (with the other guy), but no guns! Didn't London or the Free French understand how eager they were to fight? To rise up? Just like the victorious *Résistance* in Corsica? This made Henry feel even more awkward.

Everything leading these men and women to this point in time felt so fast, given the rapid but multiple changes. So, what had happened to France? Before the humiliating capitulation of France came the general mobilization of September 1939. And before that? The folly of denial.

Sure, everyone had heard searing accounts from across the border about November 9th, 1938, *Kristallnacht*, the Night of Broken Glass. Tremors of war were now everywhere. Still, the rich and famous would have preferred to put these tremors, metaphorical or not, down to something like the drama and sonorous chaos of one of Elsie de Wolfe's—that is, "Lady Mendl's"—legendary parties.

The French had an unshakeable confidence in the massive Maginot Line's fortification to hold back any German advance. Therefore, Lady Mendl was entirely undeterred—continuing her plans to hold the last great Parisian party of the season on July 1st, 1939—even though history could testify that it was just two months before September's General Mobilization. It was something that wouldn't have been out of place in centuries gone by in Versailles.[57] She strode between the feet of elephants adorned with a circus whip and Cartier tiara, whisking the sweet botanical fog that hung in the warm summer air like aromatic drapery. Her frivolously opulent Circus Ball lit up the adoring eyes of seven hundred of the most fascinating and upcoming names and stars, all dressed in the most lavish couture—men in white tails and ties and women in body-hugging gowns—all immortalized by *Vogue*. Paris in the 1930s really was, in the words of the historian Oliver Bernier, "ever more determined to amuse itself."[58]

On September 3rd, 1939, when Germany refused to withdraw from Poland, France joined England in declaring war on Germany. The mobilization that followed shocked France in its familiarity. Jostling for position on the train platform at the *Gare de l'Est*, families were haunted by memories of the mobilization of the First World War, where an optimistic crowd with two billowing, gigantic *Tricolore* flags escorted the soldiers into a future that no one had ever wanted to relive.

Later, the iconic existential philosopher Jean-Paul Sartre—whose maverick-like magnetism easily outstripped his looks—would identify the mobilization as a key turning point in his thought: "I believed myself sovereign; I had to encounter the negation of my own freedom—through being mobilized—in order to become aware of the weight of the world and my links with all these other fellows and their links with me . . . You might say that in it, I passed from the individualism, the pure-individual, of before the war to the social and socialism."[59]

And yet, for a while, there was then an eerie lull, the *drôle de guerre*. For those left in Paris, like Sartre's equally brilliant companion, the philosopher and novelist Simone de Beauvoir, life had no hope of remaining the same. In *She Came to Stay*, Simone sketched her characters Pierre and Francoise—essentially Sartre and herself—as having "stood together at the center of the world which it was their compelling mission in life to explore and reveal."[60] But how do you do that away from one another? All too fast, a new dynamic took hold: loved ones now separate, thrown into a burnt-out obscurity in the eyes of others by the blunt face of war, each stranger encased in their own macabre epic with suspicion building not far beneath the surface.

57. Scheips, *Elsie de Wolfe's Paris*.
58. Bernier, *Fireworks at Dusk*, 6.
59. Sartre, *Politique et Autobiographie*, 180.
60. Beauvoir, *Prime of Life*, 338.

Once at war, life in Paris became surreal. Everyone was shutting up shop, including (for a time) their beloved *Café la Flore*, famously an epicenter for the artistic milieu of the '30s. This meant that de Beauvoir moved to *Le Dôme* to write. Children were shipped off to the country. By September 4th in Paris, obnoxiously interrupting this silence were the blasts of air raid sirens. De Beauvoir noted that initially, people ran into shelters wearing their gas masks or, failing that, using anything, even undergarments, as a substitute. But as the interruption became a more frequent part of life, Simone wasn't the only Parisian who wondered if the sirens were crying wolf.[61]

The curiously long, languid days of the *drôle de guerre* came to an abrupt end as the summer of 1940 approached. As Louis Aragon recalled, 1940 bore a "May that was cloudless and June stabbed to death."[62]

For those at home, living from one news report to the next became painfully disjointed. On May 10th, 1940, just over a month before they reached Paris, Hitler's forces entered France through the supposedly impenetrable hilly forest of the Ardennes. Their tactic had worked: tricking the French forces into expecting a repeat of World War I. France had sent her best forces further north towards the Franco-Belgian border. Not long after, on May 29th, Belgium collapsed. The newspapers called King Leopold III a traitor since he surrendered unconditionally without consulting his government.

The memory of May 1940 would be forever dominated by this impalement—sparking a Leviathanic race. The Nazi machine had descended upon Northern France, a "narrow wedge of steel which pierced right through the body of France until it came out the other side, twisting around in a wound, enlarging the hole, crushing the country's flesh."[63] While many, including General de Gaulle, fought bravely, the race culminated in a retreat at Dunkirk. To avoid the annihilation of this pocket of Allied soldiers, every seaworthy vessel in England was called upon to cross the Channel. It came down to the French and British forces being encircled on no more than thirty miles of beach and German Luftwaffe pilots charged with their obliteration. Three hundred thirty-eight thousand Allied troops were rescued in the largest military retreat in history, Operation Dynamo.

61. Beauvoir, *Prime of Life*, 383.
62. Aragon, "Lilas et Les Roses," 98.
63. Koestler, *Scum of the Earth*, 158.

§

While the forces at Dunkirk were evacuated, this was just the beginning for those who lived on in France. That first night in the farm building, Henry started to get his first insight into how hard it had been. While some of the *Résistants* initially seemed cold and distant, Henry could hear their whimpers as they slept. Many had shed more blood than they had ever wanted or dreamed—and then there were those who wished they had shed more. Both were equally tormented, it seemed. Whimpers proved much harder to ignore than screams.

Each man and woman had a story of how they ended up together in this dilapidated farm building; each fought for loved ones, alive or dead. The same was true of Matthias, who had arrived just days before with Violet as they followed orders to await Henry's arrival. Though smart and in some ways an asset, he often felt clumsy, maladroit, and useless. Yet when he couldn't propel himself, it was Plato's dark horse of passion pulling his body forward. He had never imagined a life without his wife, and certainly not this one. And yet this one he had.

Henry had wasted no time in giving the directive from de Gaulle to this local *Résistance* leader. Henry wasn't even privy to him reading it, told to leave immediately. It made sense, but he'd hoped to at least read his face. *Was it good or bad news? Wisdom or arrogance?* The transfer had been swift and straightforward, a secret even to the others. Perhaps too swift. Yet he knew it foolish to speak, nay think, too soon. The road ahead of him was long. Tomorrow, he'd be off to Paris by foot to rendezvous with Ophélie, guided by Matthias and Violet.

He still had the microfilm for Ophélie safe inside the necklace hinge pin. In exchange, Ophélie was charged with giving him intelligence, including maps. He'd been instructed to determine the significance of this intelligence with the utmost urgency so that they could act on it "yesterday." *Such fantastically realistic expectations.* Nevertheless, those were his orders. London had no hesitation in communicating that both sets of intelligence were worth more than his life.

Shortly before they left, Henry made sure to find a moment alone to place the necklace around Violet's slender neck. She swept her hair to the side, wild ringlets hanging loose. Not yet having married, the only time Henry had done something like this was for his older sister before her wedding. The clasp was incredibly small. He fumbled with just one hand, having to re-grasp the end again, not once but twice, after it fell against her neck and shirt collar. He felt foolish. He couldn't help but feel the warmth of her skin as he did so. Henry apologized, but Violet brushed it off. He'd explained that the necklace was sentimental to him but not about the microfilm. Whatever their cover story, he suggested it would be much more believable for her to have it. If only the second part of the operation had been as seamless as the first.

14

Peter

Cracks in the Beautiful Age

PARIS I

Thursday, 5th Nov 1992.

> "Mathematics, rightly viewed, possesses not only truth, but supreme beauty—a beauty cold and austere, like that of sculpture, without appeal to any part of our weaker nature, without the gorgeous trappings of painting or music, yet sublimely pure, and capable of a stern perfection such as only the greatest art can show." ~ Bertrand Russell, *A History of Western Philosophy*, 383.

The train approached the sprawling outskirts of Paris. When just fourteen, Peter had gone on a French exchange at school and royally put his foot in his mouth when asked who his hero was. "Horatio Nelson," he replied, as any good London schoolboy would. Not the smartest thing: bringing up the Napoleonic wars with a French family. Anyhow, here he was, back in the land of ideas and barricades. Thanks to Edwin and Edith, he'd heard of mid-twentieth-century philosophers like Jean-Paul Sartre and Simone de Beauvoir. And yet, an earlier golden era also jostled for his attention: *La Belle Époque*, (The Beautiful Age), comprising of the optimism and frivolity afforded by the relative peace between the Franco-Prussian War and World War One.

Bible still closed, for good as far as he was concerned, Peter was deep inside his book about the history of mathematics. He had got to the part about the 1900 *Exposition Universelle* (during *La Belle Époque*) hosted in Paris, the French-speaking capital of the world. Peter could see that Edwin was right to understand 1900 as a tipping point. Oblivious to the rapidly approaching events of the next decades that would end the world as they knew it, the *Exposition* was still unquestionably steeped in the pride and assumptions of rationalistic Enlightenment modernism— brewing since the seventeenth century and having gained momentum in the eighteenth.

And yet, the beautiful age had discontent fomenting beneath the surface. Not that you would know it for the show of self-aggrandizing humanism. A humanism where the true, good, and beautiful (the so-called transcendentals) were wrenched from any mooring in God—the legacy, in part, from the secularizing French Revolution and the Declaration of the Rights of Man.

Quantifying and brutal, Enlightenment modernism fostered a climate in which both life and warfare would never be the same. In addition to Husserl's constructive criticism, major intellectual influences of the twentieth century would emerge from this time, critical of it. The most notable being Marx, Nietzsche, and Freud, with 1900 being the year of Nietzsche's death.[64] Paul Ricœur later described this brazen "triumvirate" as the "school of suspicion."[65] While these three thinkers critiqued Enlightenment rationalism, their work also redoubled the attack on religious truth or revelation.

Why need God when humanity already considered itself deified? The *Exposition* might, without too much exaggeration, be considered to have been a phantasmagoric shrine to Enlightenment modernism. Indeed, as affluent women arrived in Paris—wearing hats topped with whole taxidermy birds—they disembarked from the steamboats with their husbands along the Seine to be confronted by a mirror image. For, while the Eiffel Tower was commissioned as the *Exposition* entrance just a few years before (no longer Venetian red but painted in multiple tones of yellow-orange), the main entrance for this *Exposition* was *La Parisienne*. She was a modernly sculpted, Parisian couture-wearing woman, ousting Greco-Roman gods from their bronze monopoly. This statue,

---

64. Note that Freud's major works happened within the twentieth century.

65. For example, Ricœur, *Freud and Philosophy*, 28–34.

indignant and powerful, stood at the very top of an exotically shaped archway—its organic curves paying homage to a Darwinian-inspired evolution of humanity from sea creatures all the way to the thinly veiled idol of capitalist consumption—Empire. She was, it seemed, the icing on the cake. Humanity had made it! Rather than conceive of humans made in the image of God, this deity-like sculpture was made in the image of humankind.

La Parisienne conferred a certain cultural acquiescence towards the playful consumption of the parasol-wielding femme that walked around the exhibition, giddy at the sight of turbans, machetes, spices, and inventions, ready to take a taste of "The World" home. Paris itself, chiseled, honed, and stuffed into a corset, presenting itself as a respectable *entrepôt* to the world. Athens? Jerusalem? Rome and Constantinople? They should all have been jealous.

However, didn't the Greeks warn of the hubris of man? Could human logic *alone* secure and sustain all it had built and loved? Among the tourists, inventors and global representatives in all their regalia also walked the finest mathematicians from around the world. While *La Parisienne* exuded humanity's self-confident dominance, the mathematicians she welcomed were fighting not to have the rug of truth pulled out from beneath them. They shuttled their papers with bated breath to the conference rooms. Together, they desperately tried to lay hold upon what was true of the world, with mathematics as its very fabric. There was nothing frivolous about the stakes of the Second International Congress of Mathematics that fittingly followed right on the heels of the Congress of Philosophy.

All this display, the industrialization, the smoke pouring out of blackened brick chimneys, interlocking gears that seemed to propel humanity into the future—not to mention hot air balloons that would have been the envy of Phileas Fogg—all of this had been achieved by layer upon layer of scientific advances. And what did this build upon? Mathematics.

Mathematics had long seemed to hold the key to certainty. And why wouldn't it? The natural sciences had long held tight to the seductively self-evident Euclidean geometry. For more than two thousand years, the word "Euclidean" was an unnecessary distinction because from the days of Plato's Academy it was the only geometry—and was therefore synonymous with truth. So much so that Plato is said to have engraved on the door, "Let no one ignorant of geometry enter here."

Mathematics rested on axioms, basic truths. From this point, you could confidently build, play, discover, and repeat for axioms under-pinned theorems, which then framed a whole world of interrelation, bequeathing further exploration. This almost unhindered growth was different than that of the natural sciences, where advances often came at the cost of ungraciously deposing a preceding theory, like Copernicus' heliocentrism overturning Aristotelian geocentrism. Here, it seemed, lay the beauty of mathematics: unmediated tantalizing truth. Cut, dry, clean—the razor edge of advance and reality. *Exactly what Peter had come to expect.*

But what if truth, or what you thought was truth, lets you down? As Pilate lucidly asked Jesus before his crucifixion, "What is truth?" Herein lay the muffled desperation at the turn of the century. While trying to prove one of Euclid's geometric axioms, the Fifth Postulate, the status of this postulate as an objective truth for all time and space was under-mined. It may sound trivial; however, these postulates formed the basis upon which everything else was established.

Carl Friedrich Gauss, perhaps as early as 1800, was the first to real-ize that negating this parallel postulate might not lead to a meaningless contradiction but something entirely new. Then, it was demonstrated that given different conceptions of space, there might be more than one parallel line possible through a point, and indeed, these lines might even meet on a curved surface![66] What these mathematicians had stumbled upon was the existence of a new geometry with an internal consistency just as strong as Euclidean geometry, even if it initially appeared false or foolish based on everyday experience.

Suddenly, a whole host of new possibilities appeared as if out of the mysterious aether. For example, every schoolboy knows that the angles in a triangle add up to 180 degrees. However, for non-Euclidean hyper-bolic geometry, the angles of any triangle add to less than 180 degrees, whereas the sum is greater than 180 if the geometry is elliptic.

Surely this all confounded "truth"? Indeed, during the Paris Con-gress, some delegates might have brought along Lewis Carroll's math-ematical work that fervently hoped to dissuade Victorians from going

66. The Russian and Hungarian mathematicians Nikolai Ivanovich Lobachevsky and János Bolyai, respectively, are both known for their development of non-Euclidean geometry.

down the rabbit hole of Wonderland into a non-Euclidean world, in his aptly titled 1879 book *Euclid and His Modern Rivals*.[67]

While this painful fear boiled within some of the men who gathered in Paris, the honest couldn't ignore the fall of Euclidean geometry from its unrivaled status. Most of them stuffed it down with hefty bouts of optimism, dense servings of camaraderie, and maybe a puff of desperation masked by the smoke drawn, perhaps, from a finely crafted meerschaum or briar pipe picked up from a nearby exhibition hall.

To further compound this situation, serious problems had also started emerging in set theory, such as the Burali-Forti paradox, discovered in 1897. Now, even set theory—that jewel in the crown of nineteenth-century mathematics—was being threatened! Still unresolved in the early 1920s, the distinguished mathematician David Hilbert would release a fervid rallying cry for others to join his program to secure these foundations through formalism. He declared, "No one shall expel us from the paradise Cantor has created for us."[68]

However, Hilbert's leadership had begun even earlier. Already, in 1900, at the International Congress of Mathematics in Paris, Hilbert had stepped up to offer clear direction in an attempt to deliver mathematics from such a vulnerable impasse. Distinctively pragmatic, on the morning of Wednesday, August 8th, Hilbert took to a platform at a hall on the Left Bank, having all retreated from the chaos of the main *Exposition* grounds. Here, he announced the first ten of his famous twenty-three problems. Having set down his floppy Panama hat before taking to the stage—an essential accessory on this hot summer day—the thirty-eight-year-old's receding hairline revealed his last few reddish wisps of hair. He was unpretentious but spoke out boldly, his bright blue eyes establishing confidence from behind his circular spectacles.[69] These problems, he thought, would have to be addressed to disarm history of the blades that threatened to disembowel the cathedral of mathematics of its axiomatic structure: to secure its legacy at the heart of logic. Each problem, once formally solved with proofs, would theoretically act like a tent peg, anchoring the whole architecture to rebuff all those within its canvas from the battering of further onslaught, this aching uncertainty. Delegates listened carefully, noting the possibility of doing something great and making a name for oneself.

67. Dodgson, *Euclid and His Modern Rivals*.
68. Hilbert, "Über das Unendliche," 170.
69. This account is based on Reid, *Hilbert*, 71–73.

Amongst those present also strode a young aristocratic Cambridge man: the beak-nosed and yet quite handsome Bertrand Russell, grandson of a prime minister who twice served Queen Victoria and godson of the secular philosopher John Stuart Mill. Freshly inspired in Paris by Hilbert's problems and Giuseppe Peano's symbolic notation, Russell and Alfred North Whitehead (his friend and former tutor) came away empowered to continue in their feverish attempt to "save" mathematics. Their approach would be to significantly develop logicism which radically asserted that all mathematical truths can be stated as logical truths and mathematical proofs must be derived from logical proofs. Confusion and tautology would be vanquished. Essentially, human logic was the key.

However, neither rescue attempt—logicism nor formalism, launched later by Hilbert—would be easy. Shortly after the Congress, Russell found a significant flaw in Gottlob Frege's attempt to derive arithmetic from pure logic. In one of the most famous correspondences in the history of mathematics, Frege responded, "A scientist can hardly meet with anything more undesirable than to have the foundations give way just as the work is finished."[70] Russell and Whitehead's program would also need to avoid any devastating paradoxes if their own project could be considered successful.

Likewise, Hilbert and his bold compatriots had twenty-three problems left to solve—and that's before we trace the fateful story of Hilbert's formalism.

An announcement came over the speaker. Peter was arriving at the Paris *Gare du Nord*. Reluctantly, he slammed the book shut. It left him with a taste in his mouth of fear and uncertainty. He had never fully appreciated the role of thought or philosophy behind mathematics. Sure, Bertrand Russell had been on the tip of his tongue to defend against any talk of faith, but their faith in mathematics and the tremulousness of it all unnerved him. He'd hoped to stay away from philosophy, having had more than his fill in Amsterdam, but this book made it seem unavoidable.

Being one of those impulsive people who skipped to the end of a book to see how things resolve, to his horror, he'd found that there is still debate about what the truth of mathematics actually relates to. If there is truth, how did it get there? Is it discovered? In which case, who put it there? Or is it created, like a language? And if created by us, who is to say it reflects "truth" at all?

---

70. Frege, *Grundgesetze der Arithmetik*, appendix.

"Who put it there?" This sounded too much like moving from philosophy to an argument for God! Peter liked his mathematics hermetically sealed. Reliable. Stoic.

15

Alexi

La Belle

PARIS I

Friday, September 4th, 2015.

Alexi had arrived at the address on the first postcard, Tristan's place. He was, according to Edwin, one of Peter's university friends. But looking at the dead and dying plants in shriveled soil pulling away from container sides, Alexi wondered what on earth she was doing knocking on this door. She'd lucked out with Edith and Edwin, and now the universe would surely balance itself out by introducing her to a serial killer.

A young blond-haired guy answered, barely able to nurture a decent beard (or trim one). He took one look at Alexi, her absorbing, reflective eyes, and flowing blond hair, and called deep into the stale apartment with American-tinged English: "Blake, it's for you." Kicking what looked like a pile of brick-like man-shoes out of the way, Sam opened the door wide before excusing himself, allowing Alexi's eyes to meet Blake's. In an instant, Alexi could tell he was looking her up and down. "I don't—" Blake, an apparently effortlessly chic student, started.

"This is a mistake," Alexi said, immediately cutting him off. Besides, no one here was old enough to know anything about her father. Pivoting in an instant, she said something even she didn't "catch," clenched her fists and let gravity pull her down the black metal steps as quickly as possible, hoping to forget it ever happened.

But she didn't expect him. She ran right into a young man coming home, still smelling of the kitchen. "Hey, hey, are you okay?" the young man, Marc, a waiter, asked. Ashamed that someone had caught her dashing off with tears welling up in her eyes, she just stared as the tears fell. "Hey, it's okay," he said.

"No offense, but you literally know nothing."

"No, I don't. But I know that it doesn't have to be like this. Do you want to come in? We can chat about it?"

Alexi would have said no. But for some reason, his care pulled out from her a reluctant, "Sure." So, with the door still partially open from her quick departure, Marc pushed it fully open.

Alexi just ignored Blake, to start with at least, and sat cautiously on a wobbly bar stool that seemed to be the best of all the options. "I'm looking for Tristin Balmer, but I think I've got the wrong place," she told Marc apologetically as he leaned on the counter. She showed him the postcard as if to justify her intrusion.

"Well, you've got the right place, but Tristin hasn't lived here for years. There's probably been five other people in the apartment since him. But if you ever find him, tell him we keep getting his junk mail!" Marc joked, interspersed with more compassion than Alexi was expecting. This invited the faintest appearance of a smile on her face; something felt unexpected but easy with Marc.

She stopped long enough to take it in. The scent of cannabis lingered in the air. Oh, and curry, Alexi realized, seeing last night's dishes in the sink.

To his credit, Blake didn't wait too long to come over and apologize. But, avoiding awkwardness, Alexi took to her feet, said everything was fine, and moved away to look at the books and movies.

"How many guys do you live with exactly?" she asked as she perused the shelf.

"Well, there's me and then three others," Marc said. "Sam's probably here somewhere," he continued, banging the grubby white wall with his fist. "We've got company," he hollered.

"We've met," Alexi offered, as she saw Sam re-emerging from some sort of lazy stupor. Sam dragged himself into the kitchen clad still in checkered pajama bottoms despite it being past 4 p.m. on a weekday. He timidly shook hands with Alexi before filling an aging plastic tumbler with milk.

"That's Sam's normal," said Marc, seeing that Alexi wasn't quite sure what to make of him.

"I'm normal?" said Sam, throwing out these words from between sips.

"I guess I do claim to be the only normal one here most of the time," said Marc, trying to get Sam going.

"What are you talking about?" said Blake authoritatively from the armchair. "You, normal? Not this bunch; though normal's overrated." Blake's long gelled fringe swept over the short sides of his manicured hair, framing a distinctive look about him that reeked of ambition. He was American, floating upon family money while sampling Paris's literary and political flavor. "*Enchanté*," he said, lifting Alexi's hand to his soft lips. He was trying to make a better impression. He couldn't handle being frozen out; girls normally pandered after him.

"Get away from her, Blake," Marc said, enjoying seeing her reject him. "Don't trust a thing he says."

"Oh really?" Alexi added, settling into the groove of her trademark sass.

"Seriously," said Marc sarcastically. "He's only ever lucid long enough to get himself arrested!"

"Burn!" said Blake more classily than any American Alexi had ever heard.

"You don't deny it, then!" added Marc, trying to make sure that Alexi knew, in all seriousness, not to give Blake a look-in.

"What does a girl have to do to get a drink around here?" Alexi interrupted, walking back into the kitchen space, now drawing from her well-rehearsed stock phrases.

Drink finally in hand, Alexi looked at the apartment properly, bantering a little. One open window led to a balcony that sagged too dramatically to be safe, despite evidence of a recent barbecue. She tried to discern who was responsible for which decorating choices. The green and white flag with a red star and crescent? It turned out to be Marc's—he was half-Algerian but grew up in France. "Okay, who does that belong to?" Alexi asked, gesturing towards the cotton Che Guevara print.

"Okay, you have to claim that one," said Marc to Blake after a couple of silent seconds.

"Guilty," he said, blushing at the stereotype. "Don't you go thinking I'm some off-the-shelf political groupie," Blake said, wanting to appear much more sophisticated.

"Didn't you say there was a fourth housemate somewhere?" Alexi suddenly asked.

"We're missing Tim; he's going straight from work to an event," Marc replied.

"An event?" Alexi was intrigued given how vaguely it was put.

"Hmm," said Marc, trying to decide whether to let her in or not.

"Oh, just tell her," Blake said. "It's not a state secret."

"It's just a community movie," said Marc, playing it down.

"*Beauty and the Beast*, right?" Blake said.

"Not the Disney one; the Jean Cocteau version from the forties."[71]

"'Love can turn a man into a beast…'" Alexi started quoting.

"But love can also make an ugly man handsome," Marc finished, cracking a smile. "I'm impressed you know it!"

"I'd watch it again, for sure," she said. "But what's was so secret about it?"

"Ah," Marc sighed. "Well, it's underground in more ways than one. Have you heard of *cataphiles*? Technically, the catacombs beneath the city have been off-limits since the mid-fifties. But for us cataphiles, we are urban explorers uncovering and reclaiming our heritage. It's not about the ossuary, the bones; that's only a small section of the mines." To whet her appetite, he shared about places like *La Plage*, a beach-like chamber with sand and art around the walls. Sure, exploring the catacombs was illegal, but that was part of the thrill of it—the police chasing them through the tunnels.

"You make it sound like that happens all the time," Blake critiqued.

"And you'd know, right?" Marc said to Blake.

"Their authority's only on the street level," Blake attested, apparently having challenged his recent ticket.

"Did you hear about the movie theater the police raided years back?" he added, to divert the conversation. "It was there for years, with a bar and room for twenty—"

"CCTV and automated guard dog sounds," Marc added. "They actually siphoned power from above," he continued, neither of them revealing the less rock-and-roll elements like the pressure cooker full of couscous the police found.

"They only found it by accident," Sam said.

71. Cocteau, *Belle et la Bête.*

"I thought it was a bitter ex-girlfriend!" Blake differed. "Anyhow, by the time the police raided it, they'd taken everything down, cut the power cables, and left just a single note: "*Ne cherchez pas.*"

"Don't search," Alexi echoed with a smirk, appreciating that touch.

"Anyhow, that was UX. They're, er, *extrêmement* secretive," Marc explained. "Tonight's not them, but it's basically the same idea."

"It's more than a movie: it's political, the community taking back the city—all layers of it," Blake added, trying to one-up Marc *and* pretend that he was part of the oppressed Parisian masses.

"Oh, I'm in!" Alexi said.

Marc offered to help her get a room at a youth hostel on the way which, surprisingly, she accepted. Having just arrived in Paris, she needed some time to orientate and decompress to get a fresh start tracing Peter's steps in the morning. Switching his apron for a worn leather satchel, Marc said with gusto, "*Allons-y!*"

16

Peter

The Last-Ditch Attempt

PARIS I

Thursday, 5th Nov 1992. La Gare du Nord, Paris.

Peter found himself swept up in the stream of people that flowed out from the train carriage and onto a gigantic arrival hall. He pressed his arm against his leather bag as they rushed past the green ironwork pillars—with orb lights clustered like grapes—that marshaled the platform.

Once past the gates and ticket inspectors, Peter looked up, attempting to orientate himself against the skyline. Tristan's apartment wasn't meant to be more than a five-minute walk away, yet he held onto his crumpled map for dear life. Overwhelmed by the sights and the people, he found comfort as a distant jet engine alerted him to a Concorde flight, eager, like a horse at the gate, to cross the Atlantic. Concorde spoke of unity in engineering from across the Channel. Funny, given that for so many centuries the neighboring nations had each other by the jugular.

Having just read about *La Belle Époque*, Peter's dark, brooding, and irrational side half-expected to turn back to the triumphal, stone-arched facade of the station to see a mangled steam locomotive stuck, the engine hanging down through the station wall. As a schoolboy, Peter had been transfixed by a picture of the 1895 train derailment at the old Montparnasse station—the image forever burnt into his memory. It had been his first real insight into a historical, tuberculosis-ridden Paris that

93

lay beyond the clichés. A brake failure and speeding driver led to several tons of highly calibrated metal crashing through the platform and concourse before falling nose-down through the outer wall and onto the cobbled street far below. It killed one woman as she stood in for her husband, selling the morning paper.

The capital stopped to take note but only for a moment. The privileged took pictures to sell for tomorrow's papers. Then, just as quickly, the shock wave passed. Nothing could loosen this city or nation of its intoxication with speed, power, and engineering. Like *La Parisienne*, the twentieth century beckoned these aspects with unbridled, supersonic optimism. Little did they know *La Belle Époque* would end with the First World War; that same power and speed turned against humanity. Advance, or science, it seemed, was amoral and mute when it came to how it was used. The heart and mind of its master made all the difference.

Paris unabashedly courts its suitors, inviting them to muse over dinner and coffee while they steep in the warm glow of the radiance of its past. In another life, Peter would have been an artist, a counterpoint, not a contradiction, to his devotion to mathematics. Choosing the path of least resistance and most affirmation, he'd buried this passion early. He'd suppressed it further these last years, hardly aware that it was still there. He'd devoted himself to his fiancée; whatever made her come alive after round and round of treatments. It had been so hard on her body and mind. He'd chosen to come second. How abruptly that chapter of life had come to an end; the past and its dreams locked behind him.

The streets oozed art like a livewire, making the anemic part of his heart twitch slightly as if waking from hibernation. Surrealists like Dali felt like long-lost friends, their anti-rationalism pushing back against the cold mechanistic modernism of the First World War. Melting clocks, bringing dreams and the unconscious back into view. Oh, how he wished to feel human again—an agent in his life, not a punching bag.

Peter made a snap decision to take the Métro and explore before his inevitable occupation of Tristan's couch, predictably permeated by the smell of burnt toast and, beneath it, a generous *accoutrement* of rat-sized dust clumps. Once in the heart of Paris, he was drawn to the *bouquinistes*, the open-air stalls that clung like dark green barnacles to the walls along the Seine: the only river in the world, some say, between two bookcases.

Stopping at one stall near Pont Neuf, he went straight to the art books: Dada, surrealism, and volumes on André Breton. The stalls had such a diversity of old books. His eyes also caught the front of a new plucky journal, where it was written in gold cursive lettering, *"Il n'y a que les imbéciles qui ne changent pas d'avis"*—that there are only imbeciles who don't change their minds or, literally, their opinions. Peter chuckled, feeling that it encapsulated what he knew of France: direct, opinionated, and convicting.

Intent to avoid the theology section entirely, there certainly was a lot about life and death in the philosophy section, and, to his chagrin, reading what he had about mathematics had put a small chink in his armor. So much of his life had been thrown into the air; how was it going to land? *A fortuitous Eton-Mess, perhaps? Who am I kidding?* Peter thought.

There were so many philosophy books. He was drawn most to the ones with eccentric marginalia, imagining the intensity with which its past owner's graphite indented the page, leaving a trail while their neurons fired. But it was honestly disorientating: everything from Enlightenment thinkers—like Rousseau's *Emile* and Voltaire's *Candide*—to the Marquis de Sade's explicit twin stories *Justine* and *Juliette*; even Deleuze and Guattari asking afresh, *What is Philosophy?* It was hardly gossamer, trifling, or insubstantial stuff. Each book a potent apothecary jar, willfully concocted to intoxicate the mind. One thing they did have in common: they were all controversial to someone, at some time.

"Are you looking for anything in particular?" asked a lovely young lady with her hair twisted back into a relaxed braid.

"Just answers!" said Peter, poking fun at the immensity of the task he'd set himself. There's no way he could just accept what Edwin and Edith had said without investigating further.

"I can't guarantee answers, but if it's opinions you want, we've got plenty of those!" she said, weightless and poised, agile wrists and nimble fingers hovering over the book spines as if beloved friends or lovers. "You can't come to France without picking up some Sartre or Voltaire," she said in her sweetly thick French accent that piqued at the mention of the mavericks. "Maybe even some Camus, a playwright and *résistant* in the war, and a close friend of Sartre . . . until he wasn't."

Pivoting to the English section, she gave Peter the Irish-born philosopher Dame Iris Murdoch's book *Sartre: Romantic Rationalist*. Peter was happy: *much shorter than* Being and Nothingness he thought. Flicking it open mid-way to where the spine was broken, he was immediately stopped in his tracks. There it was: Sartre, this atheist philosopher, arguing that "man is the being who aspires to be God."[72]

Amused by Peter's reaction, a nearby man took an interest in him. He inquired as to what he found so provoking. He wasn't much older than Peter, later twenties perhaps. His waistcoat fit, which just tipped the scales slightly from starving artist to "old money," though following that road too far wouldn't have done him justice either.

"Well then," the man replied to Peter after he'd explained, "you need to read this." He took the small book and turned two-thirds of the way through. "Here," he said, pointing to a passage. He prompted, "Murdoch argued that Sartre's philosophy was—"

Peter read: "A last-ditch attempt to the value of the individual, expressed in philosophical terms."[73] It shook Peter. "That really ups the stakes!" he exclaimed.

"Not everyone would agree of course," the man said, "but I think it explains something of why these mid-century debates were so charged and why they're still valuable."

"But surely we've figured that one out by now?"

"Turn to the last page," the man said, eager to throw more fuel on the fire.

Peter read aloud, "Sartre's 'inability to write a great novel is a tragic symptom of a situation that afflicts us all. We know the real lesson to be taught is that the human person is precious and unique; but we seem unable to set it forth except in terms of ideology and abstraction.'"[74]

"What do you think?"

"Well, she didn't hold back!" Peter answered, "I guess I'd have to read a few of his novels. But that conclusion's stinging. Was she right?"

"I mean, it's a little embarrassing for us *Homo sapiens*, but we do seem to struggle with giving consistent, coherent answers as to why anything really matters in the grand scheme of things. I also think Murdoch was right in identifying Sartre's philosophy as a critical watershed. His thought punctuated the tail end of enlightenment modernism, both steeped in the philosophical tradition of Descartes but also pushing its boundaries. It was also during his later career that postmodernism really took center stage."

72. Murdoch, *Sartre*, 58; Sartre, *Being and Nothingness*, 587. Barnes translates this same passage as "man fundamentally is the desire to be God."

73. Murdoch, *Sartre*, 102.

74. Murdoch, *Sartre*, 114.

Peter said, eager to demonstrate some understanding, "For Sartre, taking responsibility means grabbing ahold of the reins of one's own life and being the sole master of its project, right?" This met the man's approval, but there was something that had confused him in Amsterdam. Seizing the opportunity to ask in a low-stakes conversation with a gentleman he'd likely never see again, Peter said: "Since he's an atheist, man aspiring to be like God is good, right? Ousting him?"

"Not too fast," the man gently corrected him. "Aspiring to be God is Sartre's diagnosis of what ails humanity. So, not only is the aspiration undesirable but also an impossible goal—a contradiction."

"Oh, right. I'll never get this stuff," Peter sighed. "Why's it a contradiction?"

"Well, it's worth saying that Sartre even thinks the idea of God is a contradiction. Starting by defining the identity of God as absolutely fixed and complete, the supreme object, he identifies a conflict with this and the Judeo-Christian God, who is also considered thinking and self-aware."

"Where's the conflict?" Peter asked.

"The key is that Sartre considers consciousness as only arriving from an incompleteness: a mind driven by a desire that arises from lack. Thus, he argued that God is a contradiction because he cannot be both complete (not lacking) and incomplete (with lack)."

"Huh," Peter said, wincing in thought. There seemed like a lot of assumptions being made.

The man continued, "Sartre thought that humanity, on the other hand, has no fixed essence before existence; we're incomplete, conscious, and thus condemned to be free!"

"So, we're condemned, but at least we're not a contradiction!"

"But, *voilà le hic*, or as you Brits might say, here's the snag: Sartre thinks we find this tension almost unbearable, so we're willing to trade it in. Thus, we try to become this impossible, life-nullifying contradiction where we abdicate our freedom to play a role for others, becoming object-like. He called it living in 'bad faith.'"

"Isn't it all unbearable?" Peter joked.

The man chucked, "Here's the interesting thing: this means that even an atheist like Sartre finds it ironic how 'the passion of man is the reverse of Christ, for man loses himself as man in order that God may be born.'[75] The still-birth of these self-perfection projects are just as unbearable to watch as they are to live."

"All round pretty awful then," Peter laughed a little, part amusement, part desperation. "Is there a way to avoid all this?"

"That's certainly something to think about," the man agreed. "Can we actually create ourselves without turning ourselves into objects, or static idols? That was a concern for Sartre.'"

Peter recalled how Edwin and Edith had argued that self-creation threatened to further enslave, compounding the lived experience of death. From this perspective it could never be the answer. "So, what did Sartre prescribe?" Peter probed.

"He argued that we must be authentic. But he knew that this was also terribly frustrated. After all, he realized that sincerity—the opposite of bad faith—was impossible to achieve because 'that supposes that I am not originally what I am.'[76] And without God, how could that be true?"

"A fair point," Peter conceded.

"That's why Sartre spoke of an 'embarrassing constraint that we constantly experience . . . our incapacity to recognize ourselves, to constitute ourselves as being what we are.'"[77]

"We're just a complete embarrassment, aren't we!" Peter jested while his mind was working overtime. He remembered all that talk about gifts and receiving and felt desperate enough to see what this sophisticated Parisian thought. "What do you think of Christians like Gabriel Marcel who don't think God is a logical impossibility but that he offers a different mode of being, love, and relationality?" Peter asked, desperately trying to say all the right words.

"Participation?" the man asked, surprised.

"Sure . . ." Peter replied, though he didn't recall hearing this word in Amsterdam.

Intuiting this, the man unpacked, "It means close, life-giving fellowship. The idea has some merit—though merit and truth are different things. You probably know that—and full disclosure, you're speaking to an agnostic—thinking Christians will often build their case cumulatively, saying God makes the most sense of most data points."

75. Sartre, *Being and Nothingness*, 636.

76. Sartre, *Being and Nothingness*, 85.

77. Sartre, *Being and Nothingness*, 86.

"Right . . ." Peter said tentatively, curious about his agnosticism, why he'd left space for God.

The man continued, "For Christians, being is also not something that can be given abstractly as a disconnected token—"

"—like fruit thrown to Tantalus," Peter interjected, unable to help himself.

The man got the mythic reference and smiled, "Right. Participation argues that being can only truly be established within community or communion, meaning a sharing. From the Christian perspective, this personal, connected, sharing in the gift of God's Life is seen as an antidote to isolation and alienation: participation with the God who is Life."

The lady running the *bouquiniste* took advantage of the short lull in conversation to suggest that Peter may be interested in a smiling postcard of Pope John Paul II, or a book about him? It was funny seeing the Pope right next to a picture of Joe Dassin with large microphone-like hair, the title of his sixties pop-song "Aux Champs-Élysées" with the Arc de Triomphe superimposed behind it all. To her credit, they were not far from Notre Dame Cathedral, and she'd heard them mention God more than a few times. Peter tried to hold back his knee-jerk reaction. It *was* his fault for asking about Marcel. This left him unsure of what to say, made worse now that he noticed the silver cross around her neck.

The Parisian man jumped in, agile enough in both philosophy and theology to ease the awkwardness. "You know, Pope John Paul II, or Karol Wojtyła, is a formidable theologian in his own right. He offers another worthy counterpoint to Sartre. Similar to Marcel, he argued that Sartre's rejection of gifts, and in the case of God, the gift of participation in his Life, leads directly to our experience of alienation. Now, this debate isn't a peripheral concern for Wojtyła. Instead, he considers it 'the central problem of our age.'"[78]

"Why?" Peter asked.

"Because how we conclude it determines how we understand and relate to our humanity, and, as a result, what world we build and leave to the next generation. You have to admit, there's something to their response: instead of being frozen, objectified, and alienated, through participation, humans can be empowered in the pattern of the Trinitarian community to become more fully moving, active, and relational. So, rather than participation being the abdication of creative action, for

78. Wojtyła, "Participation or Alienation?," 72.

someone like Wojtyla, it's the beginning of a more glorious, life-giving mode of creative work…and play."

"He seems pretty sold on the idea," Peter joked.

"To be the Pope, I think you have to be," the man laughed.

"I guess so," Peter said, kicking himself that he didn't have a snappy riposte.

Seeing Peter's wheels still turning, the man provoked him, "Or you could stick with Sartre and conclude that man is the being who folds nothingness into the world!"[79]

Wonderful, Peter thought. *God felt so absent when I needed him, and now I can't get rid of him.* "Choose your haunting: Nothingness or God!"[80] Peter joked quietly to the man so that the lady couldn't quite hear. Regardless, he immediately felt guilty. Its harsh edge was quite out of character, though he'd been "out of character" so much recently that he now feared whether this was his new temperament. Peter couldn't disappoint the lady, especially now; and besides, she'd worked hard. He bought all three of the books placed in his hands but left the postcard of the Pope for someone else.

Then, the man properly introduced himself. "So sorry, I'm Etienne," he said.

"Peter." A clumsy handshake ensued.

"You know, Peter, if you're serious about exploring philosophy, I meet with a group of men and women a couple of times a week."

79. 'Folds' is used here to connect to the idea of creative human projects in the world. The original quote explains that humankind is, "The Being by which Nothingness arrives in the world," Sartre, *Being and Nothingness*, 47. This idea is repeated and emphasized throughout the book.

80. For nothingness 'haunting' being, see Sartre, *Being and Nothingness*, 35.

17

Alexi

Le Musée de l'Homme

PARIS I

Friday, September 4th, 2015. Trocadéro.

"I'd forgotten how hilarious the costumes are!" Alexi said, brushing her-self off after having emerged from the catacombs via a secret entrance and into Place du Trocadéro—that monumental plaza from where people gather to view the cityscape dominated by the Eiffel Tower.

"And those lines!" Mark added.

Alexi echoed the beast: "Besides being hideous, I'm not quick-witted."[81]

As Belle, Marc replied, "You're quick enough to recognize it." They laughed.

"So good! Though I've never quite understood why, when the Beast 'dies' at the end, Cocteau made him look like her other suitor. What's his name?" Alexi asked.

"Avenant?" Marc offered.

"Right."

Tim walked with them. "Really, what can't a magic arrow do?" he toyed. Tim had glasses, a good jawline, and a subtle French accent to augment his tall and gangly silhouette. Apparently, he had moved here

81. Cocteau, *Belle et la Bête*.

from England almost a decade ago for his last years of schooling. "The years where you're forced to study philosophy," he'd joked.

"Hey, it's only eleven. Why don't we do something else?" Marc asked.

The view from Trocadéro was spellbinding. Alexi became quite transfixed by the lights on the Eiffel Tower. She didn't want to be a cliché, but Marc could tell. "Hey, Tim, are you thinking what I'm thinking?" he asked. Tim lit up, immediately grabbing his museum lanyard—equipped with his digital entry card—from his bag.

Tim took the three of them around the back of the newly refurbished *Musée de l'Homme*. Since closing time, the exhibit galleries had plunged afresh the treasures of civilizations past into darkness. His entrance of choice, it turned out, was through the restaurant at the bottom— a slight giveaway that this wasn't exactly permitted. They hopped over the privacy railings and into the grand dining room. A couple of staff fire exits later, and a trip to the restaurant freezer to acquire some leftover cheesecake, and they were up on the next floor overlooking the city. They didn't turn any lights on, but that made it perfect: the moonlight beaming in effortlessly through the windows.

Tim grabbed some disposable forks from the nearby café; "We're not animals!" he joked as they peeled the plastic film from the plates.

"This is the best view of the Eiffel Tower, hands down. And Tim gets to see it every day!" Marc boasted.

"You get to escape from the crowds," Tim explained. "Out there, it's all trinkets and photographers, people selling water and bumping into you. Here's how it's meant to be: serene, dignified." They looked out, right above the head of Pommier's sculpture of Hercules taming a bison. The tower really was tantalizingly close.

A spark then came into Marc's eyes. "Didn't Gandhi detest it? The Eiffel Tower, I mean?" Marc asked Tim.

Tim was confused. Was Marc trying to anger Alexi? He assumed the opposite was the plan, but then again, Tim couldn't claim to understand girls. Reluctantly, Tim replied, "Well, yeah, Gandhi said something about there being 'no art about the Eiffel Tower,' that it didn't contribute real beauty; it was just 'the toy' of the *Exposition*."[82]

82. Gandhi, *Autobiography*, 103.

While Alexi was ready for the good-natured repartee, Marc didn't miss a beat before driving home his next point: "Even Tolstoy said it was a 'monument of man's folly, not of his wisdom.'"[83]

Alexi jumped in: "And now you're going to bring up how it almost got scrapped but it was saved as a radio tower . . . And that Hitler wanted it gone." Alexi just resisted her urge to give a dramatic fake yawn, offering a side-smile instead. "Which is funny," Alexi continued, "because he posed by it just days into the occupation." She didn't mind Marc's games—they made him more interesting.

While it had been almost unfathomable to her citizens, Hitler had long foretold of this occupation. Paris, the heart and soul of France, the birthplace of liberalism, was now in Hitler's hands. On June 14th, any Parisians who had stayed, awoke to an announcement by loudspeaker: a German-accented voice announcing that a curfew was being imposed for 8 p.m. A gigantic swastika soon flowed beneath the Arc de Triomphe and others were liberally draped around the city. "They flew the Reich's military flag from the top," Tim said, pointing to the tower.

"And Versailles," Marc added. "They were making a point: defeating the humiliating terms of the Treaty signed there, ending World War One."

"Not many people know this," Tim confided, leaning in, "but an early cell of *La Résistance Française* met here in this museum."

Now we're talking, Alexi thought. "Where?"

"They met in the basement," Tim added.

§

On June 14th, 1940, the French government declared Paris an "open city," which meant they were not going to actively defend it. In the days leading up to its almost unthinkable occupation, those who could flee generally did, grannies in wheelbarrows, babies on backs. Simone de Beauvoir was among the throng, joining her friend Bianca's family in evacuating with six million others, Parisians and refugees from the north, simply known as "the Exodus." The thread of history, once draped around the necks of philosophers during *Les Années Folles*—commentators on both life's woes and great pleasures—now seemed to have their immunity revoked. The thread tightened to pull them into line with their estranged brothers

83. Gandhi, *Autobiography*, 103.

and sisters toward a shared fate. The sharp edge of life had caught up with them. Perhaps they owed a debt.

A young and scrappy writer, Albert Camus, watched from the Hôtel Madison while the fearful mass of bodies and belongings pressed its way down the Boulevard Saint-Germain. They moved towards the Place de l'Odéon from where they would exit the city through the ancient Porte d'Italie. The living mass ground against every inch of space, piles of things built upward upon bikes, prams, wheelbarrows, all strewn along country roads when their value dwindled in comparison to survival.

Camus wasn't about to leave Paris. Besides, he'd only moved on June 4th from the bohemian hill of Montmartre—the district where many a penniless artist had swapped art for food, and Picasso had painted *Les Demoiselles d'Avignon*. The very same day as his move, in the wake of Dunkirk, England's Winston Churchill gave his "Fight them on the beaches" speech in the House of Commons, urging the nation to never give up.[84]

Camus felt like a stranger to Paris and these people: an outsider with his heart longing for home in Algeria, feeling stuck between two worlds. He pounded out this volatile and peculiar estrangement in his novel *The Stranger*.

While watching the Exodus, there was little way to predict the next few days, let alone years. However, despite Simone fleeing the city, Sartre becoming a prisoner of war, and Camus staying put, their lives would soon become entangled. Under occupation, in the years to come they would come to know each other well. "How we loved you then," Sartre said of Camus. Their wartime gatherings included acting together in private home-based plays. One, the absurdist *Le Désir attrapé par la queue*, (Desire Caught by the Tail), was written and directed by Picasso.[85] He found this pastime entertaining amid the wartime austerity, which, due to a lack of heating, could make it too cold to paint.

That June day, the "interminable procession" of humanity moved south.[86] Women shrieked uncontrollably; their children swept off in the current of chaos. Artillery fire was heard the distance: plane-mounted machine guns utterly decimating whole groups of people along the roads. The sun was masked by billowing black smoke in the distance. Cars started impeding the flow as they sat abandoned once they had run

84. Churchill, "We Shall Fight on the Beaches."
85. Beauvoir, *Prime of Life*, 568.
86. Humbert, *Résistance*, 6.

out of gas. Like fuel, food was scarce to non-existent since earlier waves of the Exodus had swept through like locusts. Money didn't mean much when there was no food left to buy; chaos was a great leveler. Likewise, people quickly lost their bodily inhibitions—you had no choice but to squat along the side of the road or help an ailing *grand-maman* up from a converted pram to relieve herself. Propriety wilted as shock and self-protection set in.

The distinguished art historian Agnès Humbert would soon return to Paris to become a core member of the resistance cell at *Le Musée de l'Homme*. But not before she, too, experienced this absurdly rapid degeneration of normalcy. During the Exodus, she attempted to staunch the blood of a dying sixteen-year-old girl, Emiliene, run over by a French army vehicle in flight from the enemy.[87] Only then did she realize how dire the situation really was. No one answered the phone at the hospital, and there was no way to hail an ambulance. When she later found one, its occupant was busy indulging in personal pleasures as if he bore no duty in the crumbling nation-state.[88]

After finding a room to stay in, Agnès, like many others, turned the knob of the wireless set, desperate for news. By fluke, she recalled it being tuned to London:

> A voice announces an appeal to be made by a French general. I don't catch his name. In a delivery that is jerky and peremptory—not at all well suited to the radio—the general urges all Frenchmen to rally round him, to carry on the struggle. I feel I have come back to life. A feeling I thought had died forever stirs within me again: hope. There is one man after all—one alone perhaps—who understands what I feel in my heart: "It's not over yet."[89]

Upon hearing this, Agnès flew out of her room "like a lunatic," thrilled to share her excitement with others. Only, she was met by an old captain who replied, "It's all a lot of nonsense . . . He's a crackpot, that de Gaulle. You mark my words."[90]

However, he wasn't a crackpot. Not really. But did he have any legitimacy from the French government, which had capitulated? Not at

87. Humbert, *Résistance*, 4.

88. Humbert, *Résistance*, 6.

89. Humbert, *Résistance*, 7.

90. Humbert, *Résistance*, 7.

all. What he was doing *was* an act of treason. The French prime minister, Paul Reynaud, had recently resigned, leaving Marshal Pétain—the eighty-four-year-old Great War hero—to sign an armistice with Germany and become chief of state of the collaborationist Vichy regime. Churchill had tried to stop the armistice, calling for the fight to continue, offering an indissoluble union between England and France. But, through the cataractous lens of rival Empires, Pétain saw this as an opportunist move and threw the gesture back in Churchill's face. Besides, Pétain argued, it would be akin to "fusion with a corpse," for "in three weeks England will have her neck rung like a chicken."[91]

Charles de Gaulle, a newly appointed brigadier-general—whose warnings about the effectiveness of modern tank warfare (essentially *Blitzkrieg* tactics) had been largely ignored by superiors—vehemently disagreed with Pétain's actions. He insisted with Major-General Edward Spears, Winston Churchill's personal envoy, that he travel with him to London on his last flight from Bordeaux. He was intent to carry on the fight for France, even from exile.

As Churchill admitted, in that small plane, de Gaulle carried with him "the honor of France."[92] When flying over the Breton peninsula—his long legs wedged up against the next seat—his treasonous intent caused him great personal anguish, and yet his resolve was unwavering. He watched from the air as smoke besieged the countryside, awash with flame as the retreating Allied forces set fire to the British fuel storage to deny the hungry Nazi machines their fuel. Yet, it was the pain of separation from his own dear family—still down there—that made it most hard to breathe. He had managed to ensure that the heavy water from the French nuclear program would reach England[93] and had begged for his wife and their daughter, Anne, to be sent for, praying earnestly that they would make the trip safely. The thought of living out the war with them in Canada came to mind.[94] But he rejected it. What kind of world would he leave for his children—or their children? For humanity? He felt no option but to lead this fight.

They saw many ships burning, especially in La Rochelle and Rochefort as they flew up the Atlantic coast.[95] Just west of La Rochelle, near

91. Churchill, *Second World War*, 213.

92. Spears, *Assignment*, 619.

93. Lacouture, *De Gaulle*, 42–54.

94. Jackson, *Certain Idea of France*, 135.

95. De Gaulle, *War Memoirs*, 80.

La Pallice, and not long after taking off, Major-General Spears mentions seeing the terrible sight of hundreds of tiny figures struggling to swim to safety.[96] Champlain, a luxury modern liner turned refugee ship, lay stricken on her side—her proud, rich-red steam tower humiliated—after being hit by a mine. This was, perhaps, symbolic of the fall of France and her mighty *Tricolour*. Her carcass was laid to rest by a torpedo from a German U-boat a few days later. The large visible wreck was to lie, embalmed *in situ*, well until the 1960s, just as the pain and shame of the occupation would dig deep into the sand-bed of public mind and memory, "the Vichy Syndrome."[97]

De Gaulle was a lone French leader in the initial days of the occupation: isolated yet impassioned. Major-General Spears, Churchill's envoy to France, famously said that the Cross Lorraine—de Gaulle's symbol for the Free French (*Résistance)* movement he led—was the hardest cross of all to bear in the war. But, while the war might have been easier to lead without him, without his clear leadership of the *Résistance* would the Allies have been as successful? What then of the world?

All over the French-speaking world, posters were put up heralding de Gaulle's appeal for *Résistance* that he gave the day after his flight, on June 18th. For, while Philippe Pétain believed this war to be just another bloody scuffle in a long line of confrontations between France and Germany, easily enough repealed in due time, de Gaulle recognized that this was not the case. While significant, land wasn't all that was at stake. Instead, this was about how humanity saw itself and what lengths humans could go to shape the world according to their values. The framework of thought—the worldview that the Nazi Regime brought within its Fascist agenda—was hostile to life, hostile to humanity. It led to claims that some human lives were "life unworthy of life" (*Lebensunwertes Leben*) and defined the worth of others based on racial terms.

Nobody wins in war. However, this fight was not *just* to hold back the assaults of the Reich against what de Gaulle saw as the prophetic "destiny" and "grandeur" of France. It was also a fight to lay ahold of something: to attempt to reclaim and secure a future that looked humane, that valued humanity in its diversity. As a Catholic, de Gaulle anchored

---

96. Spears, *Assignment*, 619. Spears notes that the *Champlain* had thousands of troops on board, but he may have confused the *Champlain* with the *Lancastria*, which was bombed later that day in one of the deadliest maritime disasters of World War II, with an estimated three thousand people lost.

97. Rousso, *Vichy Syndrome*.

this insistence on a Christian worldview which keeps central the idea of *Imago Dei*, informing the dignity and value of all humans since all are made in the image of God. Was de Gaulle a perfect leader? Absolutely not. Perhaps such things do not exist. At times, his nationalism eclipsed and even contradicted the values of his faith. But, to remain honest, did he not also accurately assess the real import of the situation when many, like Pétain, did not?

§

Just as Tim had confided, an improbable team had gathered in the museum, determined to resist. This included ethnologists, librarians—even an Egyptologist from the Louvre! Agnès Humbert wrote in her diary: "How bizarre it all is! Here we are, most of us on the wrong side of forty, careering along like students all fired up with passion and fervor, in the wake of a leader of whom we know absolutely nothing, or whom none of us has even seen a photograph."[98] Yet their hope came alive.

Alexi begged Tim to show her where the *Résistance* cell had gathered. "They called themselves a literary society, '*Les Amis d'Alain*,'" he explained.[99] "It formed around Boris Vilde, a twenty-five-year-old Russian-born ethnologist who'd been wounded and captured in the Battle of France."

"He was fighting for the French," Marc clarified.

"As he should have," Tim joked. "In early July, just weeks after the occupation of Paris had begun, Agnès saw him arrive at the museum steps, haggard after escaping imprisonment and hobbling three hundred kilometers on an injured knee but determined as ever."[100]

As Tim had tried to explain to Alexi, there wasn't any sign of the *Résistance* cell left in the basement since the Gestapo had turned it over. But Tim showed her where—in the corner with the best light—Agnès had sat faithfully typing out their bulletins. The very first was dated December 15th, 1940. "They copied it on a mimeograph machine," Tim explained, sharing how ink oozed through a stencil and onto the precious paper. "The first edition introduced themselves, eager to inspire others: 'We have only one ambition, one passion, one will . . . to see a pure and free France reborn.' This clandestine newspaper, the first of its kind, was

98. Humbert, *Résistance*, 20–21.

99. Humbert, *Résistance*, 25.

100. Humbert, *Résistance*, 18.

simply named *Résistance*. Just two weeks later, in the second edition, they shared de Gaulle's appeal. They left them on toilets and trams—anywhere subtle yet strategic."

This is where Violet and Matthias had first met—well before their trip into the lion's den at Wagner's opera house in Bayreuth—distributing *Résistance*.

Eager to curb the disappointment, Tim offered to show Alexi what treasures were in the basement: some artifacts had once belonged to private collections reaching back hundreds of years. "I've always been interested in anthropology," Alexi said, looking at the skulls and artifacts the ordinary tourist didn't get to see. She opened drawer after drawer to find things labeled with neat handwritten notes related to index cards. "It's so meticulous," she said in awe.

"It is," he smiled. "I don't know if it makes it more amusing or tragic that, after a devastating flood in 1910, one of the other Parisian museums—Le Muséum National d'Histoire Naturelle—thought for a while that they'd lost René Descartes's skull!"[101]

"No!" Alexi said, wide-eyed, picturing the philosopher's skull bobbing down the promenades. "Only thought?" she added.

Tim explained, "A little while after the flood, someone found this note about the skulls being in their collection and put two and two together."

"Imagine being the person having to break that bad news!" Marc joked.

"But the crisis was averted. Within a week it was mysteriously returned to the director of the museum. It's actually upstairs now," Tim explained.

Marc quipped, "Unless they're lying to us."

"Well, can I see it?" Alexi asked.

Marc and Alexi followed Tim back upstairs to the main exhibition taking the liberty to deactivate alarms as they went. "It's over here," Tim said, gesturing. He ran over—footsteps echoing on the newly shined floor—and turned on a singular spotlight just above it.

That's when Alexi saw it for the first time. "What's written on it?" she asked, not expecting the Latin inscriptions.

"It's a poem. The translation's here," Tim said, before reading it out:

101. Shorto, *Descartes' Bones*, 209–11.

> This small skull once belonged to the great Cartesius. The rest of his remains are hidden far away in the land of France; But all around the circle of the globe his genius is praised, and his spirit still rejoices in the sphere of heaven.[102]

Alexi asked, "He's the philosopher who said, 'I think therefore I am,' right?"

Tim nodded to agree with Alexi, adding, "He's often considered the father of modern philosophy, working in the early 1600s."

"Where's the rest of his body?" Alexi asked quite logically.

"After they dug him up, they did weird things with his bones: cults and stuff," Marc had to add, ever so precisely. "Losing the rest of them is pretty ironic when you think he helped forge an Enlightenment culture obsessed by reason and neglecting the body."[103]

From there, Marc and Tim practically tripped over each other to explain Descartes's world and thought. Alexi found it quite amusing and so, of course, she let them.

"Descartes was French but lived much of his life in Amsterdam during its Golden Age," Tim started.

"Do you know Rembrandt?" Marc jumped in.

"Of course," Alexi said with confidence. "He painted honest portraits of the middle class, rather than propaganda for the rich."

"That's him," Marc replied, impressed.

Alexi started, "But why—?"

"He's important," Tim jumped in, "because that's the milieu that helped inform Descartes's rationalist, individual—or subject-focused—philosophy. It was the time of the bewildering Scientific Revolution, overturning concepts formerly held as truth at a remarkable speed."

Marc tried to one-up Tim. "Each new discovery, whether Galileo's astronomy or William Harvey's circulatory system, seemed to undermine received truth, including official church teachings—"

"If you mean with the earth going round the sun, then Galileo's evidence helped overturn Aristotelian metaphysics, which had reigned for millennia. It was that which the church, like pretty much everyone else in Europe at the time, had adopted as fact," Tim clarified.

"What else had people of that time taken from Aristotle?" Alexi asked.

102. Shorto, *Descartes' Bones*, 146.
103. Core thesis of Shorto, *Descartes' Bones.*

"The idea of the physical world being divided into earth, air, fire, and water; and, corresponding to these, the bodily humors: all blood, phlegm, and bile," Tim replied.

Marc seized the opportunity to launch at the topic afresh: "Descartes welcomed the Scientific Revolution. He's famous for his skepticism, but he didn't feel it needed to run all the way down."

"Well," Tim clarified, "he made strategic use of doubt as a method for distilling truth. He wanted to see if there was something—some truth to anchor these new scientific discoveries into."

"I see," Alexi added, captivated by the story surrounding the man to whom the skull before her belonged. She walked around the case, to see it from different angles. "Did he find that anchor?"

"He thought so!" Marc rushed to affirm. "At bottom, one could not deny that even when having doubts—"

"—one must be thinking," Tim finished. He then extrapolated, "Upon this central lynchpin—the thinking self—now hung, it seemed, every Enlightenment ideal from democracy to the scientific method, itself underpinned by the discipline of mathematics, a fundamental building block of scientific advance."

"Yes," Marc added, "but by affirming this one part of reality so highly—the unseen, bodiless world of the mind—this added fuel to the flames of an already polarized world."

"How?" Alexi asked.

"For Descartes," Marc replied, "the foundation for what could be trusted and true was connected to the thinking mind. So then, what of the body?"

Discarded, Alexi reasoned.

Tim explained, "Descartes rendered the mind and body like polar opposites: 'I have a clear and distinct notion of myself, as a thing that thinks and occupies no extension in space, and . . . a distinct notion of my body, as a thing that has an extension and does not think.'[104] This all cracked open the issue of 'Substance Dualism.' The key question then becomes: how can two such different parts of ourselves—different substances—make up just one person?"

"Right," Alexi said, following along.

104. Descartes, *Meditations*, Meditation VI, 44.

"Descartes started making really suspect hypotheses," Mark offered, "like the idea that the pineal gland in the brain must be the magical adjoining organ—and 'the seat of the soul.'"

"Why?" Alexi asked, curious.

"Because it's not duplicated like many other organs!"[105] Marc replied.

"You're also going to blame him for the Enlightenment excesses, aren't you," Tim said with a smirk reflected in the glass case.

"Someone has to!" Marc replied. "Enlightenment rationalism emphasized mind and logic over body and world. In its quest for truth, it 'heroically' vanquished anything it didn't understand," Marc said cynically. "It thought it cornered the market in truth. So by the early twentieth century, we reached an extreme position where philosophers like Ludwig Wittgenstein argued that statements which could not be empirically verified were meaningless!"

"But there was also Romanticism, right?" Alexi pushed back, remembering images of wanderers in fog and neoclassical nymphs from taking art at school.

"Right! Peaking in the mid-nineteenth century, Romanticism pushed against reducing everything to reason. But even so, *both* of these dominant positions picked a side from the apparent mind/body divide. The question is whether we need to," Tim explained.

"You're saying it's a false binary?" Alexi asked as she looked deep into Descartes's eye socket, both repulsed and drawn in.

Tim nodded, "To be sure, there were some very good things about the Enlightenment, like the overturning of archaic pseudoscience. Such as solving everything with leeches—Descartes *really* didn't like leeches."

"For good reason!" Marc quipped.

"But," Tim continued, "I'd actually agree with you, Marc: the Enlightenment also irreparably scarred the modern era, setting it on a trajectory for two world wars." Tim stopped for a moment, unsure how much to share. He pivoted to offer with a boyish glee, "I like to think that when Descartes was down in the basement with Agnès and friends, he overheard their schemes."

"I love that," said Alexi. "What do you think he would have made of the war?"

"Interestingly enough," Tim replied, "he fought in the Thirty Years War. He calculated the trajectories of cannon balls for a while, which

---

105. Shorto, *Descartes' Bones*, 177; Lokhorst, "Descartes and the Pineal Gland."

wouldn't have harmed his handle of geometry! I also overheard someone visiting here recently who said that it was when he was stationed on the Danube that he had night visions. And in them? The seeds of his famous *cogito*: 'I think therefore I am.'"

"I'd like to sign up for some of those visions!" Marc joked.

"And there's more," Tim added swiftly. "He may have been a spy! Descartes was brought up as a Catholic but started the war on the Protestant side before switching over. This, and that fact that he somehow managed to meet up with some very important people all over Europe, and you have a compelling case!"[106]

"A double agent, hey?" Alex joked, speaking directly to the skull with admiration. "So, he *would* have been rooting for the *Résistance*?"

"I like to think so!" Tim said. "Though, by helping to set the trajectory of the Enlightenment, he may also bear some responsibility for the war's inhumane excesses."

"Why?" Alexi asked. "What does reason, mind, and truth have to do with war?"

Tim chose one path of many, albeit one close to his heart: "If we're to agree with thinkers like the Jewish philosophers Horkheimer and Adorno, then the Enlightenment is totalitarian by its very nature—it's all about fear and control."[107]

"Fear?" she said, confused.

"You know how wild animals are most dangerous when they are scared? Well, the reductionism of the Enlightenment might have been a fear response. A denial that says only this one part of reality exists or has meaning."

"Explain that," Alexi pressed.

"Because if you can't control it, then it's perhaps easier to deny it exists," Tim replied.

"These guys talk about all this fascinating stuff to do with the magic man or shaman," Marc said, realizing how fitting this was surrounded by ritual masks and regalia, seeing just the slightest glimpses gifted by the farthest reaches of moonlight.

"Right," Tim added. "They talk about the ancient shamanic practice of marking out a circle over which they would have control. The grand irony, Horkheimer and Adorno argue, is that this is exactly what

106. Grayling, *Life and Times*, 8.

107. Horkheimer and Adorno, *Dialectic of Enlightenment*, 4.

Enlightenment man does! Whether in the name of magic or science, it's just a different iteration of the same story: man trying to have control over nature. There's something to that if you think about it. The territory, for Enlightenment man, is simply what they think they can understand and what they will then use for their goals. Once reality is marked out, it is flattened out: the existence of anything uncontrollable or unquantifiable is denied.[108] Violence thrives in this climate," Tim argued. "Nothing is safe: with nothing holy and untouchable, even the parts of reality—the world and community—that are acknowledged are truncated and corralled within the sphere of control to be edited and manipulated at will. It's ironic, isn't it?" he suggested. "I've often thought that this isn't a free, enlightened position but looks more like chains and impotence! In thought, I mean," Tim clarified as Marc laughed.

Alexi found their passion—and teasing—amusing. "You guys really like this stuff, hey?" Alexi said to Tim, much to Marc's chagrin.

"Like I said, we do philosophy in school here. Besides," Tim added as he pointed towards the collections still tantalizingly bathed in darkness, "I have to think about something while I'm around here all day, and it's fun listening out for those extra nuggets."

"This connects back again to the Second World War," Marc offered, eager for the spotlight to shift back toward him. "Descartes's skull is interesting, right, because it is small.[109] See, compared to the others? If Enlightenment rationalism is all about measuring and controlling, vanquishing myths and fairy tales, and treating the human body like a thing, then it's partly Descartes' fault for letting this out of Pandora's Box. But his skull is also analogous to its weakness."

"Why?" Alexi asked.

"Because it helped show that stripping everything back to numbers and stats—quantifying everything—can't explain everything."

Marc explained, "At the dawn of the turn of the century, much faith was put in the pseudoscience of phrenology, studying skulls. According to this, the reason for his genius should have required a larger brain, and so . . ."

"A bigger skull?" Alexi guessed.

---

108. "For the Enlightenment, anything which cannot be resolved into numbers, and ultimately into one, is illusion; modern positivism consigns it to poetry. Unity remains the watchword from Parmenides to Russell. All gods and qualities must be destroyed," Horkheimer and Adorno, *Dialectic of Enlightenment*, 4.

109. On phrenology, see Shorto, *Descartes' Bones*, 167–76.

"Right!" Marc said.

"And yet it's small. Well, in comparison," Alexi reasoned.

Marc agreed, "Now, that sort of quantification of the human body was rampant in the colonial world. Dehumanizing, really."

"Right. It was one of the root causes of the Rwandan genocide," Tim explained. "The Belgian colonial authorities attempted to solidify the ethnic distinctions between Hutu and Tutsi populations by pseudoscientifically measuring noses and other facial features."

"Which is exactly the sort of thing that the Nazis did to the Jewish population," Alexi said, perceiving where Marc was going.

"And others." Marc pulled himself together to add, "If you look back at the occupation, at those jackboots and *panzer* tanks rolling in—how they categorized and rounded up people—that's the dark side of the European Enlightenment. That's why Sartre's friend, Frantz Fanon, a radical Afro-Caribbean psychologist, could say it was simply colonialism coming home."[110]

"That's chilling. But I see it," Alexi said as Tim flicked off the light above Descartes.

---

110. "A colonial system in the very heart of Europe." Fanon, *Black Skin, White Masks*, 33. Sartre wrote the preface. By 1964 even Sartre could attest to the paradoxically dehumanizing nature of European "humanism." See Sartre, *Colonialism and Neocolonialism*, 160–69.

18

Peter

The Community

PARIS I

Wednesday, 11th November 1992. Le Dôme Café,
Montparnasse.

Peter had arrived at the threshold of his future. Intrepid? Not so much.
He doubted whether he was serious enough about philosophy to have
accepted the invitation, but the mix of boredom and his promise to Edith
and Edwin had brought him to it. The café buzzed with a residual charge
of passion and promise, hitting him as soon as he opened the door.

Without wasting time, Jean-Paul made himself known to Peter,
pulling up a chair next to him. This was almost certainly not his real
name, but it was what he chose to go by in France. It was so terribly cliché
that it worked well as a mode of anonymity. Otherwise, he was far from
forgettable, with a chiseled jaw almost as sharp as his tongue and wit. He
also had a tight beard, still commendable even if only a shadow of its former glory, having protected his face from the pleasantries of windburn in
Siberia. He confronted Peter: "I hear you've been reading Sartre?"

The question was easy enough. But responding to him? "Er, yes,
yes. I'm trying to figure out if I agree with him," Peter said awkwardly as
if being called to account for his presence. Everyone *was* trying to make
a measure of this inoffensive-looking Brit who had somehow found his

way into the epicenter of heated debate. Jean-Paul was just more direct about it.

Nervously thumbing through his book and missing his place a number of times, Peter came upon a section he'd highlighted—it felt safer to at least use Sartre's words than throw out any half-baked conclusions of his own.

> . . . man first of all exists: he materializes in the world, encounters himself, and only afterward defines himself . . . to begin with he is nothing. He will not be anything until later, and then he will be what he makes of himself.[111]

He read the quote and then nervously drew his eyes up from the book.

"Very representative," said Bernard, an older, more welcoming gentleman, whose wizardly graying dark hair and beard made up in volume—and potentially foreign bodies, burrs, and the like—what it lacked in density.

"But do you agree?" Jean-Paul demanded.

"Like I said, I'm not sure," Peter reaffirmed.

Bernard diffused the inquisition by offering a thought: "It seems to me like you're on a blue flower quest." As he said it, he looked at Peter intently, searching for his response. Though, in truth, only one eye did, for Bernard's lazy eye kept watch over his inner world. A seething, solemn realm, it needed watching over.

"Sorry?" said Peter, perplexed.

"A blue flower quest," Antonio clarified. "It's a symbol from German Romanticism that speaks to hope, beauty, and the metaphysical striving for the unreachable." Antonio was an interesting fellow. His fiery-red Viking hair made him hard to miss, as did the whites of his eyes, which stood out more glaringly than the average man—especially when he was thinking deeply . . . which happened sometimes. Other times, he was intent on bobbing along in the currents of life. Antonio continued, "It's Bernard's way of saying that you're trying to figure this maddening life out, right?"

"Young man, I can speak for myself," Bernard asserted, with fondness curbing frustration. Dignified though somewhat disheveled, clothed in a green woolen cardigan and a twenty-year-old checked cotton shirt, Bernard continued, "Antonio is right. Novalis wrote about Heinrich, his

---

111. Sartre, *Existentialism Is a Humanism*, 22.

protagonist, dreaming about a blue flower. It called to him, absorbing his attention and setting him off on a quest."

Peter thought of responding that he was pushed, not pulled, but he wasn't ready for that level of vulnerability. Instead, he gathered his words, "Do you think that I am just wasting my time on existentialism? If the whole point is that there isn't a point and that we have to make it up, then am I just stuck in a pointless circle of chatter?"

"I like to think that nothing is a waste of time; as long as we master it, it doesn't master us," replied Bernard. "It all becomes a tool in some way. Plus, there's more to it than meets the eye. Why do you think someone would be drawn to it?"

Seeing Peter start to panic, Etienne jumped in. "Care to weigh in, Antonio? You see, he *is* an existentialist, born and bred. Well, perhaps not *born*." The group laughed. Peter felt obliged to join in.

"Existentialists are my people," Antonio admitted. "They stick their face right in the gaudy sarcophagus of death—looking it right in the face—and then try to figure out if it is possible to live."

Is it? Peter desperately wanted to ask, still bleeding out. Instead asking, "Are you all existentialists?"

"Oh no, pretty much only Antonio!" Etienne joked. "Take Jean-Paul, for example. He's more the depressing Russian literature kind of guy." This made Jean-Paul smirk. "You don't want to put him in a box," Etienne added, triggering an amused outburst.

"I'm that intimidating?"

"Now we're doing proper introductions; this is Bernard," said Etienne in a familial way. "He's our oracle; our wise safe. I guess you could say he's both our revolutionary and our brakes, telling us to pause and recalibrate."

How old was Bernard exactly? Peter found it hard to tell.

"I'm Andrea," interjected the self-assured African-American lady on the far side, jumping in. She introduced herself with a firm handshake instead of the customary kiss, refusing to be introduced by someone else. Peter was perfectly fine with this, especially since his fumbles with that earlier in the evening. After growing up in Chicago, she had been a social worker in both Kenya and Europe and was now convinced that society, if not humanity, was rotten to the core. She was versed in philosophy but not ruled by it.

"You'll meet Hélène at some point," said Bernard in a particularly grandfatherly manner. "Oh, and Amy. They sometimes join us . . . Amy's busy with bedtimes." Of course, this was just one of the many tables buzzing with activity, albeit the one that entertained most of the main players.

Later in the evening, Peter would also meet Lavinia and Ritesh. He found them easy to talk to—an artistic couple boldly wearing the marks of a nomadic life. Ritesh was half-Nepalese, while Lavinia had grown up as part of a Romani community traveling Europe as the seasons cycled. They met each other when traveling in India and had entwined lives ever since.

"To circle back to Existentialism, you'll figure out what I think about that, and many other things sooner or later," Etienne quipped, evidently enjoying some cloak of mystery. Etienne was complex, like a burnished spirit—a scotch or whisky—with notes that made themselves known in different contexts. Almost impossible to fully predict—though his girlfriend, Hélène, tried in vain.

"Somebody ought to get his boy an apricot cocktail!" Bernard announced like a jovial grandpa with a nod to Sartre's epiphany. "He can't be empty-handed when discussing Sartre!"

"I'll just say one thing," Etienne offered, "Regardless of my other opinions, I think Sartre helps bring life into perspective. He uses the example of a *serveur* in the café as an example of taking on a role for his job and thus being restrained by what he called 'bad faith,' a sort of self-deception."

"Right?" Peter recalled.

Jean-Paul asserted, "Think about it: the belief that life has to be the way it is is compounded by the machine of capitalism. Humanity becomes a self-restrained automaton going through the required motions."

Antonio jumped in, "Everyday life can be absurd, and the facticity of it all quite nauseous. So why not change it?"

"Though we have to remember that de Beauvoir brought a corrective to Sartre, reminding him that we are not practically free to make every change we might want to make," Andrea added with force.

"A good reminder, of course," Etienne pacified.

"Women simply don't have the same blank slate as men, Peter," Andrea compounded, her words tinged with frustration.

Wanting the last word, Jean-Paul piped up again: "Sartre thought we have a duty to break out of both the mundane and moral constraints that work alongside 'bad faith' to keep us trapped. We're condemned to be free, but it is only in defining and creating meaning for own lives that we take this responsibility seriously."

"So, do you agree with your namesake?" Peter asked, shocking himself at the audacity with which he now turned Jean-Paul's earlier question back towards him.

"You're a bold one," said Antonio, as if he knew something that Peter didn't. Honestly, Peter had immediately regretted asking the question.

"On bad faith? Vehemently," Jean-Paul boldly announced. Then, as if sinking a dagger right in the middle of their discussion, he continued, "On others? Absolutely not." He found Sartre's philosophy idealistic, made worse by its tendency to be popularized, grossly misunderstood and repackaged as therapeutic. Besides, if he had to take sides, he much preferred Heidegger's "being-towards-death."

"Well then, with all due respect," Peter said, still floating on being called bold for possibly the first time in his life, "Can anyone live like this? Do you all action these ideas—like getting free from these everyday restraints—or do you just meet in a café to discuss them?"

"He's got a point," Andrea added, pointing to Peter.

Etienne's eyes widened. *He knew something.* He watched Jean-Paul like a hawk.

"How out-of-the-box do you want?" Jean-Paul smirked as he made Etienne squirm. *Was he going to disclose some cloak-and-dagger secret?*

"It's not time," Etienne said between his teeth with a subtle headshake.

Attempting to draw a line under it all, Etienne interjected loudly, "Hey, Peter, didn't anyone tell you that the first round's on the new guy?"

"Sir, you need say no more," Peter replied.

As Peter stood at the warmly lit bar, he reflected that, thus far, it hadn't been altogether horrible. They seemed interesting and interested in him. He rehearsed the order: red wine, bourbon, gin, coffee, and whisky times two. *Okay, that's what an order looked like for an eclectic group of academics and radicals on a Wednesday night.*

"Oh, and one tea, please. English tea . . . do you have that?" Peter hastily added when the time came.

"I've got Darjeeling, Indian tea, Chinese tea but no English tea, *monsieur*," the waiter said with a straight face. Before Peter could get too caught up in trying to figure out where his French had let him down, the man smirked, "English breakfast coming right up."

"Actually, no. Make that an apricot cocktail," he said before apologizing for all the fuss.

Thankfully oblivious, those in the philosophy "circle" continued to hurl jargon-laden bombs at each other—a huge problem if they didn't enjoy it so much. They packed out at least a half-dozen tables, squeezing in as many extra chairs as they could. Peter could understand enough to make out the broad strokes of the impassioned debate at one nearby table. Housing was a right, not a commodity! A position liberally littered with obscenities directed towards President Mitterrand.

Peter walked past that table to sit back down with Etienne's group. "You really want to wind him up and let him go, don't you!" Peter heard Etienne saying to Antonio as he set down the drinks.

"Me?" Antonio pledged innocence, more mischievous than malevolent.

"You know I can take care of myself," Bernard huffed. "If you're going to convince me that cyborg-esque transhuman existence is *really* freeing for the individual, then you'd have to be first in line for the upgrade!"

"Just playing devil's advocate, Bernie," Antonio smirked fondly. "You know that."

"Sorry, what are we talking about now?" Peter asked.

"Just corrupting the youth," Andrea jumped in.

"That's what the philosopher Socrates was accused of in Athens before being sentenced to death," Etienne said, helpfully decoding. "He's the philosopher that said that the unexamined life is not worth living."

"So, you're examining whether being a cyborg—tech upgrades and all that—is freeing?" Peter inquired.

"Antonio knows that's a slippery slope. But he brought it up to make a point as part of a bigger question," Etienne explained.

"Which is?"

"Whether the world is structured in such a way to enable human flourishing . . . or whether it's just inherently hostile to humanity," Etienne replied.

Antonio jumped in, "Perhaps we're just biding our time before the heat death of the universe? In which case, why not optimize our fleshy bodies and overcome limits?"

"If I had a body like yours, I'd want to optimize it too," Andrea joked in a dry way that only she could get away with. It helped that they had been friends for years. She put up with his oddities, while he put up with her way of dealing with it.

"He's looking for a reaction," Bernie explained to Peter. "Antonio knows that overcoming our limits in this way would leave us all the more enslaved, editing our lives and that of our loved ones."

"He does?" Antonio jibed, not always able to read a room.

"But it's a good question, isn't it?" Etienne suggested. "It connects to the idea of not living in bad faith, for after asking what's next, we must ask: what are our options? Indeed, is reality structured in such a way so as to enable human flourishing? And can we restructure our lives within it to give ourselves a better chance of flourishing?"

"I wouldn't know where to start," Peter admitted.

"One could start by breaking it down into smaller questions, like: What is the structure of reality? What is the human? How might a human flourish in this reality? If we extend the flourishing analogy, one encourages this by rooting into what? Liberty? Hope? Should we comport towards a future? Or are we to resign ourselves to brute facts and expect less and, in doing so, be happier?"

"So, what are we talking? Philosophy or politics?" Peter asked.

"Are they really separate?" Andrea quipped.

Peter responded, "If I'm honest, I associate the first with endless questions and the second with action."

Antonio burst out laughing: "You associate politics with action? Is it possible that they know something in England that we do not?"

This got Jean-Paul's attention. "Surely not!" he teased as he walked back over after having an animated conversation at another table. Curious, he perched himself attentively.

"We do need action, Peter," Etienne explained, "So if the government isn't going to address the sorry state of society, we have to ask, who will?"

"You're saying that society needs to be restructured for human flourishing?" Peter asked.

"We couldn't get much further away, could we?" Andrea added.

A round-faced man from an adjacent table leaned over: "Human flourishing? Is there even such a thing? And if there is, who's to say it's the same for everyone? What if your heaven's my hell?"

"Don't listen to him," Andrea said shutting the man down as if batting down a jumping dog. "He's mostly messing with you."

"Mostly! Ha," the man laughed impishly before turning back.

Peter didn't know what to do. That comment put him in a bit of a tailspin. "Okay. Um. Well, what alternatives do we really have?" he asked.

"According to Francis Fukuyama, nothing. Not really. We've reached the end of history; liberal capitalism has won,"[112] Etienne explained.

"And that's bad news?" Peter asked, with scenes of the Berlin Wall falling and the joy of those who had been stuck under the hold of Soviet regimes being free to move West.

"Good news if you want Levi's and Coke but bad news if you're a human who wants to do more than consume," Andrea explained.

"What allows for the flourishing or good fruit in our lives?" Bernard asked, like a sage of old. "If you want to change the fruit you have to change the root. Are we rooted deeply into a reality that is alive and humanizing? Or is it dead like the soil we keep abusing with our bigger and chemically intoxicated agricultural practices?"

"You lost him with all the roots and land talk, Bernie," Jean-Paul joked.

Before Peter could protest, Bernard clarified, "You can have all the choice, free will, and responsibility you like, but if you're not set up for success in a society structured with values and an internal architecture that allows you to be human, then what's the point?"

"And that's why we're doing it, right, Etienne?" Jean-Paul said.

Etienne stared back with daggers in his eyes.

"It will never be time," Jean-Paul snapped as covertly as possible.

"Ascona!" Jean-Paul then exclaimed, loud and unashamed.

That means something to these folks? Peter thought, seeing their reaction. "What, er, is 'Ascona?'" Peter asked. "Did I miss something?

"Well, you've got to tell him now," Andrea said, giving Jean-Paul the extra authority he'd been waiting for.

Scared Jean-Paul would run away with the whole thing, Etienne grabbed the bull by the horns, interjecting, "You're absolutely right, Peter. We need action."

"Between the First and Second World Wars, philosophers, and free-thinkers . . ." Jean-Paul started.

". . . and nudists," Antonio interrupted with a little too much glee.

"Sunseekers," Etienne clarified, in a slightly amused yet authoritative tone, "as well as artisans and intellectuals from around the globe, converged upon a small Swiss town from the 1920s onwards. They sought to redefine humanity and redefine their lives away from the repression of that age."

112. Fukuyama, *End of History*.

"Many people do not realize the extent of its legacy," added Antonio. "It was quite the hub for counterculture." You could see the wheels turning for Antonio. "So why not do something here?" Antonio reasoned, being drawn along. "France is not just home to the Declaration of the Rights of Man; it's the home of the Revolution!"

"I bet you Amy and Jacob would be in," Andrea said. "They've been wanting to shift the rhythm of their lives for a while now."

"It's fortuitous that tonight I was going to share about the next steps," said Etienne, hoping this forward approach would help hide his knee-jerk justification. Jean-Paul had jumped the gun. Again. But with such a livewire, it was easier to keep him on side.

"Peter," Andrea said, turning to him amongst the excited chatter, "there has been a loss of meaning in all our lives due to the imposed sterility of the modern world. Its technology, its expectations, the fetish of commodities, as Marx would have put it. It's only getting worse today." Peter nodded along.

Eager to re-cement his leadership, Etienne jumped on a chair to share—with the refined skills of a Grecian orator—the vision more widely. "As you all know, Francis Fukuyama has just declared to the world that the Cold War and the fall of the Berlin Wall are all signs of the end. An end to our sociocultural evolution, the 'End of History.' Fukuyama says that liberal democracy, in bed with capitalism, is the final, victorious form of government for all nations." Etienne added, "These nation-states just flex technology to reinforce their own power. However," he said, drawing the crowd closer, "I refuse to surrender all hope for another world so easily, to allow commodities to bribe my conscience into being complicit with subjugation. We can still make and change history today—and we must!"

Jean-Paul added, "Indeed we must. Besides, Derrida says we shouldn't try to assume the death of Marx so quickly!"[113]

Jean-Paul's mention of Marx took Peter aback. He didn't realize this was still a thing after the Berlin Wall fell. Later, Peter would learn that this group was split over its approach to transforming the world. Some held a neo-Marxist agenda to overturn oppressive power structures, while others were anarchists looking to create an independent alternative world.

Etienne's speech continued. The onlookers tracked with him, seeming to jump from thought to thought with agility. Etienne reaffirmed,

---

113. Derrida, *Specters of Marx*.

"I refuse to believe that we have to resign ourselves to capitalism and technology dictating the content of our lives."

Peter watched it all, intrigued but truthfully a little scared. He awkwardly stirred his cocktail, flirting with what was going on but not knowing what to make of it all. He hadn't meant to pull the pin on this with his cheeky comment about bad faith. *Had he?* This must have been lurking right beneath the surface. The vision seemed steeped in hope, and if anyone could, these guys exuded both the confidence and intellect to pull it off.

"Now is the time to fight for humanity," Etienne said, rallying the group around each and every word.

"But how?" a bold voice shouted.

"A community like Ascona," Etienne confirmed decisively.[114]

"Exactly," Jean-Paul added. His unwavering support made Etienne worry whether this help came with some serious strings attached.

Immediately, men and women started to shout out, bubbling up with thoughts and ideas. "Yes! That's good!" said Lavinia and Ritesh. Etienne raised his hands as if beckoning an orchestral crescendo. "This will be a community where ideas can grow, be refined and nourished—to impact culture. Rather than planning to rupture the facade of capitalism, we can subvert it from within by offering something stronger, more alive, injecting a strong tangible flow of ideas."

Jean-Paul piped up, seeing the opportunity to impact the vision: "Yes, like a virus into the system. But here's what we must remember: our future stands and falls on our integrity to our vision. To succeed, we cannot simply recreate a place like Ascona. We need to learn from where they went off course. Most importantly, we must not conjure up some pseudo-meaning for ourselves within the New Age movement. What's the point of replacing narratives forged in 'bad faith' with mystical replacements?" he said, conjuring a spell of his own.

Etienne replied with an unsubtle corrective to appease the artisans: "We need to replace the straitjacket of Apollo: stagnant, outdated modernist reason and identities. We will have space to release who we really are, evolving, creating." The relief was almost palpable.

Jean-Paul was smarter than starting a spat out in a public place. He just held onto offense for later and continued to plow the soil where the

114. See, for example, Green, *Mountain of Truth*. Also, Fondazione Monte Verità, "History."

group was in agreement. "We must occupy our life, or it will be occupied for us. We must choose now!" Jean-Paul said, forcing an imminent choice.

"Where will it be?" someone shouted, holding a drink and high expectations.

"Where do you think it will be?" Jean-Paul questioned back, causing everyone to burst out laughing, even Etienne. "*Les Vosges!*" Jean-Paul confirmed. "Where else would this madman want us to put down roots? Where heroes are made! Right, Etienne?"

The love and laughter were infectious. It helped knock off those radical edges just a little, convincing Peter that it was going to be okay.

"Have you heard about his grandmother yet, Peter?" Jean-Paul asked, still quite publicly.

Peter shook his head.

"Well, wait another twenty minutes," he joked to a riot of belly laughs. "Okay, who's in?" Jean-Paul asked the chaotic chorus.

Hands raised. Everyone besides just one. Peter was free . . . he hardly knew them. He *could* disappoint them. But would he?

Peter turned inward: he'd given his all these last years, emptied himself, and it had been for what? Did he have anything left to give? But maybe this was a way to make his life matter. To leave even just a small legacy for humanity so that when his moment under the sun was gone, holding the baton in this race of life, he'd leave the world better than before. *I have to take responsibility*, he thought. *What else can I do—keep going through the motions and live in bad faith? What if there is another way to structure life? To truly live? To flourish? I would be able to tell Edwin I've found community* . . . All of a sudden, hardly believing it himself, his arm rose from the table sprung by the promise of purpose.

"Ahhhh! Even the Brit's in!" Jean-Paul explained to everyone, clinching rapturous excitement.

What had he signed up for? Etienne swiftly came to stand behind Peter, wrapping both his hands over his shoulders from behind—thumbs left on his shoulder blades—to form a strong and comforting v-shape. In a quiet and yet assured tone, he bent down to his ear so that Peter could hear him amongst the uproar and said earnestly, "Excited to have you, Peter. You won't regret it."

ACT TWO

The Rubicon

19

Peter

Fire, Foundations, & Four Bullets

LES VOSGES I

Sunday, August 1st, 1993.

It was the height of summer. The day had finally come to move into the Vosges Mountains and embrace a new communal way of life. The old hunting cabins were surrounded by a lush, wooded valley, occluded and yet close enough to a small village to gather supplies from select, noble sources. Water surged down the nearby mountainside even in drought, enabling a basic waterwheel to be set up. This swiftly developed into a rudimentary, though surprisingly effective, hydroelectric project.

Martagon lilies, with freckled bright petals and proud, protruding stamens, stained the woodland the color of crushed berries. Ferns, too, sprouted with the promise of ever more fronds sprung like piglet tails. Nestled in the mossy-moist undergrowth, they brought forth a yeast-like aroma that clung to the vapor, hanging poised within the folds of the earth where one thread of the landscape feathered into the next: farmland into hedgerow, hedgerow into pasture, trees, lakes, and mountains.

Beyond that formidable natural boundary of the Rhine, the Vosges were mirrored by the German Black Forest. While this all lay beneath a sky that rang with a timbre of eternal glory, it was not immutable. Rather than a hollowness, it was dense with the vitality of adrenaline-fueled surges of history—contingencies that carved the world as we know it.

For example, during the Gallic Wars the land had absorbed the sights, sounds, and smells of the Battle of Vosges in 58 BC. Ariovistus, leader of the Germanic tribe of the Suebi, had brazenly attempted to seize land in Gaul from the Roman Empire. After all these years, the land still clung to the defiant words of Ariovistus, who told its defender, the great Gaius Julius Caesar, that if he killed him, many in Rome might be pleased. How different history might have been had that been the case! Instead, the land—unable to act but only wait, receptive to the bodies of the dead—bore witness to Caesar's skillful rallying of his legions. He took them from the fear-inspired knife edge of mutiny to fanatical loyalty; from being surrounded to pursuing the invaders back across the Rhine.

History infused this deliciously arcadian place, layer upon layer of passion and promise. Bearing a vision of romantic pastoralism and harmony with the natural world, people flocked to it, their number multiplying daily. Many learned of it by word of mouth. They all wanted hope of some kind. The modern world, ever increasing in speed, had wrung them dry, leaving a clawing thirst for change.

They were housed in cabins made from partially stripped wooden logs or repurposed wood from farm buildings. Insulation was stuffed in the large cracks, and on many of the cabins, the A-frame had been crudely extended with a basic porch. The cabins clustered in several groups extending deeper and deeper into the deciduous strata of forest. By contrast, the communal area consisted of a more modern lodge before it opened onto the fire pit. Not far beyond lay the first splattering of lakes, where water pooled and breathed temporarily before its next descent.

Everyone came equipped with their own dreams and visions. Truth be told (but not to any living soul), Etienne already regretted allowing Jean-Paul to twist his arm that night in Paris. They had launched with a premature vision. How he wished they had distilled the limits and goals more concretely, for this choice would almost certainly bite him. The council couldn't even agree on a name. Some, almost sarcastically at first, called it *Le Rubicon*—the river that Caesar crossed when marching on Rome, intent to defeat Pompey's forces and take power from the Senate. Crossing that point showed that he really meant business: that there was no turning back. It worked even better since the nearby river had burst its bank when the lead group had visited the land for the first time. Apparently, it had been quite the torrent to drive through right before the entrance. The unofficial name had stuck. Only Etienne minded.

A habit quickly grew of gathering each night by a grand fire. Each family brought an offering of kindling or logs. While the outbreaks of merriment and music soon became less spontaneous over time, they remained, nonetheless, intoxicating. As the sun arched to its rest, the fire's burnt-orange light brushed up against cheekbones. Like a divine confluence, something loosely akin to a Gaelic *cèilidh* entwined the path of dancers. Most joined, aside from the elderly or those too engrossed in conversation. Flying strands of hair sliced through humidity as fiddlers from Ireland joined goat-skin *bodhrán* drummers in pounding out a rhythm that grounded hearts and souls in joint pursuit. A group of guitars was often joined by a scar-marked sitar. An older, rounder man plucked a melody on it that laced through the air. While his body could no longer dance, his music was eager to play this role for him.

The human soul swung wide to optimism: it was the early '90s! Anything was possible, and history was in the making. After all, hadn't humanity won? The guards on the Berlin Wall were unable to hold back the tide. And so, defying all models and expectations, the Cold War was effectively over and the new was stirring.

This particular evening, Jean-Paul was out hunting. However, more often than not, he could be found pacing with his dogs through long grass in a field nearby, angered at the dangerously liminal zeal that peaked into a thinly veiled spiritualism, when veiled at all. Conversely, Etienne saw the need for laughter, merriment, and, perhaps most importantly, rhythm. As anthropologist Marcel Mauss—the father of French ethnology—pointed out, rhythm had a unique power in being able to bind groups in cohesive movement.[115] This became both critical and almost magical when different people had different, often conflicting, needs. If only Etienne, too, could have laughed and lost himself in the merriment. He longed for it, but there was so much pressure to get this right.

Peter made a habit of sitting with his coterie of new friends, Antonio, Andrea, Bernard, and sometimes Etienne—that is, when he could sit down and someone didn't want a "quick" word about something. The drama of life was everywhere, vying for his attention. To punctuate this particular evening, Ritesh and Lavinia sat with these friends, inviting them to join them in lighting candles. The wick was dipped in ghee; the golden purity of this, they explained, symbolized sacrifice for safe passage.

---

115. See Michon, *Marcel Mauss Retrouvé.*

"For what?" Peter gently inquired.

"For the community to be successful as it grows," Lavinia explained, drawing from the Hindu culture of Ritesh's upbringing. The friends paused for a moment, honoring and embracing its meaning.

They then found themselves flung back into the drama. Bernard stopped two little children, Evan and Liesel, cousins, as they ran past barefoot. They each gave a *myrtille*-stained grin as Bernie did magic, revealing that a coin had been hiding in Evan's ear. Funny, this spoon-shaped inner cartilage contained more than a healthy amount of dirt, mirrored by the semi-circle creases under his lower eyelids, ordinarily quite invisible.

Antonio's whole body laughed. He pointed out that there was also a certain irony about this place. As he had already brought up a little too often—slow to catch onto social cues—he joked that Peter had come to "find himself" in this land of contested identity. Alsace-Lorraine had, after all, been subject to an embittered tug-of-war between France and Germany during most major conflicts since the early 1600s.

"You're still reading that, hey?" Andrea inquired, looking over Peter's shoulder as she brought over another heaped plate of food to share. Most people found Peter's obsession with mathematics endearing. Everyone else, it seemed, was throwing out random quotes from Friedrich Nietzsche, who, Peter had recently found out, was the philosopher whose character, a madman in a marketplace, had cried, "God is dead!" Or they were debating the merits of Marxist philosopher Henri Lefebvre's last book, *Rhythmanalysis: Space, Time and Everyday Life*. It had just been released and spoke of the effects of rhythms in urban spaces upon the human being.

In fairness, it *was* quite humorous. Perhaps Peter was scared to be done with his book? While he was still reading it there was hope, it seemed, to simplify life and neatly package it. Some slim hope. He was looking for this hope like a door, even if just a little open. Yet the irony was that the opposite was happening. Rather than opening up to certainty, the evidence gestured to a reality that testified to, or opened onto, "more." And that more? It seemed to be what philosophy (at best) and theology (at worst) tried to describe. He clung to the book like a safety blanket—or better, a life vest—while dipping his toes into the water of philosophy.

Bernard joked that if Peter had expected mathematics to stay in a neat little circle—as either the heavenly gift of the gods or as a surprisingly useful language of the earth—then he was bound to be disappointed, just like in the story of Archimedes.

"What story?" Andrea inquired.

Bernard leaned in, each of them drawing closer in response. "Legend has it that when Roman soldiers came to seize Archimedes after the Siege of Syracuse, they found him working on geometry in the sand." He paused.

"And?" Peter asked.

"Against their orders, they slew him. But with his last words he cried out: 'Do not disturb my circles!'"

Antonio immediately flew back, letting out a laugh. But Bernard drew them back in with a serious whisper: "Reality doesn't stay in neat little circles. You ignore the overlap of the seen and unseen, thought and the world, at your peril."

This reminder of complexity resonated with what Peter was learning about the crisis in the foundations of mathematics. It seemed just as fascinating as it was tragic.

The year David Hilbert turned sixty—incensed at young mathematicians being drawn towards programs that he felt would mutilate mathematics—he launched a project to secure the foundations of mathematics unlike any other.[116] Beginning with number theory, Hilbert's goal was to rebuild from the bottom up, formalizing mathematics by axiomatizing it. With Russell's paradox as a cautionary tale, each formal system would need to be proven to be consistent—that is, that it does not produce contradictions—by finitary means. In other words, can it bear up to the pressure of revealing truth and marking out the rules of the game?

Eight years later, in the fall of 1930, Hilbert was given an honorary citizenship of his hometown, Königsberg, where Immanuel Kant had been born, lived most of his life, and died.[117] At this event, Hilbert gave his retirement speech. As he rallied the next generation behind his project, he could not fail to draw upon their beloved luminary, connecting mathematics to the nature of reality. Like any good Königsberg boy, Hilbert had grown up paying homage to Kant at his cathedral-adjacent crypt each April on the day of Kant's birth. There was no getting away from him; this man who'd made being awkwardly eccentric—such as scripting his dinner parties—seem obligatory for genius. The statue Hilbert

---

116. Hilbert was concerned over Intuitionism. See Reid, *Hilbert*, 156.

117. Awarded at a meeting of the Society of German Scientists and Physicians.

had walked past each day—tricorne hat in one hand and the other hand held out as if in dialogue—simply read: KANT. No other explanation was necessary for the Enlightenment thinker whose "Copernican Turn" had changed the trajectory of human thought forever.

The worldview in Hilbert's retirement speech was clear and crisp. In his mind, everything collapsed down to mathematics, the true hinge of reality. Echoing Kant, he asserted: "Only one who has learned the language and signs in which nature speaks to us can understand nature . . . This language . . . is mathematics."[118] Mathematical truths, after all, had been identified by Kant as belonging to a unique sort of knowledge, uniquely accessible *a priori*. This meant that they were thought to be true and reliable without being first derived *a posteriori* from elsewhere, for example, through logic or experience.

For Hilbert, mathematics set the foundation for everything else. What then, was more pressing than securing these foundations? Had Kant not also said that 'genuine scientific content can be found only in so far as mathematics is contained therein'?[119] Thus even the entire magisterium of science seemed to rest on this project being taken to completion.

However, while Hilbert eagerly invoked Kant to bolster his arguments—also having defended him fiercely in the doctoral project of his youth—over time, Hilbert had become far more reductionist. Before his retirement speech Hilbert had even confided in a young relative that much of what Kant had said he now considered "pure nonsense."[120]

Kant's idea of what the mind could directly experience (*phenomena*) and categorize—in his theory of transcendental idealism—left space for the possible independent existence of God and other *noumena*, or things in themselves. However, Hilbert became explicit in his desire to free Kant's *a priori* theory from all its "anthropomorphic dross" to found a "pure mathematical knowledge."[121] This would be independent from metaphysics and included cutting the God hypothesis loose as irrelevant.

Indeed, while Hilbert's methodology was famously compared to a work of theology, Hilbert is often considered to have been agnostic. Hilbert certainly did not go out of his way to consider or protect any sacred territory in the landscape of truth. "Mathematics was a presuppositionless

118. Hilbert, "Naturerkennen und Logik."
119. Hilbert, "Naturerkennen und Logik."
120. Reid, *Hilbert*, 194.
121. Reid, *Hilbert*, 195.

science," he had asserted, "to found it, I do not need God."[122] Hilbert was thus after an entirely autonomous, axiomatic foundation.

Hilbert ended his retirement speech with a rallying cry that countered the famous nineteenth-century German physiologist Emil du Bois-Reymond and his famous *ignorabimus*. Du Bois-Reymond had argued that in relation to certain questions, one must accept the harder truth that we cannot know the answers. Defiant, Hilbert drove it home: "We must know. We will know!" When this ending was recorded later in the day, it captured for posterity his free-flowing laugh that followed it, optimistic and jovial.[123]

Tragically, however, mathematics proved unyielding to Hilbert's project. A young man named Kurt Gödel had made a quiet but incredibly inconvenient announcement just two days before Hilbert's retirement speech. During a round-table discussion on epistemology, the nature of knowledge, Gödel revealed the existence of his Incompleteness Theorem.[124] Essentially, while he had earnestly sought to contribute to Hilbert's program, quite the opposite had transpired. It was a depth bomb, for it gradually became clear that his findings meant that the complete formalization of mathematics was impossible.

As a student in Vienna, Gödel had seen Hilbert's rigor and reductionism inspire many. Invited by his supervisor, Hans Hahn, the young Gödel listened to the back and forth of the Vienna Circle, possibly the most important philosophical group of the twentieth century. This exclusive group of great minds met regularly between 1924 and 1936, bouncing ideas off marble tables as they also sounded the limits of human reason. In addition to highly venerating Hilbert, they also held Einstein in the highest esteem. It was hard not to! Moritz Schlick, the nominal leader, was particularly enamored by Einstein, who had used both non-Newtonian mechanics and non-Euclidean geometry in his theories of special and general relativity.

Unofficially binding the Vienna Circle was also their mutual admiration of the aristocratic, unruly former student of Russell, Ludwig Wittgenstein. Wittgenstein was a man with both piercing eyes and intellect. With God anathema, his *Tractatus Logico-Philosophicus* became the Circle's dogmatic touchstone. Committed to the reductive philosophical

122. This was shared at Hilbert's 1927 Hamburg address. See van Heijenoort, *From Frege to Gödel*, 479.

123. Reid, *Hilbert*, 196.

124. Wang, *Reflections*, 85–86.

tenant of logical positivism, many of the Vienna Circle balked at Gödel's honest suggestion of incompleteness and its possible implications for both mathematics and logic. That is, before its conclusive findings rendered it impossible to avoid.

However, few might have heard about the young Gödel's findings if it were not for a senior mathematician, John von Neumann, cornering the young man after the roundtable discussion in 1930. He had to ask if Gödel was really suggesting what he thought he was: *Incompleteness!?*[125]

Gödel had a proof demonstrating that a project like Hilbert's formalization could never succeed. As Solomon Feferman has eruditely summarized, "Hilbert had conjectured that number theory is complete and that its consistency can be proved by finitary means."[126] Yet Gödel revealed that no system/mathematical language or axiom set could contain all the elements it required to be self-sufficient or self-evident. Essentially, there would always be truth outside of these systems, unable to be captured by it.[127] Later, Gödel summarized the incompleteness theorems as demonstrating that "there are arithmetical propositions that are true but neither provable nor unprovable within their own calculus, so that arithmetic is intrinsically incomplete."[128]

In a sense, Hilbert's reductionism could not outmaneuver Kant's wisdom in keeping the door open to "more." It is fitting, perhaps, that Gödel's findings first came by way of revealing a paradox, showing an arithmetically true statement that was not provable. For, akin to how Immanuel Kant had famously used reason to critique reason, demonstrating its limits, the aforementioned paradox meant that, even if unintentionally at first, Gödel had used mathematics to critique mathematics, finding its limit.

The possibility of truth beyond what one can logically prove within a formal system? This was scandalous. Painful. Possibly indecent. This had been the first takeaway for Peter: that, while evidence can absolutely point in certain directions, truth might still exceed what is formally provable. And second? There were limits to reductionism: if you reduce too

125. Budiansky, *Journey*, 132.

126. Feferman, "Provenly Unprovable."

127. In layman's terms, Gödel's famous incompleteness theorems demonstrated that for any computable axiomatic system that is powerful enough to describe an arithmetic for the natural numbers, the following would hold: 1) If a logical or axiomatic formal system is consistent, it cannot be complete; 2) The consistency of the entire system cannot be proven by that system alone.

128. Gödel, "Modern Development," 383.

far you are in serious danger of excluding or shaving off vital and true information about reality. Peter discovered that Gödel considered this the danger of materialistic philosophy (or what he called the leftward view),[129] the dominant worldview on the continent at the time; the view the Vienna Circle had propagated.

Peter was surprised to read that while Gödel's finding had immediate implications on these discussions about mathematics, truth, and logic, it continues to inform discussions regarding the possible limits of artificial intelligence. Gödel's biographer Stephen Budiansky summarized that in his later years, Gödel "firmly believed that his proof was profoundly encouraging for human creativity" because human minds—more than computational brains—will "always be able to recognize some truths through intuition . . . that can never be established by the most advanced computing machine."[130] They have access to something the algorithms don't.

While the news of his brain not being entirely inferior to a computer was of some comfort to Peter, the rest of these revelations grated on him like a pernicious irritant. It was not lost on him that if truth can exist beyond what one can prove by normal, formal, logical means, then this might open up the possibility of "necessary truth" or a source of truth in some sort of beyond, whatever that meant.

Upon learning this, Peter had done what he always did to avoid spinning out: he had dug his heels into the facts. He was shocked to learn that while Gödel changed the field of mathematics forever, at 9:20 a.m. on June 22, 1936, something happened that likewise irreparably changed the trajectory of Gödel's life. Moritz Schlick—core to the Vienna Circle and the man who first got Gödel interested in logic—was mortally betrayed by a student. Four bullets from a 6.35mm caliber pistol filled his body. He bled out on the university stairway that should have led to his morning lecture. Why? Because Schlick was mistaken for having been Jewish, and an unemployed, radicalized student chose murder.

Gödel had long worried about his health, but when he heard of the assassination, this triggered a severe nervous crisis. This included a fear of being poisoned, the same fear that decades later claimed his life. As the 1930s wore on, so did the fear and the genuine threats; for while Gödel was not Jewish, he was often mistaken for being so. This brought

129. Gödel, "Modern Development," 377.
130. Budiansky, *Journey*, 280.

with it real danger. At one time, Einstein had a $5,000 bounty on his head. "Not yet hanged," the caption read. "Jewish intellectualism is dead," Propaganda Minister Joseph Goebbels proclaimed.[131]

Gödel and his beloved—a divorcé dancer, Adele, of whom his parents thoroughly disapproved—fled to the United States upon the start of World War II, going east via Russia and Japan. They ended up at Princeton University, where he became the friend that Einstein said was the reason he went to work. Why? For the privilege of walking home with him.[132] They were utterly different in their temperament and quirks but mutually enriched each other's ideas, genuinely enjoying time together.

Princeton was also where Bertrand Russell temporarily resided in 1944. Here, Russell joined Gödel and Wolfgang Pauli in weekly discussions at 112 Mercer Street, Einstein's house. So, what of Russell and Whitehead? Was their attempt at founding a logical system of mathematics more successful than Hilbert's? Peter was still tracing their story.

Why did this logical underpinning to mathematics matter for Peter? If everything was mathematized, a big machine, and (with science collapsed down into it) mathematics equated to the sum total of truth, then everything could be complete. Settled. While Hilbert's formalization seemed untenable after Gödel, Peter hoped that other attempts at mathematical foundations might have fared better. Maybe a different approach could offer him at least some sense of peace. Then, perhaps, all the personal pain didn't really matter—just the messy froth of humanity spinning its wheels? And beyond that? There might be no room for God. He'd heard it somewhere that, like a Greek deity, God could be edited out—a "god of the gaps"—just as Zeus was no longer needed to explain the existence of lightning once humanity knew more.

Despite his better judgment, Peter had written to Edwin about these thoughts right before leaving Paris. He wasn't expecting a reply now that he was in the Vosges. Honestly, he didn't really want one. Perhaps he just wanted to feel connected to a friend with whom he actually had some history? This was, after all, his "safe" subject.

§

Peter shook his head. He had a habit of withdrawing into this space in his mind. But a commotion drew him out of it. Jean-Paul was back with

131. United States Holocaust Memorial Museum, "Books Burn as Goebbels Speaks."
132. Yourgrau, *World Without Time*, 94.

138

a hunting party. It seemed that they had been remarkably successful. A number of women fawned over the men, who seemed more than happy to receive the hero's welcome. Some women were shouting congratulations, while a couple of the men took to howling, their chins tipped towards the moon and engaged diaphragms gleefully at playing this prehistoric role.

"Neanderthals," Andrea said under her breath at the ungainly parade as she kept her head down. Peter caught her whispering, as she had done by habit many times before, recalling some poem she'd once heard about husbands and their foolishness like Icarus.[133]

"Oh, you're married?" Peter asked, startling her a little. She hadn't bargained for an audience.

"Good God, no! I'd probably do away with myself if I'd married one of. . ." she bit her tongue. Probably best. Redirecting, she explained that it was just so typical: this sort of grandiose pantomime. "Women bring back food and clothes all the time," she added as a side comment. "Why men have to have this sort of pomp and pride, I will never understand."

Curiosity got the better of Peter. "What did you mean about Icarus?" he pressed, familiar with the myth where he flew too close to the sun.

"Well, his wings held together with wax!" Antonio chimed in.

"Exactly," Andrea said, looking over at them all. "Hubris led to Icarus's downfall in more ways than one."

The hunters did seem to be basking in their own praise. Peter grinned awkwardly to appease Andrea, unable to think of any other legitimate response. Thankfully, she found it somewhat endearing.

Mothers and fathers brought their kids to watch Jean-Paul expertly skin and dismember animals, ranging from the big to the small that they had snared. Many hoped to desensitize their youngsters and teach them about their food. The children seemed fascinated. Honestly, some of the little boys looked as if they'd waited their whole lives for this.

"Is he not more like Prometheus, stealing fire from the gods?" Bernard joked as Jean-Paul stole hot coals from the large bonfire to make a roasting pit. Above it, he lent the large animals over the smoldering pit, having pinned them to long poles using all his bodily force. He scored chest cavities, holding them open with cross beams and scavenged cast-iron dowels. Soon, all could hear the fat of the animals burn up as the melted droplets landed on the super-heated rocks. The crowd waited as

133. Duffy, "Mrs. Icarus."

patiently as they could, barely making a dent in the feast of foraged berries, wine, and local cheeses.

Jean-Paul's hunting dogs obsessively guarded the meat, stuck to the spot but shivering in anticipation. Only the occasional small head of fox daring to peep above the ground could draw them away. In such a moment, they fled as one raptor-like pack of demoniacal hounds into the outer wilderness. Their pure speed scooped air into the depths of their lungs, pressing against their chests from the inside, narrowly outwitting the suffocating attempts of the shadows.

20

WW2

Bone Armor

LES VOSGES I

Sunday, October 3rd, 1943.

Matthias woke up on the forest floor before the dappled dawn light, with a crick in his neck and leaf-litter in his hair that left him smelling like decaying mushrooms and mold. If he had been any less exhausted, he wouldn't have slept, fearing that the incessant Nazi activity in the area would cause them to stumble upon them. He woke up to Violet's eyes staring into his. In another time it might have been romantic. Instead, it jolted him into realizing that he was, in fact, a widower. What a funny, unfamiliar, heart-wrenching term that was now forever true. He and Violet were so different, but fate had bonded them from those very first days distributing resistance pamphlets in Paris. They knew the risk they were taking; but it's one thing losing your own life, another having the life of your loved one taken out from under your watch. Blown by the wind, face-down in the foundation, it impaled him afresh daily. He felt her in his arms. How could that have been the end of their story, a story that started in such joy? He hated what the Nazis had destroyed, for him and so many.

He was also jealous of Henry. He was jealous that he didn't have someone that close to lose. No wife, no kids. He honestly felt guilty being jealous of a man with one hand; in all probability a brave man, probably braver and more capable than he was, he thought. Yet jealous he was. He'd seen the looks. The little glances of admiration. He wanted to protect Violet. He owed her husband that much, didn't he? After all, it was only by sheer luck that he hadn't been there when the rest of them were arrested.

"Look, we need to move, quickly. I know a place," Violet forcefully whispered to the two men.

They jumped to it, gathering all their things and sweeping back the forest floor to leave no trace. They left the dwindling safety of the dense forest in these early hours to find a dirt road. "It's not far," Violet told them. While he couldn't lead, Henry used his SOE training to keep watch both in front and behind them, a rear guard as they contoured the occupied land. Each one of Henry's senses bristled.

They needed to adjust course a couple of times before Violet finally led them to a stone barn. They climbed the ladder and positioned what was left of the straw around them the best they could. "I can't believe how much activity there is right now," Matthias said to Violet.

"They're on the move," Violet agreed.

"I hate to think," Henry added.

"It must be to do with Natzweiler-Struthof," Matthias whispered to Henry the moment Violet was occupied downstairs. He knew Violet couldn't handle it. They were close to the concentration camp, but it was not as if she were unaware.

"It's not safe out there," Violet said when she climbed back up, ignoring the gentle swell of unwelcome tears. "Do you have enough water if we wait a little while?"

She hadn't wanted to leave the Vosges by going north. After all, Paris was west. But the roadblocks had made it impossible. There were so many they hadn't anticipated. They must have been expanding the camp. If it was just she and Matthias, they may have taken a chance, but they needed to protect Henry and the mission above all. Yet the irony was that heading north pushed them closer and closer to the main camp. Each road west was blocked and each trail showed signs of excessive use. This was not normal. Mercifully, the occasional friendly farmer warned them about what they knew.

This was Violet's worst nightmare. Could she stay level-headed enough? If she were going this way anyway, would she be brave enough to look for him? That is, her husband's brother. He too had been caught up in what the papers had called the *Musée de l'Homme* affair. It was all very public. Many were martyred for the cause, but others were shipped out to concentration camps. There had been whispers about him being at Natzweiler-Struthof. But what were the chances of him still being alive? Many friends had been brought here to labor hard: some to death in the granite quarries, the majority of them delivered under Hitler's *Nacht und Nebel* directive specifically targeting spies and the *Résistance*.

When the time came, fully clothed in the itchy hay loft, Violet tried to sleep. She needed to. But her sleep was broken by vivid dreams, her mind feeling wide awake. They started with her trying to free Jérôme and then being lunged at by a German Shepherd. It tore at her. Then, it went darker still. She was back in Paris, watching it all unfold. One lady, whom she knew all too well in real life, condemned her, shouting that she was the traitor. She shouted it louder and louder, as Violet watched most of their group, including her husband, Jérôme, being manhandled, arms behind their backs and marched out of the museum. They had been caught red-handed. Violet's memory snagged, just as it did in the daytime, obsessing over the way Jérôme's eyes found her, catching them right before he disappeared. It lasted just a second, but it had absolutely unwound her. It is not as if this had been a surprise; they knew it could have ended this way. What truly bothered her was that, ordinarily, she could always read him. Yet in that one glance, there were so many interwoven truths that she couldn't plumb its depths. He seemed to say: "I love you" and "Protect yourself." The glance was honest, defiant, and brave in its acknowledgement of fear. But did it also reveal shame? What about disappointment? Did he think she could have betrayed them? Surely not. But did he? Had his mind been poisoned? Did he blame her? Had not the last few years taught them that everything is possible in war?

The lady's accusations droned over that memory, intensifying it, strangling it. It morphed unrecognizably yet remained so familiar as to be like her own blood circling her veins. This lady had always been jealous of Violet marrying Jérôme. She never hid that—not from Violet. The rumor—the accusation—now spread in Violet's mind as a disease. Surely, he wouldn't have believed them. But was there disappointment in his gaze? She wished she could decipher it completely. She protested in her sleep, writhing painfully. *Why would she betray the group? Why would she do something that triggered the death of her own husband?*

"*Tu va bien?*" Matthias asked Violet.

She woke from that liminal torture. "I'm okay," she said, reaching into her pocket. The scute was there. That's what she cared about: one little piece of bone armor from an armadillo. Jérôme had been, after all, overseeing the collections at the *Muséum national d'histoire naturelle*. He had given it to her the first time she delivered the Résistance pamphlets without him. It was good luck and was meant to remind her that she had armor on the outside—she was stronger than she gave herself credit. She now knew every part of the curious little thing, even its slight ridges, by touch, squeezing it tight.

21

Peter

The Mediterranean Storm

LES VOSGES I

Saturday, August 21st, 1993.

Time stretched for friends old and new, bent by the Einsteinian gravity of excitement as they explored the possibilities of this Eden. Even before the first week had fully passed, Peter noticed that families had acclimatized: pre-teens, once wallowing in shame as their father's generous shape appeared bare-chested, now accepted it (however reluctantly) as the new norm.

Like ducks to water, the young boys around the camp had started whittling sticks, attempting to stalk and hunt prey of their own. They particularly delighted in giving passersby heart attacks by rustling hedgerows. One ran past Peter with an impressive mustache of caked-on dirt that had adhered to a trail of smeared snot. Stirring up trouble, they led the younger kids like a gaggle of "lost boys" defending Neverland from Captain Hook and a whole hoard of beastly enemies. It reminded Peter of distant times, now vignettes in his mind, when he had fully convinced himself that running off to sea at six—to be like Captain James Cook (who he liked to imagine was his great-great grandfather)—was his destiny. He did it to spite his parents but turned around when it got dark, as he missed Nana. He really needed a hug. Though it would have been nice if his parents had noticed that he had been missing.

145

Mothers in the community had switched babies to cloth nappies despite the extra work, thankful to newly adoptive grandparents to help. The community seemed to flourish as if it was all that was ever needed for humanity to click back in sync with itself. Peter was hopeful. *Perhaps the biggest problems of all were simply the modern pressures and inhumane rhythms of life?* he thought, remembering the Henri Lefebvre book the others liked. Peter was just feeling lucky that he had been at the right place at the right time to jump on board. This felt meaningful. It felt good to have vision again. There was talk about needing to turn people away soon.

Before the sun went down, Peter started asking around to find where he could make himself useful. He went to check on Etienne.

Etienne was just finishing a radio broadcast. It turned out that, in those days, sharing a frequency was common. That worked well for them starting up a broadcast—they didn't need to fill it the whole time. Etienne wanted to give a voice to the community and impact the wider world. He also wanted to freely educate people and encourage good dialogue, arguing that we live in a culture of amnesia. Etienne asked, astutely, "How can we navigate into the future if we don't even know our current trajectory? And how can we do that without plotting at least two points over time to find our bearing?" History—including how humanity has understood itself, its call and obligations over time—is essential, and Peter was starting to agree.

Waiting quietly for it to end, Peter's eyes darted around. There were so many books and documents, records and cassettes packed into this small cabin. Peeling off the headphones once finished, Etienne apologized to Peter.

"Don't worry at all," Peter replied. "I was the one who intruded!"

"You're never an intrusion," Etienne replied, kindly.

"The show was fascinating—at least the part that I heard," Peter said.

Etienne was laying foundations by talking about the use of political violence and whether it was ever justified. To do so, he had shared part of the story of Albert Camus. Today, he had started from the late forties at a party thrown by the French polymath Boris Vian. Why? Because this way, Etienne could sketch the conflicts and contours of the debate through the intellectuals and bohemians of the Left Bank.

Camus, it turned out, was that suave, French-Algerian thinker who loved life while also being determined to stare at its gruesome underbelly. He thought humanity foolish to keep looking for an overarching reason or unity to existence, calling it an absurd pursuit. He compared this desire, in his book *The Myth of Sisyphus*, to "a man armed only with a sword" attacking a group of machine guns. Absurdity bursts forth, he argued, "from the comparison between a bare fact and a certain reality, between an action and the world that transcends it."[134] For Camus, life unabashedly exceeded the bounds of the rational and justified. As an absurdist—familiar with theology and with his finger on the pulse of atheistic existentialism—Camus did not think that humanity should just throw its hands up into the air and surrender nor try to escape this reality. Instead, he thought that one should engage with the heart of it, for he argued that being human means to rebel, to stand against suffering and injustice.[135] Primed and passionate, he became ever more concerned about the fate of humanity rather than choosing a particular political tribe. But in doing so, Camus found himself on a collision course with the dominant thinkers of his time.

Etienne had skillfully set the scene: Paris, in the spring of 1947, American jazz pouring out jubilant clouds of ecstatic elation upon esteemed guests from Vian's phonograph. This was fitting for a man famous in his own right in the jazz scene, though he also wrote playful articles and novels dripping—like the juice from a ripe pear—with surreal parody. This included, written that same year, his caricature of Sartre in *Froth on the Daydream* where "Jean-Sol Patre" traveled to lectures on elephants, adoring audiences were addressed from a throne—joined by others parachuting in—only for many of them to be drowned by firefighters' hoses.[136] The prime days of Sartre's fame really was—*almost*—that chaotic!

It was a time of the feverously new: new tastes in politics as well as philosophy, though the two often came interwoven. France had bled dearly for her freedom. So, while the Left Bank—with Sartre at the helm—gladly received the music surging from the veins of their African American brothers and sisters, they were unwilling to submit to what was perceived as another occupation: a cultural infestation that had

134. Camus, *Myth of Sisyphus*, 22.

135. "I rebel—therefore we exist," Camus, *Rebel*, 22. "When he rebels, a man identifies himself with other men, and so surpasses himself . . . human solidarity is metaphysical . . . solidarity that is born in chains," Camus, *Rebel*, 17.

136. Vian, *Froth on the Daydream*, 80–85.

supposedly clung to GI boots epitomized by Coca-Colonization, ostensibly the envoy of White American Capitalism.[137]

Capitalism and communism were largely seen as the exclusive political options in this early Cold War era, and Communism was, ostensibly, the lesser of two evils. In fact, in 1947, Maurice Merleau-Ponty, a friend and colleague of Sartre with whom he had launched *Les Temps modernes*, released a series of three articles, "Humanism and Terror,"[138] later a book. While he would later change his position,[139] at the time, Merleau-Ponty fervently defended the 1936 Moscow show trials and claimed that since violence was inherent to all politics and regimes, "what we have to discuss is not violence, but its sense or its future."[140]

Albert Camus wasn't having any of it. The way Etienne explained it, Peter could see it playing out in his mind's eye. In 1947, fresh from a trip abroad, the tanned, football-loving ladies' man of a novelist and philosopher burst into Vian's party. He made a beeline past fluted champagne glasses. They shuddered. He then astonished guests as he launched his attack without hesitation: proverbially leaping for Merleau-Ponty's jugular. *Did he not realize what he was justifying?*

Merleau-Ponty defended himself before Sartre jumped to his aid, everyone aghast. Camus abhorred this betrayal; Sartre had been more than just a friend, some claiming that Camus likened him to an older brother, if not a father figure. After all, Camus's own father died young in World War I.

Camus stormed out. As if summoning a Mediterranean storm, full of power and potentiality, he slammed the door. Everything shook. The whip of the wind incised the room with the bitter residue of this smoldering, relational asphyxiate.

Sartre, hardly svelte, ran after Camus and into the cobbled street. There was no going back to the party *or* the embrace of friendship. Etienne underscored that afterward, Camus wrote, "Today things are clear and what belongs to the concentration camp, even socialism, must be called a concentration camp. In a sense, I shall never again be polite."[141]

---

137. Marling, "Coca-colonization," 731–39.

138. Merleau-Ponty, *Humanisme et terreur*, was first split between three issues of *Les Temps modernes*. Published by Gallimard the same year, 1947.

139. For this change of position, see Merleau-Ponty, *Adventures of the Dialectic*.

140. Merleau-Ponty, *Humanisme et terreur*, 109.

141. Camus, *Notebooks 1942–1951*, 211.

§

"I'm glad you enjoyed the episode!" Etienne replied. "It's all about the conflict of ideas. Really, the twentieth century can be read as the playing field upon which enlightened humanity rejoiced in having liberated itself from God. It had slayed all infantile delusion, and now it was the turn of ideologies—such as fascism and communism—to try to bend the world into their utopic visions."

"That optimism is chilling," said Peter. He then asked quizzically, "I thought Camus and Sartre were close friends. But that was the beginning of the end?"

"Ah! You've seen those pictures of them in Paris together during the occupation—right? But Camus was always more radical and hands-on, incarnating the spirit of resistance from the start. Sartre and de Beauvoir briefly considered more tangible resistance, cycling around France talking to friends, but then they went back to writing. In Sartre's case, even performing shows under the occupation. A lot more happened after Vian's party, but these events were just the tip of the iceberg, testifying to an ideological rupture."

"Can you help me understand why they saw things so differently?" Peter asked.

"I can try! As I think you heard, after the war much of the intellectual scene in Paris reacted to fascism and turned towards the USSR, avoiding the capitalism they saw in the West. Mind you, the irony was not lost on everyone. For example, Raymond Aron pointed something out. Know that he was the same friend who had introduced Sartre and Simone de Beauvoir—when still in their exuberant, optimistic twenties—to the field of phenomenology—"

"—over apricot cocktails at the Bec-de-Gaz."

"Right. A key philosophical steppingstone on their way to their particular brand of existentialism."

"So, what did Aron say?" Peter was intrigued.

"That, while Marx said that religion was the 'opium of the people,'[142] communism had become 'the opium of the intellectuals.'[143] In a way, while Sartre and de Beauvoir, for example, rejected God from starting principles, it seemed that they had made this treacherous, secular leap of political faith."

142. Marx, *Critique of Hegel's Philosophy of Right*, 131.

143. Aron, *Opium of the Intellectuals*.

"That does seem inconsistent," Peter acknowledged.

"Most importantly, Camus was not having it," Etienne replied, avoiding the implications regarding religious faith. He hadn't meant to reveal that vein of human life. Not now, not yet. He liked to share about topics he felt he had mastered and could look behind. Yet somehow this area, so intertwined with human longing, seemed unyielding. He could not master it as anything more than a strawman, and this did not suffice. Without mastering it, he could not vanquish its spectral presence.

"Why did Camus see this when the others didn't?" Peter mercifully asked.

This was a question Etienne could answer: "Camus felt that it was abundantly clear that the Soviet gulag was no better than the concentration camp; ideology didn't change a thing in this respect. Do you know much about them, Peter?"

"Not really."

"Aleksandr Solzhenitsyn, a former captain of the Red Army, gave a detailed first-hand account in *The Gulag Archipelago*. It's worth reading. He calls it that because these forced labor prison camps spread like islands all over Siberia. Solzhenitsyn explains how, if you fell out of favor, you would get flushed down metaphorical sewer pipes into the prison system: 'The prison sewers were never empty. The blood, the sweat, and the urine into which we were pulped, pulsed through them.'"[144]

"And you're saying that Sartre, de Beauvoir, and co. were okay with this?"

"You have to understand that some information was sketchy at this time. Solzhenitsyn's account wasn't published until the 1970s. Of course, other accounts were building; after all, this system started back in 1919, not long after the Russian Revolution. The French Left Bank intelligentsia seemed content, for a time, to overlook these accounts."

"I see," said Peter.

"Anyhow, it became a very public feud between Camus and Sartre," Etienne added. "You know, Camus didn't think he needed to learn about poverty from Marx: he lived poverty, growing up in Algeria. A responsibility to humanity wasn't cornered by one nineteenth-century man writing from a comfortable London library."

"The man had a point."

144. Solzhenitsyn, *Gulag Archipelago*, 25.

"Indeed. He honed it in the form of the book, *The Rebel*, a punchy survey of history where Camus dared to diagnose both the roots and tragic irony of revolutionary movements.[145] He saw that humanity is rebellious at heart, driven by existential passions and eager to push against injustice. He calls this instigated by "revolt"—the very human cry of "no!" However, the challenge is the next step: revolution requires a "yes" to something, and—this is where the tragedy lies—the ideology-driven nature of revolution means that—as history has taught us—it will inevitably betray the human being."[146]

"Why did he think that?" Peter asked.

"Because revolution tries to 'fit the world in a theoretical frame.'[147] The moment the goal becomes these naked ideas, humanity suffers to achieve these goals. He particularly looked at the French and Russian revolutions. Camus points out that there is never an end, the perfect static point where the revolution has won. The possibility of the utopic ideal—for which they have already given so much—has to be maintained and protected. Those who are a threat against it need to be weeded out. Just think of the French Revolution. What came next?"

"The Reign of Terror?"

"Exactly," Etienne said. "That's what this episode was really about: Camus's pursuit of something integrally humanizing, something moderating that kept humanity at the core of the human desire for change and a better world. Without it, humans are sacrificed on the altar of achieving or maintaining this progress. You know, as the French Revolution played out, both Maximilien Robespierre (the revolutionary who led the Reign of Terror) and Marie Antoinette (wife of King Louis XVI) were murdered in the dogged pursuit of the same cause. And now? Their bones are both in the catacombs beneath Paris."

"What did Camus think was the solution?" Peter asked.

"That's the interesting part. He knew that somehow moderation needs to happen to keep humanity at the center, not these naked, enslaving ideas. But regarding how this could be achieved, he's impassioned but

---

145. Camus, *Rebel*.

146. "Rebellion is, by nature, limited in scope. It is no more than an incoherent pronouncement. Revolution, on the contrary, originates in the realm of ideas . . . revolution is an attempt to shape actions to ideas, to fit the world in a theoretical frame . . . rebellion kills men while revolution destroys both men and principles." Camus, *Rebel*, 106.

147. Camus, *Rebel*, 106.

vague. I feel as if he is almost groping around this idea at the end of *The Rebel*. Here," Etienne said, "read it for yourself. Those last pages are really interesting. Mind you, it'll make more sense if you read the rest of it first."

"Thank you," said Peter, adding it to his pile. "Just because finding the solution is hard doesn't mean Camus is wrong though, correct?"

"Indeed. Just like in medicine, diagnosing a problem is imperative to move forward. But finding a cure? That's a whole extra kettle of fish." Etienne shifted on his chair, spinning it slightly, confidently. He rested his hand against his chin, still holding the red pen with which he had marked up this evening's script.

"So, Sartre and friends didn't agree with Camus's diagnosis?" Peter inquired.

"For quite a while after the war, they continued to pivot towards Moscow. Sartre even attempted to connect Marxism and existentialism."[148]

"Just promised? So, he didn't?"

"Not with the rigor that he intended. He may have set himself an impossible task—the individual condemned to be free; and yet somehow, set within the wider framework of Marxism's deterministic historical materialism." Etienne added off the cuff, "In a certain way, though, I wonder if the depth of Sartre's support of the radical left was, indirectly, Camus's fault."

"Really? Why?"

"Because after the party incident, the feud built, peaking again when Camus published *The Rebel* in 1951. Shortly afterward, Camus publicly reminded Sartre of how, during the liberation of Paris from the Nazi occupation in 1944, he had found Sartre asleep in a theater chair. He inferred this to be analogous to his posture throughout the war. And here's my point: I think it's possible that this criticism, along with a healthy helping of guilt, provoked Sartre to double down, digging in his heels at a time when others like Maurice Merleau-Ponty were starting to have a crisis of faith in Marxism."[149]

---

148. Sartre had hoped to fully reconcile his existentialism with a communal ethic. This goal became integrating individual freedom and personal subjectivity within the context of collective social structures to sketch an improved, humanizing Marxism. While he started his attempt in *Critique of Dialectical Reason* (1960), Sartre was never able to fully deliver, not to the extent that he had hoped. This was a complex task, and he died before his second volume, *The Intelligibility of History*, was complete. However, it remains pertinent to ask whether this materialism, this reductionist understanding of reality, was ever able to deliver what he had hoped.

149. Merleau-Ponty, *Adventures of the Dialectic*.

"Ouch. I get it, but that's a low blow from Camus."

"Perhaps. But here's the wider context: when *The Rebel* came out, wonderfully imperfect and raw, Sartre and his friends used their platform—especially *Les Temps Modernes*—to push against it. Camus was being ripped to shreds: ostracized, out of favor, and standing alone. It was assumed that by using certain words and tone, he had dared to criticize the position of Sartre et al. in the penultimate chapter. It, therefore, implored a response. But Sartre didn't give Camus that dignity. *Les Temps Modernes* waited for months before releasing a review. Then, rather than having a distinguished colleague review it, they chose a younger junior member, Francis Jeanson, to assassinate the work. Which he did. Virulently."

"What happened next?"

"Camus directly replied to 'Monsieur le Directeur,' Sartre, who eventually came out of hiding to personally attack Camus's philosophy: 'And suppose you didn't reason very well? And suppose your thinking was muddled and banal?' he said. It was only after Sartre's public rant that Camus reminded Sartre of this nap at the Comédie-Française during the liberation. As a member of the *Résistance* who 'never walked away from the combats of the time,' Camus declared that he was tired of being given lessons by those who had 'never placed more than their armchairs in the direction of history.'"[150]

"So, you think that Sartre felt guilty after that and was trying to prove himself?"

"Allegations are most painful when they confirm a fear that we already have about ourselves—don't you think?"

"But how could we guess what he was thinking?"

"Playwrights can't help but share a part of themselves, just like any creative. Interestingly enough, both Sartre and Camus wrote plays shortly after the war on the topic of political violence and whether it was justified: *Dirty Hands* (1948) and *The Just Assassins* (1949), respectively."[151]

"Oh, yeah, you mentioned these," Peter said.

"Right. This is what you need to know: during the war, Sartre had sat on the sidelines, writing 'polyvalent' plays in cafés (like *Les Flies*) while German officers drank downstairs. But after the war, Sartre's *Dirty Hands* seemed to justify violence in the name of political goals.[152] Conversely,

150. Aronson, *Camus and Sartre*, 145.

151. See Aronson, *Camus and Sartre*, 133.

152. Aronson, *Camus and Sartre*, 134.

Camus's convictions were moving in the other direction. Having got his hands dirty, Camus was now more concerned with restraint. While Camus was never strictly a pacifist—and it was not a linear path—the scholar, Ronald Aronson, makes a powerful case for Camus's growing preoccupation with 'keeping his hands clean,' brought to a head with *The Just Assassins*, and later, *The Rebel*."[153]

Etienne concluded for Peter that, "after their very public break hit the Parisian and international headlines, they never spoke again. When Camus claimed his Nobel Prize for Literature, he broke his silence on the topic. He quipped that he and Sartre had an 'outstanding' relationship because the best relationships are the ones where you never see each other. However, not long before his own passing, Sartre admitted that Camus was probably his last good friend."[154]

"That's quite the unraveling," Peter said.

"True. Sartre said of Camus: 'How we loved you then.'[155] That still breaks my heart." He paused for a second, holding space.

"In the show," Peter chipped in, "I liked how you shared Camus's conviction that 'it is better to be wrong by killing no one rather than be right with mass graves,' but that it would later be said that many in the early '50s would 'rather have been wrong with Sartre than right with Camus.'[156] It makes you wonder what ideas you just go along with," Peter concluded, not fully realizing the importance of what he was saying before it left his mouth.

Over a brief, ambiguous silence, Peter tried to find the words he was after. "It's not like that at all, but, er, I hate to bring this up, but you and Jean-Paul don't exactly seem to be seeing things eye-to-eye."

Etienne tried to diffuse this immediately. "We agree on what matters," he said, more kindly than honesty demanded. People saw both of them like parents of the community and Etienne wanted to make this work. He explained further because Peter didn't seem entirely satisfied: "It's about the method. We agree on the problem, for the most part. But

---

153. Aronson, *Camus and Sartre*, 136. Aronson also explains that Camus often demonstrated a paradoxical position regarding political violence by seeing it as "at the same time unavoidable and unjustifiable." Note: Camus felt that the occupation of France had forced the situation (or imperative) of resistance. He saw this as a different situation than choosing violence, meaning that, perhaps (controversially) one's hands might remain clean. Aronson, *Camus and Sartre*, 136.

154. Aronson, *Camus and Sartre*, 4. Comment from a late interview.

155. Aronson, *Camus and Sartre*, 38.

156. Levy, *Sartre*, 313.

Jean-Paul is a little more radical than I am. I am inclined to think that force can backfire."

"Force?" That scared Peter.

Etienne sidestepped the question, instead sharing his perspective: "Just as Camus pointed out . . . we need a kinder, more humane way to change the world, or you undermine the objective."

"Which is? In a word or two?"

"I'd have to say, 'human flourishing.'"

That was interesting to Peter. "And Jean-Paul?"

"He'd probably say the same, but he'd take a different road to get there. He's worried about us making these wrong turns, especially into any sort of spiritualism. I think that comes with the territory of humans. That sense of the transcendent, of something more? I'm not sure we can really rip that out of them."

"Oh, yeah, I've seen that," Peter said, referring to Jean-Paul's pacing and gruff remarks.

"He just doesn't want us to lose any ground we gain," Etienne said generously. Peter could see Etienne was holding back. He wanted to share more. The tension was palpable; it would only grow in the months to come.

§

Bernard knocked but didn't wait for an answer. "I heard you were looking for a job, Peter?"

Despite being eager to keep talking, Peter dutifully accepted. He and Etienne would talk again. But for now, hive boxes were waiting for him to lift from the back of Bernard's car. Etienne hastily looked around for something he could write on. Peter told him the back of his Bible would do, for—despite being the least read—in that instant, it happened to be on top of the books in his bag. Etienne listed the names of some of Camus's works, putting a star by *The Plague* and *The Rebel*, saying that these, while very different from each other, were his favorites.

At the last minute, Etienne made a snap decision: "Here, you can tick one off already," he said, placing his personal copy of *The Rebel* in Peter's hands.

Peter was thankful for the gift. He could see how much Etienne valued it, and while Etienne had many books on hand, his collection was still dwarfed by Bernard's voluminous collection. Peter had become quite familiar with that when he'd helped transition to its new home. *Mercifully*, he thought, *the beekeeping supplies shouldn't take as long.*

It was endearing how excited this old man was. "They create little Edens of fruitfulness," Bernard shared eagerly with Peter, referring to how they couldn't help but pollinate the world and make it flourish. He was clearly excited to introduce Peter to his several thousand "girls," his magic ingredient for life. The colony transfer would surely make his next load an extra-exciting one!

However, before they had finished this load, the ominous clouds revealed once again the already-too-familiar capricious nature of weather in the Vosges. The sky darkened and dulled, having mastery over the colors in a way that he hadn't fully appreciated when teaching mathematics indoors or sitting in a hospital waiting room. As if it had been waiting for the cover of a darkened sky, Peter was taken aback by something altogether unexpected. Scales?! But not a snake or reptile. Or were they? Tentatively, Peter pulled back some white canvas beekeeping gear to jump back, revealing a small, stuffed mammal. Intrigued but not wishing to ostracize his eccentric friend with too many probing questions, he tried to normalize the situation. "Armadillo?" Peter said as if he saw them every day.

Bernard enjoyed Peter's playful company: "Horrice," he concluded with a nod.

"Sorry?" Peter replied.

"His name is Horrice."

"Horrice it is then!" said Peter carrying him onto the front porch of Bernard's cabin looking at the stuffed creature's mouse-like features. Placing him down, Peter checked to see Bernard wasn't watching, giving into his need to wipe his hand, in this case all over his trousers. *Could a stuffed armadillo harbor any latent bacteria?* He knew he was overcautious, but it is hard to forget after walking alongside someone—a someone whom he loved very deeply—through chemotherapy.

22

WW2

Infernal Music

LES VOSGES I

Sunday, October 3rd, 1943.

Weary from a restless night of unsettling dreams, Violet rose at the break of dawn to refill her water bottle. The others were still sound asleep. Then, she heard it: the music. At first, she dismissed it as her imagination playing tricks. But, no, it was unmistakable. It wasn't the lone melody of a wistful soul but a symphony of instruments. What could it mean? Troubled and curious, she woke them.

They agreed the music was eerie: close enough to make out the generalities but hard to decipher where it was coming from, the melody bouncing off the hills. Natzweiller was still a good fifteen kilometers or so away. However, there had been talk of satellite camps. Was this why there had been so much commotion in the area? But why would they be playing music?

Henry knew his task: to get to Paris. He knew it was of the utmost importance, but he couldn't bear to see Violet tortured like this. After a strained back and forth, he convinced Violet and Matthias that keeping their focus was important to his mission—what they had been entrusted to do. And so, if they just needed to check it out to put their minds at rest, then that is what they needed to do. The deal was—only if Henry stayed in the hay loft. He felt ever-so-foolish and extraneous but agreed.

Matthias was candid with Violet. He owed her that. He knew it wasn't a good idea, but good ideas came second to the state of her soul. The chances of her brother-in-law still being here, indeed still being alive, was almost zero. And what would they do if they found him?

The same question circled Violet's mind. If they could, no doubt about it, she would try to free him. But then, what if she failed? What about Henry? The bigger picture? What could she possibly say or do?

The music got louder, taunting. So did the noise of hammers and equipment. In recent months, the camp commander Egon Hill had transferred over from Dachau. He couldn't bear to leave his camp orchestra, so they transferred it with him. The musicians could be heard playing, melodies seized by the wind as if the breeze held its breath upon the shock of absorbing the memories of the men and women. The air gained a supernatural chill as if it had been grabbed by the collar and submersed in freezing water. To the music, the "healthy" inmates were expected to march. But what did they march to? Little is recorded regarding what was played at Natzweiler-Struthof; however, there is evidence of Wagner's music being played in Dachau in 1943 and 1944 to "re-educate political prisoners by means of exposure to 'national music.'" Given the Dachau band transferred, it would have been possible to hear Wagner in the Vosges[157] amongst a concoction of other "infernal" tunes, to borrow Primo Levi's first-hand description from Auschwitz:

> As the bread is distributed, one can hear, far from the windows, in the dark air, the band beginning to play; the healthy comrades are leaving in squads for work…The beating of the big drums and the cymbals reach us continuously and monotonously, but on this weft the musical phrases weave a pattern only intermittently, according to the caprices of the wind. We all look at each other from our [infirmary] beds, because we all feel that this music is infernal.[158]

Those working in and around the gypsum quarries were forced to march to the rhythm with their left legs. The Reich was still building some of the over fifty satellite camps to Natzweiler-Struthof, and they had stumbled across one. While not big enough to have its own band, the music from the main camp was clear enough to demand obedience.

---

157. Fackler, "Music in Concentration Camps 1933–1945." Also see: Music and the Holocaust, "Natzweiler."

158. Levi, *If This Is a Man*, 70.

Violet and Matthias stayed low, more and more accustomed to how to survive. This camp was all men. Most of them looked to be in their twenties or thirties, but it was hard to tell with them being so thin. Violet scanned the men. There was no chance, she realized now. She felt for them and the ones they had left behind. Would they ever taste freedom again? Everything in her wanted to spend her life freeing them. But even a suicide mission wouldn't change anything: they were surrounded by guards and watch towers with machine guns. Sure, there was some tree cover, but far away from where the men were.

And then she saw him. Did fate just want to spite her? Just as she had made peace with him not being there—a needle in a haystack—there he was. A bow in his back, rake-like, but it was him. No doubt.

But what could she do now? Matthias saw her, almost blue, unable to breathe. Stunned.

"Violet!" he spoke into her ear. "Violet!" He held her forearms in his hand, forcing her body to turn to his; to look him in the eyes. "What is it?"

"It's him! It's really him."

"You know you can't go out there. There's nothing we can do!" Matthias cursed the situation. He shouldn't have agreed to let them come.

It took a while before she could speak, as if her mouth couldn't keep up with her mind, filtering through different permutations. What could she do?

Finally, she realized she had something. A small thing, but he may not even want it. She fought with herself over it, as Matthias was still trying to get through to her. She was immune. She put her hand in her pocket. She felt the armadillo scute and next to it the cyanide that the Oberführer had given her. What would she want? He'd survived this long. Would he even want this way out? Or was this now patronizing? Perhaps, even if she could get it to him, this would break him. But if he were still his compassionate self, then surely he would understand . . . and if he didn't need it, maybe there was someone that did? If he were no longer that compassionate self, then perhaps he did need it after all . . .

"We have to try," Violet said, finally. "We can't shoot our way in or get them out—there's simply not enough of us. I know it's the long game . . . but I can get this to him." Matthias knew in an instant what she was talking about—the cyanide tablet. She further reasoned that the option of death might help him choose to stay alive—the gift of the dignity of free will when all else was stripped away.

Matthias didn't try to convince her otherwise. He knew how stubborn she was. He kept watch as she crept to the lonely side of the compound as the music kept going, over and over. From a distance she could see that there was only one small person over there.

> The tunes are few, a dozen, the same ones every day, morning and evening…They lie engraven on our minds and will be the last thing in Lager [the labor camp] that we shall forget; they are the voice of the Lager [the prisoners], the perceptible expression of its geometrical madness, of the resolution of others to annihilate us first as men in order to kill us more slowly afterwards.[159]

The music in the Auschwitz camp complex was varied, with prisoner bands arranging and playing for various events. This included being forced to play for the guards' dances, upbeat tunes like "Die schönste Zeit das Lebens," literally, "the most beautiful time of life."[160]

The scene Violet found was anything but beautiful. The only one somewhat close by was a boy, perhaps no older than twelve. He was skin and bones, looking, falling into the empty heart of nothingness. He sat on bare dirt without even a weed to speak of. His eyes seemed to roll back into his skull. Lice crawled upon his shaved head. He didn't even notice her approach. Neither did he startle when she made contact. What had they done to him? He must have been the youngest here, but, at one time, was considered strong enough to do the work.

Violet spoke, soothing him. Calling him back to the present. Slowly, he responded. The small arrows of his cheekbones raised to draw an unexpected smile. They hadn't killed the human in him yet. Every minute there was precious, but she talked to his heart, speaking life over him. The irony wasn't lost on her. She was going to ask this boy to deliver cyanide while she called him back to life?

All too soon, someone became suspicious. The boy was closer to the fence than normal. Ordinarily, he barely moved from his spot, tormented by a guard, scarcely eighteen, reciting Nietzsche's pity aphorisms to pass the time. This curiosity was enough for the guard to start marching towards them. This, in turn, sent the hackles up on others: the guards had been triggered.

159. Levi, *If This Is a Man*, 70.

160. To listen to a reproduction of this, visit the University of Michigan, "Die schönste Zeit des Lebens."

"I have to go," she whispered. But before she sprung away and melted back into the forest, she closed his hand upon a gift. Little did she know she also left part of her heart there, vowing to come back as soon as she could.

23

Alexi

Analogique

LES VOSGES II

Saturday, October 10th, 2015. Paris, France.

With so much information in the world how could there be so little about Peter or this community? If only he had written a return address on the second postcard. A watercolor fox, some symbols and the words "*Le Rubicon*?" How was that meant to help? What did Caesar crossing the Rubicon—an Italian river—have anything to do with the French Vosges? She could scream! She'd driven herself crazy visiting all the neighbors. The only neighbor who was around in the early '90s when Tristan had the apartment had no idea and really didn't care, eager to return to the trench he'd made in his couch.

She tried to have fun exploring Paris, hanging out mainly with Marc, sometimes Sam and Tim. But it all felt meaningless when faced with this dead end. Doubling down was wearing her out. Given that the internet seemed so incapable of helping her pull back the edge of the carpet of time to peer into the early nineties, she had started going to libraries. The silver lining was that some were utterly beautiful: encrusted in golden filigree or with a rapturous blue that drew one to look up and partake in the grand design of the constellations painted on the ceiling.

A man with short white receding hair stopped her one day. "I've seen you often," the man said. His attire screamed of an academic, undoubtedly a professor: his bowtie a rich red, and an oft-buffed pocket watch just so. "You must be working on a big project."

"You could say that," Alexi replied.

"Where do you study?" the professor asked.

Alexi tried to backpedal a little.

"Sorry, I just assumed. So, you're here by choice!" he said kindly. "Even better."

Alexi smiled, feeling a little more at ease. Before she knew it, she was explaining everything she was ready to share—which certainly wasn't it all—about her quest to find information about Peter, whom she pretended was her uncle.

"Well, if I were you," he said, "I'd check the microfiche." Alexi looked quizzically at him. "Before much of this digital stuff, we stored a lot of print information on small transparent film. If the community was notable, then perhaps there's some mention of it in the newspapers. Check the regional papers. They're sure to have some here, though not everything. If you can't find what you're looking for, then it's worth checking those small newspapers at the local libraries."

Alexi had no idea about this stuff. The librarian waved them on, assuming that Alexi was one of his students. He took her to the basement where, lo and behold, beneath a white throw cloth was a clunky greige machine. "They're basically miniatures," he explained kindly, like a grandfather. He generously orientated her, singing its praises. While admitting that it was noisy, he claimed that it was still the gold standard in analog data storage.

Perhaps this was what it was like to have grandparents? For the first time, she wondered whether—if she ever found Peter—he would introduce her to them.

24

Peter

Dancing Like Dionysus

LES VOSGES II

Wednesday, September 15th, 1993.

The Ascona community, *Monte Verità*, that had first inspired Etienne when he was still a teen, hosted famous names like the psychoanalyst Carl Jung and the Swiss-German novelist Hermann Hesse. At the dawn of the twentieth century, from above Lake Maggiore in southern Switzerland, the community welcomed visitors who were interested in a third way beyond the double bind of capitalism and communism.

This sanctuary attracted philosophers and anarchists, artists and dreamers. This included modern dance pioneer Mary Wingman. She was revolutionary, dismantling ballet's restrictive demands, including the use of pointe shoes.[161] Closer to Milan than Bern, the *Monte Verità* dancers embodied an energetic return to nature. Unfortunately, the weather in northern France, just a few hundred kilometers away, was not as conducive to open-air dancing. As autumn teased at the hems of summer and threatened cooler evenings, the community's dancers, like Lavinia and Hélène, found themselves dancing more and more in a converted barn. It wasn't the best, but they had high hopes for it.

---

161. Watson, *Age of Atheists*, 44–45.

164

Once again, the alpha males had gone hunting or doing whatever they did, and Peter found himself walking around, looking to make himself helpful. On this particular evening, Lavinia found it especially hilarious to run out to him and pull him into the barn with promises of it "not being so bad!" He found himself in the middle of a group of ladies. He had talked to them here and there, but this was . . . new.

He usually kept at a distance when he saw them going about their day. Indeed, when they had first arrived, he noticed how Hélène, Lavinia and their group of friends had quickly exchanged high heels and boots for the "liberation" of walking around the camp barefoot. He had stifled a laugh when he saw them wincing over gravel paths but was too gentlemanly to be seen to notice. Truthfully, they scared him a little.

The barn still had a dirt floor. When they danced, the powder convulsed, pulsating; it trembled in anticipation of the next movement, settling if only for a moment. The walls were covered in motivational quotes as well as organic murals to which the artistic members of the community had contributed—a work in progress.

The largest quote, written in an elaborate cursive script, said, "Le Rubicon: Being begins at every moment; the center is everywhere." It was about self-creation and drew from Nietzsche, as had the dancers in Ascona. Nietzsche had, after all been that iconic philosopher who prophesied of the utter magnitude of the devastation caused by a sterile, reason-*only* existence. This comes through vibrantly in his book *The Birth of Tragedy*, conceived at a time when he was still enamored by Wagner, temporarily a father-figure for him.

Nietzsche had been excited for the Ring Cycle and Wagner's vision of changing the world through an encounter with this fully immersive operatic experience. However, what did he see at its opening? The same static, pompous, and self-congratulatory strata of society. Nietzsche was after something deeper, richer.

Bare, brittle reason, Nietzsche thought, was exemplified by the Greek god Apollo. But why suppress the rest of life? For Nietzsche, the Dionysian needed freeing—the dark, immoral, illusive, but very honest currents of life.[162] While Wagner understood this, Nietzsche thought that his method didn't deliver. Condemned to carve an independent path, Nietzsche's thought continued to argue for a radical self-creation that embraced this Dionysian current of life. Likewise, at Ascona, "The ambition

162. Nietzsche, *Birth of Tragedy*.

. . . to replace religion was insistent," and expressive Dionysian festivals and dance were core to this.[163]

However, Nietzsche's goal was not smooth sailing. He knew that without God or a specific *telos* (meaning and purpose)—an end goal for humanity to move towards—even this initial dynamism of self-creation was threatened by the pit of nihilism, an utter purposelessness. Finally, walking around Lake Silvaplana in Switzerland, he came to a revelation: the vital importance of embracing every moment as part of a whole—the creative moment raised to the pitch of eternity. But how? Eternal return: one should live as if one might have to relive this choice eternally. Only then could it be said that "being begins at every moment; the center is everywhere."[164] This magnifies the importance of self-assertion as if walking into a cavernous cave invites us to shout and make an echo: but not just any echo—one that echoes into eternity.

For Nietzsche, receiving any meaning or identity was not an option, since for him, the concept of God had been long dead, given the growing atheistic thrust in the cultural and academic *milieu*. Indeed, he argued that it was time for humanity to grow up and do the dirty work required to clear the decks of all entanglements. This included erasing objective, normative morality. Just as the Buddha was said to leave his shadow on the wall after his death,[165] Nietzsche thought the shadow of Christian morality had overstayed its welcome in the history of humankind.

The diagnosis of the anemic enlightenment life? That was easy for anyone to see. Nietzsche's crusade against any objective sense of morality, stubbornly left over from (an ostensibly) dead God? Brave and dangerous. The solution? Much more unwieldy and polyvalent—it could and would be read in different ways. Possibly intentionally so. Indeed, Nietzsche knew that his radical thought would cause evil to be done in his name. In his preface to *The Gay Science*, he warned the reader gleefully, "'*Incipit tragoedia*,' [tragedy begins] . . . Beware! Something utterly wicked and mischievous is being announced here."[166]

---

163. Watson, *Age of Atheists*, 44–45.

164. Paraphrase of "In every Now, being begins; round every Here rolls the sphere There. The center is everywhere. Bent is the path of eternity." Nietzsche, *Thus Spoke Zarathustra*, 264.

165. Nietzsche, *Gay Science*, §108, 167.

166. Nietzsche, *Gay Science*, 51. This phrase, "*Incipit tragoedia*," also concludes *The Gay Science* and is echoed at the start of *Thus Spoke Zarathustra*.

He wasn't wrong. Indeed, the assassination of Archduke Franz Ferdinand, sparking the First World War, was committed by Gavrilo Princip, trained in his thought and known to fondly recite from Nietzsche's poem "Ecce Homo": "Insatiable as flame, I burn and consume myself."[167] While this poem is radically individualist, the fire didn't stop after consuming these one or two lives—moving far beyond even the regional goals of the Young Bosnia Movement, to engulf the world.

There was also Hitler's well-known appropriation of—and obsession with—Nietzsche, encouraged by Nietzsche's sister, Elisabeth. Indeed, Hitler used images related to Zarathustra at his Nuremberg rally as he called forth individual hearts to grasp onto creating this new world, albeit together. Dionysian passion—stripped from the anchoring restraints of Judeo-Christian morality where all are made in the *Imago Dei*—proved to be potent gunpowder.

If the passion was the gunpowder, then the fuse was the aforementioned doctrine of "eternal return" (*Ewige Wiederkunft*). He first proposed it as a thought experiment in *The Gay Science*, asking what if:

> "a demon were to steal after you into your loneliest loneliness, and say to you, 'This life as you now live it and have lived it, you will have to live once more and innumerable times more; and there will be nothing new in it, but every pain and every joy' . . . Would you . . . gnash your teeth and curse the demon . . . [or say] 'You are a god and never have I heard anything more divine.'"[168]

It was upon eternal return that Nietzsche conferred the honor of being the "fundamental idea" driving his anti-Bible *Thus Spoke Zarathustra*.[169] The protagonist, Zarathustra, moves from strongly resisting the idea to embracing it. An embrace of the full experience of it all: pain, suffering, boredom, joy. This makes sense, given that Nietzsche knew the pain of life well: internal pain (rejection in relationships) and physical pain through persistent illness. Nietzsche also connected eternal return to another concept: *amor fati*, a "love of fate." While suffering isn't directly justified, its horror is embraced and, in doing so, it is received and loved. For this reason, hundreds of thousands of copies of *Thus Spoke*

---

167. "Ecce Homo," poem 62, in Nietzsche, *Gay Science*, 85. Not to be confused with the book of the same name.

168. Nietzsche, *Gay Science*, 290. Section 341.

169. Nietzsche, *Ecce Homo*, 96.

Zarathustra were sent to the German frontlines: a call to embrace their suffering and sacrifice.

Given this embrace, perhaps talk of demigods is again appropriate: a call to make oneself great, regardless of the cost. "In man," Nietzsche wrote, "creature and creator are united; in man there is material, fragment, excess, clay, dirt, nonsense, chaos; but in man there is also creator, form-giver, hammer hardness, spectator divinity."[170]

Significantly, in his later work, Nietzsche's focus on the *Übermensch* expanded the focus of self-creation to rethinking humanity en masse. Who has a right to belong to a certain society, to dream and determine its future? Hitler found this aspect of Nietzsche's thought particularly amenable to his diagnoses of the problems in Germany after the devastation of the First World War. Certain people *were* holding the Aryan race back, Hitler thought. If only they weren't.

The community in the Vosges, of course, was more interested in seeing the fun, self-creative interpretation of Nietzsche—grabbing fate by the horns. But can one tame fate? Fate, it seems, does not love humanity back, either trampling or running away with humanity, just like Zeus in the legend where, disguised as a bull, he abducts and abuses Europa.

In those early days of the community, there was so much hope, though their reading of Nietzsche was eclectic and partial. In addition to Nietzsche, the group drew on a smorgasbord of other influences as they sought to unite their "whole self" using dance as both expression and modality. They explained that they were also breaking down barriers, helping them break out of what they had been conditioned to before being "drilled to become economically productive robots." Dancing, they explained, helped them tap into their radical freedom, creativity, and embodied nature. Peter could get on board with a lot of it, but while the problem seemed very real, the dance form or manifestation of the supposed solution seemed like it would bring him maximum humiliation. That fear was immanent: they seemed to want him to join them. No, in fact, they demanded it.

When the girls realized that Peter was inching closer and closer to the walls, Lavinia and another jumped over, playfully grabbing Peter's hand and pulling him into the center of the room to dance. "Just let your unconscious be released!" Lavinia said, enthusiastically.

---

170. Nietzsche, *Beyond Good and Evil*, 154 (aphorism 225).

Apparently too self-conscious to let his unconscious lead, Peter danced for a couple of minutes, painfully pulling out moves he hadn't used since those awful university discos. His body could never quite connect with what his mind thought would look cool or appropriate.

Just as Peter was letting his internal walls down and loosening up, Etienne and some others walked in. Great timing. To be fair, the community had been quite embracing of both men and women in the arts. A couple of guys (who certainly looked more the part) really went for it, Lavinia's Ritesh among them. Etienne did smirk a little, though kindly, upon seeing Peter's attempt.

As soon as the other men walked in, the whole dynamic changed. The girls seemed to jump higher and faster. The dirt trailed their movements to trace the very edges of mystical arcs. Etienne was swarmed, as normal, by both questions and people—or rather people with many questions. So much so, Etienne didn't notice when his girlfriend, Hélène, landed badly on her ankle. She held in her curse, her eyes immediately dashing towards Etienne. He did glance briefly when someone pointed it out, but he brushed it off as something small and planned to touch base later. "Are you okay?" he finally asked from a distance "Yes . . ." she said briskly, tears fluttering upon her lashes in embarrassment.

Immediately after, she fled the barn. Peter knew he had much to learn about women, but this he understood. He excused himself, following after—for Etienne wasn't going to. He had resumed talking about something "more important."

"I know he's busy," she said, as Peter caught up to her in a dimly lit trail.

"Can I help?" he asked.

She found him refreshingly genuine but simply replied, "It's an old injury. I'm good."

"That doesn't mean you have to be alone," Peter said, returning a tangible kindness along with the moonlight that reflected from his eyes.

By this hour, the full moon had taken center stage in the night sky. "Okay," she finally replied, wincing through the sharp stabs of pain as she walked.

"Here," Peter said, putting her arm over his back. "Where do you want to go? I can check if Marje has some ice?"

"No," she said, not wanting him to leave her side.

"Well, you don't want it to swell. The stream is cold," Peter said, since it was nearby. Hélène agreed, and they made their way to its bank.

"Are you doing okay?" Peter asked when they got there. She didn't reply. She didn't want to answer questions about the heart. He put his gray jacket around her to keep the rest of her body warm.

Silently, her pointed toe broke the water tension before she slid the rest of her foot in, bracing for the soft and slimy things that she imagined there. After a few minutes she agreed to Peter looking at it. The cold had made it almost numb. He hadn't fully appreciated how thin her wrists and ankles were before, though it was clear to everyone that she was thin, perhaps too thin. "I think it will be okay," Peter said after quickly feeling the ankle with his hands, briefly warming her chilled flesh. She then placed it back in the water.

The two sat side by side, more acutely aware by the second of the life teeming around the water as if invited into a secret. Water folded with an effortless curvature repeating against the intrusion of Hélène's apricot flesh. Life in abundance welcomed them, shy at first, flattered to hold an audience in its palm. Spindly "pond skaters" began to emerge, waltzing upon the glistening water, masterfully striding wherever the water pooled and slowed enough behind sticks and rocks. Small midges and gnats joined the symphony as they hovered right above the water, causing hundreds of micro-ripples—a ghost rain.

Spiders had been incredibly industrious with their webs between bulrushes. A small shift in Hélène's weight was enough to send frogs, recoiling their muscular legs, to torpedo into the pondweed on the other side of the bank. She jumped. "They won't hurt you," Peter consoled her. "They'll leave us well alone." He awkwardly added, "And even if they didn't, they only eat insects!" Hélène didn't mind his awkwardness, feeling a smile break through, the first genuine smile for a long time. Not giddy or silly but satisfied and deep. She liked it—she liked smiling—her face felt like it was breathing.

The safer she felt, the more Hélène melted into Peter. However, he held himself to a code of personal honor, subtly rejecting any extra closeness. She was Etienne's girlfriend, even if he was acting like a jerk. Besides, they hardly knew each other.

The silence needed breaking. "The moon seems extra big," he said, clutching at straws.

"Beautiful, isn't she?" Hélène announced.

He kicked himself. He fell into that one. He looked around. Were they being watched? He hadn't meant to make it feel romantic. He couldn't see anyone. But the nocturnal animals were out in force, an owl perched not far away.

"Is it true that we only see one face of it?" Hélène asked.

"It is," Peter said. Realizing that a couple of his trademark nerd comments might kill the mood, he continued, "It's all to do with gravity over time. Tidal locking essentially locks the moon in place so that as it orbits, we only see the one side."

That was the first time that Peter saw them: the bruises. She had been carefully hiding them under loose clothing, but as she relaxed Hélène let her guard down. He didn't think much of them then. Perhaps he should have.

The longer they sat, the more uncomfortable Peter felt. He wanted to ask. Instead, they talked about trivial things, and he encouraged Hélène about her dancing when she revealed that she thought it was pointless. Peter became more and more aware of the owl's intensely orange eyes illuminating the dark. This wasn't one of those small Tengmalm's owls—barely 120 grams of feathery mass, perfectly camouflaged against the trees—but a Eurasian eagle-owl with long ear tufts and a piercing beak that looked like a Norman helmet's noseguard. It tracked Peter, eerily, silently. No wonder that, while the Greeks thought they carried the wisdom of Athena, the Romans thought owls were an omen of death.

As if prophetically announced, the dulcet sounds of dancing bugs and frogs croaking gave way to a sharp-edged avalanche of teeth and claw, squeals and whimpers. Hélène jerked out of the water. She immediately contracted, tucking her legs up. By instinct, Peter held her, trying to discern what was going on a stone's throw away in the same field.

He jumped up. "Hey, hey, hey!" Peter screamed, bursting into a run over the uneven fallow field. He bent down under perpetual motion to pick up a large, gnarled branch.

"Get away! Away!" Peter yelled as loudly as he could, holding the branch up against the dog's perfectly white teeth.

Jean-Paul's dogs were smothered in a certain crimson vibrancy that moments before, transmitted life and were now ubiquitous with death. They were unfazed, amused perhaps, at the human's sentimental tenderness.

Hélène let out an unfettered, ugly scream upon hearing the sort of squeal where the pain itself had found its voice.

"Get off!" Peter yelled again and again, this time cracking the branch right between the eyes of one of the hunting dogs. The skull was thick. It finally granted Peter the dignity of taking its eyes off a limp fox kit in its mouth and looked at Peter, defiant. Red-tinged saliva dripped gratuitously over blades of grass that clung to the dog's dark, sticky gums.

Another dog nipped at Peter's left hand, a warning for daring to interfere. He then hit that one, but they both went back to the kit, especially that stocky brute. The dog played with the ragged body; gleeful.

Again, Peter yelled. How many had they killed? People were starting to take note of what was happening from inside the camp. As if bored of the now lifeless carcass, the dog turned its attention back to the assailant, this time clamping vice-like upon his hand. Peter let out a sharp shout, but shock held back the blood for the first few seconds.

Watching it unfold, Hélène had risen, afraid. Ignoring her throbbing ankle and using her blanket to make herself look as big as possible, she shouted, "*Fu!*"

At that, Jean-Paul broke into a run. He barked, "*Ostav eto!*" commanding them to leave it.

His presence alone pierced the dogs' instinctive hold. They ran to him, wagging their tails as blood hit the dust in glimmering droplets. They panted, looking at him for praise. Within just a couple of minutes, the dogs had decimated an entire den.

Hélène felt superfluous despite her brief but bold stand. She hobbled back to the riverbank as the wreckage was surveyed.

"I'm okay," Peter mouthed to Hélène, putting pressure on his hand, embarrassed, though he had never once suggested he was impregnable. Peter couldn't get it in his head how the mother and cubs were here one minute and now just gone, forever.

'What are you doing here?' said Jean-Paul to Hélène, looking at her with distinct detestation, now flanked by his pack.

"My ankle," Hélène said, protesting her innocence. She looked away to loosen his interrogation.

"Errr . . ." Jean-Paul grunted with zero compassion, curling his lip and moving on before compassion hit. "If I ever see you hurt my dogs again . . ." he started to intimidate Peter. But Peter wasn't really paying attention, chilled by the lack of feeling in the dog's eyes. The canine had planned what to do. Now, the perfect little creatures torn apart lay before him. *What a waste.*

Eventually, Jean-Paul left. Peter felt burdened by virtue of his witness to do something—perhaps giving them the dignity of burial. He didn't know what to do, never having buried anything before. Perhaps he was overly sentimental. Yet he felt he had to be true to his instinct, lest he feel the guilt of his conscience. A minute or two after sitting on the ground in thought, Peter heard a snuffling. Then a small shuffle. Then another. Peter held his breath, twisting his torso slowly. One small fox kit, the runt, emerged. A welcome surprise. The kit approached him. Closer. Closer still. It searched for understanding in Peter's eyes. Then, it moved towards the warmth of Peter's humanity, bowing his head as if with the weight of grief at the bloodshed. They shared the sorrow for a distinct slice of eternity.

Peter offered his hand for the creature to smell. The little fox didn't flee. Gradually, it dipped its silky soft head underneath Peter's punctured hand, dipping its small shoulder blade by bowing a paw. Peter didn't mind, careful to avoid the kit's tender ear—it seemed that, like him, the kit was not entirely unscathed. As if a covenantal vow, the kit then orbited its soft head in around Peter's injured hand. They were now bound with mutual respect and honor. It looked up at Peter: the cat-like slits of its pupils had swollen to an almost rounded shape given the poverty of light.

"Don't worry, little guy, we'll take care of you," said Peter, now joined by Hélène. She opened Peter's coat, which she was wearing. She drew the kit into an embrace, warming him against her chest.

25

WW2

Mosaics & Michelangelo

LES VOSGES II

Tuesday, October 5th, 1943. Grand, Ancient Andesina.

The three *Résistants* had traveled from Natzweiller for the best part of three interrupted days and nights, often staying in abandoned buildings—even medieval ruins. The land was littered with small towers overlooking valleys, but not many of them were unoccupied. Violet wasn't ready to talk about what happened at the camp. Mercifully, the guards had stopped the pursuit. Only God knew why. They were now on the outskirts of Grand, just half a day's walk from the birthplace of Joan of Arc. Violet's family had come to this small village every summer during her childhood. The relief of entering into the footsteps of these golden memories was palpable.

She led them to the subterranean entrance of something old, very old. This way of life, hiding wherever they could, was now curiously familiar, so it had cultivated within them the faintest hope of safety. However, this place felt unusual and different—their spirits both awakened and on edge. It was like no place they had yet visited. They squeezed down through an occluded hole surrounded by bushes. Violet had done this as a kid many times, not knowing what she was rehearsing for. They dropped down into something.

From the way the sounds were held, Henry could already tell the place was big, though the ceiling was not too high. They had entered into the bowels of a 17,000 seat Gallo-Roman amphitheater, for Grand was ancient Andesina—that is, what was left of it. It was now insulated by thousands of tons of dirt, leaving just an impression on the surface.

They had been preserving their flashlights for this. They finally turned them on as Violet squatted down, her mushroom-colored pants dutifully folding on command. It took a good few seconds for their eyes to adjust. "Over there, they kept the prisoners. And there? The wild beasts. But look right here," she added, as she cleared dirt from the floor.

"A mosaic?" Henry said.

"Not just any mosaic," Violet said.

"Oh wow," Matthias said, joining his light to the other two, further illuminating the space. They helped to uncover more using their feet. An almost unbroken image regained its force, proud.

"One treasure the Nazis know nothing about," Violet said, smiling.

"Just like that. *Spectaculaire!*" Matthias offered.

"There's a bigger one in the basilica in the village. But there's no doubt they know about that one."

"What is it like?" Henry asked.

"I'd show you if I could. It depicts a Greek comedy, most likely *Phasma* by Menander. It's been a while, but I still remember all the details, especially the animals on the four corners. One of them is a panther."

"A panther?" Matthias recognized the symbol with excitement.

"The cult of Dionysus," said Henry, happy to win that one before Matthias had a chance. "The Romans loved to appropriate Greek culture."

"Right," Violet said, impressed.

They spent the next little while settling in, including getting a little airflow so they could start a small fire. It was going to be another interesting place to sleep. As they ate their last supplies, Violet felt confident that she could slip into the town early in the morning. She knew many of the shop owners.

"You know," Henry said around the fire as they finished their meager meal. "It's said that over Apollo's temple in Delphi, was written, 'Know thyself.' But do you think that's fixed? Who you are, I mean? And our fate written in the stars?"

"Fate? Put it this way, the Nazis won't win as long as I can help it!" Matthias replied.

"I hope not!" said Violet.

"But do you think there is an essential part of who you are?" Henry asked.

"I'm no expert," Violet said, "but my father found joy in finding underappreciated art and filling the farmhouse with it—he joked that he'd be a penniless artist in Montmartre if it wasn't for his love for my mother and the Vosges. When I was young, he told me something about Michelangelo that's always stuck with me. When asked about how he went about carving such spectacular sculptures, he said: 'I saw the angel in the marble and carved until I set him free.'"

"I like that," Henry replied. "Like, who we are just needs to be set free?"

"Right. Like there's some sort of essence already there that can be revealed and encouraged or suppressed. You know," Violet added, "I grew up with one older sister and four younger siblings. It never failed to astound me how each of the little-ones seemed to come into the world with who they were packed into a tiny bud-like body. They already had certain ways about them, even habits."

Matthias agreed. "Michelangelo's angel comment says something profound about how he saw the world."

"Which was?" Henry asked.

"Early on, he was pulled into the humanistic orbit of Renaissance Florence and Lorenzo the Magnificent, but he later saw the depth beneath what he was painting, to venerate a designer—a loving one. I memorized one of his late poems once," Matthias offered, "'Neither painting nor sculpture will be able. . . to,'" Matthias tried to remember, "'—calm my soul, now turned toward that divine love that opened his arms on the cross to take us in.'"[171]

"So, he was a Christian?" Henry asked.

"It seems so," Matthias teased, happy to flex his knowledge.

"Are you?" Henry asked them both boldly, before tempering it: "I mean, I grew up with it . . . but I thought we just grow out of it." He caught himself again, "I don't mean . . ."

"No, it's a good question," Violet said. "If we can face the Nazis, I'm pretty sure we can handle a question or two about faith!"

"It's the only thing that's got me this far," Matthias said vaguely, not having told Henry anything about his wife and not intending to.

---

171. Michelangelo, *Complete Poems*, 141. (Poem 285, written in 1554).

"But how, when some of the Nazis wear crosses around their necks?" Henry said, meaning the Iron Cross he'd seen.

"Half of the churches in Germany supported the rise of Hitler. But half of them didn't," Violet calmly explained. "Those who've pushed back are the 'Confessing Church.'"

"The true believers?" Henry asked, unsure how to phrase it.

"Well, they stood against power and for humanity, knowing they'd probably be killed for it," Matthias replied with an edge.

"So then, why *do* the Nazis wear those?" Henry asked.

Matthias replied, "The Iron Cross goes back to the Napoleonic wars. It's got more do with history and nations, not faith. And, honestly, Hitler's a populist. He uses anything he can for power. So, at least to begin with, he's wanted to appear Christian.[172] Like anything with social capital, religion is a clear target to either co-opt and twist, or silence." Matthias explained, "In this case, it's both."

"At first?" Henry asked.

Violet replied, "I've heard that Hitler and Himmler 'intend to eradicate Christianity just as ruthlessly as any other rival ideology' even if they're 'content to make compromises with it' right now."[173]

Matthias added, "Really, the high-ups are obsessed with the Greco-Roman—all this stuff." He said, shining his light back on the mosaic floor, "Egyptology, the occult . . . anything that could provide them with the foundations or legitimacy and power that they otherwise lack."

"As with anything," Violet said, "the devil's in the details, like how some people claim that the Greek god Dionysus is just like Jesus. And

---

172. See, for example: Blamires, *World Fascism*, xliii. While Himmler is known to have been more overtly pagan, Hitler's thoughts on religion and cultural reform continue to be debated, in part because politically motivated messaging is not a reliable account of personal belief. Notably, Richard Weikart has rejected Richard Steigmann-Gall's account that Hitler was "a sincere Christian, at least until 1937" (Weikart, *Hitler's Religion*, 71), concluding: "the evidence is preponderant against Hitler embracing any form of Christianity for most of his adult life" (105). Instead, Weikart argued that, consonant with Hitler's admiration of Nietzsche's "primacy of the will to power" (23), Hitler was most likely a scientific pantheist, believing that the brutal laws of nature demanded "uninterrupted killing, so that the better will live" (269). Nevertheless, Nicholas Goodrick-Clarke argues that, despite Hitler's rejection of certain occult factions, esoteric or pagan elements were leveraged to mythologize the regime and justify Aryan supremacy (Goodrick-Clarke, *The Occult Roots of Nazism*). Consider, to this end, Bruce Lincoln's thesis that myth is ideology in narrative form (Lincoln, *Theorizing Myth*).

173. Blamires, *World Fascism*, xliii.

so, Jesus is just these old myths—rinsed and recycled. But it couldn't be further from the truth."[174]

"Why?" Henry asked eagerly, long having absorbed this allegation as his own.

As if igniting the pitch-black silence under the amphitheater beyond the fire's glow, Violet replied, impassioned, "Yes, according to the myths, Dionysus was a son of the powerful god, Zeus, and in some stories was dead and then raised again to life. But that sort of parallel is superficial and misses everything characteristic about Dionysus and Jesus. Dionysus takes life; a master of chaos, inciting intoxication and revenge, where people are ripped to shreds while he watches with a gleeful smile. Whereas Jesus gives his life for others, pouring out the fullness of his life to establish peace. In doing so, Jesus inverts the values of the Greco-Roman world—casting out darkness with a piercing heavenly light where all are invited to flourish and come alive. Jesus is utterly different, unique, and revolutionary."[175]

174. "In comparative mythology, the (controversial) category of "dying-and-rising gods" was first proposed by James Frazer's *The Golden Bough* (1890). Frazer's examples included: Osiris, Tammuz, Adonis and Attis, Zagreus, Dionysus, and Jesus. See: Mettinger, "The 'Dying and Rising God': A Survey of Research from Frazer to the Present Day," 373–86. Regarding Dionysus, at least one story variation contained a resurrection-like story after being dismembered by the Titans. See Cook, *Empty Tomb*, 132–40. Christian responses to this allegation that the resurrection of Jesus is not unique, range from Athanasius' explicit denial of significant parallels (*On the Incarnation*, 89) to J. R. R. Tolkien and C.S. Lewis' identification of Jesus as the "one true myth," upon which others (to be expected) are shadows/trace this arc. See: Lewis, "Myth Became Fact," 63–67."

175. N.T. Wright has argued, "Did any worshipper in these cults, from Egypt to Norway, at any time in antiquity, think that actual human beings, having died, actually came back to life? Of course not. These multifarious and sophisticated cults enacted the god's death and resurrection as a metaphor." (Wright, *The Resurrection of the Son of God*, 80). Further, this is a confounding change in paradigm. Despite superficial similarities, such as the worshipful use of bread in communion, Wright points out that "the set of beliefs and aims that were generated from within their [Christian] worldview were simply not on the same map . . . evidence suggests that they [non-Christians] were more likely to be puzzled or to mock. When Paul preaches in Athens, nobody said, 'Ah, yes, a new version of Osiris and such like. The Homeric assumption remained in force. Whatever the gods—of the crops—might do, humans did not rise again from the dead." (Wright, *The Resurrection of the Son of God*, 81.) Thus, the assertion that Jesus genuinely rose from the dead is a significant categorical difference. Further, as K. R. Harriman points out: Jesus' resurrection is unique in that it provides a way for resurrection/everlasting life for others; for us. See: Harriman, "Early Christian Responses."

As Henry thought it through, his eyes were drawn to their long shadows cast upon the ancient stone walls by the fire, framed by a deep orange glow.

"So that claim about Jesus being just like Dionysus, and those like it, doesn't hold," Matthias clarified.

"And Jesus is a real historical figure," Violet said, referring to records from historians at the time who were not Christians, like Josephus, who had no reason to make a fraudulent claim.

"Okay. Say we acknowledge there's a difference," Henry said. "Why can't Hitler just build his own cult without co-opting Christianity or ancient myths?"

Violet replied, "Even the Roman emperors of old drew in what cultural capital they could, realizing that to build anything lasting, you must secure it on a foundation of something. Foundations are essential. You can do without them for a while, but sooner or later, things will start to crumble without them."

"That's also why someone like Descartes in the seventeenth century was intent on finding a foundation for knowledge during the Scientific Revolution," Matthias added.

Violet shared, with the images vivid in her mind, "You know, Hitler loves Wagner's Ring Cycle. In it, there's a battle between the love of power and the power of love. To support his pro-Aryan but otherwise very anti-human worldview, he's reaching for foundations that he thinks may be able to cement his beloved power—to help him bend the world into the image or 'Eden' of his making."[176]

"If I am honest, the thought of them trying to secure their power is overwhelming. I mean—" Henry backpedaled, but Violet respected him more for him sharing that truth, "—are the Nazis here to stay? Are they dug in?"

"We'd be foolish if we didn't take seriously what we're up against," Violet said. As she prodded the fire, a glowing log fell inward, casting sparks upward. "But here's what helps me. I like to think of it in a different way. Once upon a time, the Greco-Roman love of power was eroded by the power of love."

"It was?" Henry asked.

---

176. Regarding Hitler and Wagner, see Spotts, *Power of Aesthetics*, 223–65. Spotts also notes Hitler's "dream to create a culture-state" after his own image—that is, his aesthetic taste and passions (401).

"Yes. Big, powerful emperors like Nero, who outwardly were afraid of nothing, became petrified of normal people—slaves even—who were willing to give their lives because they saw another way to live because it eroded their chokehold on power," Violet said. "They saw Jesus."

"They refused to bow down to the emperor," Matthias added.

"Love. It was, and is, powerful," Violet said, "like the ocean undercutting a mighty cliff."

Later, as the long dark evening under the amphitheater wore on, Violet revealed that her middle name, given upon her first communion, was Felicity, after St. Felicity. "The story goes that Felicity, a servant, was in prison for her faith in the amphitheater at Carthage with Perpetua, the lady she served. Felicity was pregnant and gave birth in the prison. "Can you imagine it? Like in the cell over there," Violet exclaimed somberly.

Matthias couldn't help but think of his late wife. How they had longed to see a child make it to term. They had been through not one but two miscarriages. At least their innocent little eyes never had to see what had become of their homeland.

Violet continued, "The guards taunted Felicity for the pain she went through. After all, they reminded her that she was destined to be killed by wild beasts. Speaking about the comfort she found in Jesus, Felicity replied, 'Now alone I suffer what I am suffering, but then there will be another inside me who will suffer for me because I am going to suffer for him.'"[177]

Henry looked up to see her expression. He was not disappointed. Violet remained resolute, explaining that the story meant just as much to her today as when she first heard it shortly before her first communion—possibly even more now, given that she knew much greater depths of pain. "You see," she explained, "the story is not saying that suffering is okay. Nor is it suggesting a full embrace of suffering, like Nietzsche's love of fate. Nor does it dismiss suffering as easy. Instead, in and through suffering, there remains a loving relationship, the presence of someone—Jesus—and that changes everything. His loving, resurrecting presence is closer than one's own heartbeat, even when everything else is stripped away."

---

177. Paraphrase of the account in Perpetua's prison diary. See Musurillo, "The Martyrdom of Perpetua and Felicitas," 123–25.

26

———————————

Peter

Marje's Kitchen

LES VOSGES II

Thursday, November 4th, 1993.

It was early November, and the day was frosted and fresh. The night before, Ritesh had invited Peter to celebrate Diwali, the Hindu festival of
lights. It had truly captured Peter's imagination against the dark, damp
forest: a sacred gift. But if he were honest, he had desired for the light not
to stop, for it to go far deeper inside his heart. If only it could have. He
knew he needed a resuscitation, a resurrection of sorts, for it had helped
him realize that so much of his heart had turned to stone. What could he
do but keep trying to warm himself up with good conversations and hot
apple cider?

"You stay here," Peter told the fox kit, tying it loosely with his chilled
fingers outside the community kitchen. They had been together for over
a month now, and Peter's hand was finally out of bandages, though he
despised the exercises. Peter ducked under the large apple tree bough
that, over the course of time, had come to rest over the kitchen's door
frame. He touched a cluster of leaves with his fingertips; they would fall
soon. Funny, he now noticed these things. He paused briefly before stepping down into the cool workspace, bucolic but welcoming, hunkered
down in the dirt.

It was like entering the warm, busy engine room of an old steamship. "Peter! Come in, come in!" said Marje, her thick Estonian accent lovingly holding together her broken English. She invited Peter into the kitchen. Marje was the type of spritely great-grandmother who still crushed every eggshell, having learned that otherwise the witches might use them to sail out to sea and bring misery upon mariners. Foolishness, she knew, but it still informed her habit of not leaving even one shell intact. Besides, Bernie wanted shells crushed to the size of oats to help in his crusade against the slugs and snails.

"Does he want a little water?" Marje asked. Without waiting for a reply, she paused making breakfast to fetch some for the fox—who was delighted.

Littering her counter space and the far pantry were what seemed like hundreds of little science experiments marinating in time beneath an inverted sea of hanging herbs, drying to a fragile crisp in twine-bound bundles. "Those will get us through the winter," said Marje, directly addressing the Englishman's worry.

"What exactly are they?' Peter asked, trying to hide his repulsion with a healthier sense of curiosity.

"Why don't I just get you to taste some?" said Marje, wearing (as always) her trusty apron which could have been used for everything from carrying eggs to wiping children's noses. She was the type of cook who knew every contour of a bird's carcass after ensuring that nothing, for more than half a century, had gone to waste.

Quite amused at the cultural distance between Peter and herself, she loaded a small amount of the contents of one jar onto the end of the spoon. "Don't look so worried!" she said in good spirits as she lifted it to his lips. Peter ducked quickly out the way to avoid the food being ladled into his mouth. He was stopped fast—his head colliding painfully with a hanging pan.

Moving first and thinking afterward, Peter felt ashamed that he had flung himself out of the way.

"I am so sorry," said Peter sincerely, masking the pain. "It's not about the . . . er . . . food," Peter said. "It's just that I've always had this thing about someone else feeding me. It's a wonder I made it as a kid!" he explained, hoping she would look upon the funny side of his phobia.

"Ah, it's not to worry," she said the best she could, "though you'd think I was poisoning you." Her cheekbones cradled a wide, forgiving smile. "Here," she said, offering Peter the spoon.

Realizing that there wasn't really an opt-out clause for over-friendly grandmothers, Peter reached for it. Overly aware of Marje waiting for him, he forced a smile—the sort that left lines upon his face. Peter opened and closed his mouth nervously upon its tangy contents.

"How is it?" said Marje, jovially.

"Good! Hmm, what is that?" said Peter, pleasantly surprised as the flavors continued to permeate his mouth.

"Well, that's a family recipe. But if you treat it with honor, I could share it with you," Marje said.

"Oh, so it's not that big of a secret then?" Peter said with a cheeky smirk.

"The best things are made to be shared," Marje added, smiling at the prospect of educating this delightfully engaging twenty-something with memories from her homeland. "Really not that bad, hey?" she added.

"Are they all the same?" Peter asked, gesturing towards all of the jars. "Oh no," she said, "there's a lot of different things in here. Each has a story."

"What is that!?" Peter asked.

"I thought you might have known that one," Marje added, as a mother and daughter came in. The daughter, Liesel, brought corn right to the wooden table before making a beeline back to the door to tickle the kit's little belly. It wasn't complaining.

"Sauerkraut?" said Peter.

"Right!" replied Marje. "Tonight, I'm going to make *mulgikapsad*: pork with sauerkraut and barley."

"And that?"

"That's going to be *sült*," Marje said, referring to a pan with leftover meat ready to be turned into a sort of jelly. "Very good for you." Marje picked and processed everything that she could get her hands on, working from memory or old handwritten recipes marked by spillages past.

"Oh, my dear," said Marje in thanks, as Liesel obeyed her mother's silent cues to leave the kit and bring Marje the milk they'd also collected from the neighboring dairy farm.

"You've heard about the meeting after breakfast?" Amy said to Peter.

"Oh?" he replied.

"Just make sure you're there," Amy replied, tight-lipped.

Peter took the hint. They didn't need to bother Marje with it. He hated nothing more than a mysterious meeting. It gnawed at him. He always thought the problem was him. He tried as he could to relax into the magic of this bubbling, effervescent, and sage-scented world.

"What are you planning to make?" young Liesel asked Marje, with wide hazel eyes.

"Cheese!" Marje said while leaning in, eagerly anticipating the little girl's reaction.

Right on cue, little Liesel jumped up and down, "Yes, yes!" she screamed, pulling down on her mother's jumper and causing her ringlets to take flight.

"Let's see if we can't make something we'll be proud of!"

The natural flow of joy between the generations generously filled Peter's heart like water rippling over the sides of a majestic fountain. They were a family that chose each other. It made him think of Nana again. What a gift that was; and how the loss of her in his life made those beautiful memories sting. Liesel switched between languages in an instant with Marje.

"You see here," said Marje, hunched over, showing Peter, "this is the magic—tiny bacteria in the oak will make this the best cheese you've ever tasted." Peter looked green.

"You do realize that even if the food that you eat was completely dead, as soon as you put it in your mouth, you'd have contaminated it?" said the mother, Amy, eager to prompt Peter's reaction.

"Well, don't rub it in," said Peter whilst making a funny face that made Liesel bend over laughing. "Are you trying to give me a complex?"

"Food is meant to be alive, teeming with good bacteria. How else is it meant to help keep us alive?" Amy added.

"Well, I think it's pretty cool," said Liesel, puffing out her chest, Marje and Amy muffling their laughter. Her gappy smile simply accentuated her point.

"I see," Peter echoed like a jovial uncle.

"You seemed quite happy drinking that kombucha last night," Amy couldn't help but add.

"What ghastly wizardry?" Peter exclaimed, making another funny face at Liesel, whose now uncontrollable giggle was augmented by a little snort.

"You really want to know?" replied Liesel, skipping straight over to an old ceramic vessel. "Come, have a look," she said, lifting the muslin.

Peter almost gagged. It looked like one those anemic specimens he saw during nightmare-inducing trips to the Natural History Museum as a child. He leaned over to Marje: "You've got some explaining to do, *Madame!*"

"Nothing wrong with that, Peter. It keeps you regular, you know, your gut," Marje protested.

"Oh, Marje!" Peter grinned. "I'm quite private about those unmentionable matters!"

Marje finally understood that Peter was having fun with her.

Amy was even more abrupt than normal. She cut straight to the point: "Peter, if you wanted to live a sterile existence, you couldn't—you'd die. The microbial colonies living within and on your body weigh more than your brain. To thrive we need to take this seriously. We're dependent on these little things whether we like it or not." She was preaching to his cultural bias.

Nagging at the back of his now inferior-feeling brain, Peter wondered about whether the culture in which he grew up had also sterilized other out-of-sight critical components of life? *If we're not as independent as we like to think, then what about what Edwin was saying about dependence upon God? Could we suffer a withdrawal, like a stunted plant? But more painfully so given our awareness; spinning into anxiety?*

"Don't be sad," Liesel said, snapping him back into the present. "There's a letter for you," she added, hoping to make him smile.

"Oh, wow. Thank you. I'm not sad, just thinking. You've given me lots to chew on. I'll go read this in the garden with Bernie." The hot apple cider could wait.

"Speak up later," Amy said covertly to Peter, out of Marje's earshot.

"Do take a bun with you, dear," Marje told Peter, well-worn words from her loving on her now-grown sons and daughters. She couldn't have him "suffering" without one. "Oh, and tell Bernard that I am *very* anticipating some leeks!" she added, shouting when he was already halfway across the main field, the fox kit stuck to his side.

27

Peter

Gödel in the Garden

LES VOSGES II

Thursday, November 4th, 1993.

Out of breath and having long devoured Marje's bun, Peter, still flanked by his fox, broke free from the forest tracks and into Bernard's sunny garden plateau. It was now more than cool enough for a mist to have formed over the lower valley areas. It made for a glorious treat after climbing the hill. They had broken through the clouds so that they now stood above them, overlooking this mystical ceiling. It was the first inversion that Peter had seen since they had arrived. It felt liberating to be blissfully immune to the graveyard-gray sky and its muting of colors—met by unfiltered access to the honeyed autumnal sun.

Bernard was wearing a tweed waistcoat, which—despite being tailored for a very different environment—seemed utterly convinced of its prerogative to be present in the loamy dirt after decades of participating in this, Bernard's beloved labor. Peter found him leveraging his whole body to turn his fork. This was risky given that he was trying to avoid wrenching the metal any further away from the wooden handle, a casualty of an already over-zealous morning.

"Oh, Peter! How delightful!" Bernard said, having first assumed that he was Etienne emerging from his ritual of sweat-drenched solitude.

"Bernie, how long have you been here?" Peter asked, noticing a long train of overturned beds.

"Probably longer than you'd like to know!"

Bernard already had a small pile of treasures found in the early hours. These included chunky squared Roman nails and shards of pottery that were stashed by his overcoat, which further confirmed his suspicions that a Roman villa had been here. This made sense to him, given they were close to a road that connected Lyon and Trier to the sprawling Roman Empire that once ran from modern-day England to Egypt. Somehow, Bernard was incapable of living in just one era. His mind flitted between them—and why not? Ages past shouted at him from every degree of vision: insatiable layer upon layer, as if the land had found someone with whom it could finally entrust its secrets.

"Can we join you?" Peter asked, pausing. "It's okay if you'd rather be alone."

"Please do. What are you going to call the little guy?"

"I'm not sure yet . . . nothing quite fits," Peter said, rubbing under its chin.

Bernard smiled, "Sorry, do go ahead! You have a letter I see!"

"It's from Edwin, my friend."

"Ah, yes."

"I guess Tristan took pity on me and mailed it on." That unexpected kindness was welcome, but Peter felt bad. He'd peeked into the envelope on his way over. The letter looked detailed and meticulous, written in a beautiful cursive. Should he have expected anything less? Edwin had certainly given a lot of time to his queries, but Peter could barely remember what he had asked.

The kit circled to a stop on Peter's lap after they had found a place to sit under a knotted apple tree. The grassy bank was festooned with inspired, translucent threads, each spiraling out from a velvety moss that harbored a whole world of tiny insects.

Peter pulled out the letter. It opened with fantastic news: Edith was pregnant! This touched Peter deeply, knowing how deep the desire to become parents had been for them. Beyond the family updates, Edwin was kind enough to speak to Peter's preoccupation. It began with context about Bertrand Russell. What he needed to know, Edwin wrote, was that the story of Russell and Alfred North Whitehead and their approach of logicism corresponded to the first of what Ernst Snapper called the three

"Crises in Mathematics: Logicism, Intuitionism, and Formalism," while the story of Hilbert and Gödel had related to the last. [178]

Edwin explained that Russell was a figurehead for the British atheist movement—the Richard Dawkins of his age—and faced Frederick Copleston on the famous 1948 BBC debate on the existence of God. However, to Peter's surprise, Edwin revealed how Russell still felt the need to give a sort of disclaimer when speaking "truthfully and with rigor." While he thought that God almost certainly did not exist, he had to admit that agnosticism, not atheism, was, unfortunately, the more accurate label for his position. This was largely because science actually refers to a methodology where hypotheses are accepted or rejected in an attempt to illuminate or excavate truth. Consequently, Edwin explained that, while it can amass evidence, the scientific method cannot logically prove or disprove something conclusively for all time, just as the famous discovery of black swans in Australia disproved the maxim that all swans were white—no matter the number of confirming white swan reports in Europe. The same was true regarding the existence of God. Russell had written:

> In regard to the Olympic gods, speaking to a purely philosophical audience, I would say that I am an Agnostic. But speaking popularly, I think that all of us would say in regard to those gods that we were Atheists. In regard to the Christian God, I should, I think, take exactly the same line.[179]

Edwin went on to explain that this is where we can also see that Russell sadly missed something critical: the comparison was flawed. In making it, Russell was honestly speaking of the Victorian, moralistic god of his childhood. However, this austere, uncaring projection was not the God of the Bible, not the one that Jesus demonstrated. Instead, as Nietzsche even pointed out with venomous jest, this was a shadow that the British, in particular, were prone to confuse with the real thing.[180] While this misguided projection may overlap with the Olympic gods, the truth of the Christian God was utterly different. Different in message or meaning, and categorically different. In terms of message, following Jesus, the Crucified God, was so different and utterly scandalous to the Greco-Roman world that Christianity turned it upside down and inside out. God dying a slave's death to love and redeem humanity? That was an

178. Snapper, "Three Crises."
179. Russell, "Am I an Atheist?"
180. Nietzsche, *Gay Science*, 167.

abomination to the followers of someone like Zeus, who was squabbling, petty, and serially abusive. And, as ever, as one's god is, the followers are also.

The fox lifted his head; one of Bernard's small honeybees had zipped past. This drew Peter's eyes briefly from the page and towards the forest. Inside, there were all sorts of treasures from rare orchids to uninterpreted pagan carvings frequented in the twilight hours by lynx.

Peter returned to reading, awoken afresh to the depth of creation. Gods like Zeus, Edwin had explained, were also categorically different: they were "gods of the gap." Conversely, the Christian God isn't a place-holder for knowledge; he is the author of all knowledge and creator of everything.[181] Everything includes that which is already unveiled scientifically and that which is not, or not yet. Since the Christian God is of an entirely different category, rather than being intimidated by science—as if the ground of belief was lost or God deposed with each advance—Christ's followers can delight in seeing scientific advances. Science isn't simply compatible with Biblical worship; it is the "glory of kings is to search out a matter."[182] What a privilege, Edwin asserted, to, as Johannes Kepler said, think "God's thoughts after him."[183] So, while Russell made a good point about the difference between atheism and agnosticism, in regard to his opinion on Christianity more generally, Edwin concluded that Russell (like Dawkins) had conflated two very different things.

As he read, Peter found it curious that rather than attempt to vanquish science to keep the object of his faith intact, Edwin deeply valued the discipline. Indeed, the central question that Edwin spoke to in his letter became: Since mathematics and logic are so successful in explaining the physical world, it leads us to ask where this truth comes from. How do we ground truth?

For Edwin, the evidence was clear. Physics, for example, smuggles in the idea of objective truth through its use of the abstract, like logic and mathematics. But if physics can't provide those things itself, where are they coming from?

181. Lennox, *Can Science Explain Everything?*

182. Prov 25:2.

183. A common summary of "those laws [of nature] are within the grasp of the human mind; God wanted us to recognize them by creating us after his own image so that we could share in his own thoughts." Baumgardt and Callan, *Johannes*, 50. Kepler wrote this to Herwart von Hohenburg, April 9/10th, 1599.

"If we avoid circular reasoning," Edwin argued, "then anything we try and put into that blank starts to look suspiciously like a rational and intelligent mind. Indeed," he explained, "the astrophysicist, mathematician, and Nobel Laureate in physics, Sir Roger Penrose (who would not call himself Christian), has suggested that the "mental" is one of the three "worlds" underpinning reality.[184] Together, I find this to be compelling evidence for an intelligence behind this world," he opined.[185]

Peter found this intriguing and was drawn to read on. "For science, a discipline so driven by the pursuit of truth," Edwin wrote, "to ignore this logical problem is confused at best and hypocritical at worst. Likewise, in a concise and stinging way, Gödel called it 'apriorism with its sign reversed.'"[186] Gödel meant that while empiricists who assert that the only trustworthy knowledge that we have is attained via human bodily senses—with stricter versions requiring this knowledge to be verifiable by scientific experimentation—might actually suffer from the very same disorder that they claim to find undermining the thought of others (including men and women of faith). That is, choosing a philosophical side or "truth" before testing or looking into the matter. "Have empiricists (or scientific materialists)," Edwin asked, "not chosen their philosophical team before looking at the full weight of the evidence?" He passionately asserted, "Does not honesty demand, as with any of us, that they acknowledge their blind spots and dependency?"

The logical positivism of the Vienna Circle of the early twentieth century offers the classic example of the fragility of this position. While the meaning of logical positivism evolved, the verification principle, core to their initial philosophical position, held that statements are only meaningful if they convey truths that are empirically verifiable.[187] Yet, here is the problem: that sentence is self-refuting. Why? Because that is a philosophical statement and cannot be proven by the means stated. The Vienna Circle thus imploded under the weight of its own burden of evidence.[188]

---

184. Penrose, *Shadows of the Mind*.

185. Thanks to the scholar, astrophysicist, and apologist Dr. Michael Butler for this informed and succinct articulation.

186. Gödel, "Modern Development," 383.

187. Later, after criticism, evolving into the falsification principle.

188. See, for example, Craig, "William Lane Craig on Logical Positivism"; Craig, "Religious Epistemology."

Peter took a deep breath. He shifted his body as he took that in, eager to read on. To his surprise, given that Gödel had sat and observed the Vienna Circle from the inside, Edwin shared how Gödel spoke directly about the dangers of that sort of reductionist worldview. Gödel did so with shocking humility. Rather than inflate the importance of his own theory, he framed the whole drama by suggesting that the "uproar" in mathematics around the turn of the century regarding the antinomies of set theory (and new types of geometry) were "exaggerated by skeptics and empiricists . . . as a pretext for the leftward upheaval."[189]

Peter was stunned. Not only was that humility refreshing, but it was paired with a bold claim. Gödel made it sound like there had been an opportunist revolution of sorts, driving home materialistic philosophy or empiricism to vanquish otherness—that pesky residue of Platonism or God. But, if so, why? Edwin argued this was "because it was inconvenient: it didn't affirm how they understood the world." Indeed, Gödel assessed that, while Hilbert uniquely related mathematics to *a priori* knowledge, the hinge of engaging with reality—he still attempted to tame (or reduce) mathematics to fit in the box of the materialist worldview![190] But it categorically doesn't fit. It is, perhaps, too wild and glorious for that.

Clearly, while Gödel's bodily constitution was that of a fragile man plagued by the fears of the heart and mind, he made up for it by pulling some weighty intellectual punches. Peter let out a short burst of shock when he read that Gödel called Hilbert's project a "curious hermaphroditic thing, for it sought to do justice both to the spirit of the time and to the nature of mathematics."[191] Gödel concluded, "The Hilbertian combination of materialism and aspects of classical mathematics thus proves to be impossible."[192]

---

189. Gödel, "Modern Development," 377.

190. Gödel, "Modern Development," 381. Gödel also wrote, "And thus came into being that curious hermaphroditic thing that Hilbert's formalism represents, which sought to do justice both to the spirit of the time and to the nature of mathematics. It consists in the following: on the one hand, in conformity with the ideas prevailing in today's philosophy, it is acknowledged that the truth of the axioms from which mathematics starts out cannot be justified or recognized in any way, and therefore the drawing of consequences from them has meaning only in a hypothetical sense, whereby this drawing of consequences itself (in order to satisfy even further the spirit of the time) is construed as a mere game with symbols according to certain rules, likewise not supported by insight." Gödel, "Modern Development," 379.

191. Gödel, "Modern Development," 379.

192. Gödel, "Modern Development," 379.

"However, as is often the way, evidence *this* inconvenient is blatantly ignored," Edwin had written. He then painted Gödel's frustration well by sharing his argument that "while these turn-of-the-century crises have been resolved 'in a manner that is completely satisfactory and, for everyone who understands the theory, nearly obvious,' (in no small part to his incompleteness theorems), such arguments are 'however, of no use against the spirit of the time.'"[193]

"The spirit of the time?" Peter read out loud to Bernard, seeking understanding. "Like the Spirit of the Age?"

Bernard turned in a series of deliberate movements to face him. His body wasn't quite as flexible as he thought it still to be. "I would think so," he replied. "The *zeitgeist*—what people are generally thinking—which doesn't make it true or good, mind you."

"Right," Peter said, thoughtfully. "And Gödel talked about a leftward upheaval before. What does that actually mean?"

"Read it to me," Bernard said, perched on his spade, attentive, his skin drinking in the morning sun like a sail yearns for the wind. His waistcoat now shed.

Peter backed up a little to read a passage right from Gödel. The best way to gain "an overall view of the possible world-views will be to divide them up according to the degree and the manner of their affinity to or, respectively, turning away from metaphysics (or religion). In this way we immediately obtain a division into two groups: skepticism, materialism and positivism stand on one side, spiritualism, idealism and theology on the other."[194] Peter also read the clarification: *a priorism* (given or self-evident truth) belongs "on the right and empiricism on the left side."[195]

"Ah, yes. I see what he's saying," Bernard said, "but it's a lot. Let's strip it down a bit."

Bernard drove the spade into the ground and came over to sit down with them on the bank but not before he walked to the stream that fed his irrigation lines and pulled out a couple of chilled bottles of his home-made mead.

He spoke as he settled himself, "You know, worldview is critical to understand. Wittgenstein talked about worldview or world-image—as

193. Gödel, "Modern Development," 379.

194. Gödel explains that there can also be "degrees of difference in this sequence, in that skepticism [for example] stands even farther away from theology than does materialism." Gödel, "Modern Development," 364.

195. Gödel, "Modern Development," 383.

the type of 'certainties' that we people harden in our thinking about the world—as a 'river-bed for thoughts.'"[196]

"So, channeling all other thoughts?"

"Exactly, channeling them round bends to reaching certain conclusions. A worldview structures or organizes our attempt at understanding those big things of life, such as: what (if anything) is wrong with the world and how to fix or navigate it. Wittgenstein also calls them hinges and axes, but I like the riverbed metaphor best."

"Me, too."

"Here," said Bernard, handing him a bottle.

"Drinking in the morning now, hey?" Peter joked as he reached out his hand.

They clinked bottles before taking the first sips. The taste lingered as they paused to watch how the unashamed morning sun warmed the garden beds despite its shallow autumnal arc. Steam rose, releasing an honest aroma. The soil that had been turned first was now noticeably drier than the following rows, far richer in color as they remained moist.

Bernard couldn't help but engage with Peter's questions, for they tapped into the very nature of reality itself which had long plagued and perplexed him. "Distinguishing worldviews in this way is not altogether novel. What I believe Gödel means by left and right, I would normally call 'lower and upper narratives,' respectively, because it ties into the Greek imagery a little better." He took another sip. "Here is the context: Like us, Hilbert and company lived in a post-Kantian world. A world awoken to the painful reality of the 'homelessness of humanity.'[197] This is important: it impacts how we think of ourselves—as alone and suspended no matter how much we thrash around to make our mark on the world." Bernard took a few more generous gulps as if to get the taste of that reality out of his mouth, readying himself to move forward. "I'm going to go quickly, so hang with me. You know Descartes and Kant, right?"

"Just a little," Peter said.

"Kant's focus on the individual's thought-world emphasizes one half of the mind-body duality that Descartes framed when he re-scored the distinction between two perceivable layers of reality, which some have called the lower narrative and the upper narrative."[198]

---

196. Wittgenstein, *On Certainty*, 34. Section 97.

197. Pacini, *Through Narcissus' Glass Darkly*, 7, 23, 48.

198. Francis Shaeffer famously identified these upper and lower narratives. First published widely in Schaeffer, *God Who Is There*.

"Right, Descartes effectively split the thinking mind and body."

"Essentially, yes, though he still sought in vain to ascertain how they were connected. These two layers have been relabeled throughout history. The most famous early philosophical depiction of this distinction is immortalized in Raphael's painting *The School of Athens*. Have you seen it?"

"I can't say I have," Peter answered. "Where is it?"

"The Vatican," Bernard jested.

"I must have missed it on my last visit," Peter said, making Bernard chuckle.

"Raphael has Plato and Aristotle standing right in the center, on the academy's steps. Referring to Plato's allegory of the cave, Plato is painted pointing upwards, to the real truth that he finds in a transcendent, ideal world of perfect forms away from our shadowy, imperfect life. Conversely, his student, Aristotle, holds his palm downwards to emphasize the real value of particulars on the earth. Plato was an idealist, whereas Aristotle prioritized and embraced the natural world, often liking to swim around his favorite Mediterranean islands, studying sea life."

"You're saying both emphasize one layer of reality over the other?"

"Right," Benard replied. "And that's only possible because the fabric of reality was thought to have been disconnected—split in two. Ruptured, perhaps."

"Can you explain that?"

"Absolutely," Bernard said.

Carefully finding somewhere that resembled flat, Bernard put down his bottle so that he could pick up a large gnarly chunk of bark shed from the base of the tree. Woodlice scattered. "This is the fabric of reality," he said, "a continuum, a tapestry." As he raised it before them, Peter noticed how Bernard's hands were laced with spider webs of soil. He cracked the bark in an instant. The fox jumped to its feet. "Sorry, boy," he said.

Bernard then held the two pieces, one in each hand. "Once you have broken and separated reality into two different categories, you can turn them in opposition to each other." He held the two chunks of bark to face each other. "Now you can present something that could have been continuous, tied together or even mutually reinforcing, as polar opposites."

"But should you?" Peter asked. The fox kit was now on edge, nuzzling Peter's hand for comfort. When Peter obliged, the kit immediately relaxed like a spill on the mossy bank, training Peter's hand to move from his neck to soft belly. Thinking and listening, it seemed, did not have to mean neglecting this duty.

Bernard replied, "Well, let's see how it plays out. This logic of opposites reaches its zenith in modernity, intent on clarity by framing the world in couplets—as opposites—day and night, right and wrong, man and woman."

"Aren't they?"

"You can have distinction without these things being polar opposites or warring against each other."

"I see. So, opposing them is wrong?"

"It's about the logic that follows from this modernist opposition. You see, by labeling one narrative as true or good, the other (that used to flow with it seamlessly as a unity) is now condemned to be . . .?"

"False, bad, or less than?"

"Right! Or at least not objectively true. With this logic superimposed upon the whole of reality, the upper narrative—which traditionally includes ideas of God and any eternal attributes he might have like love and justice—is relabeled as false or at least subjective."

"A delusion."

"Possibly a pernicious, dangerous delusion," Bernard explained with a hint of satire. "Interesting, that degeneration, isn't it? It all comes down to that break and trajectory of thinking. From there, the modern Enlightenment mindset takes off: a crusade to eliminate anything that it does not consider truth."

"So, seeing the fabric of reality as broken apart has consequences?"

"Oh, yes, Peter. What starts as a movement of naked thought ends up costing human lives—it has real consequences. This crusade against the upper narrative has proven to be a little too useful politically, especially for those wanting to unplug a population from any objective morality, intent to have the state define what is justified in the name of progress. You know, whether he realizes it or not, Jean-Paul—with all his huffing and puffing about anything spiritual—is a student of that world."

"Why do you say that?"

"After the Bolshevik Revolution, the Soviet state was determined to bring re-education. After all, history was, they thought, on a trajectory that couldn't, or shouldn't, be stopped. Any faith aside from that towards the state was steamrolled, ridiculed, and replaced. I think it was Anatoly Lunacharsky—who, interestingly enough, was a fan of Wagner's idea of using culture to stimulate social change—said, 'We have got to change our god . . . it is necessary . . . to invent a new faith . . . to create a god for all.'"[199]

"Replaced by . . . what? The god of the state? Because Christianity was a threat?"

"Exactly. Back in the ancient world, Roman emperors like Nero persecuted Christians for daring to have not just one God instead of many, but one whose call to love spoke louder than the demands of the emperor. In a similar way, the Soviet leadership saw Christianity as a threat to people falling in line with their demands. As a result, Orthodox priests perished (alongside others) in the years following the Russian Revolution in particularly high numbers."

"Flushed down the sewers," Peter said, remembering what Etienne had shared about Solzhenitsyn, whose first-hand account had revealed the sordid architecture of the gulags spread over Siberia.

"I've always thought that if you need to kill people who, because of their worldview, stand in the way of you killing other people, then it says something," Bernard said soberly.

Peter was shocked. Just something? Or did it say everything? "So they re-educated people?"

"Those they didn't kill. Education is powerful. And Lunacharsky? He became the first people's commissar for education. After the revolution, Christian festivals like Christmas were replaced by secular alternatives that decapitated the upper narrative or spiritual element of life. That sort of replacement was rampant through the lifespan of the larger Soviet Union, with first communions replaced by pleading allegiance to the state—that kind of thing.[200] Science, of course, was held up as a replacement for the delusion of faith," Bernard explained. "The propaganda was all about them being in conflict."

"But it's not as simple as that," Peter admitted under his breath, a surprise even to himself. He was finally starting to understand why Edwin was so passionate about this. Conclusions about whether science and faith, for example, are in conflict have real human consequences. It really matters.

"So, what do we do?" Peter asked. Putting his bottle between his legs, he picked up the two pieces of bark, juxtaposing and peering

---

199. Watson, *Age of Atheists*, 209. Lunacharsky famously propounded a theory of *bogostroitel'stvo*, "God-Building." See Lunacharsky, *Religion and Socialism*. For talk of "the invention of supplementary lies," also see Lunacharsky, *On Education*, 37.

200. For further examples, see Brother Andrew, *God's Smuggler*.

between them. "Is religion the only way to solve the problem of these two narratives? Where do we go from here?"

"That's a great question," Bernard admitted. "We don't like tension and complexity, do we?"

"True . . ."

"We can either keep the tension and try to acknowledge both layers," Bernard explained.

"Or . . .?"

"Or attempt to depose of one, making the executive decision that only one layer—or narrative—is able to exclusively speak the truth about reality."

"Do not disturb my circles!" Peter jested, echoing what Bernard had shared that late-summer evening about Archimedes's last words.

Bernard laughed. "Let's start with the first instance: keeping both layers. From a Judeo-Christian perspective, your friend Edwin's, a rip or tear in reality isn't radical news—it is expected—a radical disconnection resulting from 'the fall,' right?"

"And so?" Peter asked. "We have to muddle through or try to figure out how to mitigate this disconnection?"

"Yes and no. For them, the two narratives or layers may also loosely relate to heaven and earth; seen and unseen. Rather than just muddling through, as I understand it, what Jesus achieves on the cross impacts the whole of reality. The idea is that Jesus started—and continues through his church, empowered by his Spirit—to create vibrant pockets of peace where heaven and earth reconnect as originally designed. Is that where your friend goes in the letter?"

"Somewhat. But he was answering my questions, so he connects worldview back to Gödel."

"How so?" Bernard inquired.

"There's a part here," Peter explained, taking a moment to find the place, "where he mentions Gödel's last public presentation, the 1951 Gibb Lectures. Gödel argued against the position where mathematics is understood as just an invented language but is discovered. Edwin said that Gödel ended by quoting Charles Hermite."

"Ah, yes, the nineteenth-century mathematician. This debate continues today. Do share, Peter."

"He said, 'There is, if I am not mistaken, a whole world which is the set of mathematical truths, into which we gain access only through intelligence, just as there is a world of physical realities; the one and the other are independent of us, both of a creation divine."[201]

Peter could almost hear Edwin's voice harmonizing as he read it, called up within the dawn chorus in which he and Bernard sat, embedded. This idea of a mathematical world moved dangerously close to acknowledging an unseen but essential land. A land where the full depth of its reality may outstrip the faculties of the human mind, but the faculties of faith may take the lead in exploring its contours.

The letter continued with Edwin sharing that as we allow ourselves to spiritually draw closer towards these truths that first appear to be entrenched in fog—the fog burns up, allowing us to encounter a nourishing homeland so heavenly that it outstrips all comprehension or attempts to tame it.[202] This brave approach into "more" has been called many things, but for some it looks like worship—that is, digging wells of wonder. Even now, reacquainted with these vibrant thoughts, Peter couldn't help but imagine a bucket plunging into a surging underground stream. Once again, living water, just like Edwin had driven home by pointing to the rings of the Amsterdam canals. "But that's foolish, isn't it, Bernie?" Peter said, after trying his best to summarize these scattered thoughts.

At that moment, a sweet little honeybee came to rest on Bernard's hand. Completely unfazed, Bernard gently orchestrated his fingers to be a playground for its exploration. "I don't know about that, Peter." He looked at the bee's fluffy little body with proud orange stripes. "Visible light reveals just a fragment of reality to the naked eye, but a whole world exists beyond it, where bees and other insects navigate using ultraviolet markings."

"Like on flowers?"

"Exactly. They have little runways! Peter, as infuriating as this is to Enlightenment man, just because human reason can't master something does not mean it is not true, necessary, real, or good."

"Just as in the night an inability to see in the dark does not dissolve the world around us of its being?" Peter reasoned.

"Precisely."

"Huh," Peter said, thinking it through.

---

201. Gödel, "Some Basic Theorems," 323.

202. Paradox might even draw us in. For Milbank, the "misty," opaque quality of paradox "is in no way static...[venturing] to ensure [one] reaches further out toward that alterity." See Milbank and Žižek, *Monstrosity of Christ*, 198.

"I think there is more than we give credit to. But the height and depth of this? I don't know, Peter."

Peter picked up the letter afresh, pulling it out from under the fox. The crinkle was audible. He then studied it intently. "You were right: Edwin claims that the world is this integration of seen and unseen, and that we are made for an overlapping of heaven and earth."

"Let me see," Bernard said, intrigued. "Yes. He thinks we're like fish out of water, a complicated composite of soul, spirit, and flesh," he said after scanning it quickly. "I can resonate with that. Given that in the Christian understanding, the world is affected by the fall of humanity, some of us—or even one part of us—tries to find a home in this unseen, spiritually engaged world while another part of us feels more at home on the earth." Bernard handed the letter back.

"So, we can feel torn—homeless—like you said before," Peter reasoned. "Untethered." Peter pointed to a section, "Here, he calls this gap in the structure and fabric of reality a 'metaphysical wound.'"

"Isn't that interesting!" Bernard replied.

Peter couldn't help but connect to that. Feeling, yes, homeless, but also like he was bleeding out. A metaphysical wound: a rip in reality, perhaps made worse by our botched way of navigating it.

Bernard agreed. "Does he say anything about the Dutch mathematician L. E. J. Brouwer?"

"I don't think so."

"Surprising. He studied at the University of Amsterdam. Anyhow, Brouwer is the last of those three attempts to found mathematics, leading the intuitionist camp. His project was the one that Hilbert reacted against and Russell wanted to vanquish. Not only does Brouwer talk of how he believes that for our consciousness, "the deepest home vaguely beckons,"[203] but this also connects to his concept of how 'when the basic intuition of mathematics is left to free unfolding,' we start to discern certain 'harmonies' and beauty.[204] I'm especially surprised that your friend—"

"—Edwin—"

"—didn't mention him because he argued that this beauty 'awakens in our diseased bodies the frozen consciousness of God.'"[205]

203. From Brouwer's 1948 Amsterdam address, "Consciousness, Philosophy, and Mathematics," in, Brouwer, *Collected Works*, 487.

204. Brouwer, *Collected Works*, 484.

205. Van Dalen, *L. E. J. Brouwer*, 282.

Peter didn't say another word, for he was stunned. Upon that utterance he had felt the undeniable sensation of his frozen heart starting to thaw. It reached right into him, without the mediation of his will. It was not wholly unwelcome, but he wanted to fight it. He didn't like the long-ago discarded idea of God.

Perceiving that the finest wisps of something—for lack of better words—holy and ineffable had begun, Bernard let them breathe for a moment. Who was he to interrupt? He encouraged Peter to set aside his lonely mental wrestle—less a buttressing castle and more of a prison—to instead be present to the reality in which he found himself. Nevertheless, resistance was written all over Peter's face. His inside world had been fighting to protect itself for so long.

After some moments, Bernard simply suggested, "Rather than suture that metaphysical wound, we have so often drawn attention to one part of reality and suppressed the other. But, oh, isn't it magical when it comes together?" That helped Peter put his guard down for a second, teasing him back out of that chilled tight knot. He began feeling. Hearing. Smelling. Noticing beauty. Birds fighting over grubs in the overturned soil. Butterflies flew, encircling each other as if caught in a tumbleweed, so infatuated that they were unable to fly straight, grazing Peter's chin.

"It is," Peter said tentatively. It felt good to agree with Edwin, and, indeed, Bernard also. But it also felt unnerving to have his resistance to some sort of holistic spiritual life eroding. He decided to lean back against the familiar controls of his rational mind: "So the alternative is just choosing one layer, right?"

"Exactly," Bernard said, perceiving this pivot but ready to dignify his question. "As Gödel points out, like so many others of his age and our own, Hilbert attempts to bring peace to this tension by choosing a path of refusal—reducing and simplifying."

"And while that works for fractions, it doesn't work so well for reality," Peter joked. Jokes had often proved themselves reliable for keeping things surface-level.

"It was the same with Russell and Whitehead's logicism," Bernard explained.

"How so?" Peter asked.

"First, you need to know that Russell's love affair with mathematics started at just eleven years old when his brother, Frank, introduced him to Euclid. He said finding Euclid was one of the great events of his life, 'as dazzling as first love,'[206] and that his thirst to learn more had saved him from suicide."[207]

"So, Russell tried to save mathematics after it had saved him?"

"Something like that. Now, between Hilbert's twenty-three problems and his ill-fated formalist program, Russell had dreamt of *replacing* Kantian intuition with rock-solid mathematics via logical rigor."

"Right," Peter said, recalling that from his book.

"But as I said," Bernard explained, "it didn't go to plan. After almost killing themselves patching holes again and again in the logical edifice, Russell and Whitehead left *Principia Mathematica* unfinished. They had planned a fourth volume."

"That tracks. Edwin quotes Russell," Peter offered, finding the spot. "Here it is: 'The splendid certainty which I had always hoped to find in mathematics was lost in a bewildering maze.'"[208]

"Exactly. He and Whitehead had given it all. But Russell came to realize that they had allowed abstract mathematical work to 'destroy one's humanity' admitting to raising 'a monument which is at the same time a tomb.'"[209]

Peter read out from the letter for them both: "With the fresh sting of his approach, or theory of knowledge being critiqued by his former student, Wittgenstein, Russell felt the gravity of reality. He had watched 'young men embarking in troop trains to be slaughtered on the Somme because generals were stupid.'[210] In this world the value of mathematics and 'abstraction' were lost. And yet in former times, he wrote, he had been drawn to this 'enchanted region' of mathematics because in 'thinking about it we [had] become gods.'"[211]

"You know," Bernard said, to give the bigger picture, "Whitehead and Russell clashed over World War I. Russell was imprisoned for a time due to his pacifist stance and activism, while Whitehead had a son who died in the war. Funnily enough, despite these differences, both moved from studying mathematical philosophy to philosophy more specifically. Whitehead was especially passionate about diagnosing the cause of the inhumane world wars."

206. Russell, *Autobiography*, 30.

207. Russell, *Autobiography*, 38.

208. Russell, *My Philosophical Development*, 157.

209. Russell, *Autobiography*, 168.

210. Russell, *My Philosophical Development*, 157.

211. Russell, *Autobiography*, 167–68.

"And what did he think?" Peter asked.

"Well, what does your friend Edwin say?" Bernard asked, having caught a glimpse of Whitehead's name on the page.

Peter looked down, studying it for a second. "He traces it back to Enlightenment thinkers. Whitehead argues that the views of Sir Isaac Newton and David Hume were 'gravely defective. They are right as far as they go,' but, taken by themselves, they omit 'our intuitive modes of understanding.'[212] Whitehead concluded that science fails 'to endow its formulae for activity with any meaning.'"[213]

"Right," Bernard affirmed. "So, after this, Whitehead goes the other way from a bare-bones logicism. He became the father of Process Philosophy, a very immanent, meaning-drenched way of seeing reality."

"That's quite a difference," Peter acknowledged, placing the letter down again.

Bernard agreed. "Many wanted different."

"Explain that."

"Well, in observing that modern Enlightenment man had lost the ability to see the world as saturated with any objective received meaning, those like Whitehead observed that it was then easy for humankind to surge forth and force meaning upon the world—to shape it to their will. To build a kingdom of their own values."

"And that's when Enlightenment man gets a taste for blood?" Peter reasoned.

"There's the motive, the means, and the muting of morality," Bernard said.

"Like in the war?" Peter said.

"Yes," Bernard answered, subdued and hesitant.

"I mean, the Second World War," Peter prompted him.

Bernard dutifully answered, slowly and more humanly, "Yes. You see a backhanded acknowledgment of this insecurity when, in searching for foundations, Hitler became obsessed with Greco-Roman culture.[214] But

---

212. Whitehead, *Nature and Life*, 26.

213. Whitehead, *Nature and Life*, 65.

214. Consider Hitler's cultural aspirations for his Führermuseum, part of his "dream to create a culture-state" (Spotts, *Power of Aesthetics*, 401), that "drew from what [in his terminology] racially similar peoples—meaning the Greeks and Romans—had developed in the past" (316). Hitler was, as Joseph Goebbells reflected, back in 1926, "thoroughly the architect" (73).

these man-made elements had no ability to make their captor more humane."

"Quite the opposite," Peter agreed soberly.

Just then, Etienne emerged from the forest.

The fox kit jumped.

"Exactly, Peter, exactly," Bernard said, obscuring the end of these words as he turned away and rose to his feet, finding the air between them oddly chilled.

28

Peter

Skulls & Scandals

LES VOSGES II

Thursday, November 4th, 1993. Bernard's Garden.

"Oh, Peter! *Bonne journée*! Care to accompany me to breakfast?" He knew there was no point in inviting Bernard. Anyhow, it was not uncommon to see traces of a fried egg and tomato and foraged mushrooms later in his cabin. He related to others on his own time and terms.

Just as Etienne said that, the bell rang out. All the people housed in the lower valley shifted in an instant.

"Good timing," Peter said, rising to join him.

"Is that a letter from home?" Etienne asked.

"From my friend Edwin in Amsterdam."

"Ah, yes! How is he doing?"

"Well," Peter said confidently, a little embarrassed about the content regarding God. He promptly stuffed the letter back inside his pocket.

As they left the garden plateau, touching Bernard's arm gently, Peter said, "I'll come by later, Bernie." He received a courteous but paled response. He wanted to see if Bernie was okay, but it was clear he didn't want a fuss. And so, Peter left. This was a mistake but an honest one.

Peter and Etienne headed down the wooded mountainside, the fox kit staying for an extra second circling Bernard to say goodbye, pausing to lean its forehead against his shin before looking up into Bernard's misty eyes. They were like a screen behind which flashed a zoetrope of images, each vying for attention. When Peter came by later, Bernard's door was locked, though, without a doubt, he was inside.

Despite Peter's attempt to change the subject as they descended, Etienne returned to the letter. While he was bound to be more intellectually generous about Etienne's opinions than Jean-Paul, Peter only got him up to speed on select themes.

"Ah, Gödel is an interesting one, isn't he. On the one hand, as Gödel quite humbly admitted, his theories don't change much—that is, about the vast majority of mathematics can continue unhindered."

"Right, and he thought the crisis might have been deliberately overblown by the dominant reductionist worldview. I mean, it makes sense if some part of them wanted an opportunity to definitively drive home their position," Peter said.

"Indeed! But on the other hand, they are still earth-shattering because they challenge assumptions about truth that have doggedly held their ground since the birth of philosophy.[215] People are split as to the full consequence of it all."

As they got into single-file woodland tracks, it gave Peter a second to reflect on what he had read about this. Sir Roger Penrose had resurfaced in the letter. Why? Because he'd argued that in light of the incompleteness theorems, artificial intelligence would inevitably fall short of replicating the functions of the mind, as it operates within the confines of formal axiomatic systems. For Penrose, because the mind is more than just the function of the physical brain, humans can intuitively recognize truths that are unprovable within such systems.[216]

It turned out that, like mathematics, which Edwin thought belonged in the "upper narrative," there were also all these other "*M*'s"—such as mind, morality, and music—that are essential to human life and yet resist reductionism in that the lower narrative cannot exhaust their full meaning.[217] Essentially, these realities can't be pinned down like a butterfly on a dissector's board for empirical study. Central among these, Edwin

---

215. For example: "Gödel's work raises the question of whether or not reality itself is fully rational. In this sense, the demonstration of Gödel's incompleteness theorems struck a mortal blow to aspirations and assumptions stretching all the way back to the origins of Western philosophy." Fosl and Baggini, *Philosopher's Toolkit*, 314.

216. Penrose, *Emperor's New Mind*; Penrose, *Shadows of the Mind*; Megill, "Lucas-Penrose Argument." On the mind-brain distinction, also see: Dirckx, *Am I Just My Brain?*

217. This insight/phrasing about the *M*-words is from UK apologist Glen Scrivener.

argued, was the mind. For, whatever it is, the conscious mind is necessary to perceive mathematical truths, beautiful music, or any objective value to human life undergirding any moral system we feel compelled to hold ourselves or others to.

Like Penrose, the Oxford philosopher J. R. Lucas assessed in 1961 that "Gödel's theorem seems to me to prove that mechanism is false . . . We are trying to produce a model of the mind which is mechanical—which is essentially dead—but the mind, being in fact 'alive,' can always go one better than any formal, ossified, dead system can. [218] Thanks to Gödel's theory, the mind always has the last word."[219]

While he underplayed it, Peter was also perceptive and sharp. He connected the dots between the beginning and end of Edwin's letter. While he didn't like the conclusions, he reasoned that if the mind is not the same as, or entirely reducible to, a material brain and its electrical impulses—but is instead distinctly valuable and real—then making space for its existence also opens up the rational possibility of a God of this sort of "mind stuff." A mind behind the mind: something—or someone—alive. Not dead or machine-like.[220]

The narrow path opened upon a lower field. The two men were finally able to walk alongside one another. "You know," Etienne said, "regardless of where we land with the implications of Gödel's work, I think that what it brings up about the human mind is essential to consider."

Peter chuckled to himself about the timing. Was Etienne also telepathic?

218. Lucas, "Minds, Machines and Gödel," 116.

219. Even if AI becomes computationally superior to the human brain, the question remains whether a machine mind is possible. There is a difference between the understanding afforded by a mind and performing as if there is understanding. See, for example, the "Chinese room" thought experiment in Searle, "Minds, Brains, and Programs." Recently, by using modal logic and drawing on Polanyi's work, Andy Steiger has argued that even if a computer mind is possible, it would remain categorically (ontologically) different than a human or animal mind. Steiger, "Critical Exploration and Theological Critique," 230–39.

220. Sharon Dirckx, who holds a PhD in brain imaging from the University of Cambridge, suggests that accounting for the existence of the human mind starting with non-conscious matter continues to pose a problem for materialist accounts of existence. This development seems almost, or perhaps more, miraculous as turning water into wine! Conversely, the Christian theist account of existence that starts with a thinking, rational, intentional creator accounts for this much more readily. See Dirckx, *Am I Just My Brain?*

"To quote the essayist Marilynne Robinson," Etienne said, "whoever controls the definition of mind controls the definition of humankind itself."[221]

That quote dropped like an anchor in Peter's spirit. He'd never heard something that clear and direct on the topic.

Antonio and Andrea, whose cabins were close to each other, overheard this as they joined them. Antonio couldn't hold back. It was right up his alley to share a slightly gruesome but true story.

"Do you know the story of Einstein's brain?"

"Right before breakfast?" Andrea said, rolling her eyes.

"Well, he can't leave me hanging now!" Peter smirked.

Antonio seized the opportunity. "This is what I *will* say," he said as if he were going to hold back. "When he died in 1955, Einstein's brain was stolen." Antonio came alive as he set the scene: "His iconic white hair that spun outwards to connect previously disparate, nebulous ideas of the cosmos was cast aside and his brain pried from his cranium without prior consent." He continued, "The same sort of sordid thing that happened to Descartes's bones, you know. Just like with René Descartes's skull, the goal was to show the world how different and superior his brain was—to explain his genius. Finding Einstein on his cold, hard slab, the doctor no doubt wanted to weigh in on the same centuries-old debates that had ensnared Descartes's skull in Paris: the first of which crudely reasons that if all that matters is matter, then a genius must have a bigger brain capable of complex thought."[222]

"And was it bigger or more complex?"

"That's the thing," Antonio answered. "Just like with Descartes's skull, not really: 1230 grams! It was 'unremarkable' and even in the lower-to-average range for a man his age. There were some normal human variances, but nothing that shouted 'genius.' Mind you, that didn't stop Dr. Harvey slicing up his brain and keeping some of it in mason jars in his basement in Kansas." Antonio, you see, was wonderfully neurodivergent and able to recall details when they interested him almost exactly and almost indefinitely. Even more than learning about them, he loved sharing them.

Antonio couldn't help but draw another parallel to Descartes. As a curious precursor in the accordion-like deep pockets of history, Antonio

221. Robinson, *Absence of Mind*, 32.

222. Shorto, *Descartes' Bones*, 167–76.

explained that just as the brief loss of Descartes's skull had caused a city-wide crisis—thinking that it had been carried away after the 1910 floods—Einstein's brain was lost to the world for twenty-three years. You know," Antonio touched back, "They didn't even realize that Descartes's skull was in their collection until they found a letter in 1912 about it being transferred to a museum in Paris in the early 1820s."

"I would have hated to be the one that found the letter and had to break the bad news!" Peter said, as if setting off an echo in time that channeled his daughter's steps towards her discovery of Descartes at the Musée de l'Homme decades later.

Antonio enjoyed seeing Peter appreciate his tale. He continued, "It wasn't until 1978 that a young journalist, Steven Levy, realized that Einstein's brain was missing. After finding Dr. Harvey and pressing him on the issue, eventually he's said to have turned with a 'sheepish grin,' retreated to the corner of his basement, and brought out a couple of samples. He'd kept samples of the brain in a beer cooler within a box labeled 'Costa Cider,' split between two large mason jars. Levy said that the first jar contained what looked like 'a conch shell-shaped mass of wrinkly material the color of clay after firing. A fist-sized chunk of grayish, lined substance, the apparent consistency of sponge. And in a separate pouch, a mass of pinkish-white strings resembling bloated dental floss.' The second had 'dozens of rectangular translucent blocks, the size of Goldenberg's Peanut Chews!'"[223]

Andrea shook her head. "Revolting," she said.

This gave Antonio even more gumption. "National Geographic called it 'The Tragic Story of How Einstein's Brain Was Stolen and Wasn't Even Special.'[224] While Einstein's parietal lobes had some differences, they may have just been regular variations between people. One respected neurologist said, 'If you put my feet to the fire and you say, "Where's special relativity? Where did general relativity come from?"—we have no idea.'"[225]

"But what happened right after they found out the doctor had it?" Peter asked.

"After Levy broke the scandal," Antonio explained, "his front lawn was full of press. Soon after, the doctor sent new samples away for further analysis. Some, in Cool-Whip containers."

223. Levy, "My Search for Einstein's Brain." Also in Kremer, "Strange Afterlife."
224. Hughes, "Tragic Story."
225. The neurologist was Dr. Frederick Lepore. See Kremer, "Strange Afterlife."

While Andrea already knew about it, hearing it afresh made her gag.

"Antonio's right," Etienne added. "It's a good example that goes back to what we said: whoever controls the definition of mind controls the definition of humankind itself.[226] Because what happens when you reduce humanity to just matter, to a thing? You treat it as a thing. What we think about ourselves has consequences, let alone what we think about others."

"I can see that," Peter reasoned. "So, somehow, we need to keep a wider view." Though quite what this needed to be or how it was to be secured, he didn't know. Peter suddenly realized that this was, in some ways, simply the transposition of Camus's concern in *The Rebel* to secure humanity against the excesses of perpetual, violent revolution.

"You know, Peter," Etienne added, as the friends walked deeper into the heart of the community, "Despite his nervous disposition, Gödel took care of some very human things after Einstein died."

"Oh?" Peter replied, intrigued.

Etienne replied, "Gödel and Einstein's last research partner—Bruria Kaufmann, if I recall correctly—undertook the task of cleaning Einstein's office."

Andrea shared, "That's so hard; sorting through the possessions of a friend after they pass." The others agreed, each mind excavating its own memories.

Etienne then continued solemnly, "Einstein left an office and whiteboard full of his work: equations that lead to nowhere as he attempted to subsume the advances of physics within a new, eloquent equation aiming for a 'unified field theory.'" Etienne clarified, "He'd attempted to do so without the need for quantum theory, which seemed to clash with his theories of relativity in regard to central concepts such as time and probability."

"$E=mc^2$ was so neat. You can see why he was confident," Andrea answered.

"So, he wasn't able to get there?" Peter asked.

"Not by reducing everything down to one theory," Andrea replied.

Peter could imagine Gödel right there, in a cloud of chalk that had once been formulas hanging in the air around him, tickling his throat. So final. Even these equations—white on black—had been so much more:

---

226. Robinson, *Absence of Mind*, 32.

the product of an impassioned genius's search; but there was no choice but to rub them off.

"Did incompleteness make it a fool's errand?" Peter asked them all, curious.

"Unified field theory is still an open line of work," Etienne explained. "Incompleteness doesn't necessarily rule it out, nor a 'theory of everything,' in part because physicists are still debating what such a thing might look like and what scope it would have."

Andrea added, humbly. "Regarding a theory of everything, I am inclined to think the fabric of reality is much greater than one theory can ever do justice to."

§

NOTE: In 2003, at his Dirac Centennial lecture, "Gödel and the End of Physics,"[227] Stephen Hawking, author of *The Theory of Everything*,[228] controversially revealed a significant change in the trajectory of his thought. Gödel's incompleteness theorems had helped convince Hawking that such a goal—at least as he saw it—was impossible. Nevertheless, Hawking saw the positive side, arguing that acknowledging incompleteness wasn't defeatist but inspiring, for it meant that there were many more great discoveries to come.

Hawking, no doubt, was in favor of widening explanations horizontally, on the scientific materialist plane or narrative, and never argued in favor of the existence of God. But once that more generous posture is justified, could a case not also be made for widening the types of explanations that we offer when considering the true fullness of reality in which we find ourselves? Perhaps even vertically, to include the upper narrative? After all, materialistic explanations address causal questions within the created world but offer little to answer different types of questions, such as: Why?[229]

§

As the friends walked towards breakfast, Etienne shared, "The effect of losing Einstein on Gödel, each other's closest friend and confidant, was huge. He spiraled further into isolation and anxiety. Many trying years

227. Hawking, "Gödel and the End of Physics."
228. Hawking, *Theory of Everything*.
229. Lennox, *Can Science Explain Everything?*

later, after his wife—who he alone trusted to prepare his food—was admitted to hospital, he, too, was eventually hospitalized before later dying of starvation."

"What a fascinating life," Peter said just as they arrived. "Both of them," he added.

Andrea agreed, asking Peter, "You've heard Einstein's phrase: 'God does not play dice with the universe?'"

Before Peter could agree, Antonio took the spotlight: "I think Einstein needed to stop telling God what to do with his dice!" The group laughed.

Breakfast looked like porridge made with the milk Amy and Liesel had brought and a couple of other protein-heavy options. Before the little group integrated and Etienne was torn away from them, Andrea made sure to say, "You know, Gödel must have been devastated in losing Einstein and packing away his unfinished work, but I've always thought that he must have been so proud that his brilliant friend tried until the end. And that's all we can do, right? Try?"

Peter passed out glasses filled with wild berry juice.

"To trying!" they said, raising their glasses in a toast, the bright morning light brilliantly bouncing off the edges.

As they did so, Peter caught sight of Jean-Paul staring at them.

Jean-Paul broke his gaze and turned quickly, taking his conversation further into the shadows.

It didn't occur to Peter that Andrea had been desperately trying to encourage Etienne. She knew the honeymoon was over. Honestly, so did Etienne.

The meeting after breakfast exposed the cracks in the community, many of which extended far deeper, finding their origin in human hearts. The same fears and worries that they had borne before in their old lives now seemed transplanted there, like a virus. Etienne had suddenly become "just like" someone's awful uncle, hated mayor, or even despised head of state.

This was the community that was going to change the world? Peter did speak up but not as much as he later wished he had.

29

WW2

Trouble & Tuberculosis

LES VOSGES III

Wednesday, October 6th, 1943.

They entered the town of Grand in the early morning, hungry, met by walls plastered with the faces of *Résistance* fighters: those either wanted or soon to be executed. Henry had seen some of these posters before that first night in the *Résistance* hideout in the Vosges, displayed boldly in solidarity with their kin and as a sign that it was working: they were getting to the Nazis. It was, however, another thing to see these posters in the wild, on the street—the very same streets upon which the enemy was walking. "You can't let it get to you," Violet whispered to Henry. "That's suicide."

Henry saw another warning about reprisals—where any resistance activity would be met by the death of innocent local people. *What a vicious, charged situation*, he thought. In one sense, it made one question what to do. However, in another, what could he do but keep moving forward and following orders?

Violet immediately recognized many of the older generation. But the young and able-bodied men that she had known in her youth were emptied out, gutted from its streets, mobilized either by the French, or later, by the Germans. This meant that it would be suspicious for Violet to be accompanied by two men in their prime. Henry at least had an alibi: his missing hand. But that also made him stand out. Bearing this in mind, Matthias opted to put his Vichy uniform back on. This was a rare sight in the north, especially in such ceremonial dress, but Matthias couldn't pass for a German. Plus, leaning into who he really was—a Parisian bureaucrat—was easy. Truth, the best cover of all.

The local population was suffering. Anything good was shipped out, the status quo for years now. After a final check that she had all the leaf litter out from her hair, Violet joined the early morning lineup at the *boulangerie*. She came supplied with a ration book. However, just because you could claim food or supplies didn't mean it was available.

As she waited, the men stayed close enough to watch at a distance, while still spreading out their unfamiliar faces. Before they parted ways, Henry rebuked Matthias, "Stick your chest out, look proud! It's still your homeland." Matthias did not appreciate being educated on what to do by this green SOE officer. Henry continued, "If the *Boche* greets you, you've got to look happy—you're on the same team for goodness's sake!"

"I see them every day," Matthias snapped.

They parted. The crisp morning didn't hide anything, unlike moist, humid, foggy days. They couldn't argue here.

Blown and damp, a page ripped from *L'Illustration* flew onto Matthias's polished boot. Though faded, it was clearly a chocolate advertisement with a smiling Aryan child proclaiming her loyalty to Pétain's new "moral" order. He hated it. He hated all of it, wishing to crumple it up with what strength he had left, wishing it all into oblivion. But eyes were everywhere. He stoically walked it to a *poubelle* not far from the café.

The baker knew Violet from the fading dream of her teenage years, though she still had to slip past a hovering guard: a gossiping pack of aging ladies. The bakery was clean but cold. It hadn't been heated all winter, the family relying on the residual oven heat to keep them warm upstairs.

The small baker with white, wispy hair had seen her as soon as she walked in, stifling a smile. Good news was rare, and seeing her alive after all this time and all this change was certainly that. She was mindful to keep her head down as if she had lost her inner fight. After a considerable wait, it was her turn. The baker was considerably thinner than she remembered. He slipped her some extra bread while acting as if he wasn't overly fond of her. It wasn't the first time she had called in this favor, but he knew she was worth investing into.

The pack of women started talking, piquing the interest of a nearby officer. Matthias and Henry could only watch helplessly as the officer started to follow Violet across the square. Surely he couldn't have guessed? Individually, they picked up their pace as much as possible without looking suspicious, Henry stopping to look at the meager offering of vegetables and Matthias a café menu. That was Matthias's mistake. Every morning without fail, the higher echelons of the Nazi operation in the area gathered to begin the day over a civilized cup of coffee. "*Heil Hitler*," an almost angel-faced young officer said, greeting Matthias.

Why is this so hard? He said good morning to Nazis all the time. "*Heil Hitler*," Matthias replied, switching on his charm and allowing his right arm to fly to the correct angle. It felt so jarring to click back into doing this. But he had it down. In the beginning he'd crafted a sparkling, accompanying veneer while he hid his embittered internal world. Then they shot his wife, leaving her face-down in the fountain. This veneer morphed into an impenetrable shield-like persona that he held out right in front of him, giving extra room for a whole other person to be forged by the currents of the raging river within. He smiled at the young man, wondering if he was really old enough to wear the uniform.

The young German officer continued to share pleasantries. Upon learning of his role at the Vichy Ministry of Culture, they quickly moved onto German culture. "Bayreuth? Was the Ring Cycle as magical as they say?" the officer asked, quizzing Matthias out of curiosity rather than suspicion. This caught him a little off-guard but made sense: the officer had been commissioned to break up meetings late at night or pull women off bikes as they passed notes from place to place. Alone, Matthias was an anomaly but not a worry: *Résistance* fighters wouldn't have access to such a clean Vichy-emblazoned uniform, let alone the audacity to pull it off.

Seeing Matthias caught up in conversation, Henry was solo in following Violet and the officer. He could tell she was scared, even if she hid it well.

The young Nazi officer at the café saw Matthias divert his gaze to the street. He saw Violet, bread cradled in towards her body, crossing the road. "You like the look of her?" the officer asked Matthias, with a smile.

They couldn't afford slip ups; he was angry at himself for drawing suspicion. "No, no."

"Well, there are many lonely women here," he said looking at the breadline and butcher shop. "You can afford to be picky."

His heart gripped him: fear, sadness, longing, all in one. This was what France had become. Matthias knew that Violet was beautiful. He had known that for as long as he had known her, back to those long evenings as couples, together, at the beginning of the occupation of Paris and in the basement of the Musée de l'Homme. He was protective of her, absolutely.

If honest, like so many others, he had also been jealous of her husband, while the women all seemed jealous of her. As a couple, Violet and Jérôme had seemed untouchable, perfect. Yet the war ripped them apart, one stuck in life and the other in death. Matthias told himself he loved her like a sister, protecting her. He didn't like how Henry looked at her; but, more pressingly, he was afraid that the German officer following her was thinking what he thought he was thinking. At least Henry was getting close. It killed him to watch while talking pleasantries.

"*Mein Herr*, are these your matches?" Henry called down into the small alleyway, at a loss for what to say. As he approached, he could see the officer saying something to Violet, having cornered her in a section usually frequented just by skinny cats and hanging laundry.

"What a beautiful necklace," Henry overheard the officer say as he got closer.

"Are these yours?" Henry asked again, interrupting. The officer finally turned around. He checked his pocket.

"*Nein*, I have mine," he said, trying to shoo Henry away.

"Sister," Henry said, having come upon them. Henry made sure that the officer could see that he only had one hand, so that he wasn't a threat. The officer said something to Violet. *I look awful*, she thought, after all the camping, and yet he *still* followed her. She was dying inside, embarrassment compounded by fear.

"Tell your sister that the future looks brighter now that our nations are united."

Violet had clearly pushed back any advances, graciously at first and now as overtly as she could without provoking him to turn on her in anger.

"I could keep this safe for you?" the officer said, holding the locket that Henry had given her. "There are those who would covet this."

"Suit yourself," he replied when she kindly declined.

Violet was shaking inside. So was Henry.

"I'm not a monster," the officer said as he turned, releasing her. "But I could do with some matches," he said, snatching them from Henry and cutting his losses. What a relief to still have the microfilm safe. It was worth much more than one of them, considering they were expected to put their lives on the line to protect it.

It was torture for Matthias to walk stoically past the officers after parting with another obligatory *"Heil Hitler,"* eager to find out what was happening.

The blessed relief of seeing the other officer emerge from the alleyway and then Henry and Violet safely together was short lived. After the officer who had followed Violet went back to the café, there was some animated talking. It piqued the interest of a senior officer. He'd just heard about a woman and two men (one with only one hand) who had been seen suspiciously close to one of Natzweiler-Struthof's satellite camps.

Violet and Henry had a head start out of town, while Matthias went a different way to avoid them being seen together. They didn't yet seem to know that Matthias was with them. The plan was to meet back at the amphitheater or, failing that, a farm she knew that supported the *Résistance*.

Upon being given the order, two of the Nazi officers jumped on motorcycles parked right outside the café. Given that they were nowhere near any front lines, these were just a couple of old BMW R11s, but they still instilled fear. The second Matthias saw the motorcycles, he knew Violet and Matthias had no chance. They didn't even make it out of the village.

Matthias slipped into in a nearby house. Watching the two of them being forced into a van was bloodcurdling. They acted shocked and claimed innocence, but their protest did nothing. *Did the Nazis really know who they were? Or was the officer that had talked to Violet just trying to take advantage of the situation?* Whatever the motivation, it wasn't good.

Matthias crouched behind the house's front window. *What to do? What to do?* Until now, Violet had taken the lead. But in this moment, it all hinged on him and his element of surprise. Henry was meant to be meeting Ophélie in Paris in just a few days' time. *What would happen if no one were there to meet her? Who would die? How many?* That was above his pay grade. Not that any of this was about money.

Henry and Violet sat silently on the wooden benches of a modified, dark-green Opel Blitz, accompanied by a guard. Even there, they could hear the café phones ringing, officers eager to ask for further direction regarding the reinforcements that had been requested. For, if they were right about the two of them, they knew there could be at least one more *Résistant* somewhere, perhaps many more.

Matthias scanned every detail of the truck with his eyes, calculating. Removing his gaze for just a second, he was confronted by a picture in a frame; almost everything else of worth had been stolen, likely by a neighbor. At first Matthias saw the man in the kepi hat staring back at him. *How did I get here?* Then his eyes adjusted, reminding him why he was here. "I wonder what's happened to you?" Matthias whispered, as he looked at the beautiful family staring back at him—a father surrounded by his wife and small children. He could have been mobilized early and was still stuck somewhere. Or perhaps he was called upon to work in factories in Germany, making planes or ammunition? Perhaps he was Jewish. As he swallowed, he felt the tightness of his shirt collar.

The crowd dispersed around the green truck as quickly as it had gathered for fear of showing too much sympathy and becoming embroiled with suspicion. Then Matthias saw his chance. For a split second, no one was guarding the outside; the driver had set down his gun and gone to talk to his superiors. Matthias took a deep breath and ran for it, darting out of the door, across the cobbles and right into the driver's seat. That was part one. He claimed the gun on the passenger seat, for they had left theirs in the amphitheater. Now he had to use it.

He jumped out, hidden between the metal vehicle and stone shop facades, mercifully covered in newspaper. He felt the trigger. *Can I?*

Inside the truck, the guard seemed unnerved by the stillness with which Violet and Henry sat, as if they'd already made peace with what awaited them. She coughed. She noticed that the guard sat opposite her moved way when she did that. Instinctively, she dared to try something. Hands in chains but spirit alive—a wild, unbroken pony, as Jérôme had affectionately called her—she started coughing harder. The guard shuffled over again. Then, with all the gumption she could muster, shielding her face, she bit down on her tongue.

Outside, Matthias double-checked that the gun was loaded. He slowed his breath, knowing that at any time the backup would come and he too would be arrested.

With her next round of coughs, Violet bit her tongue and launched blood right at him. It perfectly flung into his eye. Fearing it was tuberculosis, the officer threw the door open. Matthias jumped back, having expected to be the one opening the door.

The officer immediately saw Matthias's gun. His eyes widened. It silenced him. He raised his hands. It was the same young officer that he had talked to earlier.

The air bristled, charged. Matthias waved him into the back of the truck, and Violet and Henry out, indicating that he was going to use the gun if he made a sound. The young Nazi officer didn't dare swallow. Neither did Matthias, though cool and collected on the outside. His hand shook as he bolted the door from the exterior, his body shot through with adrenaline.

Immediately, Matthias was hit with regret. It was foolish, perhaps, to keep the officer alive. He recalled their earlier conversation about culture. His cover was blown. But he couldn't freeze up now. "This way," he directed Henry and Violet with a lump in his throat.

30

Peter

The Human Face

LES VOSGES III

Sunday, March 13th, 1994.

The great chilling yawn of winter had come and gone for the community, gaping wide to expose both the best and worst of humanity. Some had celebrated Hanukkah, others Christmas. Many embraced the winter solstice and the promise of days getting longer, while all had rejoiced at seeing the first hints of spring in one way or another.

Young boys and girls had stopped coming home after long expeditions in the bush, soaked through from shaking down upon each other the resting snow that had perched, tantalizingly, upon the tree branches. Instead, they came with mud liberally flicked up behind their backs and twisted ankles from the fresh thrill of running over almost iceless paths.

Since that day reading the letter in the garden, Bernard had been distant, when present at all. Etienne said it was typical for Bernie in the winter season. That didn't satisfy Peter. He couldn't handle how they were so close one minute and so distant the next. He must have hit a nerve. Confused and frustrated at being so oblivious, he had tried over and over through the winter season to connect, rethinking the end of their conversation. This had lasted too long.

Peter walked, resolute, to Bernard's cabin. Bernie was an obsessive tinkerer. He always had a part, something he could retrofit to make his vision work. Now that it was spring, the next project was under construction, extending from the cabin deck to the grass beyond. Peter had seen it growing over the last weeks. Whatever it was going to turn into, he was impressed. Perhaps they could talk about that. He weaved his way through the pieces on the way to the door with the fox trailing behind him. Then he saw some goodies. *Perfect.* "Bernie," he shouted in, "there are some cookies out here on the deck for you!"

"Do bring them in, Peter. Thank you," he replied from the halo under his reading light. The rest of his room was dense and dark but bristling with the passions of generations: books everywhere, the obsessions of lives. "Come join me," Bernard added. Peter was relieved at the invitation. He had dwelt here often in the early days of the community, but not in the last months, and had truly missed it.

Trying to hide the softness with which he tentatively stepped, Peter offered Bernard a cookie from the plate. Peter then balanced it on a stack of papers between them while Bernard's pipe smoked, perched loosely between his lips.

The fox had been into Bernard's cabin many times when just a kit but for some reason now took particular exception to the armadillo on its perch above the sink. It shocked him. He raised his hackles. "It's okay, boy. You know Horrice," Peter reassured him, pulling him upon his lap on the free armchair opposite Bernard.

"What's the story of that little guy?" Peter asked regarding Horrice, taking Bernard's lead to act as if nothing had happened when he knew something had—just not exactly what.

"Ah, that's a story for another time." Bernard paused, patting down his wild beard to seem a little more put together. "Enough small talk. Why don't you tell me what you've been working on recently? Did you ever finish reading that book about the crisis in the foundations of mathematics?"

"I'm reading it over again. I know, I know. It's my emotional support!" he said, poking fun at himself.

"Well, you have this little guy now," Benard said, pointing with the pipe's flattened end towards the fox.

"Can you believe he's almost six months?" Peter wasn't quite sure if he would be able to release him or what that looked like. He wasn't ready to think about it, though the thought accosted him daily. They had bonded deeply while he nursed him into a strong, dashing-looking fox with quite a taste for little rodents—one that was really quite naughty.

"You know that beautiful oak door I made with Antonio and the others last week?" Peter asked.

"Aye," Bernard replied.

"He already scratched it!"

"It's like what young mothers say, you're making memories, Peter! Besides, you don't want to kill the wild in him."

Peter smiled, scratching the little fox behind the ears. He was like a dog: if you scratched him in the right place, you could make his leg twitch. "I did finish the letter, though," Peter said, realizing as he said it that this victory sounded mighty small. However, whether motivated by guilt or passion, he still couldn't help but think over and over about every last sentence Edwin had written.

"And what conclusion did you come to?"

"That anchoring the foundations of mathematics is just one piece of the puzzle in anchoring humanity."

"Oh, so your friend *did* disrupt your circle!" Bernard joked, as if Peter had been Archimedes with his head in geometric clouds, detached from the brute force of the rest of reality. "You know, Peter, as important as metaphysics and ontology—the study of being—are, they can't be studied in abstraction. If we're talking about anchoring our humanity, that's got to acknowledge our lived, communal attempts. In fact, it's almost impossible to understand the major philosophical movements of the twentieth century without understanding them as embedded within politics."

"Teach me," Peter challenged, eager to see the old Bernard flushed with passion again.

Bernard readied himself: "Well, I've come to think that politics largely relates to different visions of humanity and, by corollary, human flourishing." He paused, "Do you remember how Andrea shut Timo's comment down at Le Dôme?

"About whether there's even such a thing as human flourishing?"

"Right. It's a good question."

"Is there?"

"That's loaded. And, as with anything, it depends largely on how we define it. The idea of flourishing connects back to Aristotle's *eudaimonia*, central to his *Nicomachean Ethics*. He explained it as realizing one's full potential through the cultivation of rationality and moral virtues that align with our nature as human beings. Of course, the presumption of a shared human nature causes problems today," he said leadingly, followed with a puff from his pipe.

"I see."

"On the one hand, I can understand those who argue that some virtues may be culturally dependent and that flourishing may look different for different people. But on the other, I've always been amazed at how connected I feel to other human beings of entirely different backgrounds. Even when we don't share the same conclusions, coping mechanisms, or religion, I find we seem to share the same pains. I've never found someone who can't relate to the pain of exclusion or someone who's lived a full life without the searing pain of loss."

"So, how would you define it?" Peter urged, thrilled that his plan to reanimate his friend seemed to be working.

"Ha! I'm a nobody, Peter. A magpie at best."

"You can't tell me you haven't given it thought."

"Too much, Peter, too much. Some connect human flourishing to autonomy, being free to pursue personal goals, like Robert Nozick, and having the resources to do so. However, I find the most compelling definitions as those that connect—but don't sacrifice—individual flourishing to that of the community. I'm thinking of works like Alasdair MacIntyre's *After Virtue*, where virtues are cultivated through relationships and communal practices, meaning that human flourishing is intertwined with the well-being of the community. Why else do you think I put up with you all?" He smirked.

"Happy to help," Peter joked.

"Assuming that we agree there's some merit to the concept of human flourishing—perhaps a sort of positive growth where we might be more alive and humane to ourselves and others—then I think it's also worth asking whether the world we find ourselves in is even capable of supporting this vision. Or if, despite our grand notions, we're doomed to being endlessly frustrated."

"Is the soil good?" Peter offered.

"Yes! That's basically been my life, Peter, a grand experiment asking with exhausting urgency: is this it? Is absurdity and inhumane violence all we can expect? Or can something more beautiful grow?"

"Well, is it?" Peter provoked.

"Peter, I've felt the pulse of each of the major philosophical movements in the twentieth century as they've run their course. I wasn't the only one asking these questions." Bernard paused. He didn't want to offer a trite answer. He started again, clothing his story with honest vulnerability: "The Second World War defined some of my most formative years. I was barely a teen when it ended. Part of me just wanted a quiet life, but the other part knew I was too young to give up yet. I became convinced that I could take my anger and use it positively to change the world somehow."

"Now you're just old and wanting to change the world?" Peter teased.

"Ha!" Bernard said, thankful that Peter had finally taken the kid gloves off. "As you know," Bernard continued, "I still have a strong propensity for the quiet life. But if I'm honest, I'm scared to disconnect entirely, Peter. The moment I do, I might as well be dead."

Peter wasn't used to hearing quite that amount of honesty from someone other than his own mind. "What did you do after the war?" he asked.

"The only thing anyone could: find somewhere safe to plant oneself, *then* figure out what life looked like now. I was thankful to find a job at the Peugeot factory just outside Paris. With a heritage stretching back to Napoleonic times, it couldn't have been more French. I think they made coffee grinders before cars, but during the occupation it had been converted to make munitions and vehicles for the German war effort. They were still reconstructing the factory floor when I got there."

"Wow."

"But what was most disorientating, Peter, was seeing the adults who struggled around me. Almost without exception, the war had visited upon them tragedy. Some hid it better than others, but it leached out of them like sweat, betraying their attempts at stoicism with the scent of moral torture. Some who had worked there during the war began to tell stories of how they had resisted, sabotaging bombs and such. Others stayed quiet. The tension on the factory floor peaked during the Épuration: for fear of the law, or worse, vigilantes. For some people, the end of the war was just the start of another nightmare." Bernard paused, tapping his glass three times as he remembered. "There was this fervor to purify ourselves of collaborators. I remember some men rushing in and dragging out a quiet man. I'd never suspected anything. He was the sort of man who ate dry bread and kept to himself. I still don't know if he was guilty," Bernard trailed off.

"That must have been so scary."

"It was. But you keep going. You have to."

"What helped?"

"I realized that I didn't have a man to look up to in my life. My heart needed that. I found what approximated one in Benoît. He was all that was left of his natural family. He wasn't emotionally available but was willing to carve out a little space in his life for me if I was willing to tag along. Before the war, like Sartre, Benoît had been to the École normale supérieure. Here he was, a literal genius working at a car factory. But he was also Jewish." Bernard froze for a moment. Peter couldn't make out what his eyes were looking at, as if they focused on something unseen before him. Bernard continued, "I think that after the war he was afraid to stick out. Seeing people you'd trusted turn on you, betray and attempt to kill you . . . you struggle to trust again."

"Absolutely," Peter acknowledged softly, not deeming himself worthy to come alongside these weighty memories.

"It was Benoît who showed how me how ideas have consequences: that philosophy can be a tool to help us excavate truth, but it can also inadvertently help us dig ourselves into treacherously deep holes."

"Noted," Peter said.

"I was there, Peter, at Sartre's 'Existentialism is a Humanism' lecture. Benoît told me that I had to go, that it was history in the making. He wasn't wrong. We were there among the crowds, and, according to the papers, Lawrence of Arabia—not that I saw him. Over the years, I've come to think it was ironic: that Sartre was saying there was nothing in the world to orientate us, and yet all of Paris seemed to cling onto him for dear life, as if a wise sage had come to deliver us from our purgatory. I think people found it helpful: how he said that in many instances there wasn't a right answer, like going to war or staying home to help with an ailing parent. But we had to live with whatever we chose."

"Huh," Peter said. "What did you learn?"

"The next decades were full of hard lessons and hope returning void. Of course, the trade union at the factory leaned politically left, just like Sartre and the bulk of the intelligentsia at that time. Sartre even tried to marry his brand of existentialism with Marxism. Etienne shared with you about Camus's frustration with all this, right?"

Peter replied, "How he thought it hypocritical that they'd ignored the damning reports of gulags when they'd just fought against the evil epitomized by the concentration camps?"

"Exactly," Bernard replied. "Camus was rightly livid. Those next years and decades felt especially politically charged. We watched the world change and tried to change our corner of it the best we could. The big change was the growth of the Soviet Union. But then the growing pains came. Like Sartre, most of us were in denial. There were some other lone voices, however, like Raymond Aron—"

"—the apricot cocktails guy?"

"The one and only. Aron certainly poked a bear when he bounced Marx's condemnation of religion right back at the Parisian Marxists by calling it the 'opium of the intellectual.' But the honeymoon didn't last forever. The first disenchanting shock was the USSR's invasion of Hungary in 1956. We all felt the sting of that. I remember someone running into the factory, sheet-white and livid, holding up the front page of the newspaper for us all to see."

"You must have been at the factory for quite a while?"

"On and off," Bernard replied mysteriously. He continued, "While Sartre was never officially a French Communist Party member, for a time he was one of the best-known advocates for Communism in France. He and de Beauvoir even visited Cuba in early 1960, meeting both Fidel Castro and Che Guevara there. He wrote admiring articles under the series title 'Hurricane over Sugar.' He publicly condemned the invasion of Hungary in 1956 'wholeheartedly and without any reservation.' But he didn't really part ways for over a decade."

"Then what made that happen?"

"In 1968, the USSR brutally suppressed Czechoslovakia's 'Prague Spring.' Under Brezhnev's leadership, the Soviet Union effectively rolled tanks over Alexander Dubcek's attempt at reform: 'Communism with a human face.' I find it almost too fitting of an analogy for the sacrifice of humanity to the enforcement of an ideal."

"So, Camus was vindicated?"

"You don't want to be right about predicting bloodshed," Bernard said. "Besides," he added solemnly, "Camus didn't live long enough to see it. He was killed in a tragic, meaningless, ultimately absurd car crash in 1960. But yes, Peter, I think so. Essentially, as I'm sure you remember, Camus argued that—in the name of perfecting naked, revolutionary ideas—living, breathing, enfleshed humanity is sacrificed."

"He urged moderation, right?"

"Right. He thought that if we're human we're going to rebel. But the issue is the lack of any moderation of revolutionary fervor. How do we keep it humane and not become the new oppressors—the very thing we despise?"

"Such an important question," Peter agreed.

"Over the years, I saw those around me struggle to find the perfect movement to align with. The existentialists I knew tended to follow Sartre's lead towards Marxism. Dare I say it, I had a fair few Maoist friends for a while! But as the years wore on, more and more friends moved towards neo-Marxism, which widened the concern of Marxism, class oppression, to recognize other forms of oppression; and to explicitly call all people, not just workers, to actively transform society. Neo-Marxism has proven central to many justice movements this century. Though, I don't think it is the only foundation to fight for these causes. Regardless, they were particularly central to the May '68 protests in Paris."

"Don't you Parisians protest against everything?"

"Ha. But this was one of those 'once in a generation' moments. Between us workers and students, we brought Paris to a standstill and almost toppled the government." As he said that, he vividly remembered the surreal yet satisfying feel of pulling up cobbled streets, literally enacting the slogan "*Sous les pavés, la plage*" ("Under the paving stones, the beach"). Less satisfying was the force of the water cannon that followed, ploughing him and others off their feet. "I remember turning the corner one day to see Sartre standing on a soapbox. A few workers paid attention, but it seemed as if Paris had moved on. It really moved me. I think it taught me how ideas had their own seasons and how I needed to be as agile as I could with being able to see, the best I could, what motivated them and where they were going."

"So neo-Marxism became really important?"

"Right! Their insights are compelling! Like the urgency of escaping the "spectacle of society"—Guy Debord and all that—that attempts to lull us to sleep. But there were also other radical political currents jostling for attention at that time."

"The most important?"

"Without doubt, postmodernism."

"What does that *actually* mean? I've heard it enough," Peter asked.

"Ah, well, that's hard to nail down with something that slippery—"

"Fantastic," Peter joked.

"—but," Bernard conceded, "in *The Postmodern Condition*, Jean-François Lyotard famously explained it as an 'incredulity toward metanarratives,' those big, all-encompassing, and oversimplifying stories that modernity loved. Beyond that, the best way to explore this constellation of thinkers might be to start with context."[230]

"Let me guess . . . France?"

"Indubitably. Paris was not just the stage but the crucible. Given the postmodern rejection of the fixity of labels, few thinkers really embrace the term, but we're basically talking about philosophers like Lyotard and Baudrillard. However, my favorite thinkers who engage at least some core postmodern themes are, without doubt, Michel Foucault and Gilles Deleuze."

"It was one of those movements that brewed for a long time before hitting center stage. It turns out that while Benoît and I, along with the rest of Paris, were enamored by Sartre, there were some that already deplored it as not being radical enough."

"Oh?"

"Foucault and Deleuze, for example, were not much older than me: nineteen and twenty at the time of Sartre's lecture. They weren't disappointed by his lecture because they agreed with the classical Christian Thomistic position of essence preceding existence, but because they thought that Sartre hadn't gone far enough."

"Why?" Peter asked.

"Because they observed that issues of identity had animated the war, particularly fascism. Therefore, these thinkers and those like them flew in completely the other direction, ostensibly rejecting the obsession over identity: or analogously, the form of the human face."

"They have a point," Peter said.

"Indeed. Sartre had been Deleuze's philosophical hero—knowing *Being and Nothingness* by heart—but found, in his words, their 'master rummaging around in the garbage can where we had thrown this worn out idiocy, stinking with the sweat of the interior life—humanism.'[231] Even a self-creating humanism was thought to condemn humanity to repeat the past since the idea of fixed identity had been so explosive during the war."

Peter started writing down these core ideas as quickly as he could while his mind sparked, afraid of losing track.

"I remember it vividly," Bernard shared. "Like Deleuze, Foucault saw 'postwar society as turning its youth into subjects who would continue

---

230. Lyotard, *Postmodern Condition*, XXIV.

231. Dosse, *Gilles Deleuze/Félix Guattari*, 118, 120; Gutting, *Thinking the Impossible*, 18.

the sordid history that had produced war.'[232] Instead, Foucault argued that the majority of French youth "wanted a world and a society that were not only different but that would be an alternate version of ourselves... completely other in a completely different world.'"[233]

Peter conjectured, "Different from a society that had collaborated with Nazism?"

"Without doubt."

"They had a point! So how?'"

"Foucault argued for 'experiences in which the subject might be able to dissociate from itself, sever the relation with itself, lose its [received] identity.'"[234]

"He's not messing around."

"Indeed." Bernard added, "Now catch this: like Sartre's existentialism, postmodernism values self-creation, meaning that they superficially sound like similar projects. But they are not."

"For example?"

Bernard dug around to find his Foucault books.

Peter offered, "Sartre said that 'in life, man commits himself and draws his own portrait, outside of which there is nothing,'[235] right?"

"Right! Likewise," Bernard shared, now having found what he was looking for, "Foucault said that 'we have to create ourselves as works of art.'[236] Blink and you miss it, right?'"

"Sure," Peter affirmed.

"But herein lies the difference. The existential responsibility to self-create almost gives way to an urgency in Foucault to acknowledge the historically contingent elements of human identity, deconstruct, and rewrite them."

"So, more excavation?"

"Right. Inspired by Nietzsche, Foucault called it genealogy. This was compelling because it meant that something different could be built. Even our understanding of humankind is seen as historically contingent, built upon all these twists and turns of history. Foucault's famous quote

232. Gutting, *Thinking the Impossible*, 34.

233. Gutting, *Thinking the Impossible*, 33; Foucault, "Interview with Michel Foucault," 247–8.

234. Foucault, "Interview with Michel Foucault," 248.

235. Gutting, *Thinking the Impossible*, 34; Sartre, *Existentialism Is a Humanism*, 37.

236. Gutting, *Thinking the Impossible*, 72; Foucault, "On the Genealogy of Ethics," 262.

is from the end of *Les Mots et les Choses*: "Man is an invention of recent date. And one perhaps nearing its end. If those arrangements were to disappear as they appeared . . . then one can certainly wager that man would be erased, like a face drawn in sand at the edge of the sea."[237]

"I see," Peter said. "But you don't sound convinced?"

"Not by postmodernism; not anymore. I still think the importance of understanding dynamics related to identity is right on. But I think this approach makes presumptions about reality which undermines it."

"Like what?"

"About what being is, the technical term being 'ontology.' This is, perhaps, easiest to explain . . . No, that's a lie. It is most *fun* for me to explain by pointing back to the Greeks, as Heidegger might have suggested we do. Despite having but fragments from the pre-Socratic philosophers, there is reason to believe that even then, there were distinct paradigms for conceptualizing being. The most significant are those associated with Parmenides and Heraclitus."

"Parma ham and Hercules?" Peter joked, embarrassing himself with surprising ease. Bernard looked pained. Peter showed Bernard his notes to show to prove he *was* taking it seriously—just in case he had any doubts.

"Now, Parmenides," Bernard continued, "is associated with seeing identity as complete, fixed, and rigid. Conversely, Heraclitus is oft considered the philosopher of flux. For thinkers associated with postmodernism, like Foucault, and even those who influenced them like Nietzsche, there's arguably been a tendency to see the being akin to Heraclitus: as tumultuous, like a churning sea. With this ontological paradigm, there's no objective meaning to find in the world. Identities are not fixed but might be violently renegotiated through power and cultural forces. Ultimately, as a worldview, postmodernism can encourage us to fight to do our best in a hostile world, perhaps even overcome restrictions nature placed upon us—even attempting to foil death by prolonging life using science and technology! But at base, there's no reason to *expect* human flourishing or agree on what it means."

"I see that; living longer is different than living better."

"Indeed. Now, I think a real strength of postmodernism was its perception of the damage that the Enlightenment vision of progress had on human life. However, it responds by flying in the opposite direction

237. Foucault, *Order of Things*, 422.

and throwing out the concept of objective truth and received identity altogether. Truth is given over to be picked clean."

"And in its place?" Peter asked.

"Values."

"But which values?" Peter inquired.

"That opens a can of worms. It depends on the vision for humanity we're aiming at. For example, Nietzsche thought that Pauline Christianity had suppressed the development of humanity by prioritizing the weak. He called it a slave morality. Instead, Nietzsche made a bold attempt to go beyond 'good' and 'evil' to establish new values."

"So, he identified new values?"

"He attempted to order values but didn't finish. Now, going beyond good and evil is clearly a seductive idea to fascist movements. For if the sanctity of human life is not a central value, then the ends might justify the means of a different political vision." Bernard continued, "As you probably know, Nietzsche's sister Elisabeth Förster-Nietzsche was quick to portray his work as amenable to the values of the Nazi party, with Joseph Goebbels (the Nazi Minister of Propaganda) selectively drawing themes and images from Nietzsche's work to support his messaging. This appropriation is undoubtedly a distortion of Nietzsche's work, but certain aspects of it lent itself to such a distortion, a misuse he predicted."

"If he predicted it, then surely he bears some responsibility?"

"Perhaps," Bernard replied, sounding distanced. "Ironically, as if repeating a scene from a Dostoyevsky novel, one of his last sane acts was to protect the weak. After seeing a horse being whipped in a square in Turin, he ran and threw his arms around the horse . . . I'm also told that you can see in the Nietzsche Museum in Weimar his last earnest attempts at working on these values. Yet over them, he wrote a shopping list, including a note for a toothbrush. You could absolutely disagree, but I wonder if that's not a sign of a man giving up. Hardly the care afforded to your greatest work." He whispered, "I can't bring myself to visit it, of course."

"Why not?" Peter inquired.

"I'm just a curmudgeonly old man, that's why," he said with a weakened smile. "So, back to Foucault and postmodernism," Bernard restarted at pace. "In three words? Flux, conflict, and insecurity."

"Ah, thank you," Peter said, clearly having touched a nerve.

"What I've seen is that—rather than releasing humanity from the burden and pains of identity formation—this insecurity can make the desire to control and secure identity even more pressing. This induces a critical, pain-saturated coma that spills over as violence against ourselves and others. To continue our analogy, Peter: if the Enlightenment atomized the human face, measuring and objectifying it unto oblivion, then under postmodernism, it is swept away in the sea, or, at the very least, blurred. That's why 'expressive individualism' has grown so readily in this soil,[238] a perpetual readjusting of the proverbial lens to try to find a crisp, authentic image of one's inside world. Some might still find postmodernism and its related ideas liberating, as I once did. But, in my experience, the sweet fruit I was promised tasted bitter."

"But if that's how the world is, you just have to accept it though, right?"

"Right. So, the fundamental question becomes: Is this how the world is? What worldview best aligns with what we know about reality?"

---

238. For this term and context, see Trueman, *Rise and Triumph of the Modern Self*.

31

WW2

Jackboots

LES VOSGES III

Wednesday, October 6th, 1943.

Everything was hanging by a thin, treacherous thread. There was a cluster of bikes Matthias had eyed, but they would be fools to think they could out-cycle the Nazis. Violet had a better idea. They broke a nearby basement window and climbed in. From the window on the opposite side, they could see the back of the *boulangerie* in a quiet alley. While she had been waiting in line, Violet had noticed a truck—well, a converted Citroën B12. It looked ready to head out. And to where? The lettering, at least, said "Paris."

Chaos reigned. They had stirred up a hornets' nest. Given that Henry and Violet had initially tried to run out of town, the Nazis expected that to be where they had now fled—helpful, for now. They kept close watch on the truck until there was some movement. By some small miracle, it hadn't departed. Seizing the opportunity, the three of them darted into the back of the truck, swiftly adjusting the canvas door behind them. It was one of those trucks with the bed made out of wood and sides a meter or so high—the rest was soft, like a tent, but large enough.

It was immediately clear that the truck was picking up the best tastes of France for those commanding the Reich. Cars converted into trucks were more common than you would think, for the Germans only

232

issued fuel to commercial vehicles used in essential services like food production—so a truck was much better than a car. The Nazis were specifically interested in supplying vineyard owners with petrol to secure better-quality wine. This truck had it all: wine, cheese, meat. It must have been destined for leaders. The extravagance of it made them feel sick. All this was destined for the enemies of the land that had produced it. For a second, Violet thought about doing something, perhaps poisoning it. But how could they be sure this wouldn't hurt anyone else? Perhaps the driver or a family spending their last resources for something on the black market for a birthday. Or someone like Oberführer Schultz, invaluable for fighting from the inside. There was too much uncertainty.

Violet would have been even more incensed were it not for the indeterminacy of the next few minutes. Suddenly, their hearts lifted: the driver's door slammed shut. It felt as if a dark cloud lifted from their hearts as the truck moved outside of town. Light filtered through the canvas cover, the dappled patterns changing as they passed tall hedgerows and trees. After that silent jubilation, they stopped just a minute down the road. It was a cattle farm. The smell of the manure and noise were unmistakable. Violet remembered playing with children who once lived there.

As soon as they stopped, there was a rumbling of other vehicles, distant but approaching. Matthias panicked. What would happen to them? Surely the Nazis were searching for them? They would be made an example of. The driver would likely be shot with them.

The truck bed shuddered as the front door opened and slammed again. They held their breath. Then . . . a voice. "Quickly," said the old French driver to someone. Violet was confused. In the front, they heard items being loaded. The truck started up again. They, too, had something to hide. Though it was one thing to hide some extra cheese and quite another, fugitives.

The vehicles moved closer still. There was only one way out. A long country driveway. Henry's heart seized when through the canvas stitches, he saw a Nazi vehicle approaching them. Surely those were the reinforcements, looking for them.

The truck stopped right by them, tilted on the verge. They couldn't believe it. Matthias bit down into his hand to occupy his fear with a different site of pain. They froze in the very back, afraid of just a slight creaking sound betraying them all. It was quiet enough to hear each individual cricket in the long verge grass. They didn't dare shift even a little weight.

Jackboots on gravel. "*Heil Hitler*," the Nazi officer said, having walked to the window.

"*Heil Hitler*," the driver replied.

"Here," the driver said. Perhaps he gave him it all, or just a portion of what he had picked up? Regardless, they had some sort of ongoing understanding. He turned a blind eye—for what? Eggs, dairy, cheese? This officer must not have heard the news yet.

Only when the truck started off again was there any real hope of getting out of Grand alive. Violet rubbed her lips—her hands coming back red: her mouth had started bleeding again. But what was a little blood in comparison to captivity? Hopefully, they were now on their way to Paris. One stolen gun, one Vichy bureaucrat, one Brit, and one Violet—just as brave, smart, and stubborn as she was beautiful.

32

Peter

Beauty & Chaos

LES VOSGES III

Sunday, March 13th, 1994.

"Bernie?" Peter said, leaning over.

"So, sorry. Where was I? I must have zoned out for a second. Don't get old, Peter. If it happens again, give me a good jab in the ribs."

"Here, this'll perk you up a little," Peter said, stretching further to offer him another cookie from the plate; a real feat with the fox snug tight in his lap. Only then did he reply. "We were talking about whether there's good soil: if human flourishing is even possible or if, at base, the reality we experience is simply made from the temporary, fickle folds of a tumultuous sea of being?"

"I really went there, hey!" Bernard chuckled. "Well then, I should tell you that the first person to convincingly suggest otherwise and pull me out of my infatuation with postmodernism was the French Lithuanian philosopher Emmanuel Levinas. While he was an on-ramp to postmodernism for many, he drew me a step back. That's because he was a bit of a paradox." Bernard took a small bite of the cookie before continuing, unaware of the crumbs taking flight. "While Levinas's suspicion of totalizing systems and attention to the limits of individual experience verged on the postmodern, he also argued for an objective, transcendent source of ethics. He was Jewish and had lost close family during the war, though, if I remember correctly, his wife and daughter had been kept safe by Catholic nuns. With Benoît, I heard him speak about ethics as "first philosophy," and the idea of seeing God in the 'face'—or encounter—with another person. That's what made me reconsider the structure of reality."

"Like, if there were two layers?" Peter asked, recalling Bernard's lesson in the garden.

"Right!" Bernard explained, "For Levinas it's almost as if there's a superimposition of the Holy God—just out of reach—behind the human being that one encounters, through whom an ethical demand is issued to love." Seeing Peter's blank stare, he added, "but I'm getting ahead of myself." Bernard jumped backward in thought to start at the beginning. "Of course, Benoît had taught me about Plato and Aristotle."

"As you did for me," Peter said, making clear his thanks.

"But what I hadn't realized was how Plato navigated the tension between the metaphysics of the pre-Socratics, Parmenides and Heraclitus: who sketched a static world and a world in perpetual flux, respectively."

"Plato's the philosopher with the shadows on the back of a cave wall and the more perfect world of forms, right?" Peter asked.

"Yes, his allegory of the cave. Plato opened up the possibility of seeing the world and in a different way, identifying two layers."

"I see," said Peter, slowly.

Bernard continued, "Now, a little later, Plotinus founded Neoplatonism. This modified Platonism to suggest that life overflows, or emanates, as if from a fountain from the top layer of reality to the lower."

"Huh," said Peter.

"So your friend in Amsterdam—"

"—Edwin—"

"—Edwin's Christian thought, as far as I can gather, is that of an Augustinian Neoplatonist."

"If you say so," Peter replied. "So, Christians stole this?"

"Not exactly. Their God intentionally loves and gives of himself to his beloved creation, whereas the emanation from the one that Plotinus envisages is unthinking and unavoidable. But regarding the basic flow of life, I think it's more the case that the Neoplatonists got here first when trying to describe what they found to be true. Which should be a possibility if something is genuinely true about the world."

"Not some cultish secret knowledge," Peter suggested. "So how does this connect to being, seas, and violence?"

"As I said, it was listening to Levinas, who was also a Talmudic interpreter, that first opened my eyes to the possibility—and importance—of both the natural and supernatural, lower and upper, layers of reality and how this offered hope." Bernard continued, "Levinas made it click. It made sense. As I've said, the Enlightenment had atomized the human face. I'd even seen Marxism roll tanks over 'the human face.' Then, postmodernism normalized violence and argued that the concept of the human face is either blurred or worse, dissolves, as if drawn in the sand by the sea. But in Levinas, I saw the presence of God uphold the worth and value of the human being through an encounter with 'the face.' This encounter was a demand for justice, with the dignity and worth of each person underpinned by the Holy God. And that's what my heart was crying out for, Peter: justice!"

"You know what really bothers me, though?" Peter said, "How we're in a world starved of justice in the first place. Why is it that we humans try to create heaven but end up creating hell? Rolling tanks over human faces?"

Bernard appreciated Peter's rawness. "Levinas was the first to convince me that violence wasn't part of the fabric of reality. Instead, in a fallen reality, violence is a distortion. Primarily, it's a distortion of the relational, looking like the reduction or totalization of others. Levinas became a bridge—or gateway—to me thinking more widely. Here I found kin: those obsessed by these very questions, still reeling from the war. I soon became acquainted with the work of the Hungarian philosopher Michael Polanyi. Maybe your friend mentioned him?"

"No, I don't think so," Peter said, revealing that the letter from Edwin was still folded in his jacket pocket, "but I could have missed something." He fished it out. It now had some pretty well-worn creases.

"Stop depreciating yourself, Peter. You'd know if he'd talked about Polanyi. You don't miss much."

"Sorry?" Peter joked.

Bernard explained, "Polanyi thought our aim and miss for heaven came down to just this: how we understand the world and therefore how we define and enforce our goals. He argued that people don't set out to create a dystopia. It happens as they attempt to enforce the road to their vision of Eden. Indeed, humanity can become morally inverted, 'seeking to realize perfection on earth all the more furiously and unreservedly.'[239]

239. Polanyi, paraphrased in Hoinski and Polansky, "Modern Aristotle," 184.

Why? Because 'the whole force of his homeless moral passions' are channeled 'within a purely materialistic framework of purposes.'"[240] Bernard grabbed his pipe and stuffed it with tobacco as if the thoughts this had sparked stoked in him the need to reignite this particular vice.

"In English?" Peter said.

Taking a moment to ensure that the pipe was properly lit, he continued, "I think we humans really struggle to live in the tension of these two layers of reality, especially given that we can't tame and control the upper, supernatural layer."

"You've said we tend to simplify, reduce, and reject?" Peter reminded him gently.

"Exactly," Bernard snuck in right before he took the first full puff. "But with reality reduced down to just the lower layer—rejecting any objective morality anchored in an upper layer—all the effort of a morally inflected ideology like Marxism goes into attempting to force perfection or submission from this world so as to achieve the end vision, in this case, Communism. Ostensibly, the end justifies the means. Never mind that the utopic or complete is always an impossible task." Bernard took a second puff, his exhale clouding them, the fox's black nose starting into overdrive, raised upward to assess the threat. Peter calmed him.

"And two layers is really a solution?" Peter asked.

"Polanyi continued to think so," Bernard replied. "In 1970, just six years before his death, he revisited the question 'why did we destroy Europe?' He still identified the tragic tendency towards moral inversion, concluding that the situation 'is likely to get worse unless we can radically change and re-establish the grounds of human knowledge and thus make sense once more of man's life and of the kind of universe which is our home.'"[241]

"Of course he did; he's clearly a theist. But can that really . . .?" Peter struggled to find the words.

"I don't have all the answers, Peter. But as I've ventured through life, I've found the hypothesis of a supernatural 'ground' of being to be much more worthy of consideration than I'd originally thought. Permit me, Peter, to tell you why?"

Peter nodded, afraid, perhaps to let his tongue loose. At least the fox had settled back, melting onto him. He was light. Peter could feel his

240. Polanyi and Prosch, *Meaning.* 18.
241. Polanyi, "Why Did We Destroy Europe?" 115.

slender, bird-like bones, even though these were covered with considerably more flesh than if he'd stayed in the wild.

"Shortly before we moved here," Bernard started, "I lost a dear conversation partner, an Eastern Orthodox priest, Father Konstantino. He was old, in his late nineties before he finally reposed—that is, passed away. Born in a different century, over his lifetime, he'd seen the death throes of many regimes, so much hell as humanity had tried to save and perfect itself. He was wise. He no longer had the idealism of a young man nor an easily won skepticism. The more I learned of his story, the more I was amazed that he'd not allowed toxic cynicism to foment inside of him. He dripped with grace and understanding. He had one of those Gandalf-like beards that you could lose yourself in. We didn't see eye-to-eye on everything, of course, but I especially appreciated his take on this subject. He thought we needed a deep, double-layered concept of humanity nailed at the very center of our understanding of the world. For him, that had to be built on a person, not just an idea: Jesus. Without humanity at the very center, humans would be sacrificed in the pursuit of the next disincarnated—naked—idea."[242]

"And you agree?" Peter asked.

Bernard skirted the question, "I think it's exactly the sort of thing that Camus was groping for at the end of *The Rebel*. Instead, having rejected Jesus from the start, Camus was stuck idolizing those willing to put their own lives on the line to kill, like the Russian assassins who would give their life in place of the one they took."

"What's wrong with that?"

"To Camus's credit, he finds in their example a thoughtful step towards limiting violence by saying that if you take a life, you must be willing to give your life in exchange. This ensures that life doesn't become expendable for a cause but is weighed with the exact same value as the human who thought there was no other option but to kill. And yet, however neat the calculus of equivalence, it lacks a sustainable way to activate that sort of passion and self-sacrifice for people in everyday life."

"Against the backdrop of everyday violence," Peter reasoned. "And so?"

---

242. Recall Camus's definitions: "Rebellion is, by nature, limited in scope. It is no more than an incoherent pronouncement. Revolution, on the contrary, originates in the realm of ideas . . . revolution is an attempt to shape actions to ideas, to fit the world in a theoretical frame . . . rebellion kills men while revolution destroys both men and principles." Camus, *Rebel*, 106.

"Father Konstantino argued this brought us face-to-face with the paradox—the genius, perhaps—of Jesus. Jesus invites people into a spiritual death even while they live. After this, he preached that we are united into new life, resurrected with Jesus, empowered to live and love differently, breaking old cycles of violence and equipped to weave something altogether holy and new into creation. He suggested that instead of forcing earth to become heaven, heaven is invited to earth. Further, instead of forcing or taking life, heaven offers the gift of life."

"I guess that's one way of answering the question of how to create heaven, not hell, on earth: by literally inviting heaven," Peter said, carelessly wielding the razor edge of these words.

"But what if there's something to it, Peter?" Bernard's eyes narrowed with sincerity.

"You don't believe in God, do you, Bernard?"

"When you're my age, nothing's quite that simple," Bernard admitted, "especially something of that magnitude." Bernard leaned forward with a sudden sparkle in his eyes. "I tell you what hill I *would* die on. We need to hold on to both layers of reality." He raised his hands again, fists clenched like two solid rocks. "We must remember that there is real value in the world. The taste, touch, the sense of it all—this embodied glorious madness—and the invisible currents that infuse meaning and underpin it. If we don't, in our groping for meaning, we strangle our already-reduced world as we try to extract from it new meaning or bend it to our own definition of Eden." Bernard said this with the certitude of a man who'd come through hell and back to finally embrace the possibility of more. "What is it the agnostic novelist and statesman André Malraux said?"

"No idea," Peter replied.

"'An age that no longer finds the meaning of the world in the soul of men finds it in their actions.'[243] Something like that. He's another who saw that the Enlightenment had created this volatile 'groping attitude.'[244] It was just a matter of time before the West—drained of life and crisp like a tinder-box—was lit." Bernard steadied himself. "Another glass?"

The fox twitched his ears in anticipation. The fox knew Bernard kept snacks near the sink and trusted that, as Bernard arose, his needs would also be catered to. Peter realized that this was why the fox had

243. Malraux, *Le Triangle Noir*, 17.
244. Tannery, *Malraux*, 46.

been taking such an issue with the armadillo! Maybe he thought Horrice was going to steal them all? Bernard did better than the usual offering, throwing the fox some offcuts of meat that had been left on the cutting board. These went down rather nicely.

Peter didn't want to challenge Bernard, but he had to. He couldn't understand why this tortured genius entertained the idea of God. "Polanyi, politics and all that aside, why bother thinking of two layers? Isn't there enough mist and intrigue in this visible world? Postmodernism's also about the vibrancy of life, right?"

"It is . . . and honestly that's what initially drew me to it. It was easy to lean into since I was already waist-deep wading in Nietzsche, and the early postmodern thinkers tended to draw upon his work. Nietzsche, after all, had done to me what it does to most young folk. It felt edgy, honest, and dangerous. It whetted my appetite for an unbridled, vibrant life." He smirked. "But when talking about life, the postmodern and Christian visions are very different. Each claim to be optimal and freeing and speak to how desire functions and flows. The results are not always plain to see."

"You know I grew up in a Christian school," Peter protested. "Trust me, there wasn't any life there."

"I don't doubt it," Bernard said.

"And desire? Well, that was anathema!" Peter couldn't help but add.

Bernard responded with grace: "Far be it for me to speak for the Christians, but I learned some fascinating things from Father Konstantino that I can't unlearn. He had a generosity in thought, reading widely. He often quoted to me the mid-twentieth-century Catholic priest and theologian from the Dominican order, Marie-Dominique Chenu."

"Why?"

"To make sure that I knew how grievous it was that all the good, life-giving stuff, the Augustinian sap and the mysticism of pseudo-Denis, had been allowed to leak out of the different expressions of his faith."[245]

Peter tentatively backed down, open to consider what Bernard had to say. *Was there a different rendering?* Embarrassed to realize that he'd lurched forward, Peter sat back and rounded his shoulders, drawing the fox—still blissfully licking his lips—back with him. "Okay. So, postmodernism and this *better* God stuff? They've got two different concepts of life and desire?"

§

245. This summary of Chenu is drawn from Kerr, "Different World," 143.

Gilles Deleuze

"Without doubt. Now, the model par-excellence of the postmodern affirmation of life comes from Deleuze," Bernard explained.

"The young man disappointed with Sartre's lecture?" Peter asked.

"Indeed. Like Foucault, Deleuze reached back to Nietzsche to help establish his ontology—his idea of what being was really like."

"Which was?"

Peter waited patiently as Bernard readied himself to explain. Bernard plucked a handful of books as he would tulips. Despite having just sat down, the inconvenience for Bernard of leaving and returning to his armchair again—each movement punctuated with a groan—was nothing compared to the joy with which Bernard greeted these sincere questions. Of course, properly opening the cover of these dear friends necessitated that their reacquaintance be accompanied by the restoration of his pipe to its rightful perch. *Now* he could launch into what Deleuze's vision of a one-layered, Dionysian world—a passionate Heraclitean clamor—looked like. Muffled, Bernard read, "'A single and same voice for the whole thousand-voices multiple, a single and same Ocean for all the drops, a single clamor of Being for all beings.'"[246]

It does sound intoxicating, Peter thought.

Bernard then explained that while this chaos creates, this creation is ultimately undone by the depth of the sea churning beneath it. What is created will eventually be reabsorbed, like Foucault's face drawn in the sand."

"But this world isn't all chaotic!" Peter protested.

Bernard explained, "Deleuze argued that what we experience as distinct things are, at base, the temporary 'composed chaos' of what is given.'[247] It's been called a chaosmos—"

"From chaos and . . .?"

"Cosmos," Bernard answered.[248] "Now, Peter, this is what really matters: in this ontological vision, all confidence, all joy, rests on life doing

---

246. Deleuze, *Difference and Repetition*, 304.

247. Simpson, *Deleuze and Theology*, 20; Deleuze and Guattari, *What Is Philosophy?*, 204.

248. This term originated in James Joyce's novel, *Finnegans Wake*. Also see Simpson, *Deleuze and Theology*, 20.

what life does. Life alone: 'unknown, resilient, obscure, stubborn life.'[249] Any attempt to curb or order life is thought to betray, kill, or poison it."[250]

"Like modernity?" Peter offered.

"Right, God or modernity. Ultimately, Deleuze argued that 'life does not need to be judged, justified, measured, or redeemed.'"[251]

"Ooo, I hear him. So, what was his solution?" Peter asked.

"Get out from anything that kills or truncates life—any hierarchy— and let life do its thing in all its difference and diversity."

"But then what?"

"In one sense, that's it. For this moving oneness, "difference is behind everything . . . but behind difference there is nothing."[252] There is no other goal aside from allowing life to fly or take flight in the direction of desire; pure expression. There's no grand scheme or design behind it all. To borrow from Antonin Artaud, there are just "crowned anarchies."[253]

"Anarchy?"

"The undermining of hierarchies," Bernard shared.

"Oh right! I forgot it's all connected to politics."

"This sort of inversion sounds good," Bernard warned, "but it's unwieldy and dangerous. A civilization that idolizes movement without telos (a purposeful becoming into), is haunted by the tortured cry of the displaced. Peter, they talk about nomads, but I've sat weeping in the dirt with nomads forced into a foreign land: those who were attuned to each whisper of the wind through the grass-lands, displaced into barren camps as if their movement meant they had no sense of home or its rhythms. In reality, their movement was not anarchic but purposeful and sacred." At sharing this, Bernard found himself besieged with an indignation laced afresh by vivid smells, sounds and compassion from his time south of the Sahara; a time long ago, when he sported a naked chin. Pushing this wave of emotion downward, he approached from another direction: "You appreciate the classics, don't you Peter. It's not wholly unlike how the wild god Dionysus humbles King Pentheus in Euripides's play *The Bacchae*."

"That's a kind way to put it." Peter recalled. "The king's driven mad and then ripped apart in a cultic, joy-infused frenzy by his mother and

---

249. Deleuze and Parnet, *Dialogues II*, 45.

250. Simpson, *Deleuze and Theology*, 13. See, for example, Deleuze, *Nietzsche and Philosophy*, 13, 16, 100.

251. Simpson, *Deleuze and Theology*, 13.

252. Deleuze, *Difference and Repetition*, 57, 266–67.

253. Simpson, *Deleuze*, 17; Deleuze, *Difference and Repetition*, 37, 41, 278, 304.

the rest of Dionysus' followers." *Wow*, that gave Peter flashbacks to performing the play in classics class. It still gave him chills. *Whatever happened to being tree number three?*

Bernard skipped back, "Some have called Deleuze's philosophy a 'cult of affirmation and joy.'"[254]

"Then, what does Deleuze mean by joy?" Peter asked.

"Complete power, complete bliss; the immanent affirmation of being, raw creative power. The freedom to take flight in any direction of desire is itself joy, right there in that action. But Peter, if you ask me, however majestic this vision, it's not all it's cracked up to be."

"Then what do you think joy is?" Peter asked.

"Defining joy? That's a hard one."

"But you must have tried!" Peter pushed. "Otherwise, what good are all these books?"

"Ha!" Bernard said, as he quickly chose his bearing. "I'm not as optimistic as Deleuze in thinking that any trajectory set by desire—any expression—*is* joy. I've entrapped myself, hitting too many dead ends that way. It left me dry and desperate for something real. While creative activity is key to who we are, there's also joy in waiting and receiving." Bernard paused, filtering his many thoughts: "I now think joy needs to be found or founded in some way."

"Founded on what?" Peter asked, having noticed the connection between founding and grounding immediately.

"Well, what do you think?" Bernard said, turning the question back toward him.

"A discovery or reception of something?" As the words left his mouth, Peter felt foolish. He'd tried not to dwell on all that gift nonsense. Now he feared that by pushing it down he'd only driven it deeper inside of himself.

"I'm inclined to agree," Bernard replied.

Peter was surprised. *Clearly Bernard was flirting with theism. But this?*

Bernard felt the need to explain himself. "Can joy not be the response to the fulfillment of a desire? Like finally seeing a flower bloom? I take real joy in that."

"And so you should!" Peter encouraged.

254. Simpson, *Deleuze*, 46; Deleuze, *Pure Immanence*, 84.

With an additional uptick in passion, Bernard added, "Peter, doesn't that spark joy? Seeing life flourish? And there's still a place for thinking desire in this theistic vision, perhaps even centrally so if God is Love."

Wow, that was explicit, Peter thought. "How so?"

"Peter, I don't just see chaos. I see absurdity in life's tortured dimensions but also order and regularity where life flourishes."

"A rhythm and a trajectory to life?"

"Right. Not just local and temporary rhythms but also on a grand scale," Bernard said. "Does not the sun shine forth its rays? Does not water run down the slope? Do not the seasons cycle? Peter, the sap of life is powerful, but it only flows one way, just like the blood in your veins."

"So where does that leave us?" Peter inquired.

"For Deleuze, all transcendence—any consideration of an upper layer—is seen as dangerous and antithetical to life: it's ultimately a 'failure to think of immanence.'[255] He claims all transcendence 'arrests' and artificially 'orders the movement of immanence.'"[256]

"And you're saying transcendence is *not* the enemy of life?" Peter interjected, seeking clarity.

"Peter, I think there's a sense in which our life depends on it."

"Prove it." Peter caught himself. "Sorry, Bernie. I mean, I get you love the created world, but how do you get from plant sap to Augustinian sap, or whatever? I still don't see why you bother keeping the case for God open!"

"Maybe I'm too much of a romantic, but the strongest case for me was, and remains, beauty. While Levinas's ethics provoked me to reconsider a source of goodness and truth, speaking to my desire for justice, beauty has always whispered potently, satiating a different dimension of desire. Peter, beauty is the reason I keep the door cracked open; beauty provokes connection and response."

Beauty? This word didn't carry the depth of meaning for Peter that it did for Bernard.

"Peter, is it not the beauty found in witnessing or experiencing flourishing that elicits joy? Not just flowers but in all of life. Beauty can be fragile, evoking awe, but it can also be powerful and essential. The natural world teems with life, in all its texture and dimension. In it all, I

255. Simpson, *Deleuze and Theology*, 18; Deleuze and Guattari, *What Is Philosophy?*, 47, 59.

256. Simpson, *Deleuze and Theology*, 18; Deleuze and Guattari, *What Is Philosophy?*, 47, 59.

hear harmony. Life *is* beautiful in its difference and divergence but it's not a chaotic mass, a tangled rhizomatic cacophony that decomposes without form, purpose, and direction. Instead, the beauty of this world points like a fully nourished, filled out, orchestral symphony beyond itself, as a sign and symbol. It takes us somewhere. It testifies to more. To a source, where in seeing the beautiful as good, truth is also unveiled."

Peter struggled against his resistance to consider this fairly. *Was this really evidence?* The talk of rhizomes did make him think of the ginger he'd buy semi-regularly with the best intentions of recreating the comfort of Nana's Jamaican food. Inevitably, he'd find it months later, half-spouted—both leathery and liquid—sitting in a dingy brown-grey sludge. He always felt guilty. It had hoped to flourish but was not planted nor delighted in. Its promise and exuberance had come to nothing, just decomposition. Expression alone, frightfully fizzling out. *Is that us, if not planted or rooted properly?*

Bernard warned, "We're invited to respond to the symphony, Peter. But beauty is not to be owned, captured, or engorged upon so that we become fat and lazy, frozen as we take beauty for granted. Instead, to hear or partake in the riches of beauty invites us to move deeper, to come alive. Perhaps even take a seat and join the orchestra."

"No offence, Bernie, but I've missed you these last months. You hardly seem fully alive." *Or stable,* Peter thought.

"Ha! The orchestra's better off without me, Peter." Bernard sought for the right words: "Don't judge any of this on me. I follow the music just far enough to feel the mist of the land bead upon my face."

"Why not plunge into the waterfalls or deep wells or whatever?"

"I'm scared of water," Bernard said sarcastically. "I must have drowned in another life."

Peter couldn't see behind the curtain of these words, no matter how obviously flimsy they were. This irked him, but since they'd only just reconnected, Peter didn't want to press further. He shifted his critique: "Deleuze seems like a genius. If what you're saying has merit—and it seems intuitive enough—why would Deleuze have dismissed *all* transcendence? Why wouldn't he have seen or appreciated this?"

§

La Nouvelle Théologie

"In his defense," Bernard replied, "the stronger counterpoints—the positive sketches of transcendence in France—were being actively suppressed in his formative years."

"Really? By whom?"

"For a time, the Catholic church rejected the French, predominantly Jesuit movement, *La Nouvelle Théologie*. This movement included thinkers like Chenu and the formidable Henri de Lubac," Bernard added.

"The new theology?"

"The name gives you a clue about what they initially thought about it."

"Oh, I see," Peter smirked.

"The irony is that, each in their own way, the *Nouvelle* theologians attempted an intentional recovery or *ressourcement* of the old riches of the Christian tradition, especially from the early church fathers. Father Konstantino loved this stuff, seeing in it hope for the reconvergence of the major streams of the faith. The hope was that by reinfusing Christianity with its 'Augustinian sap,' it might fulfill its potential as a viable alternative to secular humanism, able to shift culture.[257] Common to their projects was a compelling case for transcendence or an upper—grace-saturated—supernatural layer to life."

"The source of the symphony," Peter reasoned. "But you said their teaching was suppressed?"

"That's right. Henri de Lubac's story is a good example of this. During the war he opposed Nazi and Vichy propaganda by writing for underground journals. He also equipped Jewish people with new identities, helping them escape Nazi-occupied areas. As a result, he had to go into hiding from the Gestapo."

"He sounds like one of the good ones."

"Indeed. A good human but also a good theologian," Bernard asserted.

---

257. At this time, Neo-Scholasticism had responded to the threat of secular modernism by redoubling its rationalism and emphasizing a systematic, manualist approach to training church leaders. While there is some merit here, it was pointed out that responding in kind by appealing almost exclusively to rationalism may disenfranchise the faith of its most potent response: something different and imbued with the Life of the World. As a result, the place of faith alongside reason was a core conversation at this moment in Catholic Church history, as was a renewed interest in metaphysics and the riches of the faith in the early church.

"How on earth would you measure that?"

"I believe, like Camus, that if you're going to believe something, then at least believe it resolutely. Camus once said that there is nothing as bad as an anti-clerical cleric, and I'm inclined to agree."

"Fair," Peter replied. *Then what about Bernard himself?* It seemed to Peter that Bernard practically believed—he saw a beauty in it and talked with conviction—but stared longingly just behind the threshold. *What prevented him?*

Bernard continued, "De Lubac was an intellectual force. He stood by his work and theological beliefs resolutely, despite being censured and condemned by the Vatican. But here's the twist: a decade later, not only was he restored but also appointed as a theological advisor to the Second Vatican Council, the most important revitalization of Catholic theology in the twentieth century. His vision of grace and nature—two integrally interconnected layers of reality—was especially important in countering the naturalistic, reductionist worldview of the time and modernism influencing theological circles."

"Just a little whiplash!"

"Ah, yes, but you haven't heard the best of it yet. During a meeting at the Vatican in the '80s, Pope John Paul II is said to have bowed his head in a gesture of thanks to him."

"That seems sacrilegious!"

"Perhaps. That's all to say," Bernard continued, "not all concepts of transcendence or even God are alike. The *Nouvelle* theologians remade the compelling case for God as the source of everything good, true, and beautiful—not a moralistic oppressor suffocating life as Nietzsche et al. made him out to be." Bernard added, blinking as he fought back the sting of tears, "You know, Peter, Father Konstantinos was unquestionably more concerned about my soul than I was. He borrowed from de Lubac to warn me over and over: 'Don't get stuck, like Nietzsche's Dionysian myth, of a spirituality 'emanating from earth.'[258] Instead, let it call you deeper still, into mystery, God's mystery."[259]

"And you let beauty take you to the mist but not over the threshold?" Peter now found himself saying out loud.

Bernard shifted uncomfortably. At arm's length he stubbornly continued, "Father Konstantinos wasn't trying to convert me. The Eastern

258. De Lubac, *Drama of Atheist Humanism*, 91.
259. De Lubac, *Drama of Atheist Humanism*, 91.

Orthodox church doesn't seem to go after you like some. Instead, as I sat by his bedside, he just shared his life with me, his world. It changed me, Peter. It was much more astute and psychological, more healing than I'd ever imagined."

"I see," Peter said, making the fox squirm. *He doesn't want God, but he wants this for me?*

Bernard continued to share his gift of knowledge, "This all brings me to John Milbank. He was influenced by de Lubac. Have you heard of him?"

"I can't say I have," Peter answered.

"Milbank's a strong counterpoint to postmodernism," Bernard shared. "In his last months, Father Konstantinos was especially excited about a movement called Radical Orthodoxy from England—your homeland. Milbank's been at the front of this wave. He's bold, provocative, and radical. He's even blamed the church for inadvertently setting off a chain of events that made secularism and postmodernism possible."

"Really? How?"

"He argued that Duns Scotus and other theologians during the Middle Ages scored a sharp distinction between grace and nature: the supernatural and natural layers of reality. While the attempt was to preserve the idea of God's life-giving grace as an intentional gift, the unintended result seems to have been a rendering of the natural world as functionally independent from God's grace. After distancing the natural and supernatural, or lower and upper layers in this way, humanity finds itself just one step away from discarding the top supernatural layer altogether."

Peter suggested, "Like in the garden when you broke the bark—the fabric of reality—apart."

"Exactly. Since life limps on, once scored and split apart, it's easy to juxtapose the two layers. If the natural layer represents all truth, then the supernatural layer is not just irrelevant but a lie. In this climate, the disenchanted world of the secular enlightenment thrived; self-satisfied and mechanistic.

"And this world decomposes further into postmodernism?" Peter reasoned.

"Exactly. However, as complicit as the church may have been, Milbank and company also see in Christianity the antidote for this cultural carnage. In inviting humanity into relationship with the relational God, the church has a vital, irreplaceable ability to transform culture, singularly holding the keys to re-enchanting the world (*wiederverzauberung*)."

"How?"

"Rethinking desire, life, beauty, and joy is a good start. Because what we believe impacts what we think is possible and, in turn, what we do. The crux of it all is that, instead of transcendence limiting the flow of desire, as Deleuze claimed, Milbank argued that the very opposite is what inhibits flow: 'the failure to "refer" our desire to God . . .'[260] This connects to Augustine's definition of virtue as 'rightly ordered love.'[261] Peter, desire is not bad! Instead, what determines if our desires drive us into self-destruction or towards flourishing is where we take—or how we organize—them.[262] Even on a bigger scale, this agrees with de Lubac when he claimed that 'it is not true that one cannot organize the world without God. And yet, without God, he can ultimately only organize it against man. Exclusive humanism is inhuman humanism.'[263] For Milbank, failure to refer desire to God's life-giving relational pattern doesn't just inhibit this flow but also results in 'a false, ugly misdirection of flow.'"[264]

"It's a bit backwards, but what would ugly actually look like?" Peter asked.

"For Milbank, there's reason to think of it as a sort of evil, as a 'denial of hope'—or flourishing—for community."[265] Bernard continued passionately, "Peter, what if the world is not at base a violent clamor of desire or desperate survival of the fittest without hope, but instead there is an ontology of peace we can participate in?

Ah, that word again, Peter thought.

Bernard continued, "For Milbank, it 'provides the only alternative to a nihilistic outlook.'[266] This challenged my thinking, Peter, including some of what I'd taken from Levinas. You see, Levinas anchored peace (and the source of ethics) beyond and before ontology, while Milbank argued that peace can only be anchored though ontology, through presence. For Levinas, the presence of God seems to withdraw as one approaches, while central to Milbank's understanding of the world is the

260. Milbank, *Theology and Social Theory*, 439.

261. Milbank, *Theology and Social Theory*, 440. Virtue defined as "rightly ordered love" is found throughout Augustine's work, including *Contra Donatistas* and *De Moribus Ecclesiae*.

262. Milbank, *Theology and Social Theory*, 439.

263. De Lubac, *Drama of Atheist Humanism*, 14.

264. Milbank, *Theology and Social Theory*, 439.

265. Milbank, *Theology and Social Theory*, 440.

266. Milbank, *Theology and Social Theory*, 442.

incarnated, Christian inflection of God; a God who is close and near. Father Konstantino believed that if we can recognize, re-order, or re-synchronize our communities and lives to this deep truth—to God—then there is real reason for hope."

"And you agree?" Peter asked.

"I agree that grounding culture into a deep lasting peace seems preferable to a violent Dionysian death," Bernard quipped.

But is it true? Peter leaned in to hear Bernard beyond the buzz of his mind. "Bernie, just tell me how it would impact the world."

"It already has and does."

"What?"

"The early church undermined violent and bloodthirsty power structures to find a more peaceful, harmonious, originary form: a kingdom behind the clamor, chaos, and noise. The tune of a different kingdom which they could dance to, even if it meant death. And that changed the world."

"But how is this possible?" Peter asked.

"It's all about an ontology of peace, possible because of the Trinitarian God of Love, who—they say— invites us to share in his life. Father Konstantino would explain it to me circularly, almost like what he was describing. The triune community of God is caught up in a joyful perichoretic dance, where each person gives space and preference to the other with a loving intensity that can't help but overflow. Space is given for diversity to flourish. After the pattern of the Trinity, the good, the true, and the beautiful—the transcendentals—are founded and work together. Interwoven and interpenetrating, they invite us to move closer to partake in their source. Father Konstantino took great pains to make sure that I had at least a glimpse of what it had taken him a lifetime to fully appreciate." Bernard admitted bashfully, "he would have explained it much better than me."

Ah, Bernard feels a burden to pass this onto me, Peter reasoned. *The beauty, harmony, rhythms and music, again.* Peter instinctively imagined a divine whirlpool. While being enraptured by it, he was also released and blessed by it. Peter caught himself. "What if I don't want to receive meaning and purpose?" he said.

"You think you can do a better job creating it?" Bernard snapped, revealing an urgency. "You'll try to find meaning and purpose somewhere. And when you do, life will test it. First, you'll be enslaved by it, and then you'll lose all hope in it. You'll wonder why you gave it so much of your life and affection."

That stung. "I guess," Peter answered, looking away.

Embarrassed, Bernard made sure to reconnect with—and speak directly into—Peter's eyes. He shared, "I know, Peter, because I've lived it. I've seen it lived over and over, the best of my friends betrayed by their own genius. Building their own towers of isolation, desire causes them to hunger so deeply that they've gnawed themselves down to the bone. They had every potential to flourish but shriveled. No one talks of how the jealous pain of seeing a friend succeed over you is far less than the pain and fear of seeing a brilliant friend implode."

Peter felt in this the soft underbelly of Bernard's brute honesty. *He doesn't care about himself but cares about me. The lecture, the words, this is his way of showing love. Is he trying to save me? How far gone does he think I am?* Peter took some solace: *As long as he's preaching, I can't be a completely lost cause.*

Peter wasn't sure how to put it, but gently pushed back, "That's all well and good, but it still assumes God is true!" Peter then paused, teetering near the frayed edges of his soul. "But if God . . . I mean . . ." He squeaked, "Does God *really* encounter people?" The fox looked up at him, worried. Peter stroked him firmly to soothe them both.

Bernard answered indirectly, "In his last days, Father Konstantinos wanted us to read the Orthodox scholar John D. Zizioulas's remarkable book *Being as Communion* together. I sat by his bedside. The book talked about how taking communion together affects our reality so profoundly as if to open up time itself to encounter the eternal. He loved that part. He made me highlight it, I think because it put words to what he felt. He deeply missed attending the church prayer services, Vespers. They have a beautiful rhythm to them, with the prayers sung. Not long before he passed, a younger priest came to offer him holy communion. I swear I saw the smile of a man whose spirit had peered into the throne room. I have his copy of the book right over there. 'Time dilates,' it says, 'to the infinite dimensions of the *eschata*.'"[267]

"The *eschata*?"

"The fullness of the coming kingdom of God, saturated by his heavenly presence—of love, truth, and life—revealed even now to those who seek it out."

---

267. Zizioulas, *Being as Communion*, 22.

"That's beautiful, but do *you* believe that?" Peter asked, searching his face for any incongruity in his answer.

"I believe . . . No, *I know*," Bernard stressed, "that he'd touched the hem of some sort of peace.[268] Not just in that moment but over and over. The joy that he had despite his intense bodily suffering made no logical sense. He confided he'd rooted in the strength and knowledge of heaven—the presence of the God of Life. We joked that if he were rooted like this, then he was like an upside-down tree. And that, if so, he was surely a gnarly but majestic one." Bernard took another long puff of his pipe.

"Thank you for sharing," Peter said, seeing the fresh tenderness behind Bernard's memories. "If you believe it, even part of it, why don't you jump in?"

"Me? No, no. I'd create too many ripples," Bernard joked, trying to convince Peter that he meant this literally, given his rounding belly.

"I'm sorry if I've been too harsh about the Christian thing," Peter said kindly. "Don't let me stop you."

"God and I have an understanding: we give each other distance," Bernard said. As Peter began to speak again, he shut it down by adding abruptly, "Peter, you'll never understand!"

"Let me try!" Peter protested.

"Not now, Peter! Forget it all," Bernard snapped, throwing his beloved books into the unlit recesses of the room. After a few moments, he gathered himself, embarrassed. "Let's go find the others." Bernard rose up for the door. "Go ahead," he encouraged Peter, gruffly. "Here's the plate. You can eat the rest."

Peter obediently grabbed the plate and walked outside. The fox teetered on his pin-like legs, dazed after being rudely awoken and shooed

268. The concept of participation is not restricted to the Orthodox expression of Christianity. For example, consider its connection to real presence and communion. Notice the use of participation in this context: "Is not the cup of thanksgiving for which we give thanks a participation in the blood of Christ? And is not the bread that we break a participation in the body of Christ?" (1 Cor 10:16). The word for "participation" here is drawn from the Greek *koinōnia*, meaning fellowship. Recently, Gareth Ortlund, from Truth Unites (promoting historical Protestant Christianity), has taught on this topic. Ortlund argued that commentators on this verse who have emphasized participation/fellowship are diverse, including, for example, the Reformed Baptist Charles Spurgeon. See Spurgeon, "Communion with Christ and His People." Alongside other arguments, Ortlund also reminded his audience that the early church held to the idea of real presence in communion. For example, St. Cyril of Jerusalem Catechetical Lectures 22:6. Note that the concept of "participation" is not the same as transubstantiation. See Ortlund, "Baptist Case."

into the light. Only Bernard didn't follow. It was then, as the door closed behind them, that Peter noticed a small rectangular box-like thing glimmering on his right door frame. Given the visual clutter of all Bernard's projects, Peter hadn't noticed it before. *A mezuzah? Is Bernard Jewish?*

33

WW2

The Arrival

PARIS II

Wednesday, October 6th, 1943.

Henry stared at the last pins of light that made it through the eyelets of the cream truck canvas. He realized that he had been in occupied France for over a week now. Would Max—the "pianist" who had landed with him in the Vosges—have survived this long? He dearly hoped so, but the stats weren't good.

Both Matthias and Violet were asleep, surrounded by meat, cheese, and wine. They must have been getting close. The truck stopped a couple extra times, but the early winter evening was drawing the curtains on the day.

Violet could hear de Gaulle's broadcasts in her sleep: "*Ici Londres! Les Français parlent aux Français.*" ("This is London! The French speak to the French"). She remembered the way they had run around Paris in the summer of '41, writing "V" for victory everywhere they could as an act of subversion. How alive and giddy they had felt. She even had the gall to scratch it into a *Wehrmacht* vehicle as Jérôme stood guard.

Out of the blue, the truck in which they were hiding stopped. Then, a subtle tapping came from the front cabin. Violet and Matthias awoke in an instant. The tapping came one more time. Three dots and dash! "He knows," Violet whispered, smiling. It was clearly the dot, dot, and dash—Morse code for the letter *V* in "Victory"—the same call-sign that began de Gaulle's Radio Londres broadcasts in the form of the first four notes of Beethoven's Fifth. The *Résistance* knew this in their sleep. While the Nazis tried to jam the radio, often it could still be heard through the noise and static.

Violet looked out of the canvas. It was now pitch-black, but there was a checkpoint ahead. She could tell by the lights and distant talking. And beyond it? Unequivocally Paris! Violet returned the Morse code, a recognition and thank you. The driver waited for them to run into the bush, having stopped strategically near an entrance that the Parisians had kept from the Nazis. This wasn't any entrance. It led to the subterranean world of the catacombs.

34

Peter

Honesty

FRANCE

Saturday, March 19th, 1994.

Bernard wasn't in his cabin. Peter blamed himself for allowing them to pretend that everything was normal. He wasn't going to leave it so long to address the problem this time.

Given that it was early spring, where else would he be but in his garden tending to his bees? Peter arrived to see Bernard's hive smoker—steadily burning through dry leaves and pinecones—in hand. While Peter had unpacked Bernard's beekeeping suit for him when they moved in, it was unclear why he bothered bringing it for he never used it. He and the bees seemed to have a certain understanding, a tenderness. Bernard had waited until the temperatures had stabilized to crack open the hives. He'd chosen a sunny day with minimal wind so that the bees could forage among the fresh spring sprouts, especially dandelion and coltsfoot, without risking hypothermia.

Peter approached, bearing gifts. Was there any question of Bernard accepting him when he came with Marje's baklava?"

It was oozing. "Is this my honey?" Bernard asked.

"What else?" Peter replied, having passed the test.

"You didn't have to," Bernard said, visibly thankful. "How goes it in Etienne's Eden?"

"I did," Peter said, intent on changing the subject back. "I hurt you. I'm so sorry."

"That's my problem, Peter, not yours. Besides, we have a more pressing issue."

"But—"

"Peter, look," Bernard said, frustrated, pointing with the sharp edge of his hive tool. "The queen of the large hive has stopped laying. I need to re-queen it. And this one? The bees are taking things into their own hands. Look!" he said, lifting the frame for Peter to see.

"What is that?" Peter asked, yielding. He looked at the large globular cell.

"A queen cell. But there isn't just one, there are four on this frame alone. This is a huge problem. The girls are trying to make a new queen. But more than one and they'll take off. They'll swarm."

"Then what happens?" Peter asked.

"Well, that's anyone's guess. They'll try to find somewhere else to go."

"The whole hive leaves?"

"They'll split! Peter, we want to avoid that at all costs!"

"What can you do?"

"I'll have to get rid of every queen cell in here. I promise that beekeeping isn't normally this bloodthirsty," Bernard joked.

"Glad to hear it!" Peter joked. They talked a little more about the bees. Bernard even had a chance to bite into the baklava, honey oozing out between the flaky pastry. But Peter wanted to reconcile properly. "Can I ask what I said that was—"

"Let's forget it, Peter, and move along," Bernard insisted.

"But I just want to—" Peter pressed a couple more times.

"Look, Peter. You should be less concerned about an old man like me and more concerned about yourself." While Bernard felt Peter's care as both endearing and unmerited, he saw himself as a lost cause. Father Konstantino had left an indelible mark on him, but he felt too old to learn new tricks, scared, perhaps that had lived this many years crippled by sorrow when there may have been an answer.

Bernard clarified gruffly, "What is it that you actually want to know?"

"I'm just curious," Peter replied.

"No, you're not. Curious is taking a peek in a cupboard. You have motivation, drive, and it's not just to know about dead and dying scholars."

"Well, you like them," Peter deflected with a gentle but irreverent smirk.

"But what's your itch, Peter?"

"Sorry?"

"Your itch! What do you *really* want to know?" Bernard asked afresh. "Let's not beat around the bush."

"I don't know." Peter looked down at the dirt ground and wild grass.

"Look. Everyone has their reasons. I don't need you to tell me yours. I won't tell you mine. We're even. But you need to confront your why." Fear blocked Bernard's ascent to peace, but he couldn't stand to see another friend, with so much life still ahead of him, implode. If Peter really wanted to help, then Bernard felt that he should face reality—perhaps even Father Konstantino's peace—the sooner the better.

"I don't understand," Peter said.

"Descartes?" Bernard started, "He began as a mathematician but started mining fundamental questions about truth and existence after his beloved daughter, Francine, died. It was scarlet fever, and she was just five years old. And Russell?"

"When he realized it was all pointless compared to the realities of war," Peter recalled.

"Exactly. I don't want you to spin your wheels on this obsession with mathematics and the like when what you really care about is—." The next word seemed to take an age to come out of Bernard's mouth. He took pains to clothe it in comfort. "Suffering."

Peter's knees collapsed under his weight. He lost all control of his emotions. Bernard was right, because it's also what he knew. All that talk about—even about creating hell on earth—it was still one step removed from acknowledging the pain of his personal hell.

They embraced. Everything that they had been talking about didn't seem so academic anymore. *The story of the human face?* That haunted Peter. Why? Because he'd been that face, run over in the mud. His ex-fiancé had treated him inhumanely, but he hadn't wanted to acknowledge it. He'd loved her. Truly. He'd been there for her every step of her journey . . . and then? What? He now reminded her too much of the season that she needed to get past? Sure, she said she felt awful, but she'd discarded him like nothing. Garbage. Like a mangled toothpaste tube she'd used up. He was left a shell of a man, and he hated it. He hated himself for letting this happen.

Bernard wrapped his arms around Peter. He wasn't going anywhere. Thick like tree trunks. Sturdy. He felt Bernie's large thumbs soothing his back. He didn't even mind the proximity of his beard. It felt soft. There was a little baklava in it, but Peter didn't care one bit. The moment hung for an age, the birds and bees officiating this holy moment of friendship.

"Bernie, thank you," Peter said, having felt the floodgates open. There was so much, but this relief of pressure was incredibly welcome. He hadn't realized it, but the last time he had cried was pulling away from the house in Runnymede, knowing she wasn't going to change her mind. He had done everything he could; they'd beaten her cancer together! But it still wasn't enough. She said she couldn't go forward in life with him as an ever-present reminder of that season. They both "deserved to be free."

But was freedom being condemned to this wandering death? How he craved a freedom unto life. This liminal space was torture. He needed something real. Yes, something true, good, and beautiful.

35

Alexi
Murder & Microfiche

PARIS II

Thursday, October 22nd, 2015.

While staying at the hostel in Paris, Alexi had made a habit of sharing meals with the boys. Sam probably wouldn't eat anything nutritious otherwise, and Marc was too busy to cook, training for mountain biking events. She might have joined him were it not for the bad concussion that haunted her from messing around in a bike park in her youth. At least the boys ate decently this way. Blake also joined when he wasn't at some important seminar, sucking up to professors, or on a date. She didn't mind, both at a loss for another mode of interaction and playing games to keep the distance.

Her days were spent obsessively. She was committed but the grind was wearing her out. She would jog along the Seine before getting ready for the library. She could have done it in her sleep now: carefully opening envelopes of microfiche before pushing one into the machine, the glass cover snapping shut, navigating through the images and focusing. She switched the soundtrack in her ears to keep it somewhat fresh.

Lunch meant emerging from the library basement to people-watch by a fountain or lie on the grass when it wasn't wet; but the ever-graying winter skies meant that recently she had been going back to the Musée de l'Homme. She would sneak a hug from Tim and then try to eat her lunch in the café, staring at the Eiffel Tower, hoping that no one would notice that she didn't actually buy anything. She was sure they'd caught on to her by now, but Tim's friends didn't seem in a rush to betray her audacity. And for that she was thankful. At the end of the day, before bringing groceries to the boys' house, she would sometimes stop to try on some vintage couture and dream. She lived for the rare evening when Marc was free. Their last adventure was to L'Opéra Garnier to find the Phantom.

Life had a certain rhythm about it. Occasionally, she'd reply to Edwin and Edith's emails, but with nothing much to report, she wasn't really sure what to say. Each time, they offered a warm invitation for her to visit again. Time seemed to float like an iridescent bubble, like those days between Christmas and New Year's. That was, until that paradoxically merciful but painful day that it burst.

It had started, as ever, with the kind librarian hoping for an update. She had become quite invested after she had helped Alexi narrow down the publications, but, beyond that, neither of them really knew what to look for. "Le Rubicon?" Alternative Community? It was a guessing game. Despite the time span not being too long, it was surprising how much material there was to look through. *Why would they even be in the news?* Alexi had started to convince herself that no news was good news.

The questions ended when her worst fears were confirmed. A newspaper article from July 24th, 1994: breaking news about a radical community called "Le Rubicon." Police had been called to the scene after a disturbance: a suspicious death. The journalist didn't give much more. Alexi's heart was in her mouth. She retched. Blood surged into her ears so loudly she was sure they would burst.

No one was there to share this moment, not even the librarian. But there, in the basement, in a corner, in the dark, she knew her world had just changed. She just didn't know how. *Was this why Peter had disappeared?*

36

Peter

Charlemagne & Wolf's Bane

LES VOSGES IV

Tuesday, April 12th, 1994.

Despite the outward success of the community, inwardly it was crumbling. It was hard for Peter to watch Etienne's rising paranoia. It would be hard for anyone to hold all of these conflicting ideas together—not just the differences between his moderate anarchist tendencies and Jean-Paul's neo-Marxist goals but all the disparate voices. As a safer place than Jean-Paul, all the complaints and "suggestions" came to him.

Etienne continued to give Peter favor, often getting him on the radio. Peter put it down to his British accent, but Etienne said it was because of his insightful questions. In this respect, Jean-Paul was either jealous or curious. Perhaps he didn't even know. It led him to offer the inoffensive Brit a place among the other men—all hand-chosen—on his next adventure. Having been left so many times—instead, reading bedtime stories to Liesel and Evan to help Amy and Jacob or hanging out with Andrea and Antonio—it was nice to be invited. Jean-Paul told Peter to leave the fox with Bernie, but Peter wouldn't have risked it anyhow, given the presence of the dogs. But he could invite Antonio, who was thrilled.

Peter hadn't yet explored too far beyond the forest that immediately encircled the community, aside from a couple of day hikes. Over the next few days, the men went deeper and deeper beyond the typical biking and hiking tracks where they might see others and into another world. The relief changed as they went north. The dramatic northern, or "lower," Vosges offered intriguing terrain in times of both war and peace. Though they rise to less than half the height of the rounded, glacially sculpted southern "high" Vosges, these more jagged, northerly hills are nevertheless steeped in cunning, converting their commitment to conceal surprises round each corner.

The woodland thickets still smelled the same as in the early Middle Ages when King Charlemagne would come to this, his royal domain, and hunt, departing from nearby Metz, where he liked to govern the Carolingian Empire when not in Aachen. In April, that meant the primal smell of rotting leaves newly released from their snow-covered hibernation, intermixed with the fresh hope of spring flowers and resinous pines. Their tender, fresh growth was as vibrant, in its bright chartreuse, as its scent when crushed between thumb and forefinger. By royal decree, hunting rights in these forests were reserved for the king and his nobles, with poaching severely punished.

As king of the Franks, the Germanic tribal peoples after whom France would later be named, Charlemagne widened their influence, most notably by leading an army over the Alps to come to the Pope's aid. This led to him being crowned emperor of the Romans on Christmas Day in AD 800. However, this did not mean that he ruled in the cruciform heart-posture of Jesus—a posture saturated with love and devotion, inaugurating a movement that empowered all, even down to the slaves. It was a movement so radical that it had caused fear to rise in great Roman emperors afraid of losing their death grip of control over the empire. Instead, like so many powerful rulers, Charlemagne built his kingdom just as these emperors had: largely based on violence. In all, this legendary king gathered much of the land equating to modern-day France, Belgium, Luxembourg, the Netherlands, and Western Germany. Later, the division of the Carolingian Empire between Charlemagne's three grandsons, codified in the Treaty of Verdun in AD 843, set the stage for long-lasting divisions that would influence the future political landscape. This included the rise of the Holy Roman Empire in the tenth century and its impact on European borders and power structures up to the present day.

Unusually tall for the Middle Ages, six feet or more, and clad in a blue cloak, Charlemagne was accompanied by his faithful sword, "Joyeuse." It was forged, the legends say, to contain the Lance of Longinus, which pierced Jesus's side. He was the epitome of eighth-century

Frankish manhood: determined, handsome, and strong-nosed, with white hair blowing in the wind: the model for the king of hearts in a pack of playing cards.

Just as Charlemagne had been, Peter was entranced by how the water from on high gathered, incessantly, into timeless pools—perfect to swim in. There was also the same subtle spring of leaves underfoot, that in times past had helped absorb the sound of dismounting men, especially helpful during stalking hunts (*chasse à l'approche*).

Upon alighting, Charlemagne grabbed a handful of long, thick grass into his hands, smelling it. He had observed everything, including the direction of the broken stalks. He knew they were here; he didn't need the grass to tell him. Still, he wished to soak it in: all the visceral elements leading up to the kill.

His party's cross-gartered legs approached the deer. As the most prominent member, the kill was his. Both parties paused. Eyes locked. The royal red deer's perfectly formed ears swiveled near-instantly to isolate the direction of the threat. Joints frozen, muscles taut. Tired, the stag's chest was full with waves of a long red mane, eclipsed only by the cloud of his breath. Veins throbbed, relentlessly close to the surface of his neck and head, full of surging pressure below purple-gray velveteen antlers; this springtime encounter being before the late-summer velvet shed and staining when, for many years, the resonant sound of this stag, his loud bugle, had confirmed his dominance throughout the valley. This stag was much more than a "hart of ten" considered worthy of hunting; but in this unique instance, the king uncharacteristically resolved to offer grace, befitting for the magnificence of this particular specimen. Charlemagne departed with a nod, recognizing the stag's royalty.

Close to the same location, Jean-Paul came alongside Peter on the ancient, spore-infused path, well-worn by both man and beast. He whispered to Peter, "Wolves still prowl these forests." He was yet to make his verdict on Peter and was testing him. He carefully studied Peter's expression as it shifted from intrigue to a knowing smile behind an ever-intensifying veil of rain.

"And bears," added one of his men, knowing full-well that the last known story of a bear in the area was in the Munster Valley in the late eighteenth century while crops failed and revolutionary sentiment in Paris grew close to boiling point. The same infamous revolution that began the democratization of hunting and land ownership. One of the first actions of the National Assembly was to abolish feudalism, thereby ending seigneurial rights, those special privileges enjoyed by the nobility (*seigneurs*) and landowners.

This was a wet and moody land. As the group approached a waterfall just south of Nideck Castle, a shard of golden light effortlessly peeked through the dark clouds to permeate the cascade, timelessly teasing of its magic. Gleeful, perhaps for new visitors. The home of giants, the legends say, the castle's square keep still rises, determined, from the forest. The wild beauty was entrancing, but it felt like a place where anything could happen. The hair on Peter's neck raised. He brushed it off, but his instincts weren't entirely wrong.

When would they get there? Peter thought. He was not prepared for the miles or the weather.

"Forgot your brolly, sir?" One of the men jeered in a ridiculous attempt at a British accent, clipping him as he walked back to the front of the pack after emptying his bowels.

Seemingly isolated pockets of dissent in the community had fomented into this group. They seemed sharp and acerbic, sparking live wires. Without partnering with mystery, the higher rhythms of the heavens, or even mythos, the rhythms of the earth—peace proved impossible to anchor.

Of course, Etienne was no idiot. He had seen it brewing: first, the conversations in dark corners. Then the "discussions." Now, this dense group pulling away more and more frequently. But what could he do? Clamp down on them and confirm the whispers of his despotic thirst for power? Utterly laughable and yet, for these receptive minds, oddly possible now this thought had been cultivated. Etienne was at a loss. He simply redoubled his work and hard conversations. Peter saw the strain on his face and personal life—his many actions trying to free himself from this siege—that outstripped the foundations of his soul. Peter felt awkward hiking with this group but told himself it couldn't be that bad. Perhaps he could understand what they valued and help mend the rift.

It was now hours after Peter had first hoped for a rest. As the wind picked up, he could see the rain drive against Jean-Paul's chilled face as if suggesting that it too had been glaciated.

Noticing his gaze, Jean-Paul joked, "Cleanest I've ever seen you!"

"Talk for yourself," Peter replied, regretting it immediately, though it did get Jean-Paul to look at him sideways.

Soon after, Jean-Paul began to get a rather persistent smirk on his face. Then the others, who had hitherto raucously thrown around any lewd joke with ever-increasing appetite proportional to tiredness, grew silent as they reached a forgettable farm on a crest in the land. It clearly concealed some sort of secret to which Antonio and Peter were not yet privy.

"We're here," Jean-Paul announced. "Time to warm up with a fire," he added, gesturing towards what outwardly looked like a derelict barn. Nestled into the hillside, it was dwarfed by a large oak draped in old man's beard. Appearing terribly tortured, the barn seemed to have absorbed more pain than it could bear, suffering vicariously on behalf of its long-gone inhabitants.

On it lay a sign with the crisp, black-on-white words: "*Propriété privée accès interdit sous peine de poursuites,*" leaving no margin for misinterpretation even between the deafening howls of the wind. Even Peter could figure out what it meant: it's private. Go in and be prosecuted. *But why?* It looked insignificant. Old, undeniably, and long-abandoned. *Liability, perhaps?* Peter reasoned.

When it was Peter's turn to enter from the side door, it was altogether different than he expected. Cold, wet, and hungry, Peter was not in the mood for any surprises. *What is this?*

With Antonio and a couple of other stragglers behind him, Peter's eyes swelled in search of light as a claustrophobic dank tunnel led to another door. It went downward. Then, a door—the real entrance—kept swinging shut, promising much by teasing with an intermittent yellow light. Seizing the handle, Peter opened it, finally able to see what it was guarding: a subterranean cavernous grotto turned eighteenth-century Romantic folly.

Intrigue gripped his childlike heart. The first light of a fresh fire greeted Peter's eyes with comfort as he searched for greater clarity, the smoke escaping through natural cracks in the cave ceiling. Peter could hardly believe his eyes as the day's sights were subsumed by such treasures shining forth, piercing even. *Where to look first?* There was an opulent collection of ancient prizes and trinkets—only slightly tarnished by the weight of ages—left by empires as if by their waves as they receded. Huge hart heads—those not as lucky as Charlemagne's monarch—hung on the wall alongside an ancient bear skin and a Persian rug, once the prize of a distant market stall along the Silk Road. Who knew what else was hidden? For example, what was behind the dark Coromandel-lacquer Chinese screen, the type that made Coco Chanel swoon with all the glints of promise afforded by its mother-of-pearl inlay?

Peter had just enough time to notice how the cave-like walls had been decorated with features like rounded castle turrets made from perfectly fitted stone. Someone had taken real care in securing this secret place, along with their coveted, carefully curated treasures. But then, Jean-Paul pivoted. Something wild and Dionysian came over him. He placed a long-forgotten twelfth-century crusader's helmet over his own head, grains of sand from the Levant still hidden within its articulations. "*En guard!*" he said playfully, but with a manic look in his eyes, grabbing another helmet and throwing it at Peter, his opponent. "It's only fair," he added.

"Fair? A warning would have been ni—?" Peter began.

"Just fight!" one of the hunters shouted, gunning for sport and entertainment.

"What, a fancy naval school doesn't teach you to fence?" Jean-Paul said, reading his grip on his sword of choice.

"No, I. I mean . . . I," Peter stuttered under the pressure.

"That's right. I know you learned," Jean-Paul said, unnerving Peter. Had he overhead his conversations with Bernard or Antonio? "So," Jean-Paul continued, "shall we see what you're made of?"

"Look, I really don't want to," Peter casually replied.

Jean-Paul lunged forward and played with the top of Peter's shirt with the edge of his dueling sword. This seemed utterly ridiculous to Peter. *What is this?* The onlookers found it enthralling, oohing. "Do I need to push you, Peter? Like this? Just a little?" Jean-Paul added.

"That's funny," Peter said, trying to laugh it off and move to go sit at the fire. He then thought of backing up. He tried to turn around, but men blocked the narrow pathway. *Was this planned?*

"I don't want to," Peter said when incited again.

"Do you always get to do what you want, Peter? Did Daddy and Mummy hold your hand as you walked to school and sent you off to yacht lessons in the summer?" He emphasized the 'u' in mummy, while pouting his lower lip and murdering a British accent.

"You have no idea—"

"Oh, that works, does it? Were they absent? Neglectful? You don't even have a right to feel—"

"How would you know?" Peter said with distaste.

Someone shouted out, "You won the lottery, mate. England! Do you know how many would kill to have your passport?"

"So, you're jealous?" Peter asked.

"Tell you what. I could fight Antonio," Jean-Paul said, turning his sword on him.

Antonio looked at Peter, his eyes wide with fear. This was insane. *Is he just a bully? Is this what they do all the time out here?* Nothing in Peter wanted to accept, but Jean-Paul wasn't having it. He couldn't let Antonio try—despite the fact Antonio probably thought otherwise, Peter knew he'd just be humiliated. *What a stupid, stupid situation. Perhaps Andrea was right, calling them Neanderthals.*

"I should fight him, right?" Jean-Paul suggested to the group. The group replied with a Colosseum-worthy roar. Jean-Paul reached behind the door and threw Peter a long rapier that had long been stored there. "Show us what you're made of!" he said. The hand guard, ironically, rapped his knuckles, offering up a first blunt serving of pain. "Here," Jean-Paul added, sending another through the air to Antonio to invite the extra interest of two against one.

What a prideful, sleek-moving monster, Antonio thought. But there wasn't time to sneak that through his chapped lips.

"Jean-Paul! Jean-Paul!" the men began to shout as he took both of them on.

Immediately, the men collided into artifacts ranging from the time of Charlemagne through that of the crusading knights and into the early modern world. Ordinarily, Peter would have been horrified at the ignobility of it all; yet the intensity of the attack did not wane, to the delight of the onlookers, oohing at every blow and fall.

"It's not fun if there are no real consequences," Jean-Paul offered as if an undeniable truth.

Without wasting any more time, Jean-Paul took the opportunity to both interrogate and publicly humiliate. "What were you doing with Hélène by the river?" he asked.

"Nothing. She just got hurt!" Peter said, finding a blunt blade up against his Adam's apple. "Her ankle, I mean—"

Antonio wasn't sure what to do. It was clear that Jean-Paul was only interested in Peter. But he couldn't just stand there and leave Peter to it.

"You stay away!" Jean-Paul warned Peter regarding Hélène, before turning his attention to Antonio, batting him away like a fly.

"She needed help," Peter protested, fighting back and protecting Antonio by jumping between them. "What was I supposed to do? Besides, that was months ago."

"And they say chivalry's dead." He smirked, launching another assault, which, this time, Peter masterfully blocked with the mid-section of his blade. It was clear that he still wasn't properly engaging, only defending when he needed to.

"Why are you really here? What does Etienne want from you?" Jean-Paul continued, launching forward, showing his skill. He was dancing rings round them, playing them like marionettes.

"I don't know!" Peter admitted. "I just stumbled here, honestly." They crossed swords again, and again, and again, sapping what was left of the Brit's energy. Antonio helped relieve it a little, but he had no skill to counterweight his poverty of balance.

"'Honestly'? People only say that when they make a habit of lying," Jean-Paul said, adding audacious flourishes to show the ease with which he could intimidate. "So, what do you want?" Jean-Paul asked, pushing upon Peter's internal world as he harassed the external, somehow able to cross those invisible lines.

"I don't know! Peace, I guess. Peace for my soul." Peter said, breathing heavily between each truth. He kicked himself for allowing the marrow of his heart to be displayed to this pack of ravaging wolves.

"His soul?!" Jean-Paul joked, poking fun in front of the attentive, bearded crowd. Funny: they'd all started to look more like their idol, remaking themselves in Jean-Paul's image.

"And we should care about your soul?" someone laughed.

"Don't be so cruel!" Jean-Paul replied in jest.

"Etienne sees something in you, *boy.*"

"I am not a boy!" Peter said.

"Oh, but *he* is," Jean-Paul said. Peter had seen that sort of look before, right before the trigger was flipped to attack. Peter wasn't having any of it. To protect Antonio properly, he finally fought back with actual weight behind his blow.

"Finally, he does have some fight!" Jean-Paul smiled as Peter raged forward. "We need a man with fight, not emotional weaklings. Changing the world is not for the weak. If you aren't willing to die," Jean-Paul said as he fought him back, "how will you be willing to live devoted to a cause that demands choices—a death to comfort—everyday?"

"Yes!" Jean-Paul vocalized as they started to draw out the best in each other. The intensity had vastly increased, and with it the stakes. Antonio stepped back. They commanded the floor all the more. The blows, both physical and verbal, escalated. Beads of sweat ran down their faces.

Peter stumbled over something small. Taking that as an indication of his prowess, Jean-Paul then turned back to the crowd. "What about this one?" Jean-Paul asked the onlooking men, directing their attention again towards Antonio, who had hoped it was over for him.

As he looked away, Peter grabbed a candlestick adjacent to a complete suit of armor. With his free hand, he threw it hard toward Jean-Paul, preferring blunt force and bruises to inflicting any sharp wound.

"That's not fair, Peter," Jean-Paul said, noticeably pained.

"Is life fair?" Peter replied to the amusement of the crowd.

"Touché?" Jean-Paul replied with a smile. He rebounded more furiously until he came to the sharp end of Peter's sword.

Peter thought the fight was over. He had won. Thankful to be done, he turned away. But Jean-Paul's submission was a trick. As soon as Peter let his guard down, Jean-Paul made a gash in Peter's shoulder with the tip of his sword. *Surely they saw what he did?*

"Didn't you say life's not fair?" Jean-Paul smirked.

Peter responded, using his skill to force Jean-Paul back. "We're done, Jean-Paul," Peter said forcefully. "You've had your show."

Ignorant of the antiques behind him, Jean-Paul suddenly tripped, landing on the floor. Peter then had him. There seemed no other option but to speak his language. Antonio joined in directing his weapon towards Jean-Paul.

It looked like Jean-Paul had finally accepted defeat, reaching an arm up. But then he snapped his legs to propel his body forward and beyond them! Once again, Jean-Paul caught them off guard by reshaping the rules any which way he wanted.

The result was swift and effective. In just one carefully calculated move, he was able to turn Peter and Antonio's offensive weapons, which had been aimed at him, against each other. The result was seriously close to catastrophe, narrowly missing each other, but also hilarious to the observers. Jean-Paul flung his arms wide open as if a ringmaster before them, bowing to the crowd. After gladly receiving praise for conjuring such a spectacle, he laughed, "What fun! Go get a drink!"

Antonio and Peter were stunned. "Everyone has an initiation," one man said, attempting to normalize it.

It took a while for Peter to remember that he was bleeding. Only now did he feel it. He added pressure while thinking. Were they humiliated? Were they welcome? Did they pass? *What am I meant to do now?*

Peter stumbled to a perch on a centuries-old trunk. Someone had shoved a drink in his hand. The layers of history shifted in and out of his focus as he was still struggling to take it all in.

Once his body had settled, accepting that the threat had passed, Peter was finally free to appreciate how absolutely absurd the group looked. Around the crackling fire sat men in silver breastplates and arm guards, others (now the joviality had passed) fitting themselves into full suits of armor, while still more toasted bread on genuine daggers. Without remorse, all of them liberally guzzled silver goblets full of mead that they had clearly stolen from Bernard.

The cavernous room was flanked by the paintings of European nobles; still others filed away in undignified piles. This was the perfect place for Jean-Paul to share about his plans and struggles as if a disheveled prince in exile. He made Peter wait, perhaps even hours. But when it suited him, he made his move.

"You can thank me now," Jean-Paul said, strutting over to Peter.

"Thank you?"

"The men didn't respect you. They called you Etienne's pet. They do now."

Peter thought about it. Jean-Paul had pushed and pushed until it forced him to dig deep.

"If I had just told you to man up, would you have done that?" Jean-Paul added before being called over by a group of his riotously drunk men.

Sitting alone, Peter realized that some of what he was saying was the truth. He hadn't thought much about it; but, honestly, many of them just saw him reading books and moping around. It had been worse since his breakdown with Bernard. In a way, he was thankful. Bernard had helped him realize what was really driving his pursuit of answers—but now, what was he meant to do with that? It was like unearthing an unexploded bomb from the Blitz. He knew it was there, and he'd exposed it. How was he meant to diffuse it? Sure, talking about it helped a little, but that pain of the injustice of it all—suffering—how was anyone meant to deal with that? It's the common human experience, Peter knew, but why then were some people walking around embracing the day while he still felt like he was just a hair's breadth away from death? He tried to be happy and enjoyed sparking joy in others—like little Liesel and Evan. But that didn't mean he really was.

If suffering is so common, how do other people live? That question bothered Peter. Crossing to this other modality of life seemed like a path locked against him from the other side, shrouded in mystery. He wondered if Camus was happy? Sure, Camus made much of the rebellion of Sisyphus, condemned by the Greek gods to roll a big boulder up a hill for eternity, only for it to roll back down again. Sisyphus couldn't change the absurdity of it all, but in making peace with this lot he could be happy.[269] But did it actually work for Camus? Could this rebellion translate to actual happiness? *Maybe*, Peter reasoned, *I'm not doing it right.*

As the night wore on, the alcohol both numbed the pain and stimulated reckless questioning, most of it incoherent. Peter caught Jean-Paul's attention again. Jean-Paul took his time, easing his thick, muscular thighs into a crouch alongside him, backlit by the growing fire. "Why are you so concerned about them respecting me?"

Just then, one of his clowns flung a glug of rum into the fire. Immediately, the place erupted in a jeer and flash of light. "Watch yourself!" Jean-Paul shouted, causing them all to jump more than after the blast itself. No one owned up, unsurprisingly.

"You can't *do* much without respect, Peter."

Peter didn't know what to say. What was he expected to "do"? Peter took into his hands the blade that Jean-Paul had given, finally able to appreciate both the honor and humor of it all.

"That one has the mark Klingenthal Coulaux. Look, there," Jean-Paul said, turning the sword to show him. "Back in the 1700s, they made these in the Ehn Valley just north of here. They called it Klingenthal— The Valley of Blades. This was strategic. France needed to keep its supply of weapons close."

"Your damn arm!" Jean-Paul said, as if he somehow wasn't meant to bleed. Peter looked down to see that while his mind had been occupied, he hadn't been applying as much pressure, and his arm had been steadily leaking blood onto his shirt. Jean-Paul rounded off his harshness with unexpected tenderness: "Let's deal with you." He set his glass down and pulled a small leather pouch from his pocket. Unwinding the long leather lace, he removed a needle. That made Peter uneasy. He placed it in the fire.

Jean-Paul moved a lantern to better see the extent of the wound, a minute later offering him a concoction made with wolf's bane. "Drink

269. Camus, *Myth of Sisyphus*, 91.

this," Jean-Paul said, explaining that it was a natural analgesic made from a scrappy little weed of a plant from the sunflower family. He tended to keep some on hand, especially when he knew blood might be spilled.

The wound itself wasn't too big: just a couple of inches long and not too deep. But who knew what bacteria lay on those old swords? Peter reluctantly extended his arm before offering his glass of mead to clean it. "You'll need something much stronger than that," Jean-Paul said, pulling a silver flask from his pocket. It made his arm sting like hell.

"You know, it could have been worse. There's a long history of dueling or bragging scars right here, across the cheek." Jean-Paul traced its path on Peter. "It was the mark of the nobility, showing that you had the strength to stand there and take a blow or two. The man who collected this stuff even had one. Many still had them in the First and Second World Wars. You know, I could give you one. Apparently, it made you good husband material!"

"You know there's nothing going on with Hélène and me," Peter said, switching gears.

The suturing needle was ready. It glowed red, leaving a little black soot where it cooled. Peter was not ready for this. He tried to stay calm.

"I believe you," Jean-Paul said as he drew close with the needle, but with the ghost of an inflection that made Peter question afresh if he believed Jean-Paul. "What's the deal with her?" Jean-Paul asked. He was direct but somehow imbued it with compassion.

Peter looked away as Jean-Paul took his arm. With his body being vulnerable, he was unexpectedly vulnerable with his heart. "I think she just needs a safe place. I'm worried about her."

"Oh?" Jean-Paul replied.

"She gets these bruises. . ." Peter took in a quick breath of air—the needle was sharp, but the thread tugged through his flesh.

"How bad? How many?"

"Bad enough. I'm not sure how many," he said, trying to steady his breath. "She hides them. But I'm sure the number's growing."

"Do you think it's Etienne?"

"No! Not at all," Peter said, his mind rapidly searching through his conversations.

"It would explain why he seems to ignore her so much, even though they're dating . . . and why she'd be looking for a different, safe place," Jean-Paul suggested, working on a second stitch.

Peter protected Etienne. He was his friend and had proven to be anything but violent. But what if what Jean-Paul said were true? People were complicated. Could he be taking his pain out on the person closest to him? Peter didn't want to think about it. But that doubt that Jean-Paul had sown . . . He felt it lodge inside of him.

"Well, I am sure she appreciates you being there," Jean-Paul said.

I don't know. I don't want to make anything worse, Peter thought for a second. "You know, I don't think I worry about being respected so much as I don't want to disappoint anyone."

"I don't think anyone can avoid that," Jean-Paul shared as he drew a knife to cut short the thread on Peter's stitches. "It just needed a couple," he said.

37

Alexi

Dungeon Master

LES VOSGES IV

Monday, October 26th, 2015.

Alexi still bristled with fear. She had poured through the microfiche for further information about the suspicious death, but she couldn't find anything. Yet she couldn't just sit there in Paris wondering what had happened.

When Marc revealed that his next mountain biking event was in the Vosges Mountains, Alexi took it as a sign. The next thing she knew, she was diving out of the incessant rain and into the back of a two-door Peugeot.

"The French don't flaunt fancy cars. That's a little too bourgeois," Alexi had heard someone joke. It looked ridiculous: the car, turtle-like, given the two big mountain bikes strapped to the back. Apparently, for Marc and friends, having a bike more expensive than your car was imperative. The small heating fan struggled to keep up despite its incessant whirring. It had seen better days.

A friend she had only seen a couple of times before was co-piloting. "Nice haircut!" Marc said from the driver's seat. Alexi was surprised that Marc had noticed. *Funny how those small things matter.*

Despite Marc wanting Alexi to come out and support him, Alexi was single-minded. *Marc just didn't get it*, she thought. He had two loving parents and a sport he was passionate about and good at. She didn't have that. She never had. Questions teased her. *If Peter had died, had he been in pain? Why was it suspicious?*

The first few days were spent poring over old boxes of newspapers and talking to old ladies who were curious about her. But there was nothing. Less than nothing. In July of 1994, they just went on about forest fires all across the continent. It seemed to drown out everything else that month.

On day three, their hosts and Marc's long-term friends, Kai and Hannah, convinced her to take a break. She made a sudden pivot. After telling Marc she was too busy to see him in the semifinals but that she'd come to see him in the final (for she was sure he'd make it), she changed her plan, agreeing to do something new with Kai and Hannah: metal-detecting. Though initially resistant to pause her search, Alexi realized that the futility of it all was affecting her mood. She used to be carefree. Now Marc was angry at her—but she was also angry at him. *Could he not even try to understand how important this was to her?* She knew this pivot wasn't going to make anything easier, but she made peace with twisting the knife a little.

Kai and Hannah rented an older house with friends, and while they struggled with damp and cold, they had some great space. Swagged velvet curtains covered the living room windows, contrasting with modern red-leather gaming chairs. It was a shared and eclectic space, augmented with many props because a number of the roommates were involved in live action role play. "A d-120! Fun!" Alexi said, having barely had time to look around until now. She was drawn towards the 120-sided die among a shelf of many others, even a two-sided die with Viking runic markings. She picked them up.

As a mathematician, Peter would have immediately recognized the Platonic solids represented heavily among the dice: a special, almost mystically perfect set of polyhedrons that Plato described, having equivalent faces, edges, and vertices. Such precise geometry helped support the case for a beautifully designed world. Rather than mathematics being just a language, there is good reason to argue that, while it involves language elements, the signs and symbols try to articulate something deeper: a world of *a priori* truths like these shapes to discover, a true but invisible world underpinning the material.

But while Peter would have seen the Platonic solids, Alexi saw Dungeons & Dragons.

"Do you play?"

"Of course. Kai's an excellent dungeon master."

Kai, however, was engrossed in something else. He was hunched over a map in the best of the lamplight with another friend. They looked like Napoleonic generals perfecting their battle plan.

"Alexi, what do you think? Kai asked.

"Think about what?" she said, taken aback.

"Should we look for World War One or Two relics?"

"Well, what are our chances of actually finding something?" Alexi inquired.

"Pretty good," Kai said, pointing to the shelf above the dice that she had completely missed.

"Seriously?" she replied in awe.

"There's more out there than people think. Just waiting to be discovered. The first thing I ever got was a *Reichsadler*—the imperial eagle from a Nazi *Schirmmütze*—their peaked caps. It's second on that shelf. That had me hooked." Alexi's eyes widened as Kai continued, "I know, that was one in a million."

"Okay, World War Two. Absolutely."

"I think we'll go to this area," Kai showed, pointing at the map. "You can take an hour or two off, right, Alexi?" She was torn but already there in her mind.

Before long, everyone was in waterproof gear that rustled when they moved, Alexi rocking some really fun '80s colors that Hannah had lying in the back of her closet from thrift stores and family. Amongst the bags and other gear, they'd definitely packed more Thermoses than people. Some soup but also leftover pie.

Only twenty minutes after piling into an old brown van, they arrived at a sodden, tree-flanked field. "There's some good spots we can try here," Kai said. Alexi immediately felt guilty about not telling Marc she was going. She could—perhaps should—have been supporting him. She *had* promised but said she was too busy with her research. Well, it was too late now. She hoped that, during the day, she could plan her excuse.

Kai and Hannah oriented Alexi to the basics of metal-detecting while their friends jumped right in. They dug up a couple of small finds early on. It did get quite exciting, using the smaller finger-like detector as they zoned in to the find before discovering what had been hidden there.

Alexi hoped that each beep could be something spectacular. After an hour or so, amid cold hands and the lull of a toilet break, she broke her determination to deal with the Marc problem later. She needed to text now.

Returning to the car, where Kai was eating a quick granola bar, she pulled her phone from her Aztec-patterned bag. She needed to apologize to Marc before he found out another way. To her dismay, her journal and a few things Edwin had given her fell into the puddle. For some stupid reason, she had brought them along.

Immediately, Kai jumped to action like a gentleman. But, as he handed the postcard over to her, something caught his eye. *Le Rubicon*—and those signs . . . *Where had he heard of that before?* "Are these important to you, Alexi?" he said. "I'm so sorry." Kai didn't know much about what Alexi was researching, but he knew a little from Hannah. "I could be totally losing the plot here, but I swear I saw a sign with that phrase on it at a weird old hunting village place about twenty miles from here."

"Really?!" Alexi said as she dried off the postcard.

"Does that help?" Kai asked.

Within minutes, the whole team were on their way to the site as a matter of urgency. Alexi could barely control her anticipation. Kai braced Alexi with the reality that it could be absolutely nothing. She bounded out of the car regardless.

"There used to be some World War Two stuff over the hill, but that's been cleared out for decades now. Cowboys," Kai explained, perturbed by the lack of good judgment and etiquette he felt many others displayed (really an echo of his own father who had complained about it many times). "But what I did see last time I was here was . . . just over there!" Stuffing his keys into one of his many pockets, he ran straight over to a tall pile of wood, Alexi alongside him. The rain had picked up, blowing sideways.

The pile looked like it had been collected for burning. "Just in time, I'd say," Kai said. "A farmer's probably bought it and wants to reclaim the land."

And there it lay, beneath tortured wood and layers of branches, just visible: a flakey, white-painted old wooden board with *"Le Rubicon"* written on it and the station for *"Radio le Rubicon"* added with imprecise brush strokes. Blue graffiti was scrawled on the side.

"Is this it?" he asked. But he need not have: "That is it! That is actually it, Kai!" Alexi said, wrestling with the deadfall and soon holding the sign up to the others who were all rooting for her. She jumped, throwing her arms around Kai in pure, unexpected joy. She'd expected to greet disappointment, for they were old friends. In an instant, old walls broke down. She had forgotten what it meant to smile. "In that case, you should probably have a look down there," Kai said, reflecting even just half of her giddy glee.

Kai led Alexi down an overgrown route, Hannah just behind. The path was still worn, for where there had been a lot of traffic and compression over the years it had prevented seedlings from totally recolonizing the path. They climbed over fallen trees. And then she saw it: the path opened up into a fascinating network of run-down A-frame cabins.

"It looks like they left in a hurry," Hannah said, having caught up, while Sam remained silent and exhausted but by her side. Old, reused glass bottles seemed to be everywhere, and there were newspapers stuffed into all the cabin cracks for insulation. "'1993,' this one says," Hannah read, having exhumed one.

"There—if I'm not mistaken—that's where they broadcast from," Kai said, having scouted this area before, led by his quizzical nature. "It's been like this ever since I was a kid—my papa took me out."

Alexi looked at the door of the hut with a network of wires fed through the apex. She placed her palm firmly against her inflated, still chest, bracing herself. Pulling out a bent hanger sort of makeshift metal piece, shoved through loops made for a real padlock, she pushed it. It opened.

Inside the dark dusty building was a mess. "It's probably been rifled through in here. Youths will have taken anything of value," Kai said.

The scene was heartbreaking—betrayed and devalued by man. But even that couldn't eclipse Alexi's joy. After visiting Edwin's house in Amsterdam, she thought she had lost the trail. And now she was in this place! A place Peter had been proud enough to write to Edwin about after sharing his congratulations about their good news. He had glowed about the radio show, saying, "Listen if you can!"

She sat on the swiveling chair despite the mouse droppings and despite almost falling right over. A cloud of dust blew upward. Tears welled up amidst the shock and chaos of it all—she really didn't care if they saw.

Her long fingers began sorting through the scattered papers by the equipment tower. And there she saw them: handwritten annotations in red pen, Peter was set to talk about mathematics and the search for truth. She learned so much about him from just that little note. He must have been smart! At least it seemed so. She wondered what he thought of art, for she certainly didn't get her artistic traits from her mother, who had refused to engage with or support anything in the arts.

Alexi looked around for anything else. In time, she came out into the blindingly blue daylight. She sat on the broken wood steps. She never wanted to leave. Was this even a place of happiness for Peter? She hoped so. But what of the newspaper article?

They spent the day trying to piece together the various layers of what had happened. It was the summer of '96 when Kai said he first came there, and even then, it was already an abandoned mess. Funny—in the sunken kitchen there were still pickled some vegetables eager to nourish a starving soul with the warmth of Estonian hospitality. Some of them probably could have!

Alexi investigated for hours trying to figure out which cabin was Peter's. She could imagine him as she stepped into each. It was frustrating: so much of it was destroyed, and the scale was bewildering. One of the large cabins had its window completely broken but with forbidding jagged glass teeth occupying the corners. Something big must have been thrown right through it.

Then, she remembered the bizarre little detail about the fox. Running round a loop of the houses again, she didn't see anything . . . until she returned to one small cabin, partially obscured. *Scratches! Could they have belonged to the fox that Peter told Edwin about on the postcard?* She swung open the door. *It should have creaked, shouldn't it?* But it didn't. It just swung open silently as if she were meant to be here.

There was a little fireplace, old tatty furniture, and old sheets—who knows who last slept here—even a kettle. But there wasn't anything truly meaningful. Deflated, after a few minutes, she turned.

Immediately, a tug on her soul pulled her back to take one last look. Compelled to lie down upon the dusty floor, under the off-white tail of a sheet that hung limp as if grounding it, was her reward: a small black book, and another behind it. She jumped up and grabbed a broom from the corner of the room. She used the pole end to pull the books toward herself, dust collecting and tumbling with them.

"Did you find something?" Hannah asked, walking in on this curious sight.

Alexi grabbed the first and Hannah cracked open the second. Alexi's book was a small Bible. Her response held back, along with her breath. There, in black-and-white, Edwin had dedicated it to Peter. Her heart warmed.

Upon looking up, Hannah cried, "Alexi!"

"What?"

Hannah's face looked horrified.

"What? You're scaring me."

In her joy, Alexi had been blind to it: the bottom edge of the book pages was covered with dry blood.

38

Peter

Leverage

LES VOSGES IV

Friday, May 20th, 1994.

Etienne now seemed chronically fatigued, with blue-black circles under his eyes. He'd been swimming upstream for too long. He'd even started to entertain the idea that human flourishing wasn't possible after all. "It doesn't matter what we do out here—," Etienne said to Peter after cornering him on the trail back to cabins one dark evening, sloppy and drunk. It hurt to see him like this. "—When—" Etienne continued, unable to grasp hold of the words or form them well, "—we all bring the mess in here," he said finally, tapping hard on Peter's chest. It was quite possibly the loudest "quiet chat" imaginable.

Peter got it. It reminded him of what Edwin had said about the Israelites being free from Egypt but needing to know the reason for their continued slavery: chains on the inside. He also remembered celebrating Diwali and desperately wanting the light to go deeper still. Change required something to shift in the human heart, or community would never flourish. No rhythm of the earth had been enough for this deep work. The mythic grounding rhythms of dance, music, and nature were powerful but not powerful enough to rebuff the strong undercurrent of violence. It superficially knit them for a time, but it could not bind human hearts into the deep, enduring mystery of peace and rest.

Some residents now openly called the community a cult—this place that Etienne had earnestly carved out for serious thought, study, and intentional patterns of life! It would be hilarious if some people weren't seriously alleging it. These voices wanted to discredit him, take the reins, and build their own personal Edens regardless of what others wanted.

The insight of Polanyi haunted Etienne increasingly: the "moral inversion" that occurs in the intensified pursuit of creating a utopia or Eden through reductionist means. For, as Bernard told Peter, that is how the dystopic begins.[270]

All Etienne could do was try to allay the—often-contradictory—fears and share his story. If they worked together, despite all odds, they could fight for change just like French *Résistance*. This was the shared story of France, as well as his own. His grandmother, after all, had been a hero of the *Résistance*. This gave him an undisputed anchor in real history. She had, Etienne shared, navigated these very forests as part of the Free French, even guiding SOE operatives. "*Résistance* starts with the hearts and minds of men. Then real change can happen!" Etienne tried to remind them. Without the French *Résistance*, he argued, the Allies would not have won. In the same way, he told them, "We must not infight when they have a real enemy!" Their war, he explained, was against the capitalist way of life that held humanity in a headlock, saying that there was no alternative but to consume and be consumed. The change, he argued, had to start with them. They needed to live and embody a grounded alternative. He reminded them again of the manifesto they had written a year before, when their dreams were fresh and untainted. Yet people were selfish. Without feeling an imminent threat, as in the Second World War, there was less to bind them; less willingness to sacrifice personal ambition.

Given Etienne's condition, Peter was fearful about him being taken advantage of. He had seen a few hasty deals in the shadows. Surely, Peter thought, it wasn't drugs? Etienne had been so vigilant about keeping them out of the community. Regardless, Etienne looked ill, his body struggling. It was as if, in offering his life as a sacrifice for humanity, Etienne's spirit had been devoured by aching humanity without regret, as if it were their right. Not only were they not thankful, but they were hungry again and looking for someone to blame.

---

270. For example, Polanyi, *Beyond Nihilism*, 20, 25–26; Polanyi and Prosch, *Meaning*, 18.

Peter also felt for Hélène, who seemed more and more lonely through it all. She often sought Peter in those quiet moments. She was subtle about it, but Peter could see her thirst for closeness: to be seen, known, and genuinely loved.

Not long after this evening, Etienne snapped at Peter. He normally found Peter's thirst for knowledge endearing, but at that moment, this was just another need pulling on him. Peter gave him space. He took the fox cub with him out for a walk alone in the cool evening before turning into bed. With everything so still, it was the type of evening when sounds took on an almost opaque, concrete quality.

There was a gentle crack in the woods behind him. He turned to see Hélène there. She was silent but crying. He looked around, more aware now of prying eyes after what Jean-Paul had said. But there was no one around, and he couldn't leave her like that. He would have sent her back to Etienne, but what reception would she get this evening?

"Can I just be with you?" Hélène pleaded. She wasn't wearing much, and the night was much colder than it should have been in late May. He would have invited her onto the deck of his cabin, but he didn't want everyone to see. Instead, he made a snap decision to invite her in. The fox was thankful, leaping against the door with a mischievous boldness, adding yet another scratch. Hélène laughed through her tears. "Isn't he made for the outdoors?" she asked.

"Oh, but now he knows the difference!" Peter said, offering joy to attend to her sadness.

"Tea?" the Brit suggested.

"Thank you. You know, I think Chestnut is a good name for him," she said through her tears.

"I think he likes it!" Peter said, the fox yipping with excitement.

Hélène's giggle briefly animated her inflamed face before it broke back into the sort of grimace that only deep pain could induce. She turned, hiding her face with her cuff.

Peter didn't know what to do. He only had himself to offer, and that stability was barely enough for himself. Clutching at straws, he heard himself say, "Have you tried meditation?"

"You sound like Ritesh," Hélène replied. After an awkward silence, she answered, "A bit."

Peter knew that was a nice way of saying no. But what did it matter? Had meditation and chanting really helped him? He was more open to the spiritual now, and a holistic life seemed appealing, but how was this meant to look? In his braver moments, he had attempted to understand and join Ritesh, whose spiritual practice was eclectic but grounded by his upbringing in Nepal. Apparently, it all aimed to train his mind to avoid thoughts and actions that would store up bad karma. Yet, Peter remained frustrated. Despite his efforts, these practices hadn't led to inner transformation. It sometimes helped him calm down, but in the end, he was just as embittered and pierced. The blood kept flowing, the internal wound growing darker and black. He had no real peace. None that stayed. The emptiness was ripe as a vacuum for fears to sweep right in. He found the Hindu practices rich in grounding his body and was thankful for them, but found little to help restore or redeem. Likewise, because of the concept of karma, there was little compassion for suffering. Finally, forgiveness, the very thing that he both wanted to ignore but knew he needed to walk through—especially now that Bernard had encouraged him to confront his suffering—he found to be just a peripheral issue in Hinduism.

Peter wasn't going to call Hélène out. Who was he to say anything? "Good," Peter said, at a loss for what to suggest now.

He apologized for the length of time the kettle took to heat. The vapor slowly pooled below the cabinet. He decided to keep it simple, show her the compassion that he also desired—the type that felt natural to his heart. Gently, Peter started to encouraged Hélène to share, but she offered just the surface layer. Peter studied her, trying to hear what she wasn't saying.

Then he saw them: new bruises. One right below her clavicle. He interrupted as he rushed over from the kitchen, flushed with compassion. "What happened? Are you okay?"

Hélène protested that she just wanted tea with him. But Peter was concerned, more so after what Jean-Paul had said. This bruise didn't look normal. It couldn't be shrugged off as an accident. All of a sudden, Peter put two and two together. All Hélène said when pushed was that she hated herself. She said nothing about Etienne. It reminded Peter of what Edwin said at school after being bullied.

Peter was livid. He blamed himself for not doing anything to stop it. Of course, Hélène denied anyone hurting her—but what was he meant to believe? She adamantly forbade him from interfering.

The questions made Hélène more anxious. She tried to change the conversation. She saw the tag left over from his flight to Amsterdam on the bag slid under his bed: 31 Gooseberry Crescent, Egham, Middlesex. She joked it was the most British address she'd ever seen.

When the questions kept coming, she threatened to go. But Peter knew he needed to be a safe place. The rest of the evening unwound in a daze, emotions clouding thoughts and conviction. Peter brushed her hair behind her right ear. She took the palm of his hand and rested her face against it. She smelled of jasmine-infused honey. Hélène looked at him with affection. This was different, new. He brushed a large bruise on her arm with compassion. Their eyes locked before he kissed it, gently, chivalrous. Hélène's heart fluttered with hope, stirring in Peter an unfamiliar ardor. The gathering darkness formed a blanket over the cabin in which the regular rules seemed not to apply, suspended for their irrelevance. Present to both themselves and each other, they embraced.

It was Chestnut who alerted them to the start of a new day. Hélène left without a word as the morning sun still fought for its strength against the clutches of night. Peter instantly regretted everything—not the compassion but everything beyond it. He was tormented by a deluge of emotions, his mind litigating against himself. What would he ever say to Etienne? How would he look at him again through both anger and shame?

The weeks rolled by. Nothing changed, but neither did anything heal. The tension, the mess in between, just festered. Peter pretended things were okay, grinning through an ever-deepening despair. Etienne wouldn't just be disappointed at him: this was the full-on betrayal of a friend. To make things worse, Jean-Paul became more critical of Etienne at the community council. Apparently, he was tired of "playing politics" and needed a more radical approach. People needed to be fully in—with their finances, with their time—and they needed to start being offensive, not just defensive. This didn't seem like the utopia that they had been dreaming of in Paris—the prototype to start a new more humane world.

By the time Jean-Paul came to visit Peter in his cabin, Peter was more wary of him than ever.

"What do you want?" Peter said, before his brain had caught up with his mouth.

"We need to chat," Jean-Paul replied, forcing his way in.

Chestnut growled at Jean-Paul, so Peter locked him away in his room.

"I think you were right," Jean-Paul said.

"About what?"

"About Etienne abusing Hélène," Jean-Paul replied.

They both knew that had originally been Jean-Paul's diagnosis, but because of his recent revelation, Peter let it slide. "You know," Jean-Paul added, "I'd forgive you if that was the reason I saw Hélène sneaking out of here a few weeks ago."

Peter panicked, flushed with blood. What was he meant to do? Jean-Paul point-blank confronted him. "I don't want to talk about it," Peter said.

"I respect that," Jean-Paul replied. "I just needed you to know that I will keep your secret," he added.

But at what cost? Peter realized.

39

Peter

The Woman

LES VOSGES IV

Friday, July 22nd, 1994.

A few months had passed, and the spring had long given way to the July heat. The persimmon sky of the last days would have been idyllic were it not for its permanence. By day and night its glow testified to the wildfires all over the continent. Smoke blew in all the way from Spain, Portugal, and Italy. Even the Vosges were becoming brittle in the heat, ever more vulnerable. Moss exposed to the sun turned to powder when crunched underfoot. The land cried out for rain. Rumor had it there was even a nearby fire that had sparked up. Some blamed lightning. Others, cigarettes.

Hearing a serious commotion down by the fire pit, Peter ran down there, fox in tow. No fires had been lit in it during the drought, but still there should have been music playing. Instead, something raw was happening in the core of a mob of people; some were standing on tables to get a better view.

As Peter approached, it became clear that in the midst of it all were Etienne and Jean-Paul. *He must have finally snapped. But,* Peter thought, *whatever he's done, he doesn't deserve this in public.*

The fox stayed at a distance as Peter entered the human mass. The deeper he went, the darker the sky turned. Chestnut whined anxiously.

Smoke filtered the sunlight to the color of an old albumen print. Etienne was livid, but so was Jean-Paul. Peter tried subtly asking what had started it, but no one replied. The men were getting into it. Some of the allegations were about leadership and the direction in which the community was going in. But the rest? It was getting personal.

"You just want a comfortable feudal kingdom where everyone honors the lord of the manor!" Jean-Paul alleged.

"Stop being ridiculous. Do you see how ridiculous he is being?" Etienne implored the crowd, relieved to see that Peter had arrived.

Peter could see that Etienne was almost out of tears, his face red and swollen. He had never seen him in such a state. "Here, come with me," Peter said, coming between Etienne and Jean-Paul. Etienne was not himself. "Look at me," Peter said again, putting his hands on the sides of Etienne's face.

"He's not finished," said Jean-Paul. "Go on, Etienne—tell us why you made that decision!"

"For you," Etienne replied. "For you all!" Etienne was backed into a corner, and Jean-Paul knew it. Etienne had placed his whole life and reputation on this. All his eggs in one basket. They were right. Once *Le Rubicon* was crossed, there was no going back. It was either a success, or it was all pointless. If he couldn't meaningfully change the world then what was the point?

"They don't care how much you have sacrificed, Etienne. Everyone else here has sacrificed, too," Jean-Paul said, pushing and pushing.

Peter almost succeeded in smuggling Etienne out with him, but then he stopped. Etienne felt he had to reply. "We're not done here, Jean-Paul. We can't build a new world on anger and violence."

"It looks just fine on you," Jean-Paul said even more loudly.

"Excuse me?" Etienne shouted.

Jean-Paul put his hand on Peter's shoulder. Peter's heart fell. "Tell them, Peter. Tell them what Etienne did!"

"I don't—"

Jean-Paul stared at Peter; he felt it reach inside of him, seizing and twisting at his heart. "Tell them, Peter!" he insisted.

"Tell us what?" some of the people started to shout.

"We need the truth, Peter," Jean-Paul said.

Peter knew Jean-Paul was leveraging him. He felt trapped. He had to say something. It was clear what Jean-Paul wanted, but Peter didn't think he should say anything about Helen's bruises.

The only way he could free himself from the blackmail was to admit to what had happened between him and Hélène. But what would that accomplish? It would make them both pariahs. If it were just his neck on the line, he could do it—but Hélène? She had been through enough. Did he really have to choose between Etienne and Hélène?

"Peter?" Jean-Paul said. "You need to protect Hélène. You need to tell them."

"Hélène?" The people started whispering among themselves. Thank goodness she wasn't there to see it. She and Lavinia were still in the dance studio.

Peter knew he had to say something. "There were bruises," he finally said, quietly.

"Did you hear that?" Jean-Paul said loudly, "Etienne has been physically abusing Hélène!"

Etienne looked at Peter immediately as if he were Judas. Peter could never erase the sting of those eyes: the disappointment, the pain, the deep, dark sadness.

A broken man, Etienne tried to get away to his cabin, but Jean-Paul and the people came after him. *Can they not see that Jean-Paul is a bully?* Having killed this soul, Peter felt the blood on his hands, sticky and putrid.

The next thing Peter knew, the door to Etienne's cabin was swung wide. Scores of people had followed Etienne inside and many more outside, bringing with them something beyond the sum of their parts, something fetid and violent. By the time he had squeezed inside, Etienne was standing behind his desk. After collecting himself for a second, he stood on his desk chair. He stared at them with both love and disappointment, inducing everyone into an eerie stillness. He picked up a picture of his grandmother, Violet, from the war. She was beautiful, her smile honest and strong. "Look!" Etienne said. "This is my grandmother, Violet. Her first husband was killed at the start of the Nazi occupation of Paris. But she didn't back down. She continued to put her life on the line for freedom, again and again. To see France set free. She was one of the heroes of her generation. In the same way, my dream has and will always be to free France—free humanity. We're not fighting the Nazis, but the danger is just as real. We fight the slavery of a living death."

He held the photo up, proud, for others to see. People seemed to resonate with what he was saying. It made sense. Peter thought that everything might be okay, that Etienne might be okay.

Waiting for the crowd's murmurs to die down, Jean-Paul chose the perfect lull from which to deal his death blow. "She was a hero, was she? Guided the *Résistance*? Fought during the liberation? You've all heard the stories, but what about the truth?"

"That is the truth!" Etienne said dismissively, finally starting to feel more in control.

"What I have here seems to say otherwise!" Jean-Paul fetched a picture from his pocket. *How long had it been there? Waiting?*

In the book of Genesis, God spoke to Cain when anything, it seems, could have happened. God says, "Sin is crouching at your door; it desires to have you, but you must rule over it." In this case, Jean-Paul desired to have the last word, to excise Etienne's leadership; and despite his wise attempts, Etienne had not been able to rule over him.

Jean-Paul revealed a picture of a woman, half-naked, with a shaved head, being escorted by gleeful, gun-wielding *Résistance* fighters. He seized Etienne's picture to show the comparison. "It's the same woman!"

Etienne took it from him, took a look, and immediately crumbled. He couldn't believe it. His whole life he had heard of his grandmother, the hero. Every night his parents had shared another piece of the puzzle, another way she'd helped win the war and changed the world—in the same way they said that he would.

Once he had heard something from another child. Something about her being a collaborator, but his parents had said it was just the jealousy and foolishness of children, and so he'd dismissed it entirely. *And now it turns out to have been true?* Etienne knew what the picture meant. That sort of public humiliation was reserved in the days of the liberation of Paris for what they called *collaboration horizontale*. Those collaborators who had sexual relations with the enemy; a real betrayal of those fighting.

Jean-Paul didn't stop humiliating the man on the floor: "And what does he have? A smiling woman? What is behind that smile? He has no proof. It's all fabrication! This is all the proof we need," he said, taking the picture from Etienne's hands and displaying it brazenly.

Etienne got to his feet, ripped the photo out of Jean-Paul's hands, throwing both it and the framed picture onto the floor. The frame shattered. "Leave me alone," Etienne shouted as he stormed out. He banged his hip on the edge of his desk as he moved around people in an attempt to escape. He ran into the forest.

Peter ran after him.

"Who even are you, Peter?" Etienne cried, turning briefly as he fled. "Leave me alone!"

When turned from Peter, Etienne instinctively reached into his pocket and pulled out several Valium pills.

Peter didn't know what to do. He ran to find Bernard. How could he possibly unpack what he had just been a part of?

"And you left him?" Bernard said when Peter finally found him.

Bernard didn't care about what Etienne had said. They needed to be with him. He needed someone. "His whole world is collapsing."

Peter felt an overwhelming weight of shame. They walked as quickly as Bernard could. Since Bernard's cabin was near Etienne's, the plan was to shoo any remaining people out of his house, grab some blankets, and lock it up. It was warm, too warm, but Bernard explained that Etienne was probably in shock.

Just as they were about to leave, another unbidden moment shattered the expected. "This is the photo, Peter?" Bernard asked Peter, suddenly overcome with emotion. His hand was shaking, holding Etienne's picture of Violet. "Peter, I know her. I know her!"

Peter looked over to see Bernard sheet-white.

She had long been the woman who visited him in dreams, promising, cross necklace in hand, that she would return. Bernard was immediately back there: just twelve and a bag of bones. This woman—this angel—had crept up to the fence at a satellite camp of Natzweiler-Struthof. Before she had to leave, she gave him something. He didn't know what it was at first, but she told him it was magic. It was an armadillo scute, now kept safe on Horrice's back—a slightly different color to the rest. "You're stronger than you think," she'd said. "Look, the magic's already working," she whispered, pointing to a little honeybee that flew through the fence, defying the rules of the human world. It landed on young Bernard's hand. It was in that instant that he knew he was going to be okay, that he would live. She then drew his eyes to a wild honeybee hive behind him. The bees became his friends, his way of surviving.

"Jean-Paul had proof that she was a collaborator, not a hero," Peter explained, lifting him out of his memories.

"That's a mistake, Peter!" Bernard said firmly. He even shocked himself with his intensity. "She was my hero," he said more softly. "This was the nail in the coffin? We need to find him." Bernard said, shaking but determined. Vigilantes at the liberation made many heinous mistakes.

Bernard began running as if he had regained the vigor of a twelve-year-old boy that had once been stolen from him. He needed Etienne to know. *He* was the proof.

Chestnut ran up in front but became nervous: the forest was alive. The smoke from the fires was getting ever thicker. They tried to send Chestnut back, but he refused, instead sticking closer to Peter's side.

Then, as they went, it started to rain. But no: it wasn't rain! It was white. "Ash, Peter," Bernard explained through his heavy breaths, heart pounding. The forest fire was moving towards them. Forest animals came out of nowhere, running away from the fire as the men were moving towards it. This all felt wrong. Eden was burning, the inversion almost complete.

"Etienne!" Peter called over and over. They split up as the paths diverged.

Bernard thought to check his garden. After all, that's the way Etienne went on his morning walk.

"Peter!" Bernard screamed.

When Peter arrived, he saw Bernard sitting on the floor, cradling Etienne's limp body, ash falling around them. It looked like he'd tried to hang himself on the oak tree but had been disoriented and lacked the coordination. In frustration, he'd taken a knife and tried to stab himself. He had collapsed with an empty alcohol bottle next to him. His body was cool, too cool. "Go get help, Peter. Go get help."

"But—!"

"Go get help!" Bernard bellowed with all he could.

Etienne's breathing was shallow. Bernard applied pressure on the wound, whispering into his ear over and over: "She was a hero, Etienne. She was a hero. She was my hero."

Peter ran. All he remembered was the persistent taste of vomit in his mouth as he'd retched but kept running. Then, the flashing lights.

ACT THREE

The In Between

40

Peter

What Sacred Games?

LES VOSGES V

> God is dead. God remains dead. And we have killed him. How shall we comfort ourselves, the murderers of all murderers? . . . who will wipe this blood off us? What water is there for us to clean ourselves? What festivals of atonement, what sacred games shall we have to invent? Is not the greatness of this deed too great for us? Must we ourselves not become gods simply to appear worthy of it? ~ Friedrich Nietzsche, *The Gay Science*, 181.

The "death of God" is one thing. The death of a friend, another. But are they really that different?

Atheists today often make the "death of God" out to be nothing. A simple, self-evident liberation. But what they understood in those revolutionary years at the end of the nineteenth and the dawn of the twentieth centuries was that it changed everything. It changed how you navigated the world: how you comported yourself. Heck, it even changed what it meant to be human—and who gets to decide this.

As a substitute for God, the human god proves fickle and treacherously savage. No sooner had God been deposed of than humanity was found lamenting over its "blood-stained face."[271]

271. Camus, "Unbeliever and Christians," 71.

41

Peter

No Tattoos

Sunday, July 31st, 1994.

The community was reeling after the death of Etienne. Had he not, at one time, been a god to many of them? The one in whom they stored up hope? And yet, as nothing more or less than mortal flesh, Etienne had become the human sacrifice for Jean-Paul as he pushed for his utopic ideal.

The victory was not as sweet as it should have been. Akin to the grief of Alaric I, that king of Visigoths who in the ancient world led his fearsome Germanic tribe to achieve the unthinkable feat of sacking Rome, this victory also represented a loss. Alaric had first hoped for the honor of acceptance by the Western Roman Empire. After seeing this to be out of reach, he undermined it. Jean-Paul, too, had wanted acceptance and adoration—but only in a very particular way—he wanted his ideas to be actioned. In his mind, the fate of the world relied on it.

But how could the people love him now? He had not intended to push Etienne that far, but they saw how cool and calculated he'd remained at every step. The people were fearful of him. To make things worse, the government was now over them like a rash, trying to figure out exactly who all these people were and how much of a threat they were to the state. Apparently still not a big enough one if Jean-Paul had anything to say about it.

Continuing to live after Etienne's death—that was the hard part. While Jean-Paul had seared his own heart, insulating it from the pang of guilt, every one of Peter's good memories was tainted by Etienne's haunting stare after Peter had aired his allegation. Shame rang shrill in Peter's ears. He planned to move back to Tristan's place in Paris or even Edwin's house before the week was up.

What of Hélène? On that fateful day, upon hearing the sirens, she had run to see what the commotion was about. Held back by police, she saw the contours of his body beneath the white sheet. Her eyes widened, begging for clarity; pushing to get near. It failed. At first, no one spoke to her directly. Then she overheard a whisper. It confirmed her fear. Her scream exhumed all buried guilt for those who heard. Increasingly, smoke filled the air, leaving it blood-orange and charged like a lightning storm. *"Non, non, non!"* she cried as the ambulance pulled away.

As if Etienne had been a guardian for the community worthy of the ancient legends, just minutes after they took him away, the authorities ordered a total evacuation because of the fires. You could hear it: the crackling and distant trees falling.

Hélène and Etienne had a somewhat dysfunctional relationship, but they had loved each other in their own way. They had known each other for years; for as long as Etienne had known Jean-Paul. Etienne was the one person who truly had insight into how brilliant she was. Around others, Hélène had learned that it was safer to lean into her other talents. Besides, she was pretty, so people didn't expect much. If people caught wind of her intelligence, they assumed she was calculating or manipulating. If she were a man, they'd probably have lauded his praises and put him in charge. *People liked you more when you were carefree and giddy*, she had told herself; closing herself off to flourishing, to the real breadth of who she was. It hurt, like Chinese foot-binding for the soul. But pretty and compliant should be enough for her, right?

Given the fire, the *gendarmerie* arranged for community members to stay in old hotels in the nearby village; the type with four stories, wooden shutters, and giddy geraniums in window boxes, where the nearby church bells continued to peal gleefully throughout the day. No one saw Hélène. She confined herself to her room, sobbing incessantly even after the tears had dried up. Her body alternated between shaking and stillness; the rest of the world ignorant and indifferent.

When they were allowed back to Le Rubicon a week later, nothing felt the same. Immediately, Jean-Paul tried to steer the ship, but he lacked the moral integrity to galvanize hearts. As soon as they returned, Bernard and Peter went to clean Etienne's cabin just as Kurt Gödel had done for Einstein. The cabin was a mess after Etienne's desperate escape.

Bernard lamented that it was telling of our cultural poverty that in other cultures, they could have ministered to his body, saying goodbye as they prepared him for burial. Here, they could attend only to his things. Still, it was meaningful somehow, preeminently so. The sort of meaning that society sneers at, unable to recognize it as significant because of its hideously narrow description of worth. It failed to register, for it didn't directly relate to material transactions—or climbing a career ladder— which in turn supposedly helps you secure a life of making more of these transactions.

Bernard broke the unnerving silence. They began to talk about what to keep and what to give away. How surreal. "What about his clothes?" Peter asked.

Soon they found treasures. Old letters bundled and various curiosities. It transpired that Etienne had collected *Résistance* items with an obsession that matched his understanding. Fitting. This, it turned out, included an actual Sten gun stashed in his wardrobe and a silk map of northern France. Light and durable, this was the type of map that RAF crew were equipped with in case they found themselves shot down. It went on. There was even a necklace, old and well-made, but the picture wasn't of his grandmother. He placed it carefully on the desk.

This provoked Peter to clean up the shattered glass from the frame that had long kept Etienne's coveted, dignifying picture of his grandmother—Violet—safe. It was the least he could do.

When staying in the hotel, Peter had only managed to get fragments of information out of Bernard about how Violet was "his hero." Bernard didn't want anyone else to know. As Peter picked up the glass, he asked Bernard, "How did you know what the scute was?"

"I didn't. She seemed to me like an angel." Bernard's eyes closed, and a subtle smile came over his face as he thought about the unexpected visitation. "She told me it was magic—an "armadillo scute." Only, I didn't have the foggiest idea of what an armadillo or a scute was. It was only after American GIs liberated the camp (or what was left of it) that I learned. I was lucky, Peter. They'd left me for dead, my body weak. If they'd marched me out of there with the rest, I wouldn't have made it." His voice trailed off.

"But you don't—" Peter started as he pulled the pieces together.

"I don't have numbers tattooed on my arm because my particular slice of hell was not Auschwitz but just thirty miles from here."

"Why, Bernie? Why come back?" Peter asked, aghast.

"It's almost been fifty years, Peter. It was about time I confronted the black mark on my heart left by my memories of this land."

"But how?" Peter's cleaning ground to a halt as his mind tried to understand the magnitude of what Bernie was saying. It was good, Peter told himself, that he could speak of it.

"What better way to redeem a land of death than by inviting it to nurture new life?"

"Your garden," Peter realized.

"And my girls," by which he meant his bees. "Besides, the rhythm of the seasons is good for the soul." Bernard steadied himself as he waded back into his memories. "Shortly after they came, a GI challenged me to a game of chess. I was emptying my pockets for something to act as a rook, and the GI was really surprised to see it. That's where Horrice came from: the GI made sure I got him from another guy in the unit who had him stuffed and sitting on the dashboard of his Jeep. I was thirteen but must have looked much younger. I didn't recognize myself when I first saw my reflection in his wing mirror. The GI gave me Horrice, a Superman magazine, and a pack of gum. He'd probably have given me his Lucky Strikes if I'd asked! You could tell he felt sorry for me. Afterward, I must have looked ridiculous: not a penny to my name but a wafer-thin teenager carting that taxidermized animal around Europe, looking for family. Part of me hoped to find her. Mind you, I never did. Until now."

As Peter moved to grasp a piece of glass, the cabin door flew open. He jumped, cutting himself.

Hélène immediately launched accusations towards Peter. Someone had finally divulged what he'd said. Peter had wondered when this hammer would drop.

"Can you give us some space, Bernard? Actually, don't worry. We'll leave," Peter said, embarrassed. Peter shoved his things in his bag, including a couple of books and even the Bible that Edwin had given him. He still toted it around even if he never looked at it.

Hélène unapologetically seized hold of the necklace from the desk on her way out, as if Peter didn't even have a right to see it, let alone decide its fate. It had been so meaningful to Etienne. *How could Peter understand?* She thought. Hélène knew that it had been Violet's. Etienne shared its secrets—the secrets entrusted to him in his youth—and pledged that Hélène would have it one day.

"How could you have done that?" Hélène shouted at Peter as she stood waiting by the door, necklace clasped in hand.

"Can we talk about this?" Peter said, trying to de-escalate and move her outside. Besides, he wanted to share that what happened wasn't nearly as clear-cut as it must have seemed.

"You used me to discredit him!" Hélène cried as they approached Peter's cabin. It had been raining for the last few days, but now it picked up, carrying away her tears. She pulled her jacket right.

"Listen to me," Peter said as they walked over the threshold and into the cabin. He grabbed her hands earnestly.

She pulled her hands away and deposited the necklace safely in her pocket, frustrated. "He died thinking that I had betrayed him and—." Her face scrunched up. She couldn't bring herself to say it. Instead, she punched out every word: "You are evil, Peter. Evil!"

Peter didn't know what to say. It is rare that one sees oneself as evil since one knows one's own justifications. As the saying goes, we judge others by their actions and ourselves by our intentions . . . *But what if she was right? No, surely not*, he thought.

She was enraged that he wasn't answering her. "Don't you care?" She moved over to his small dining table. "Do you even care about people, Peter? Or do you just care about your mind games?"

"What?" Peter was confused. Hélène clearly didn't understand all of what had happened. Did she even know what role Jean-Paul had played? The cabin was cold. He started to light a fire. Perhaps they could be civil about it all.

With his back turned, Hélène wanted to do something to hurt him. She grabbed his bag and dumped out his precious books. "You think you're wise? A seeker of truth? You're a liar. You condemned him," Hélène accused, looking at the pile.

With the young fire burning, Peter took to his feet. Attempting to de-escalate again, he drew close, rounded his shoulders, and spoke calmly. It didn't work.

She shoved him away. Reviled. "You think you're better than everyone else. Think about it, Peter! You used my life to push him over the edge."

"I was trying to protect you!" He protested.

"What? By making me an accomplice? Using my story, my life, to manipulate him?"

"You really don't understand," Peter said.

"Why? You didn't publicly accuse him of hurting me?"

"At least I told the truth!"

"You think that's the truth?" Hélène said furiously, clenching her jaw. She moved her head to look away, tears trailing after.

"I was trying to protect you," Peter said again.

"You think that protected me?"

"What was I meant to do?"

"I don't know—refuse to weaponize my life!"

"I'm just doing my best like anyone else."

"So holy . . ." Hélène said, grabbing the Bible that Edwin had given Peter.

He snatched it back from her, his hand still bleeding from the glass. He'd seen her eyes dart towards the fire. He threw the Bible away from her reach, revealing his frustration. It landed with a thud before sliding under his bed.

"Look, I can do that too!" She said, snatching up Camus's *The Rebel* and throwing it in the same direction. "If it were up to me, I'd never see you again!"

Peter looked confused. *Why would it not be?* he thought.

"Everyone's already judging me. I can't tell them."

"Tell them what?" Peter's mind was running.

"You need to take me into town, Peter. I can't have your child."

42

Alexi

Blood & Streetlights

PARIS III

Friday, October 30th, 2015.

The emerald embrace of a Parisian café in the late afternoon felt both fertile and anonymous enough for the birth and death of scandalous ideas. What, after all, is fertilizer but the fruit of death?

Alexi's core concern was still whether Peter had died. *Was this his blood on the Bible? And why was it discarded?* It felt surreal to think of him as a living, breathing, bleeding human being, with dreams, hopes, and passions.

A farmer near the community had explained to Alexi that just weeks after the death and the fires, everyone dispersed, bar a few peculiar stragglers. He couldn't recall who had died. Alexi had tried to look thankful for his help but was truthfully infuriated. The only way to know, she now reasoned, was to send Edith and Edwin another email. She needed to know the date of the postmark on the last postcard: to find out whether it was before or after the date of the suspicious death.

After finding the Bible and the philosophy book, Alexi had turned the cabin over but didn't find much more. It was painful to have seen the community's disintegration: broken windows and vermin droppings. She could only imagine its former glory. The worst was the broken bottles and the soiled toilet paper, clearly the work of local youths.

Despite all the comfort of the café—a taupe foam still coating the inside of her mug—she felt real anger build within her when she thought of Marc. It was hard to separate the victories of that week from his disappointment about her missing his races. He came second, not that she cared, he alleged. Their concerns missed each other, passing like ships in the night. Nothing had been the same since. In fact, Alexi had started to hear another girl's name—Olivia—pop up. Both Sam and Blake had let things slip. Blake, perhaps, didn't do so by accident. He'd met this girl at the race. This hurt; she and Marc hadn't exactly been an item, but they hadn't decided that they weren't either.

Alexi looked at the Bible. It would be his blood, wouldn't it? Did it matter? Surely it was worse if it wasn't. A fleeting thought came to her: *I wonder blood type he was?* He had a whole history she longed to know.

Then, a putrid fear crept upon her as if dragging itself up onto her lap. What if the truth had been staring her in the face? Edwin had loved Peter so dearly. Why would Peter have rejected that? Sure, Peter could reject God, but discarding a gift of friendship like that? All she could see on the canvas of her mind were Edwin's tears and the desperation for news about him. What if that said more about the softness of Edwin's character than Peter's? Was Peter hard and callous?

What if that horrid London lady was right about Peter? She had been almost frothing! Alexi's mother certainly agreed. She had nothing but bad things to say about him, so toxic that she preferred to say nothing at all. Alexi strained to remember any specific details, but it was always the same allegation: he betrayed and then abandoned her. Alexi had thought it was just another of her mother's negative opinions, taking it with a pinch of salt. But what if there a kernel of truth? Was he the cause of her mother's trauma? The reason she was this way? This would prove him guilty, not innocent.

That all tasted foul and bitter—the kind that burnt and came with a smell that clung to the inside of one's nostrils. She couldn't get away from it. What if this whole time she'd been deceiving herself? Would else would she find? Perhaps she should just stop. Besides, if he was a monster, what did that make her?

Her mobile buzzed. She needed a distraction. Turning it upwards, she saw the text was from Marc. That was a nice surprise. She'd been giving him space. After leaving the café, the pace of the night sped up considerably. Jealousy made for an excellent motivator. She was going to apologize, practicing it over in her head: to own her stuff but also stand her ground.

She painted her nails for the first time in a while and curled her hair. Black high heels and a sophisticated tailored white dress pulled together a look that said, "I don't need you, but you should want me."

"Wow," Marc said as he rose from his barstool. The place was loud and had laser lights above to accompany the live DJ. Alexi was thrilled that Olivia wasn't there. "I hope this isn't all for me?" he said.

"Don't flatter yourself," Alexi said as Marc took her hand, helping her to her stool. This was her way of saying "I've missed you," and he knew it.

Alexi felt alive. Her mind felt quick and witty even as the night unfolded, and she tried a couple of new cocktails. *There was his smile.* She realized that she had been craving it.

"Look," said Alexi in a genuine tone, "I am so sorry for before."

"Alexi, I need to talk to you about something," Marc said.

"Fire away."

"I'd like you to meet Olivia."

Alexi didn't know what to say. Her knee-jerk reaction was "why?" but she stopped herself short of asking.

"You're important to me too, and I think you'd like each other."

"Too? What you're really saying is that she's more important?" Alexi snapped. She hated sounding like this. In an instant, everything that they'd just healed came unpicked.

"You know, a good friend would have supported me," Alexi said.

"You know I couldn't miss the competition!" Mark justified.

"There will always be another competition."

"There were other days to root around an abandoned cult, Alexi. I would have come with you."

"You don't get it. It's like I was holding my breath until I—"

"What? Until you find another cryptic clue that—"

"That what?" Alexi pressed.

"What if he's not all he's cracked up to be, Alexi? You're sacrificing your real friends for this mirage, this idealized version of a person that probably never existed. If he had a shred of decency, then he would have been in your life."

That stung. Alexi realized that part of her actually hoped that it was Peter who'd died at the community. Then he would have had an alibi, dark as it was. A martyr, a tortured soul.

But what if it wasn't him that died? Was he involved with whatever happened? Did he try to stop it? Or was he complicit? Now she remembered something that her mother had said once when regaining consciousness after surgery. Alexi had disregarded it. "He used me to kill him," she had said, clasping at Alexi's hands, sobbing. Then, she abruptly moved to laugh about something unrelated, volatile like Jekyll and Hyde. A nurse had walked by and brushed it off, saying it was normal. It seemed clear now, but at the time she had no context. Who were these men she was talking about? Had someone forced her mother to kill Peter? Or had Peter manipulated her to kill someone else? Either way, he was bad news.

Alexi's mind was racing. Strobe lights came on, chopping up their actions as her hope was also cut to pieces. Why was she so stupid? Why would her mother have put him on the child support form if he was dead? She must have at least thought he was alive when she was, what, two? So then, Peter must have manipulated her to kill someone! No wonder she was messed up, Alexi thought. For the first time in her life, she felt sympathetic to her mother.

"Alexi, do you even care?" Marc said, trying to get through to her.

"No, I mean, of course, but . . ." Alexi was in a daze.

"It's not that I don't like you, Alexi. It's just I need someone who's not so caught up in their own stuff, someone to support me."

This angered Alexi. "Support you?" she cried, the lights capturing her revulsion crisply. They both fired a couple of more blows before she stood up.

"Don't worry. I'm going," Marc said, slamming his glass down.

It seemed so final. Alexi stayed for a few minutes longer, but even the noise and buzzing of the people couldn't drown out what she now vehemently believed.

She left abruptly, stumbling a little. This caught the eye of someone. The minute she left the building and was out of the sight of the bouncers, a man approached her.

The next seconds were a blur. She was body-checked sideways into an alleyway, and her bag was stolen. It could have been much worse in that respect, but in her rebound off the wall she fell and hit her head on the cobbled street.

A sound like rushing waters filled what was left of her conscious mind. She barely heard the muffled shout of the lady who'd come over to help, just the vague impression of her red patent-leather heels as the streetlights narrowed to extinction.

43

WW2

Catacombs

PARIS III

Wednesday, October 6th, 1943.

Violet was thankful for her good leather boots, impervious to the flooded sections of the catacombs, the ones her mother had used when farming. But while her feet were equipped, Violet was silently panicking. The Vosges she knew well, but south of the Seine, beneath the city, was a vast labyrinth of interconnected tunnels, some of them already two thousand years old. This was not a section that Violet knew well, but she didn't want to show vulnerability. It might show inner strength, but in war it can also get you all killed. Confidence was everything.

Violet knew that if one could harness knowledge of the tunnel network, it could become a massive advantage. With every fiber in her being, Violet willed herself to remember the way, to unlock deep memories. She hadn't expected to traverse the tunnels without Jérôme. They had been a team. She could almost see him, walking in front. The tunnels were, after all, the same steady temperature and darkness. For a second it felt comforting to pretend.

The truck had dropped them off just south of the checkpoint at Porte d'Italie, the same ancient entrance that Simone had left through in the collision of humanity that was the Parisian Exodus.

Violet just needed to find one of the major tunnel arteries. Henry offered the use of a compass hidden in a button on his shirt. It turned out to be a lifesaver as they twisted and turned, for they had needed to abandon their navigation and other supplies in the amphitheater at Grand.

Finally, Violet recognized an inscription on the wall. If Matthias and Henry hadn't been behind her, they would have seen a large smile emerge. Within seconds, a faint whistle could be heard. There it was again.

She whistled back as loudly as she dared with a special lilt. Then, a light. And soon enough, behind the light, a face: Yves and his friend René. "Violet!" Yves beamed. His instinct was to ask immediately about Jérôme, but of course he knew. It was a sober reminder. Everyone had loved him: enigmatic, thoughtful, and a good saxophone player!

"You still come down here?" Violet asked.

"Well, it's suffocating above," Yves replied, before sweeping back his fringe.

"Is Jean…?" Her voice cracked. His absence was notable; she had to ask.

"Oh, he's fine; he's just got a night shift," René said to Violet's relief. René was a vision: while Yves exuded class and charm, René had kept his tight blond curls. It didn't quite fit with his intensity, but he liked them.

A couple of years before, Jean and René had been exploring an air raid shelter in the Sainte Anne hospital where they studied—Paris's oldest psychiatric hospital, now rapidly filling up with wounded German soldiers. One night, René had found a locked gate. He picked it. Beyond it he found a tunnel, leading to more and more. For a year, the friends spent every night they could carefully mapping the "Great Southern Network," knowing it would be helpful to the *Résistance*. Having recognized the importance of their work, Yves joined when he could, as had Jérôme.

"We need your help. We need to get to Notre-Dame du Travail by sunrise," Violet admitted.

"Ah, the 14th *arrondissement*," Yves replied.

Matthias jumped in, "Rue Vercingetorix; the closer we can get, the better. We had some problems in Grand and they could be looking for us."

Yves grabbed the latest map out of his bag. It was detailed, a work in progress. To make the map, Jean Talairach had ingeniously used inscriptions, groups of skulls, doors, and manholes—anything distinctive—as points of reference. He then measured the angles and distances between these points. Later, he would develop this method to create a 3D map of brain coordinates. The result was astounding for the medical field: he identified standard anatomical "landmarks" to draw a standardized map or atlas for neurology and neurosurgery still used today.[272]

Yves held the map up against the wall to study it by flashlight. "You can't go above ground. They don't let anything go; they'll be looking for you," he warned. "I should guide you; the Nazis are starting to use the tunnels."

"But they don't have a map?" Matthias said, worried.

"Not this one! But we recently gave Henri Rol-Tanguy—" Yves replied.

"Paris chief of the FFI, organizing the *Résistance*," Matthias explained to Henry.

"We recently gave him an annotated version," Yves restarted, "and he's going to use it. The headquarters are going to move to an air raid shelter in Montparnasse.[273] But as I said, the Nazis are using the catacombs now, too," he explained. "Most of it's safe, but you don't want to run into anything."

"We recently found them using the tunnels under the Jardin du Luxembourg and the Lycée Montaigne," René explained.

"Yeah, we can do without stumbling upon that," said Henry.

"How far is it to the church from here?" Violet asked Yves.

"We're near the hospital. So above ground, it's about thirty minutes northwest."

"And below?" she inquired.

"About an hour and a half. I guess the question is whether you want to spend the night down here or in the church?" Yves said.

"Matthias? What do you think?" Violet asked. Analyzing the patterns and movements of people and troops was more his thing. He was thankful to be asked.

"If we can get close enough, down here," Matthias suggested. Henry nodded in agreement.

"Down here it is then," Yves affirmed. "What do you think, René?"

---

272. Suttel, *Catacombes*. René Suttel helped Jean Talairach in making the map and exploring the catacombs. The René in this passage is fictional but a nod to Suttel's involvement.

273. During the liberation of Paris in August 1944, Rol-Tanguy would lead the insurrection from the air raid shelter in Montparnasse. For his map work, aiding the *Résistance*, Talairach was awarded the War Cross, France's highest military honor.

"There's been flooding, and it's rather low here," he said, stepping forward to trace their path with his finger. "We'll have to get to a *gallerie* beneath the Rue Daguerre. Then we'll join the one going north tracing the Avenue Du Main. If we need to, there is a spiral staircase we could use. But, if we can, I'd like us to get a little closer tonight. If we continue on, there are two options. After the jog right here, we can go this way, or we can continue below the Avenue Du Main until Rue Vercingétorix. We can play it by ear and keep an eye out for a place to rest."

"Thank you," said Violet sincerely to them both.

It was late. As they set off, Yves talked to Violet. "When did you leave Paris?" he asked.

"Almost three weeks ago now," she replied.

"Sleeping rough?"

"How did you ever know?" Matthias said, sarcastically.

"Well, she still looks gorgeous, but you two? Quite frankly, you look like sh*t."

"Always love a good compliment," Matthias responded.

"Let's clean you up a little before you go on the streets, okay?" Yves suggested. A razor, after all, wouldn't be too hard to acquire from the hospital.

"You can't wear that uniform. Can I burn it for you?" René teased Matthias.

They waited for twenty minutes in the tunnels below the hospital, give or take a few, while René found what they needed—and a brush for Violet, a spontaneous addition but a welcome relief. He also found a dress for Violet but wasn't wholly surprised when she ripped it to make a chic and practical turban for her hair.

At a slight distance from Matthias and Henry as they changed and shaved, Yves explained to Violet, "What you need to know is that while you've been away, the Gestapo have raided many of the safe houses."

"Delta and Echo?" Violet asked.

"Compromised. They'll be watching them," Yves replied.

"What do they know?"

"It's good to expect they know more than we think they do."

Violet sighed, feeling the weight of it all. As Matthias and Henry came over to join them, she mustered her strength: "Well then, we'll need to get him and the package out of the city as soon as the transfer is made."

"And on to England," Matthias added.

"What about Kyot—?" Violet said, suggesting another escape line.

"That's done," Yves interjected, not wishing to relive the searing pain.

Matthias piped up, "*Comete*?"

"Can you make it over the Pyrenées?" Yves asked Henry.

"Looking forward to it."

"And you can swim?" Clearly, he was concerned about Henry only having one hand.

"Like a fish."

"Okay," Yves said, "*Comete* it is. They'll likely take him to Lisbon or Gibraltar," he explained. "It won't be fast, but it's the best bet." Besides, fast didn't matter—not after he'd assessed the information and relayed his conclusions to England. "Go with René, and I'll make the arrangements tonight. They trust me," Yves assured them. "In the morning, do what you need in the church. Nothing more, nothing less. René will have your back, and I'll wait down here to receive Henry."

44

Peter

Praskovya

LES VOSGES VI

Sunday, July 31st, 1994.

Hélène studied Peter's face for a reaction. Peter's dark, dense cabin had absorbed her shouts and thuds, helping diffuse her anger and usher her back into deep sadness.

"How do you know?" asked Peter gently, stunned.

"Know? You think I'm making this up? It has to be yours, Peter."

"I didn't mean . . . So I'm going to be a dad?"

"No, you're not. Didn't you hear me?" she said, lancing his dream without compassion. "I can't do this."

"But we could; I would help you! Something good out of all this."

"All this shouldn't have happened—it can't have . . . but it has." She paused. "I shouldn't have told you." Her head hung low, her hair no longer wild and audacious but tied in a low ponytail as if it too had lost its zest for life. Perhaps in reality it was practical, away from the mess of morning sickness.

"Maybe a part of you needed to, wanted to tell me, I mean?" Peter asked gently, moving closer.

"Forget it." She launched herself back to maintain distance.

"No, you said you needed help. We can figure it out together."

"There's no 'we,' Peter. Even if, in another life, there may have been. You killed it. You didn't just betray Etienne."

Peter needed to explain. "But Jean-Paul—"

"Stop it! Just take responsibility like an adult. Or are you intent on ruining another life now?" In Hélène's mind were so many voices. Imagined conversations that she was too afraid to have. She knew what the girls would say. Some of them would basically force her to have the abortion as if to prove that she was in charge of her own body, while others would say it was a gift and she'd be belittling motherhood or something if she got rid of it. "Ahhhh!" she screamed. "I just can't handle anyone else trying to manipulate me into proving myself. I don't need you to tell me what to do."

"But—"

"I don't care. I just need one thing: I don't need this." And by this she meant the baby. "I want it all to go away. Peter, you need to take me. Please!" Hélène said, each syllable building in intensity.

"Okay," he relented. She'd already made up her mind and it was clear that anything he said would just push her in the other direction. "Just one second," he added, shoving handfuls of paper into the bin as he located his keys beneath them, fumbling around in shock.

Hélène paced in circles, tortured by the thoughts carving against the inside of her temples. The fact was, if she didn't go now, she didn't trust herself. She didn't know what she'd say or do.

On the way to the car, he quickly tied Chestnut outside of Etienne's cabin so that Bernard could watch over him. After telling Bernard just enough, he asked for his keys.

It was a blur from then on, like the countryside that was starting to disappear behind the curtains of rain. Water was surging down the hillside. The next thing Peter knew, he was in the car with Hélène screaming "drive!" hysterically.

Boom! The back of the vehicle was hit with a closed iron fist. The hunting dogs barked at the front wheels.

Peter and Hélène both instinctively scrambled to make sure the doors were locked. Hélène could see Jean-Paul's face radiating fury in the wing mirror.

"Praskovya!!" he shouted.

What? Peter was rapidly trying to understand as panic set in. Bernard's car was struggling to start. Every movement felt like a divine insult.

"Praskovya?"

"Just drive!" Mud flew everywhere. A shock after the long drought.

"I can't drive! I'll get one of the dogs," said Peter.

"I don't care!!" she shouted.

"Praskovya, I order you to get out of the car!" Jean-Paul screamed, hitting it again.

Through just a crack in the window, she made sure that he heard her as she replied in Russian. Peter didn't understand but the tone was enough to say everything.

Just then, the car jumped into action, launching out of the mud. The closest dog leapt out of the way. Peter blared the horn to warn the others.

He drove fast, faster than he ever had on a country road. Jean-Paul exuded all his energy chasing the car, mud flying off his shoes and eventually throwing a rock at the rear window. It broke it, leaving a spider's web of cracks. His screams were utterly futile, dissipating, tempered only by the screen of rain-soaked leaves.

Why was he the one that felt guilty, Peter thought, as Jean-Paul's enraged face disappeared in the rearview mirror. *He betrayed and blackmailed me!*

Immediately, Peter saw another problem. The river had burst its bank; the water unable to sink into the baked land. It raged in a torrent before them. They just had to go for it. "Hold on," he said. The muddy water slammed into the windshield. For a second, driving blind.

Then? Shaking. They were through to the other side, but Hélène shook like a leaf in a storm.

She refused his hand. Silence. Intolerable, heart-wrenching, unutterable silence aside from the car's fan struggling to warm them.

Minutes passed. Now the front windshield fogged. Despite the now-driving rain, they needed to crack the windows.

"Hélène, can you please?"

She looked away.

The country road was empty but for potholes. Keeping one hand on the wheel, he leaned over her to unwind her window a little.

"Sorry, I have to be able to see. Would you rather I call you 'Praskovya'?"

There was no response. He was trying.

"Is that your real name?"

"You think he's really called Jean-Paul?" Hélène snapped.

"Why did he think he could order you? Is he—"

"My egotistical brother? Yes," she said, so shaken her response was numb.

Peter didn't know where to go next. He had so many questions. Did this change anything he thought he knew?

"Why didn't he protect you against Etienne?"

"You know, I thought you were vindictive and scheming," she said. "But now I pity you. Perhaps you are as dumb as you look."

Peter knew she was shooting with anything she had to hurt him. "It *was* Etienne, wasn't it?"

Hélène looked away. "That's what you wanted to believe. I didn't think it made a difference."

"It did! A big one!" Peter gripped the steering wheel. "So what? Did you do all this?" Peter said, less careful with his words. He was referring to the bruises, now many colors and levels of severity.

"It's not that simple!" She sobbed without a tissue, the cuff of her cardigan doused in mucus.

"Try me," he said. "At least help me understand why I'm such a demon. I got it wrong, but you knew what I thought!"

Hélène chose silence. Oh, she could fight, but she didn't want to. Not now.

"I was such a fool," Peter interjected. "It was Jean-Paul, wasn't it?"

She closed her eyes.

Peter revealed, "He just sat there as I told him what I suspected about Etienne!" How could he have missed it? "I knew Etienne was a good man, flawed but good…but I thought he was taking the pressure out on you."

"He was a good man," she said, quietly, avoiding eye contact.

"Jean-Paul must have started scheming the moment I shared . . . He made me vulnerable and then leveraged every part of what I told him." Peter had a vision of the putrid joy that Jean-Paul must have had as he'd found an easy way for any suspicion to shift from his guilty self and onto his rival. The thought made Peter squirm. He could feel the thread tugging through his skin afresh, as if Jean-Paul was also sewing him into his plan.

"I can't call him that," Hélène said, deflecting again.

"What is his name?"

"It doesn't matter . . ."

"Brothers are meant to protect you! You could have told me. Can't you see that's all I was trying to do?" Peter protested.

"He's always loved power. He doesn't care who he stands on or trades in to get it," she continued in a whisper, "including me, apparently."

"This time he's gone too far. No one trusts him. It's not all about power; at some point there has to be care, there has to be love!"

The love of power or the power of love. Wager's Ring Cycle was right; this is the axis upon which all great stories are told and upon which the world turns.

45

Peter

Tainted

LES VOSGES VI

Sunday, July 31st, 1994.

They arrived in the town. Hélène concealed a crude address on crumpled paper. "*Ici,*" she said, wanting to walk the rest of the way alone from the town square.

Withholding her pressing tide of emotions, she leaned over to grab her bag from the backseat, intent to leave with just a sharp "thank you." But as she twisted back around in hope of leaving the car, the bag—or her knees—something—grazed Bernie's stack of cassette tapes.

Instinctively bending to pick them up, the contents of her bag spilled out. Both a French and red Soviet-style Russian passport spilled out, along with the necklace she had taken from Etienne's room. She snapped, clawing it all away from Peter.

"I don't need your help!" she screamed, flustered. She felt bad about it taking it, but she would need money. What was she going to do by herself? Life and the abortion—it was all going to cost something.

"Okay . . ." he said. "Well, let me—"

"No!"

"I can go and grab your things?"

She got out in the bitter spits of rain. "Those belong to another person," she said, no longer willing to be Hélène.

"Goodbye, Peter."

She left the door open as she walked into the maze of stone houses lapped by the unforgiving torrent, a cold blast punching Peter in his seat.

He got out, pained by her absence. He didn't even have a jacket to defend him as the rain threatened to chill him to the bone—such an abrupt change from the wildfires just a week before. He didn't care. Everything in him wanted to change the story, but he couldn't. Tears mixed with the weather, as if he wasn't even allowed to own these either.

He walked around to close the passenger door, suddenly realizing the magnitude of this moment in his life, where the small pregnant promise of a son or daughter would be no more. *Didn't it have a heartbeat already? Wasn't it human?*

Peter funneled his anger into slamming the door. It couldn't have been loud enough if he slammed it one hundred times over. It was all so messed up.

Should he have fought her veto? Use his voice? He didn't even have anything eloquent to say. But did eloquence matter? They had just argued about Jean-Paul. He felt selfish, like his parents at diplomatic parties in Cairo while he was abandoned at boarding school. He had promised himself that if he had children, then he wouldn't be selfish. He would care for them. He would fight for them. *Could I be a single dad?* But she'd said goodbye and had disappeared. She had made up her mind.

Resigned to a fate defined by regret, he sat back in the car, his body leaden. He watched the sleepy town hide from the rain through the wipers moving back and forth. Back and forth. Slowly he put the car in gear. He had done what she wanted. He drove slowly around the square and then back onto the road they had arrived on.

He drove for at least five aching minutes, but then a persistent plan hatched in his mind; pipping at first, then breaking the shell. No, more than that: he pulled a grenade pin. He manically turned, to the surprise of onlooking dairy cows, jarring the front of the car into the potholes. Given the knackered suspension, jolted forward, speeding. He didn't care.

He would propose to Hélène, Praskovya; her name didn't matter. He would do whatever it would take, remembering how much he cared for her. But would that mean enough to her?

His few possessions slid around in the car as he drove. He almost overshot the turn and would have gone straight into a hedgerow. The engine roared.

He watched the minutes climbing on the dashboard clock; he begged them to elongate.

He turned on the radio but regretted it immediately. Music painfully adjunct: either too

melancholy for his spark of hope or too joyful, given his suspense.

When he finally pulled into the town square where Hélène had walked away, his wheels sliced into the memory, determined to make a new rut in history despite the repetition.

He leapt out of the car, ripping out the key. He tried to recall the address he'd glanced at. He couldn't. Not enough. And of course there was no sign. *Now what?* he thought. There was no one out in the rain to ask. It was a Sunday. Almost everything was shut.

"Hélène?!" he shouted before pausing, listening. "Praskovya?!" Nothing. Less than nothing, aside from a twitch betraying a grandma trying to get a peek from behind her curtains. She shot backward.

If everything was closed, then surely the clinic would be too? Or maybe since it was health care . . . *Where is she?* Peter didn't know what to think. He darted, sopping wet into the cobbled streets, looking for anything. Some sign. Finally, one person was in a doorway, smoking. He didn't know. He asked his partner. Still no idea. It was hard to say thank you when steeped in so much pain, but being a good Brit, of course he did.

Peter was dizzy and disorientated. He was a rescuer by nature. He'd tried to rescue his fiancée. But then he'd been discarded because she said she couldn't think of him without being flung back into remembering her long season of illness. She said that couldn't love him the same—not really. Not the way he "deserved." All he heard was the unspoken scream: "*Tainted!*"

He truly wanted to be there for Hélène, but perhaps being a rescuer didn't work? The role wore thin. It didn't seem that humans were enough to stop each other falling; without crushing and contorting each other. Or maybe it was just him? *You're not enough,* he heard whispered into his ear in disgust and trenchant, cutting clarity. *You always disappoint those you love.* He felt stupid, naïve. Having finally, and unexpectedly, given his heart away to another, he had been discarded, defeated again.

He had no concept of time. When he returned to the car, his door was open wide; the interior chilled and wet where the rain had reached in. A fitting reflection of this heart, once again, bleeding out.

Without her, he couldn't do anything. No speech, no gesture. No second chances. The wind accompanying a nearby train whisked past him thoughtlessly, evoking an agonizingly astringent excruciation since it quickened his mind to realize that she really could be anywhere by now. This uncertainty seized his muscles and bones like tetanus setting in.

46

Hélène

The Ring

Sunday, July 31st, 1994.

An old lady invited Hélène into her house, given the rain and the dangerous content of her questions. Hélène accepted, for no one was at the address she'd been given, and she had nowhere else to go.

The lady kindly suggested that she didn't ask anyone else "those sort of things" for "they might not be so friendly," but she promised that she would find her an advocate. She scuttled off to return about ten minutes later, during which time Hélène had sat, wet, at a round, lace-covered kitchen table with some bread and butter and shelled hard-boiled eggs. She just sat there, holding a shuddering buttered knife and making a puddle.

Hélène was then shuttled into a home just off the square from where Peter had dropped her off.

The legalization of abortion in France has a volatile history. In fact, during the war, the French Vichy government was complicit in the genocide of the Holocaust—attesting that some were unworthy of life. However, they inconsistently asserted that taking the life of their unborn by abortion was an abomination. This famously led to two uses of the guillotine during this period for abortionists found guilty of the crime. Abortion debates still hinge on how we define humanity (which includes a concept of when one believes life begins) and what is a life worth living, and again, who has the right or prerogative to define this.

Simone de Beauvoir lent her fame and support to the legalization of abortion. Not only does it appear in her novels, such as its raw treatment in *The Blood of Others*,[274] but she also famously opened herself to prosecution by declaring in her 1971 article in the *Nouvel Observateur* that she and the 342 other signatories had had an abortion and was therefore one among many to demand safe, free abortion for women.[275] It was a major turning point in a furious debate.[276]

§

And so, there was Hélène watching Peter from behind a closed window two floors above. The window box spilling over frivolously with crimson blooms.

Should she call out to him?

"Praskovya?!" he called, unashamed. Desperate.

She didn't answer. He needed to try harder. Just a bit more before she—

He called again. Her heart rose. Perhaps he really did . . .?

"Hélène!" he said, with almost a whimper this time.

She looked, weighing up every option, as if this moment were a hinge on her life . . . but what was it to bear the weight of?

"Hél—"

Just as she was going to answer, his call ended.

Should I run down? She thought . . . or . . . she started to pull open the window, but it was stuck . . . She started to panic. As she wrestled with the wooden frame, he turned. She couldn't get it! She banged on the window, but with the rain he didn't hear. *Should I run down? That would take too long. Come on!!* Nothing was working. *I can't, can't I?* She should have punched that damn window. At least then the pain of her body would match her heart.

---

274. Beauvoir, *Blood of Others*. Note that Simone's protagonist, Hélène Bertrand, makes a different decision than our Hélène.

275. Beauvoir, "Manifesto of the 343."

276. On January 17th, 1975, the Veil Act was passed. A significant move towards abortion decriminalization. In 2022—the same year that the US Supreme Court overturned Roe v. Wade—France became the first country in the world to enshrine a right to abortion in their constitution.

Just as she had convinced herself to break the window, she saw him stop. He stopped calling, stopped talking to people, giving up. Past yellowing net curtains through which the previous generation had seen the last firefights of the war, Hélène saw Peter finally turn back in the direction of his car.

Was that it? He began to walk away, his whole body sunken as if someone had cut his most vital marionette string. She brought her right knuckle to the window—to bang, to stop him—to shout! But in that instant, hatred seized her heart more possessively than she had ever known. *He had given up. He had given up! Was it that easy?*

She recoiled as if to guard her very life source—her heart. Plowed down by the weight of it all, she lay on the dirty mustard rug in this foreign, moldy room. As if her soul had been wounded, it forbade her to move as Peter slipped away. While she fought it, she found she was leaking life. It pooled like blood around her, familiarly warm yet tasting of death.

It was personal. Shame-saturated, wanting to hide, feeling all alone: absolute, inexplicable torture. Herein, pain pleased itself to become her primary motivation. Not explicitly of course, for that would be far too obvious . . . but lurking there, a sulfurous, odorous cloud, growing like a cancer. It felt utterly dependent but grew stronger by the day, leaching its putrid poison into anything that threatened to become good.

She knew Jean-Paul, whose real name was Dmytro, was using her. He had been so happy when Etienne had taken an interest. But despite Jean-Paul's bouts of violence, her brother was all she had left. And leaving him just now? Well, that was one of the hardest things she had to do. They were typical siblings, but their unusual closeness had concretely begun almost eight years ago, when an emergency evacuation was declared and her first love, Ivan, had been conscripted to help with the nuclear meltdown at Chernobyl. No one in Ukraine had known for days, meaning that children had been playing as normal in the streets. Hélène herself had ridden in a yellow Ferris wheel with Ivan during that time, each capsule topped with what looked like a fanciful giant yellow bottle cap. They were gleeful and unaware of the radiation. She was a nurse but was mercifully waved from front-line care and put on the reserve list. Perhaps it would have been better if she had not. Then they could have died together. That was the last time she saw him. The radiation was so strong she couldn't even see him or take his belongings. Not even the ring that he'd almost given her on the Ferris wheel just days before. She had wondered about the bulge in his pocket. Perhaps it was better that she didn't know for sure, for it was thrown in the hospital basement with all other clothes and contaminants.

After Chernobyl and Ivan's death, Jean-Paul had felt obliged to care for her. He kept her close, which, given his own struggles, developed into control. He wasn't above using her for his own political ends, poor naive Etienne. It was easy to see him as the martyr in all this and Jean-Paul and Peter as the villains. It made the poison easier to swallow. Some rationality interrupting the irrational mess.

All the words, the lies, the justification lodged in her bones. The truth was they all hurt her, and she wasn't above it herself. The cumulative pain caused her to add to her bruises and tear at her flesh. The air boiled. It cursed her. She cursed it.

She lay again. Alone. Below was the faintest noise of someone loudly moving pots in the kitchen below—business as usual—paired with repugnantly perfect, garish birds chirping as they sheltered outside the window. She found herself doing the only thing she could- talking to the little soul she felt inside of her, the only thing that wasn't yet broken and set against her.

Finally, she let herself hold her stomach, to dream in the shadow of dreams lost. With everything having slipped through her fingers, she decided at that moment to make an about turn. She couldn't bear to lose another. She wouldn't abort the baby. "I guess it's you and me, little bean," she said between muted bouts of hysterical, tear-soaked screams that forced open her mouth, expelling seething air from perfect lips.

She vowed it would all be different: never again would she make the same mistakes, never be controlled, and never to dance again . . . "I'll make us a new life, somewhere safe."

47

Alexi

Anne

HEAVEN AND HELL

Tuesday, November 10th, 2015. Amsterdam.

Given her head injury and history of concussions, the hospital monitored Alexi for some time. They didn't want to release her without support. She was strongly encouraged to text someone. Eventually, Alexi reached out to Edith. She was embarrassed and felt like a nuisance. She wasn't expecting the warmth and care she received. If she was frustrated, Edith didn't show it. She'd driven all the way from Amsterdam, cleared out Alexi's stuff still in the hostel, and even had snacks waiting in the car for their drive back to the Netherlands.

"It's okay that you didn't find anything. What matters is that you tried," Edith said, regarding Peter. Alexi didn't want to tell her about finding the community, the blood-stained Bible, or the death. Their love for Peter seemed precious. No good would come of it.

As Edith parked, Edwin and their daughter, Lili, were already waiting at the door, smiling, welcoming. During their journey, Edith had explained that Lili had been away at a retreat center in France when she had first dropped in on them. Lili was just a little older than Alexi. She was their joy and the answer to many prayers. Indeed, unlike many young adults, she still openly shared incredible warmth with both her parents and practically everyone she met. "Don't get me wrong," Edith shared, "it was still hard, but Down's Syndrome wasn't the diagnosis we were told it would be. Sure, it was the death of a certain picture of life—the kind we can't help but project into the future—but also the birth of so many others. And isn't that always the case?" Edith asked. "Nothing is ever as we imagine."

Indeed, Edith had explained in the car that they were now part of a community that they had never known about or probably wouldn't have been connected to. The humanity of being surrounded by so many other families, supporting and celebrating each other amidst the trials and heartache? Healthy community galvanized the soul like nothing else.

"You've heard of Anne de Gaulle?" Edith had asked.

"Charles de Gaulle's wife or daughter, I presume?" Alexi said in the seat next to her.

"His beloved daughter," Edith said, her eyes smiling. Though she was driving, she pointed to her keychain. It was the type of car where they simply needed to be within the vehicle, not locked in place, so she gave them to Alexi to hold.

"What does this mean?" Alexi asked.

"It's the cross of Lorraine."

"So, a religious thing?"

"Indirectly. It is an old symbol, but it was used as the symbol of the French Forces of the Interior—*La Résistance française.*"

"That de Gaulle basically led?"

"Right. He committed treason by going to England and was ruffling feathers pretty much everywhere," Edith explained.

"And then he started the radio broadcasts."

"Right, Radio Londres, starting with Beethoven's Fifth, the notes of which made a "V" for victory in morse code."

"Yes! I've heard that somewhere," Alexi replied. The keychain was round metal, with the French Tricolor in the back and the cross with two horizontal bars on it (the first smaller, the next a normal length). She rubbed over the texture of it with her thumb while her index finger cradled it, the rest of the keys behind.

"So, Anne de Gaulle?"

"Well, Charles de Gaulle was once asked: 'Why?' Why be so exceptional, brave, daring. Not perfect, no, but why do above and beyond? Why him over the millions, billions of others? He wasn't even that high up in the ranks, and all those above him planned to capitulate."

"Basically, what made him different?"

"Exactly. I love how honest he was when he told his biographer, the late Jean Lacouture, 'Without Anne, I could never perhaps have done what I did. She gave me the heart and the inspiration.'"[277]

"That's beautiful."

"Even more so when you understand that, like Lili, Anne de Gaulle had Down's Syndrome. She was the very type of person that had no place in the world according to how the Reich saw the world."[278]

"Wow." Alexi tried to let that sink in. "He protected her."

"He understood not just her worth, but also the worth of everyone else who didn't fit in the narrow, Aryan box, those select things valued by the Reich. Before the war, he was known for visiting his family more than most soldiers and spending lots of time with Anne. Around her, he was not the rigid, stoic man that others knew. She melted him; she was 'his joy.'[279] For me, the best part is that to change the world, she didn't even have to do anything different: she simply had to be herself—a daughter beloved by her father. Sorry, I shouldn't."

"No, no. That's beautiful," Alexi said.

Gently, Edith continued, "There's a great picture of him holding her in a deckchair at the beach in Brittany. As a Catholic, de Gaulle was informed by a Christian worldview. It wasn't man's job to say who was human or not. All people, according to the Scriptures, are made in the image of God."

Alexi googled the picture on her phone. "It's funny; he's wearing a suit."

"I think that's what you wore in those times. Probably not in the water, though," Edith joked.

"So, seeing—valuing—a full humanity is what he stood for?"

"Sometimes he was consistent with this worldview, other times not as much. You have to understand that he was also influenced by his education and the milieu in which he grew up. For example, it was still the age of colonies, which is one reason the war encompassed the world. But,

277. Lacouture, *De Gaulle*, 108.

278. This extermination of those with Down's Syndrome, etc., started in 1939 under the *Aktion* T-4 campaign. Among the vast numbers who died included a 15-year-old boy, also with Down's Syndrome, who was the cousin of the future pope, Joseph Ratzinger (Pope Benedict XVI). See Pursell, *Benedict*.

279. Jean Lacouture recorded De Gaulle saying, "Her [Anne's] birth was a trial for my wife and myself. But believe me, Anne is my joy and my strength. She is the grace of God in my life... She has kept me in the security of obedience to the sovereign will of God." See Jackson, *Certain Idea*, 60.

when he was true to this vision and consistent, Alexi, that had the power to change the trajectory of the world. And I think that's true of all of us. Every decision we take to love well and deeply. To recognize the humanity of others. Like spending time talking to a stranger on a park bench…"

"Or helping clean out a hostel room," Alexi said, showing thanks. Edith passed it off as nothing.

She went on: "Yvonne and Charles de Gaulle set up the Anne de Gaulle Foundation. They're still running today and do some incredible things.[280] It's the foundation that was running the retreat for Lili last time you were here."

When they got to the familiar yellow door, Alexi went straight up to Lili. Lili beamed, deciding that she liked her new sister already.

---

280. In addition to their regular work (https://fondation-anne-de-gaulle.org), consider the social impact of the initiative to temporarily rename the Charles de Gaulle airport in 2022. See Fondation Anne de Gaulle, *Paris Anne de Gaulle.*

48

WW2

Notre-Dame-du-Travail

HEAVEN AND HELL

Thursday, October 7th, 1943. Paris.

As soon as the curfew broke at 5 a.m., Violet, Matthias, Henry, and René left the catacombs, while Yves waited there to receive Henry back and shuttle him on. This was Henry's first proper view of the legendary city. "Try not to look too much like a tourist," said Matthias, happy to give him a bit of a jab, not having forgotten how Henry had chastised him in Grand for not looking confident enough.

They started enacting the plan they'd spun in the night. Violet would accompany Henry to meet

Ophélie in the church. They were under no illusions about how important this was. By 1943, the Nazis had started testing long range "vengeance weapons," the V-1 and V-2 missiles whose range could threaten England. While the exact nature of the threat was debated, intelligence from *La* Résistance about these programs had proven to be essential, leading to Crossbow and the Operation Hydra attack on Peenemünde. Heinrich Maier, a philosopher, priest, and Austrian resistance member had sent exact V-2 drawings to the Americans. Likewise, brave members of the Polish resistance had attempted to smuggle working bombs out of occupied territories because the fuel of the V-2 had been a mystery.

Now, Henry's informant Ophélie had collected a vast amount of further information, much of it time-sensitive.

Here was the challenge: while the wireless could transmit basic information—such as the coordinates of a threat—it couldn't handle images. So too, long messages were nearly impossible to send with the Nazis breathing down their necks. Other methods existed, but none were both fast and bullet proof. For the SOE, however, Henry's performance at Operation Hillside made one thing clear: not only did accuracy and attention to detail come naturally to him, but his extraordinary ability to capture, organize, and analyze vast amounts of data set him apart. Further, through his meticulous map work, Henry had memorized the locations of countless towns and potential threats across the continent. His unique skill set made him indispensable for delivering critical insights to the Allies with unmatched speed and precision.

As Violet appreciated, every hour mattered when the outcome of the war balanced on a razor's edge.

The church seemed empty. Still, Violet and Matthias swept it for threats. "This way," Violet then whispered, holding the large wooden door slightly open for Henry.

Violet walked over to the candle table where just a solitary wick was burning. She paused, taking in the statue of Jesus, laying, dying, chin to the sky with Mary beside him kissing his hand; a suffering savior. If only she could have held Jérôme in his death. The Nazis had even stolen that from her. She knew that his last embrace with his wife haunted Matthias, but she envied him. She couldn't think of it. Not now. Not properly. Her mission wasn't over yet. She gave candles to Matthias and Henry. "For those who have come before and those who will come after," she said as she lit hers. The sun was not high enough yet to fully illuminate the church. As the daylight fanned upwards as it rose, they began to see more clearly what had only been a sketch in the low dawn light. It revealed a traditional sandstone church building upheld by a shocking rib cage-like metal structure that echoed the style of the Eiffel Tower. Some claimed that the iron was repurposed from structures in the 1855 *Exposition Universelle*.

They huddled behind an altar away from the door, able to whisper a little. The architecture paid testimony to the trades. "It helped working-class families feel more at home," Violet explained.

"Hence its name, *Notre-Dame-du-Travail*," Matthias added. "Our Lady of Labor."

Violet gestured to a painting. Small side chapels lined the nave, but one with a fresco stood out: the *Angel with Workers* by Félix Villé. The church had a long legacy of investing itself in the lives of the Parisian working class. Violet explained that under leaders like Father Soulange-Bodin, when the parish exploded in size at the dawn of the twentieth century, "they served over two thousand meals a day, ran a nursery, helped street children and working women. My grandparents on my mother's side came here from children, right up until they had their own."

"The current Archbishop, Emmanuel Suhard, would have been deported to Dachau long ago if it weren't for how loved he is by the working class," Matthias affirmed.[281]

"Why?" Henry asked.

"He's been protesting the anti-Semitic laws. They know that because of him, many followers have hidden and smuggled people out," Matthias answered.

"Then there's the Jesuit resistance movement . . ." said Violet. She wanted to say more but knew she shouldn't.

"What time is she coming?" Henry switched tracks, anxious to get this done.

Violet smiled, "6 a.m. to 'say prayers.'"

"I'll keep watch outside," Matthias offered.

---

281. Schnitker, "French Catholic Church."

49

Peter

Dilating Time

HEAVEN AND HELL

Sunday, July 31st, 1994. Les Vosges.

It had crept up on Peter, and his honor had refused to see it, but there had been the sort of forbidden intimacy between him and Hélène where absence now seared deeply and anger meant damnation.

This torturous mess was not what he wanted but thinking that Hélène wanted nothing to do with him, Peter felt he had no option but to drive off. It was not very far before he turned the car off again. What was he going to do? Jean-Paul was probably waiting for him. He couldn't face whatever scene this was going to create back at the community. Not now. Not yet.

There was one place that was open, between services. He walked into the church—past graves, pews, and shafts of light—a dead man. He collapsed but didn't hear the sound nor its echo, reality eroding around him.

A hand rested on his back. Peter didn't see him, not yet, his head bowed. They must have spoken a little, but it was of little consequence compared to what happened next.

Something rose up from Peter's stomach—an intense, loving fire. It was almost too much.

"Can I pray for you?" the man asked, helping him onto a chair.

333

"I thought . . . I thought you already had?" Peter said, struggling to speak.

"That's just Jesus wanting to get a head start! He loves you."

At that instant, God reached behind Peter's doubt to seize his heart. It was as if air rushed into asthmatic lungs. The constriction, the siege was over. His spirit could breathe! Relief was palpable.

But then the real depth of his embattled condition became evident, since he allowed himself to feel, his nerves finally alive. The floodgates opened and tear upon tear fought to pour out. He couldn't get air in quick enough to breathe through the emotion.

The priest helped him steady himself, to breathe into it. It helped. Peter finally looked at him: his eyes, his face. They felt oddly familiar and yet honestly human. Snow-white whiskers compliant, stopping crisply at his cheek, eyebrows that funneled compassion, and frown lines deep but not too stern: the face of Father Michael, a face he would grow to care deeply for.

Father Michael prayed something, inviting the Holy Spirit to be close. It was weird: as if the pain came out and something else, something deeper, flooded in. Peace. That's what it felt like: peace! Seeing Peter smile through the tears and his face change, the priest shared the words of Jesus: "Peace I leave with you; my peace I give you."[282]

Peace with content: gorgeous and satisfying. Not the boring nothingness Peter ordinarily associated with the word. This peace was a presence. The presence of love: God.

"You again!" Peter said, with broken but honest words. It was Jesus but not the Jesus he had thought—not brittle and bone-dry, accusatory and . . . Peter suddenly became enraptured in what could only be described as eternity—the eternal One—in time. He couldn't take it all in.

He felt at once suspended but also connected to everything past, present, and future that truly mattered. Wells he could drink from. It *was* like Zizioulas's dilation of time to the "infinite dimensions of the *eschata*,"[283] pregnant with the weight, truth, and present hope that transcended all reduction. This was dramatic but also enduring. In that instant, he had been desperate to keep the pathway open, like a child's waxy fingers wedged in a pantry door. But later, over time, he would learn to

---

282. John 14:27.

283. Zizioulas, *Being as Communion*, 22.

trust that it wasn't going to be taken from him. What had begun in this instant would open into an awareness that could last a lifetime.

Jesus came. Arriving in the midst of pain, his holy presence forever marked Peter with an engaged rather than a naïve hope.

Since this revelation was not the product of reason it could not be tamed by it. Yet, it was not irrational. It was not confused; it was simple and profound.

Raw, real, and powerful, this encounter lay beyond the watershed—or the "short wings"[284]—of reason alone: it quickly saturated and outstripped reason's reach. This sparked in Peter a faith that was likewise not irrational. Reason, eager to extend its reach, partnered with faith, captivated by excavating the heights and depths of what had happened even though he knew he might never complete the exploration.

284. Dante, *Divine Comedy*, 399. Canto II, line 57.

50

WW2

Gold in Its Mouth

HEAVEN AND HELL

Thursday, October 7th, 1943. Notre-Dame-du-Travail, Paris.

After Matthias left, Violet and Henry stole some quiet moments alone. She told him not to say what she knew he was going to but let their fingers brush against each other. "In another life," Violet said.

"After the war?" Henry said.

Violet didn't answer. Henry had hoped for at least a vague "perhaps." But perhaps she feared whether there would be an "after"?

Henry asked Violet for the necklace. She looked beautiful in it, as if it had always belonged to her. He felt bad taking it. He hid in the dark oak confession booth, using what was left of the flashlight's battery to see, holding it steady in his mouth. Violet kept guard, knowing better than to ask if he needed help.

The microfilm stayed tightly rolled. These orders weren't for his eyes. He placed the microfilm in the crease of his hand. Should he just give the agent the whole necklace instead? He made a snap decision. No, smaller was better. Besides, he wanted Violet to keep the necklace to remind her of him. He improvised, hiding it snugly within the Parisian "pocket litter" that London had curated for him before the mission.

In one sense, he felt like a glorified carrier pigeon, like when microfilm was first used in the Franco-Prussian War during the siege of Paris,

336

back when this church had been briefly used as a hospital. Only pigeons couldn't do what he needed to do next: quickly deciphering detailed plans and maps so that important information could be radioed back well before he or anyone else was able to get the physicals to London—if at all. This sort of information could stop the war sooner, saving lives.

London was risking a lot on Henry. But they also had much to gain. He was back waiting in the pews, but the agent didn't show. It was 6:30, then 6:45.

Finally, someone came in just shy of 7 a.m.; Violet watched from behind, cautious as ever. Henry knew what he had to do. He got out the small Paris Opera ticket Violet had kept safe—what was left of it. The agent had the exact matching rip. It had to be her. She felt safer, seeing that he also fit the description. There had been too many close calls recently. The reason she was late was for fear of being followed. Was she just paranoid now?

"Everything's in here," she said, passing over a waistcoat with the file stitched inside the back panel. "You must tell London, quickly! Then burn it." Henry nodded. He immediately slipped it on under his jacket and gave her the microfilm.

Violet looked down at her arm, her hair was raised. No sooner had the agent said, "Go quickly!" then a small rock flew against a church window. It was Matthias, warning them.

"Here!" whispered Violet, pointing towards the back of the church. She had chosen this location because her parents and grandparents had told her all of its secrets. There were secret panels leading to secret exits. Secret, as long as they hadn't already been exposed.

They ran quickly to the back of the chancel and into the vestry. But the panel wouldn't open. She forced her body into it. A sharp pain ran through her hip. The agent and Henry both added force. It moved but only an inch. What had happened? It would take too long. *What now?*

"The window!" said Henry, but it was high, starting over six feet up the wall.

Ophélie took a large brass candlestick. "Forgive me, Father," she said before making the blow. Henry could see her better now—not as young as them, late thirties perhaps, the light honest, showing her wrinkles. The vestments and communion elements were stored here. She threw up a white communion tablecloth to cover the broken glass. She got up there first. The drop looked big but not fatal. She'd done worse.

Seconds after breaking the window, the front church doors flew open. Two Gestapo officers ran in, their steps resounding in the nave. The whole steel structure then rang three times over, hit with something hard. "*Morgenstund hat Gold im Mund,*" ("The morning hour has gold in its mouth"), one shouted to them, the proverbial equivalent of the early bird catching the worm.

"Not a chance," Violet said, boosting the agent through. Matthias had run around in time to help and stand guard. She made it. "You next," she told Henry. "We've no time for arguments," she added without giving him time to protest. It was her job to make sure Henry made it.

"I've got it," Henry said, effortlessly making the leap. It was just as high off the ground on the other side. Just as in training, he rolled on his shoulder to absorb the impact.

"You cut your leg," Matthias pointed out, having scraped it on the glass.

"Try losing a hand," Henry said, making light of it.

They were close now. Very close. Violet had finished barricading the door the best she could while Henry was climbing. She tried to launch herself up. Her boots struggled to find anything to grip to. The men were coming, delayed only slightly as they searched the church. But the distinctive noise of her boots made them beeline toward the vestry.

They knew. The door handle thrown up and down. It wouldn't be long now.

Violet had climbed up on a large wood storage cabinet, stocked with elements for consecration, the doors open to use the shelves as steps. She propelled herself from them to the window.

"What's happening?" said Matthias outside, running over. It was taking Violet too long. "Why didn't you—?" He started laying into Henry. He knew why, but he was still enraged, made worse by being impotent to help.

Violet couldn't see that Henry's jump had pulled down most of the tablecloth. Her hands landed, gripping down onto the broken glass. It sliced into her flesh, yet she held on. What was left of the cloth stained red under her almost instantly. She pushed up regardless, slicing even deeper. "Go!" she shouted to Henry and Ophélie, "Both of you!"

"Violet!" Henry shouted, reaching up. He encouraged, "*Forti Nihil Difficile!*" ("To the strong [or brave], nothing is difficult").

Violet was nothing if not brave. Her head raised in response and her body did the impossible: it started through the window. Eyes indignant, determined.

But as she did, she suddenly jerked backward. They had caught her trailing leg. The blow landed her full force on the window ledge. She couldn't help but let out a cry, her ribs bruised or broken, just her clothes preventing laceration. Her head whipped. It narrowly missed slamming down into the wall. She was lucky to not have broken teeth, but even René—temporarily hidden across the way—could see the blood dripping down her chin as the impact forced her bite into her bottom lip.

René ran into the church without a plan or concern for himself.

Violet twisted and turned like a scared animal, trying to slip out of their grip. She kicked, but they moved with her.

Rivalry aside, Matthias stepped on Henry's back to get high enough to grab her shoulders. "Just do it," Violet said, seeking freedom whatever the cost. She didn't mind the impact.

Unexpectedly, one man suddenly released her. She dropped down a little, the wall now at her stomach. Then, a gunshot. "*René*?"

In the shock, Matthias was able to pull Violet down. There was no time for soft words or feeling.

Ophélie was satisfied enough to disappear just as she should have—loyal to the mission's completion. But impulsively loyal to René, Henry now started towards the church.

"No, he can't!" Violet told Matthias, through her rapidly swelling lip.

Henry reached the church just in time to see René coming out. He had been winged but was okay. "They're right behind me," he warned.

Henry tried to close the door to prevent them following. A bullet shot into it, lodged in the thick wood close to his face just moments before he succeeded. They banged. There was no way to lock it. Henry was valiant, but it was hard to keep both doors closed with just one hand to grip.

They burst it open. One grabbed Henry by the neck, tripping him onto the floor; the other chased after René across the park and into a residential area.

Henry was flipped over, face scratched and pounded into the pavement.

"No!!!" Violet said, mustering her strength. Matthias prevented her from jumping right back into the heat of everything. "I'll go," he assured.

The Gestapo agent pulled Henry's arms behind his back, but hand-cuffs don't work so well with just one hand. It threw him off. He didn't have a belt on either to attach it to. Matthias ran like a bull towards him. Though he sat on Henry, the agent instinctively guarded his face, thereby lifting his grip. What a fortuitously foolish mistake. Surely he had been trained better?

Henry bucked himself free. Matthias then took the handcuffs and turned the tables on the Gestapo agent. But it was just a small victory: they hadn't expected a third agent. He had been waiting, watching. While Violet was looking on, recovering, half-crouching, half-lying on the grass, he grabbed her hair, wrenching her head back. Her hair had come free from her turban way back in the church, and now he had it wrapped twice round his leather-covered hand. "I've been waiting to meet you," he said. Somehow he knew who she was. He smelled of oak-aged wine, Calvados apple brandy from Normandy, and Parisian cologne—and yet he wanted to extinguish the soul of Paris?

Still by the church doors, Matthias and Henry saw this too late. The agent forced Violet to stand up, first pulling her to her knees, then kicking her to move to her feet. "You haven't had enough yet? A pity," he said. Unyielding to his demand to beg, he forced Violet even higher, intensifying the pressure. Her feet dragged, desperately trying to prop her toes beneath her.

The Gestapo agent pulled her to a car, but to Henry's confusion, Matthias flashed a smile. He had covertly slashed the tires when he first saw them go into the church. Yet it barely slowed him down. The agent quickly recalculated. He made towards a police station, prepared, it seemed, to haul her the whole way. Violet struggled, twisting. The Gestapo officer moved his left hand from the bunch of fabric between her shoulder blades to pure flesh. He choked her. Her wounded ribs were already refusing full breaths.

Again, Henry wanted to charge back in. "Haven't you learned yet?" Matthias rebuked.

A shout: "Here!" It was René. He had sprinted from the church to an arms stash. While the other Gestapo agent had followed him out of the square, he hadn't yet returned. René kept one Sten gun for himself but threw the other to Henry, who caught it.

"I've got her," Matthias said. "René," he directed, "you secure an exit for the two of you. And Henry? Back me up," he added, meaning with firepower. He should have let him help, but he was damned if he'd let Violet go without a fight.

Having heard the shots, four of them now, Nazi activity started to buzz towards them. The sting of hell was close. They had seconds at most before being swarmed. Henry had trained for this. He breathed deeply, steadying the gun with his left arm so his right hand could pull the trigger. The margin for error was small, Violet's head darting in and out of the crosshairs. He felt a Scottish breeze upon his cheek, counted a beat, and squeezed.

He didn't need another shot. The Gestapo agent's body hung in the air and then fell hard. He crumbled backward, his torso weighing on Violet. Death didn't shock her anymore but life did. She gasped for air, scrambling away. Desperate, realizing she was stuck, some of her hair wrapped around his jacket button she took her hair in her hand and tore through the stands, leaving them there.

"Now go. Go, Henry! I've got her," Matthias shouted back to Peter.

"But I—"

"It's not about you. It's not about any of us."

Henry knew Matthias was right.

Motors were firing, close. A whir of voices and iron converging.

René agreed with Matthias. Guns at their side, he pulled Henry southward at speed. After darting to avoid hostile movements, he led them to one small passageway off another, away from prying eyes.

René stopped Henry still. Panting, he pulled the gun strap off and over Henry's head. Apparently, he was keeping the gun. Henry was disorientated. "Yves will find you," René said, before closing the heavy manhole cover over him, wincing from his wounded arm.

It was pitch-black. Henry shifted, by feel, down the iron rungs and back into the catacombs. It felt like another world, a world he joined as a man who had killed to save Violet. Was this ethically different than killing in cold blood? He hoped it was.

The way the sound delayed; it was a long way down. Mercifully, his one hand felt like it was able to grip well enough. His other arm looped over each rung to stabilize. This entrance had not been the plan, but at least the Parisians had enough foresight to build in redundancy.

Henry liked rhythm, pattern, and precision. He detested being dependent but knew that his life now rested on an unbroken chain of strangers, the first being Yves. He had to get out of Paris, accurately discern threats, relay the information as quickly as possible, and then get out of the country altogether.

51

Peter

Gardens of Eden

HEAVEN AND HELL

Monday, August 22nd, 1994.

The holy presence of God had entwined Peter's life with that of Father Michael, witness to the miracle of Peter's resurrection. He had a classical music-loving, book-organizing(!), overly happy demeanor. For every facet of Bernard's curmudgeonly charm, Father Michael offered a cleaner clarity. Initially, when Peter moved in, he had found this off-putting. Then he came to realize that his single-heartedness could not be mistaken for naïveté since it ran to such great depth that its engaged devotion to humanity easily outstripped any such allegation. He devoted his life to walking closely with the hurting. The doorbell, quite frankly, wouldn't stop ringing, nor the phone. Still, it took a while for Peter to allow himself to enjoy drinking from a clean white cup without pining for a stained mug—one with coffee rings inside like on a tree stump.

Once Peter was feeling brave enough, he had returned to the community, but a local farmer explained that everyone had left not soon after him. It was hard, though, ridiculously so. He wanted to go back and solve all the problems, but he couldn't. Peter abhorred not being in control of what people thought of him. Even the bees had been moved out. He found just one small carboy of mead left cooling in the river by Bernard's garden. Peter rescued it. He brought it back with him but remained

343

hesitant to crack it open. He pined for his friend. When he prayed for him, Peter imagined Bernard with Chestnut curled deeply into his lap. He liked to think that Chestnut was being a real help, faithfully accompanying Bernie as he tended to his hive—wherever they were now. In reality, the fox probably spent more energy leveraging food from Bernie and guarding it from Horrice. *Oh, Horrice!* Peter could only imagine what he had been privy to over the years.

Peter was doing everything he could to find Hélène, but each attempt came back empty. It was achingly painful. Promising leads ran dry. As avenues for his effort dwindled, the days got slower as if even they pitied him. Time lurched forwards, skipping like the tape of an old cinema film, moments of intention robbed of their footprint. He felt like a ghost. Father Michael helped Peter realize how much he had been through and how he needed time to heal and restore. He struggled to forgive himself.

On Father Michael's shelf, Peter immediately recognized Camus's *The Rebel*. Since that last day had been a blur, he'd entirely forgotten that Etienne's copy had followed his Bible, thrown under his bed. He cracked Michael's copy open, devouring it as if in doing so, Etienne was still alive and close. Foolishness, he knew, but a remarkably determined foolishness. In it, he saw the circular bloody pattern of humanity, one he recognized. A cycle where humanity felt trapped or under siege and committed to a path of rebellion. But then, the "liberating" revolutionaries became the next tyrants.

That evening, as the hot summer day relaxed into evening, Peter sat next to an open window in the living room with Father Michael both doing their best to keep cool. After allowing Peter to share his thoughts, Father Michael said, "You know, Camus knew real poverty, pain, and sacrifice. That's why he doesn't idealize revolution. In searching for moderation of revolutionary ideas, what does he come to?"

"The Russian assassins," Peter replied, fondly remembering the feeling of being couched in the bucket of an old armchair in Bernard's cabin, munching on cookies. Peter explained, "We'd been talking about whether you could create Eden without creating hell. Bernard thought that we needed a deep, double-layered concept of reality, which his late Orthodox priest friend said needed to keep humanity—a person, not an idea—at its very core: Jesus."

"I'm inclined to agree!"

It was coming back to Peter now: how Camus appreciated the ethical wrestle of the Russian assassins like Ivan Kaliayev.[285] After his assassination of the Grand Duke in 1905, his surrender unto execution contrasted with the regimes or revolutionaries who justify endless violence without personal accountability. They gave human life a value—a measure—because they wouldn't take a life without giving their own. And yet, as Bernard had pointed out, it lacked a sustainable way to activate that sort of passion in the context of everyday violence.

"And so?" Father Michael asked Socratically.

"Something about a paradox? Jesus? Death and life? Ah," Peter felt bad. "I wish I could remember more. What do you think?"

"I think you're onto something. We can get so caught up in other aspects of theology that we lose the raw weight of this revelation. We were going to die, and yet Jesus died in our place."

"My friends in Amsterdam said that: God said we'd die but not that we'd stay dead. Instead, he breaks the siege of death, darkness, and disconnection over our lives." Saying this helped him recognize how much his heart ached for them.

Father Michael nodded in agreement. He pointed to the book: "Did you read the last page?"

Peter hadn't. He passed it to him.

Father Michael opened it to where Camus summarized his core idea that idealism kills real humanity, arguing that Europeans:

> . . . no longer believe in the things that exist in the world and in living man…denying the real grandeur of life they had to stake it all on their own excellence . . . they deified themselves and their misfortunes began; these gods have had their eyes put out. Kaliayev, and his brothers . . . refuse, on the contrary to be deified in that they refuse the unlimited power to inflict death. They chose, and give us as an example the only original rule of life today: to learn to live and to die, and, in order to be a man, refuse to be god.[286]

"So explicit," Peter agreed. "So, by god he means having unlimited power to create the world how we see fit?"

"Right," Father Michael said, "the consequence of the gospel is not that we stop being creative—in fact, quite the opposite—we stop attempting to bend creation and even ourselves to our will," Father Michael

285. Ivan Kaliayev was a member of the Socialist-Revolutionary Party and assassinated Grand Duke Sergei Alexandrovich in 1905.

286. Camus, *Rebel*, 305–6.

explained. "That's where it starts to kill us and when we start to kill and suffocate others. We make ourselves and others frozen idols."

"Or objects," Peter thought, remembering Sartre's concerns.

"Right! You know, Camus turned one of his novels, *The Plague*, into a play after the war. Can you guess what he called it?"

"You'll have to tell me."

"*The State of Siege!*"

"Isn't that interesting!" Peter agreed, enthralled. Now he really was thinking of Edwin. He could hear his voice explaining again how the *Euangelion* of Jesus Christ in the time and culture meant something like "behold, the righteous king has come and broken the siege." He would write to them soon, he resolved, when he knew what to say in words. It seemed to be beyond crystallization by any combination of just twenty-six letters. How could he explain it all? Especially the parts where he felt raw and embarrassed, ashamed.

Father Michael explained, "For Camus, the title fit because the play was, after all, a metaphor for the occupation. But it also meant something wider than that. The story is about human nature when the world is in crisis, specifically in an epidemic—humanity facing the audacity of death. We could talk more about that another time, but that awareness—"

"—or denial—"

"True—of life, death, and how we respond, in large part, defines the nature of our humanity," Father Michael suggested. "You might even say that this, in part, constitutes humanity 'knowing,' living, embracing, rejecting both 'good and evil.' The highs and lows of life, the tragic and the beautiful."

"Even the beautifully tragic?"

"That too, perhaps. You might even connect it to the denial of our cultural death."

"And we're left with a choice between alienation or participation, right?" Peter recalled, his memories layered and textured. "I heard this stuff, but I thought it was fantasy. Wishful thinking, you know."

"I know, Peter. Because I thought the same. There's no shame in that. Faith cannot be second-hand. It is only by wrestling with God, with pain and death, that we are marked by the process deeply enough to give our lives to him—to really live in and through the paradox."

"Of losing our lives to save them?"

"Right. The offer of Jesus—the sharing in his life—is positioned right at the heart of this nexus, the human experience. If we die to ourselves (being a god for ourselves), then we are free to live a new life united to Christ. We don't need to self-justify or endlessly self-create; instead we can receive the truth that we are loved, that we're good enough." Father Michael needed Peter to get this: Peter needed to stop running from his shadow.

"To rest transparently in the one who created us,"[287] Peter said, surprising himself. And there he was, thinking that he hadn't remembered anything about Kierkegaard, the eccentric Dane, aside from his quirks. *Wow, these ideas sit differently after encountering the love of God,* he thought; *honeyed and welcoming instead of acerbic and threatening.*

"Yes, to rest transparently but not to disappear. Quite the opposite," Father Michael clarified. "We can receive who we are, which invites us into the joy of a lifetime as we allow that to flourish—as we become—and explore what this means."

"So, receive rather than self-create," Peter concluded, comforted. Perhaps Father Michael and Edwin did read off the same hymn book. Before his encounter with God, Peter questioned whether Edwin's life change was just an exception. Now, Peter saw that there might truly be a path to life opened for all by Jesus.

"Right," Father Michael said. "And this creativity, mercifully, doesn't come with the caveat that our creations are hot air that we have to neurotically maintain . . . or perfect." He knew that Peter could let the events he'd lived through be the end of his story, defining the rest, or the beginning, of a life imbued with more wisdom, grace, and love. "You have a hope and a future, Peter," Father Michael testified. "Maybe think about it this way," he said, connecting back. "Sartre said we're the being that—"

"The being that folds nothingness into the world!" Peter jumped in, reminded of his meal with Edith and Edwin and soon after chatting with Etienne in Paris beside the *bouquinistes,* the Île de la Cité and Notre-Dame's spire behind them. Etienne was so much more vigorous and carefree then, compared to his last days. This was how Peter wished to remember him.

"Sartre wasn't wrong," Father Michael added. "He thought that anxiety is our response to the discovery of nothingness, a lack of substantiated being. This, I believe, is the fallen, disconnected reality. This limits our creative engagement. But reconnected to the one who *is* Life,

287. Kierkegaard, *Sickness unto Death,* 41.

who is being, equips us not only to thrive but to naturally turn outwards and share this experience—"

"Like being charged up?" Peter jumped in, trying to put words to what he, too, was feeling.

"Right!" Father Michael continued. "Once we allow ourselves to know, or yes, be 'charged up,'—but in a relational, connected way—with resurrection life, then we have the distinct privilege to not keep this to ourselves but to fold this into the world. I like how Kierkegaard said 'non-being is present everywhere . . . the [Christian] task is to do away with it in order to bring forth being.'[288] He meant life—the resurrection life of the eternal one breaking in."

"Like the bees," Peter said, quietly to himself. "Sorry," Peter apologized before explaining, "my dear friend Bernard keeps bees. So, maybe in the same way that bees pollinate the world, the life of Jesus does that too?"

"Yes, Peter!" Father Michael replied, seeing this spark in Peter's mind. For him, the image immediately reconstituted majestic pages from a medieval *Book of Hours* he had once had the honor of sitting with. It was masterfully colored, illuminated, and the Virgin Mary—or the *Theotokos*, understood as the one who bears life—was covered in bees.

"Bees create Edens; lush, fruitful gardens," Peter started.

Enthralled, Father Michael amplified this, seeing where it would take them: "In the same way, we are to be sent out from the church to make pockets of heaven, where heaven and earth come together, where we are reunited with God, ourselves, others, and creation. Filled up with this love, truth, and light, we have the distinct duty and privilege to fold this into the world."

"So, the choice is folding nothingness in the world . . . or folding in love and life?" Peter asked.

"I'd never put it that way before, but I love that image. And I'm never going to see bees in the same way."

"Me neither," said Peter, missing Bernard all the more. Bernard hadn't been easy to love, but his imperfections made him human.

"Really, it's about changing the world, right?" Peter said.

"Exactly. Starting with our hearts. We're not talking about changing the world in any way: it's about how it can be made more human, how we can keep humanity at the center. From there, we're taught to understand

---

288. Kierkegaard, *Concept of Anxiety*, 75.

all of creation as a gift, deserving to be tended to rather than used and abused."

"We're called to create gardens of Eden, not hell on earth," Peter said, humbled, taking stock of the enormous repercussions of these suggestions.

52

———————————

Alexi

Love Me

HEAVEN AND HELL

Tuesday, February 2nd, 2016. Amsterdam.

This is where we first met Alexi, telling herself, "The wind whips right through me because my bones feel hollow—the marrow sucked out along with my hope, which is now dead." She could see clearly now that she had been deluding herself when she presumed, "My father is kind and gracious, everything that my mother is not." And while she had once worried whether her added weight would have crushed him, now suspecting what she did, she worried that her uncertainty about him would slowly crush her.

Seeing this trajectory, after dinner one evening, Edith was vulnerable with Alexi, sharing about the dysfunctional home that she had grown up in. Key to her healing, she said, was learning that other people—even, and perhaps most especially, parents—cannot be God for us. To hold anyone to that bar of perfection or support for our lives is always destructive, both for them and for us. Edith suggested that only by releasing Peter from that expectation might she then be able to receive him in her heart afresh as a father in all his humanness and imperfection. Alexi wasn't thrilled about an idea—*so sanctimonious and unrealistic*. But to be fair, Edith didn't know it all. *She didn't know about the death, the*

350

manipulation, Alexi thought. Maybe she didn't want to "receive him as a father" after all.

Alexi not only hated the feeling of depression and darkness closing in, but if she was brutally honest with herself, she hated how selfish it made her. For the first time in her life, she had something that approximated a family. Even a younger sister! People—who despite giving them many reasons to the contrary—seemed to want to support her. At the core of this fear was, no doubt, anxiety; Alexi feared that the intensity of their love would end, and what would be left of her when it did. Then came the worry about how to pay them back for their kindness. She couldn't pretend to be okay—not that they had communicated such a need, in fact, quite the opposite—but the self-inflicted pressure to please them remained. And it was hard to separate this misguided pressure to perform from the people she wanted to perform for, even if deep down she knew the lie. She began to hate herself—and them—for not being able to deliver on this; to thank them.

"Space" looked like going for circuitous walks, sometimes listening to music, other times audiobooks. Edith suggested jogging and stretching because she said that the body could store trauma. Sometimes she did this too. While she always lit up when Lili was around, and Lili for Alexi, days seemed long and dark. She was playing with the idea of going to university or finding a job. A café to start, perhaps. Edith agreed—it might be a nice way for her to meet others her age.

One evening, Alexi remembered the list in the back of Peter's Bible. This had first caught her attention in the hospital in those adjunct, liminal days. Etienne had written it in those very early weeks at the community when everything seemed possible and human nature less corrupt. It was nothing profound, just a brief list of some of Camus's books with Etienne's favorites starred.

Googling Camus had made her curious. Why was this smoking, pleasure-loving absurdist noted in the back of Peter's Bible? She wasn't that drawn to reading *The Rebel*, despite also finding it under the bed. But *The Plague*? A novel? The premise seemed dark and enticing, drawing her in. Why not? It resonated with her, matching her mood and, in a weird way, it made her feel less alone in a city full of happy couples and small, cute-looking children being transported in the red buckets of cargo bicycles. Perhaps they were the ones in denial?

Over a couple of days, she listened to it as an audiobook. Sometimes jogging, sometimes walking, always watching the world go by. *The Plague* was slow in places but insightful and gorgeously written. She appreciated the way the people of the coastal Algerian city of Oran first ignored the death of the rats, thinking it was a prank or would blow over . . . until it couldn't be ignored. Then, the death of the rats became the death of people. He captured humanity well. Our fickleness and attitudes.

It was one of those curious nights when, against a pitch-black sky, the moonlight reflected back from the water to make the clouds light; beautiful but somehow wrong. Edwin found Alexi with headphones in her ears, on the same bridge where he had once stood with Peter. She was staring over the water at some street art painted on a wall that jutted out into the canal. It was just two big white words in all capitals, the simple scream: "LOVE ME!"

"I thought I'd find you here," Edwin said, causing Alexi to pull her headphones down onto her shoulders. He gave her a travel mug with tea in it. It was welcome. She smiled and thanked him, before he continued, "Have you seen that graffitied in red?"

"Dripping like blood?" She said, letting the steam escape.

"Exactly."

"They're so interesting," Alexi said.

"Why do you think it resonates?"

"The contradiction: looking for love and finding pain." Alexi paused, deciding if she was brave enough to make it personal. "Edwin, what's wrong with me?" She couldn't look him in the face.

"What do you mean?"

"You're all so kind to me, and I'm truly awful."

"No, you're not," he replied. "Ok, just a little," he said to make her smile. It worked. "But that's us all, Alexi. We get afraid, and we push others away."

"I know; I'm my own worst enemy," she said, more afraid of the truth than a cliché.

"Can you try to let us love you?" he said kindly and with intent.

"Maybe," she smirked at him, before blowing on her hot tea. Rejecting them before they rejected her felt safer. But she didn't know another way. What would it even look like?

"Why do we do it?" Alexi asked, honestly.

"Why do we do anything?" Edwin replied. "I think at the end of the day, it comes down to the heart. It's the heart looking for the stability of the love it was made for. And without that, we're trying to grasp for that ourselves, trying to prove ourselves."

"Scared and impotent, like the Wizard of Oz?" she said before taking a sip. It was still a little too hot.

"Right. The fear of being found out makes us dangerous, hurting others in our desperation to be loved. Competing with others . . . all of it. We're no wonderful wizard nor God. But neither do we have to be!" He wanted Alexi to see the kindness, the grace in his eyes. "Keeping up the charade forces us to live in contradictions and instability. And are we any closer to being loved?

"No. Not really."

"Alexi, we get it! I was depressed for decades. And Edith? She traveled around the world in search of love, joy, and peace. Both of us were utterly stuck, feeling under siege, wondering how long until the walls would give way. How much longer to even try."

"What changed?"

"Edith's story is more interesting than mine. I'll let her tell the whole thing, but it started with her in India, meeting an old man on the bank of the Ganges River in Calcutta. She liked to go to the *ghats*, the riverfront steps, early in the morning, and sometimes—after their rituals—she would talk to the monks. She found them learned, kind, and devoted. She learned about different traditions and practices. She was drawn to their pursuit of peace in light of the chaos and suffering of the world."

Edwin continued, "She had been there for a couple of months when one morning she saw a young Christian nun in a white sari with three blue stripes trying to move an old, weak man. She helped her move the man to a car. After thanking her, the nun asked if she wanted to come with them. She stumbled upon the work of the Mother House, the missionary hospice that Mother Teresa had founded, giving dignity to the sick and dying, and ended up volunteering."

"Oh wow. What was Mother Teresa like?"

"Why don't you ask Edith? In just a few words: radiant humility."

"So, she just became a Christian because of the nuns?"

"It was actually because of that old man. He was weak and didn't have many days left, but he wanted to share his story with her through a translator. He shared how he had once been one of those monks, but after thirty years, he'd left that life behind."

"Why?"

"That was Edith's question, too. Because, after all the spiritual practices, bathing in the Ganges and even taking a two-thousand-mile pilgrimage across India, he didn't feel one step closer to spiritual *mok-sha*—spiritual deliverance from the weight and burden of karma.

"That's absolutely heart-wrenching."

"Right. Not one step closer to peace. He explained it like he was digging all these wells through these devoted practices but then finding no water in them.[289] You know, Gandhi experienced something similar. While Gandhi was inspired by Jesus and some notable Christians, he remained a practicing Hindu. After all he had done, in his life, all he had achieved, in his introduction to his autobiography, *The Story of My Experiments with Truth*, he humbly wrote, "What I want to achieve—what I have been striving and pining to achieve these thirty years—is self-realization, to see God face to face, to attain Moksha. I live and move and have my being in pursuit of this goal." But he ends it by saying that "it is unbroken torture to me that I am still so far from Him, who, as I fully know, governs every breadth of my life, and Whose offspring I am."[290]

"That sounds incredibly painful. So, you're saying that embracing Jesus might have helped?"

"I think so. Jesus is the human face of God. The whole premise is that he opens a pathway to real peace: a deep well that we couldn't dig but that Jesus has already dug for us, full of life-giving water. It is not a peace where we lose ourselves, disconnecting further from ourselves and others—a cold, arid, empty peace. Instead, in Jesus, we find a connected, relational, rich peace that means something. That means everything."

"Home?" Alexi said.

"Exactly."

"Did the man in Calcutta ever get there?"

"He did. Shortly before he passed, he asked a nun to pray with him. He declared something, over and over with astonishment. A nun translated for Edith: he said Jesus was taking his karma; he could feel it! It was the pure joy on his face that convinced her that despite having written off Christianity, it spoke of something deeply and profoundly true. She says that her heart started burning that day to taste some of that joy."

The hair on Alexi's arms stood up. She felt something. "How do I get there? Home, I mean. Peace," she asked.

---

289. This character is fictional. However his discovery is partly inspired by the experiences of Rahil Patel, who was a Hindu monk for twenty years, documented in Patel, *Found by Love*.

290. Gandhi, *Autobiography*, 17, 20.

"We can't seize this. It has to be relational: real love can only be a gift. The good news is that this is what Jesus does. God isn't some unmoved mover like Aristotle said, a static carved idol or logical contradiction like Sartre assumes. Instead, he offers his love, his life."

"But why is Jesus special? All of us die," Alexi interrupted.

"You're right, and many were crucified by the Romans. But since Jesus is God, he is life, and only Jesus had the ability to reconnect us to Life, eternal love, and to heal the wound within reality. To meet with us, find us, and to heal us in all the mess of earth. What he accomplishes allows us to root in this layer of reality, reinfusing our material life with meaning and joy. Jesus shares his life to resurrect and empower ours."

"Explain that more," Alexi asked.

"Think about the 'love me' sign again. It's like the art makes visible the call of humanity: asking someone, anyone, to help. Seeing our nothingness, in our anxiety, feeling this lack. Desiring to be seen, known, loved."

"Right."

"The good news is that God responds—Jesus comes. The unseen God is moved by compassion, love, to make himself visible. But not only that: this costs him something. The gift of his life. Not taken but laid down. It's like with the red, blood version of the graffiti; he offers his life in response to the 'love me' cry that bleeds."

"Mirroring it."

"Mirroring is especially apt because it also reverses things. By doing so, it can go further and really change things. Jesus gets to the real heart of the pain and bleeds and dies in response; a response that does not meet violence with violence but works in the completely other direction. Giving his life, not taking life."

"Why, though?"

"To make the cycles of violence stop. This self-giving demonstrates the weight of his love. It meant something. He inaugurated the kingdom of God in a new way, a kingdom so different than those of the world. It's often called an upside-down kingdom, as it reversed the values of the ancient world."

"But can it really change things? Jesus and the cross happened millennia ago," Alexi said, despairing.

"You're right, but through the Holy Spirit, what Jesus accomplished can impact us today. Since Jesus is the one who *is* Life, he cannot stay dead. Neither can it hold us if we have shared our lives with him, spiritually united our stories. Sin is dealt with. Pain acknowledged—and now, a resurrection future can open up in front of us. He opened up a way to break the siege. Whole communities are changed as individual lives and families are changed, transformed, and empowered. Just in the same way a small band of Jesus followers first changed the world."

"Explain that a little more," Alexi asked, eager to test its strength.

"It's about how his body was broken for us to make a way through death to life, to reconnect us with the one who is life, who is being. We're invited to join with him in passing through what the Bible calls the 'veil which is his flesh.'[291] Think of it this way: in the Old Testament tabernacle, there was a veil that separates the holy place from the holy of holies."

"The tabernacle?" Alexi interrupted.

"A sort of tent that God told his people to camp around in the wilderness. But much more than that, it was a temporary but very specific way for God to meet, rest, or dwell with his people, where heaven could reconnect with earth. Even the word, "tabernacle," means to dwell. It was a bit like this street art—a visual to help people see something, to engage with the unseen—but in this case it's a spiritual reality."

"To engage with the unseen?"

"God used it to open up a practical way to engage with his people. You see, in Eden, the picture we have is of God walking with his people in the cool of the day. But at the fall, everything was ripped at the seams. This includes heaven, the dwelling place of God, separated from earth. But we learn right away that God does not disinherit his people; he has a plan to reconnect so that they wouldn't stay dead."

"So, God showed this plan visually?"

"Right. The tabernacle was packed full of imagery and truth, that's why God gave Moses really specific instructions about how to make it."

"If it was so special, why was it temporary?"

"The tabernacle was never the end game. It was a picture foreshadowing what Jesus would do on a much bigger, more radical scale: to engage the whole world. Now get this," Edwin said passionately, "when Jesus died on the cross, the huge temple version of the tabernacle veil— the curtain to the holy of holies—was split, top to bottom."

"And if the veil meant separation, then it being split means reconnection?" Alexi reasoned.

291. Heb 10:20.

"Exactly. Reconnection, or reconciliation between humanity and God: 'For in him we live, and move, and have our being.'[292] We couldn't make this reconnection happen, but heaven could. God gives everything, emptying himself to address this issue: the rupture, the disconnection, the sin, injustice, and shame: the siege that feels like death. He doesn't sidestep any of it."

"So, the veil being torn means that the siege of sin and death has ended?"

"That's it! The Righteous King has come and broken the siege. Even today, by being united to God by his spirit, we are invited to the dynamic work of the cross to move from death to life. It's like he offers a hand we can grab hold of, pulling us through the curtain to where heaven touches earth—to where the two layers of reality are truly overlapping. By grabbing hold, our bodies and souls can be made spiritually alive, revivified."

"But Edith was saying that stepping through, making this choice, costs something, right?"

"Right," Edwin replied. "This invitation starts with letting go of old things, surrendering our old habits to get love and praise, dying to being our own gods. Only then can we grab hold, to be united in his death and resurrection. Yes, it costs, but oh, it changes everything, Alexi. If we let him, he'll even engage with the searing pain of disappointment. All that stuff that is too heavy for us to carry. If we don't? We get crushed under the weight of it."

That crushing feeling, Alexi understood.

Edwin shared a Scripture with her. "I find I can always relate to what Jesus says in Matthew: 'Come to me, all you who are weary and burdened, and I will give you rest.'"[293] Alexi looked at him, her wide eyes unleashed from the spell that had bound them, revealing the supple pools of her soul.

"A spiritual rest?"

"Right. A rest that means restoration. Healing so deeply that it affects how we then live outwardly. We could think about it this way: one of the Christians who significantly impacted Gandhi was Leo Tolstoy. Gandhi admired Tolstoy's book *The Kingdom of God Is Within You*.[294]

"What is it about?" Alexi asked, ever curious.

292. Acts 17:28.
293. Matt 11:28.
294. Tolstoy, *Kingdom*.

"That we can't change the outside world until our inside worlds are changed. Until we allow the transformation and peaceful rule of the kingdom of God in our hearts." Edwin then asked Alexi, "What do you think keeps us stuck on the inside?"

"I'm not sure," Alexi replied.

"More and more, I'm convinced the biggest obstacle is unforgiveness."

"Why?"

"Because it's the opposite of love, as it attempts to justify further disconnection."

"I don't know if I can forgive—or where to start," Alexi said, raw. Making a snap decision, she pulled out the Bible. Blood still on the side. "I'm so angry at him."

Edwin was shocked. "How did you get this?" His eyes immediately teared up, even before seeing the shocking blood stains. She gave it to him. Perhaps the devilish side of her wanted to see how forgiving he would be. But she hadn't expected how guilty she would feel.

He stood still, recalibrating, perhaps. The wind picked up a little, taking a few tears with it. They pulled their coats more closely towards themselves. The night drawing closer.

"What happened?" Edwin asked, shaken.

"Honestly? I don't even know if it's his blood or someone else's. Edwin, I've been blaming him for horrible things." As she said this, tears burst forth. It felt natural to let Edwin comfort her. She leaned into the hug, a fatherly hug—one that meant something—like she'd always wanted.

Edwin listened for a while as she shared the burden. The blood was shocking but fitting. Like the red, bleeding version of the "love me" street art and Jesus' response in pouring out his life, his blood and his body.

Once Alexi was done and he had comforted her, he chose his next words carefully. "Peter doesn't need to be perfect for us to make peace with his humanity. We're not asking him to be God, and so he doesn't need to take that central place in our hearts. Instead, making peace invites him into a manageable relationship, one where the distance shifts as we heal and sort through."

"But what if . . .?" Alexi didn't know what to say. It just felt too much.

"We may never know it all, and I'm not justifying any of it," Edwin said gently, "but I'm convinced of one thing: we're both victim and executioner. None of us are free from accusation. As Solzhenitsyn wrote, 'If only it were all so simple! If only there were evil people somewhere insidiously committing evil deeds, and it were necessary only to separate them from the rest of us and destroy them. But the line dividing good and evil cuts through the heart of every human being. And who is willing to destroy a piece of his own heart?'[295] Only Jesus breaks the siege and opens a way beyond this."

Alexi took it all in, in the same way her wide pupils attempted to absorb the evening light. Edwin gently suggested, "Allowing him to be human means you don't need to push his memory away all the time. Unforgiveness is exhausting, whether we are punishing ourselves or others by withholding love. Jesus gives the means and the power for a forgiveness that can set you free, Alexi. We are made to give love and be loved."

Edwin continued, "I can't tell you what that safe distance is right now, but once you've found it, receiving his memory to that measure might allow you time and space to heal. That way you can reject the bad things, but also receive and enjoy the good parts—that is especially important as some of these aspects may find themselves reflected in you. I've found that this really helped me."

"Where would I begin?"

"For a start, I can tell you that he was a damn good friend and an awful liar!"

"But what about the pain? The anger?" she asked honestly.

"I get it. But I'd be careful with anger. You need to feel those emotions, but it's important to try to discover what it's masking. There's a great quote that never fails to resonate with me: 'I sat with my anger long enough until she told me her real name was grief.'"[296]

As he spoke, this unlocked something in Alexi, realizing that, yes, part of her anger was grief, the death of the mirage, but also disappointment that he didn't live up to it. How he would have hated that, even disappointing people decades later. Alexi also realized, to her shock, that by remaining in unforgiveness she was essentially taking the side of her mother—the one who had made her life a living hell. She paused and pivoted, squeaking, "Where was he when I needed him?"

"I am so sorry," Edwin said sincerely. "I wish I could tell you. Forgiveness does not mean we need to justify any of it—what we know and what we don't. Recognizing those emotions and questions are really important. In time, bit by bit, it might be possible to surrender the anger,

295. Solzhenitsyn, *Gulag Archipelago*, 168.

296. Widely attributed to C. S. Lewis. This may be misattributed. For Lewis on grief, see Lewis, *Grief Observed*.

the hurt, and the pain to Jesus and in its place, receive his peace. If you do, you might find something surprising: these memories can be transformed into sites where the eternal one enters, where peace can enter, full of new, surprising, confounding hope and life."

"Life where there wasn't any?"

"A powerful creative act: life where there used to be the fuel for spirals of violence. New life is folded into the world. Life instead of death."

"There will be pain in this world, Alexi. Sadly, until Jesus comes back, far too much of it. So then, the question that really determines our future is, what will we do with our pain? Will we keep it? Or will we give it to Jesus?"

After letting Alexi think deeply for a few precious moments, Edwin couldn't help himself. He'd just remembered why he'd come to find her in the first place. "Speaking of new life, look what resurrected! It had fallen behind the drawer in my study. I'm sorry it doesn't help much."

Alexi's eyes lit up as she read the third postcard: "I'm off on another adventure. You'll be proud of this one. I'll write soon. Peter." He was right: it wasn't much, but in that moment, it was all that she needed.

Edwin's phone buzzed. "Ah, dinner's getting cold. Edith's going to kill me!"

53

Peter

What Consoling Opium?

HEAVEN AND HELL

Tuesday, August 30th, 1994. Les Vosges.

Another day of ministry was winding down for Father Michael. But he'd barely poured them each a cool glass of lemonade before the phone rang. He leaned up against the yellow plaster wall, rubbing the furrows of his brows. The news seemed to wound him with invisible arrows, one after the other. Peter knew without a shadow of a doubt what it was about.

"The gospel's not about justifying anything, but it's about bringing change, right? This hate, the bloodshed—it's the very antithesis of the call of Jesus." Peter was livid.

Father Michael's friends from the International Committee of the Red Cross had been relaying to him reports about the civil war in Yugoslavia. Until his death in 1980, Josip Broz Tito had been a strong communist leader in Yugoslavia, successfully warding off Soviet control and remaining 'non-aligned.' He had led the country since World War II, during which he commanded the Partisans, a communist resistance movement. After his death, a significant power vacuum emerged. During this time, leaders like Slobodan Milošević rose to prominence. Milošević championed Serbian nationalism, his forces becoming implicated in widespread atrocities, including ethnic cleansing and systematic killings, especially of Bosnian Muslims (Bosniaks), in what had become known as the Bosnian War. While there was little evidence that Milošević had a deeply personal faith, he leveraged religious identity, especially Serbian Orthodox Christianity, as a tool to advance his nationalist agenda.

Peter continued, incensed, "Jesus had a zeal for his Church to bring love and life to the world, not bless death or its mercenaries." Father Michael knew this anger too. He'd still be there were it not for having cultivated a structure in his internal world where peace could reign alongside zeal, a meekness. He'd come to realize that anger didn't do anything—well, nothing good—for it just created another enemy in one's mind.

"Tell me, what would you say is a mark of real faith?" Father Michael pressed him, eager to hear Peter's thoughts and get him to step back for a moment. He was not interested in making some over-pious disciple who judged others. He cared about Peter finding the pulse of Jesus' heart just as Jesus had found his.

Peter thought for a minute. How could he distill all the new things that had captivated his heart these last weeks? Landing with new understanding upon some of what Edwin had first taught him, he answered: "It's about breaking the siege—a freedom and utter change that starts on the inside and extends towards the world, to echo the truth and beauty of heaven: what heaven says over it."

"Which is what?" Father Michael asked, leadingly.

"You are seen, you are known, you are loved—you are worth fighting for."

"Good. Try to expand that. What does it look like?"

"You know," Peter said, "I've come to realize that we all want to create because God is a creating God, and so if we are made in his image, we want to be involved in making our mark on the world. But the most far-reaching act of creation that I get to be a part of isn't self-creation; it's getting to be a part of a life-giving recreation that calls creation back into order in such a beautiful way. It's all about the cross because that's the place that we meet with our creator, to be personally transformed, and then sent out with a new, deeper calibration to outward-focused compassionate love."

"I love it: the cross is a place of new creation."[297] Father Michael explained, "But partnering with new creation comes with a call and responsibility. It's easy when things are going well, but what about when

---

297. 2 Cor 5:17: "Therefore, if anyone is in Christ, the new creation has come: The old has gone, the new is here!"

they're not? What about in the world where things are so ripped at the seams? Where we are hurt and hurt others?"

Peter tried, as eloquently as he could, to tie his many thoughts together. He thought of his pain. His struggle to forgive himself and others. He shared from a place of deep knowing: "The cross is a place of ultimate creative capacity because it acknowledges the pain of victims of injustice. Then, it offers them the dignity of a choice forward when so often all other choices are robbed, defined by what has happened. It invites victims to shed the pain along with plans to be the one who brings judgment."

"Good. Justice systems and God being the true judge are important here, which releases us from needing to bear the weight and pain of this role." Father Michael said, "Keep going. What of those on the other side of this?"

"It also invites transgressors to shed the false identity of forever being condemned and either acting out of that pain or trying to fight for recognition. This gives them the grace to walk untethered into fruitful beautiful relationships again."[298]

Father Michael was quiet, as if he was tasting the flavor of what it was that Peter was saying. He began smiling, so that must have been good.

Peter continued, "And really, we're both—victim and transgressor. It's such a mess."

"And yet that's exactly where he meets us. In this mess in between."

"I also loved this quote from Jürgen Moltmann that I read a couple of days ago," Peter offered.

"Oh, which one?"

Peter leaned over as he read:

> Believing in the resurrection does not just mean assenting to a dogma and noting a historical fact. It means participating in this creative act of God's . . . Resurrection is not a consoling opium, soothing us with the promise of a better world in the hereafter. It is the energy for a rebirth of this life. The hope doesn't point to another world. It is focused on the redemption of this one.[299]

This was night and day different from the allegations of philosophers, especially Ludwig Feuerbach (1804–1872), that Peter had heard

---

298. See Volf, *Exclusion and Embrace*. Volf considers how reconciliation with God through the life and work of Jesus impacts human communal relationships.

299. Moltmann, *Jesus Christ*, 81.

while at university, who reacted against a certain historically contingent brand of "church."[300] Feuerbach undoubtedly influenced the formation of the twentieth-century zeitgeist, especially in his influence on Marx, which included arguing that it was all a deception based on the hope of another world and never concerned with this one.

But this couldn't be further from the truth. "To the redemption of this one," Father Michael toasted, raising his well-earned glass of lemonade to Peter's.

"Pockets of heaven," Peter replied, the condensation dripping down onto the fleshy shelf of his hand as the glasses clinked. "Little Edens, wherever we are."

The moment hung rich but soft, like honeysuckle on a summer's night.

This lasted until Father Michael admitted that he needed to tell Peter something: "There'll never be a good time. I wish there was." His news wasn't a huge surprise, for as long as he had been there, Father Michael had shared updates about what was happening in Yugoslavia. But he was going there—and soon—to join his friends with the Red Cross on the ground. Father Michael really appreciated their work and had volunteered before. The organization, he said, had stayed true to their mission and value of treating everyone, regardless of their side in a conflict.

Father Michael explained that someone could cover for him in the church while he was away, adding, "I know you have unfinished business here, looking for Hélène, but if and when you're ready, I've made arrangements for you to spend some time in a quiet monastery in Italy." It sounded amazing, and Father Michael had explained the importance of learning healthy rhythms in a low-pressure environment, but this hit Peter like a gut punch. He was his friend. And he was only just rebuilding all over again. But clearly, helping in a warzone took priority.

300. Feuerbach, *Essence of Christianity.*

54

Alexi

On Evil

HEAVEN AND HELL

Tuesday, February 2nd, 2016. Amsterdam.

If the brisk evening walk back from the nearby canal wasn't welcome enough, Edwin and Alexi found a hearty meal waiting for them upon their return: fish, peas, and new potatoes dripping in butter with mint on top. Around the table, the family talked about everything from Lili's swimming to news of family vacation with their church in the south of France in the summer. Alexi was invited. It sounded nice, but she wasn't sure about it.

Alexi prompted Edith to share about her time in India. It sparked tales that drew all of them in, even Edwin, who thought he'd heard most of them. But something really bothered Alexi. After all this talk about Jesus bringing and resurrecting life: if God was God, why was there evil and suffering at all? It was hard to sit down and eat peas when your mind snagged and tore itself on these big questions as if caught on a protruding nail in a coffin. The name "intrusive" did *not* do justice to the destructive incisions of these thoughts, threatening everything she knew.

Alexi waited until after supper to ask Edith about them in that lull when Lili was packing her lunch for college the next day. They'd made a habit of connecting during this time. While Alexi's soul had become a little more open to receiving the good news, the "problem of evil" felt like a huge boulder blocking the way. There was a huge difference between comprehending God's apparently game-changing response in Jesus and why all this evil and suffering was possible in the first place.

"You've both been saying that Christianity is about reconnecting with life . . . but how does it deal with evil, death, suffering, all of that? When you were talking about India and mentioned karma, I get how it can be really painful for families to be told that suffering is because it's something that they did in this, or their past life; it eroded compassion. But is it not worse to say that God justifies it all?"

"That's a fantastic question. Why do you think he justifies suffering?" Edith inquired.

Alexi jumped right to Camus's book *The Plague*, which she'd been listening to. Specifically, Father Paneleux's sermons that attempted to justify the plague.

"Oh, it's been a long time since I've read that one," Edith said, adding some cheese and crackers to her plate. "I remember how Camus was fantastic at drawing out the injustice, the pain, the bleak absurdity—"

"—and the curious, often futile ways humans attempt to navigate it all," Alexi interjected.

It started to come back to Edith. The characters in *The Plague* ranged from the hardworking Dr. Rieux to the Jesuit priest Father Paneloux.

"You know," Edith joked, "Camus once spent forty-eight hours here in Amsterdam. After that, he made it the setting of his third novel, *The Fall*. He immortalized his opinion about it through his character Clamence."

"Which was?"

"That Edwin's beloved canals were like Dante's nine circles of the underworld!"[301]

"Basically, hell on earth!" Edwin interjected from the living room.[302]

"An absolute travesty!" Alexi agreed.

"He couldn't get how different the cold and wet was from his beloved Algiers," Edwin defended before turning back to the book under his reading light, happy to have added that extra little bit of justification. He was, after all, just as loyal to the city of his birth as Camus was to his.

"While that one's up for debate, I agree with many of his other observations," Edith offered.

---

301. Camus, *Fall*, 14.

302. Bellos, "Introduction," in Camus, *Plague*, xxi.

"About what, exactly?" Alexi asked.

"The aching state of the world," Edith said. "What is it Dr. Rieux says in *The Plague*?" Edith asked rhetorically. "'He believed himself on the right road . . .' She took a while finding the other words: '. . . in fighting against creation as he found it.'[303] Something like that?"

"That sounds right on."

"Oh, good." Edith continued, "'As he found it,'—I loved that little detail when I first read it. I find Camus faithful in tracing the contours of pain."

"And our responses," Alexi added.

"Right! That idea of 'fighting against creation' as we find it is powerful, given both the beauty of creation but also its devastating unraveling. Ultimately, this is what I think the gospel does—what Jesus does powerfully and uniquely."

"Then why are Father Paneleux's sermons so objectionable?" Alexi asked.

"What is it he spoke about again?" Edith asked to clarify.

"The first justified the evil and suffering—the plague—as punishment," Alexi replied.

"Ah yes," Edith recalled.

Alexi continued, "Many of the townspeople thought this all sounded like being 'sentenced for an unknown crime, for an indeterminate period of punishment.'[304] And in his second sermon, he speaks of it all like a trial of faith, in that it gave people a clear ultimatum to believe everything or nothing."

"So bleak," Edith agreed.

Alexi continued, "It's only right before he dies of the plague himself that the townspeople decide that he wasn't quite as bad as they had first thought. That's only because he ends up working with the other protagonists side by side, helping humanity, forming a connection 'beyond blasphemy and prayers.'"[305]

"Dr. Rieux said, 'I'm glad to know he's better than his sermon,'"[306] Edith said, remembering that part well.

Even as Alexi explained it, it provoked her again, "It's the way Father Paneloux justified the plague that really bothers me," Alexi admitted. But

303. Camus, *Plague*, 114.

304. Camus, *Plague*, 90.

305. Camus, *Plague*, 193.

306. Camus, *Plague*, 135.

it also bothered her that while the fictional Father Paneloux seemed so cold in his so-called Christian thinking, Edwin and Edith—also believers—seemed the very opposite. Even their thinking seemed warm and welcoming, not obsessed with punishment and the like.

Edith explained that the difference, the humanity in their position, was because of Jesus, not in spite of him. "It's the difference," Edith offered, "between keeping Jesus at the center of Christian thought or supplanting them for naked, inhumane ideas."

"But then, since Camus gives Father Paneloux a second sermon, which is a little kinder than the first one, why isn't there a third sermon that shows another move towards . . . I don't know," Alexi stopped short.

"You're onto something," Edith encouraged her. "Jesus doesn't justify evil and suffering. Nor does he leave humanity alone in its engagement with it—which is how far Camus gets. If I were to write a third sermon, it would say how Jesus engages with death face-to-face."

"Oh wow," Alexi said, as she thought this through.

"I think Camus is brilliant in depicting some of the very real range of responses that, sadly, we all and the Church, can grab hold of. But I don't think we can swallow this humanist pill whole."

Alexi asked, "If Camus was so insightful, how could he miss some of the value of Jesus in responding to the problem of evil and suffering?"

"Like all of us, I think he misses things," Edith replied.

"Oh?" Alexi said, intrigued.

Edwin, turning around in his chair, offered, "What if there was something he couldn't quite see?"

"Like?" Alexi asked.

Edwin jumped in, leaning forward, "Do you know where he planned much of *The Plague*?" Edwin continued.

"I actually don't. Paris? Algeria?"

"Good guesses. Le Panelier, in the Auvergne, southwest of Lyon."

"Why was he there?" Alexi asked.

"His lungs needed the fresh air. If I remember correctly, he was diagnosed with tuberculosis in his late teens."

"So, why is this important?"

Edwin continued, "Ah, well, the nearby village to where he was staying, Chambon-sur-Lignon, was a center for a *Résistance* network at the time."39

"Doing what?" Alexi asked.

Edwin concluded, "Protestant priests were there saving thousands of Jewish children, and Camus seemed none the wiser."[307]

"It certainly doesn't come through in *The Plague*, even though it's a thinly veiled reflection on the occupation of France," Edith said.

"So, you're saying even an insightful man doesn't catch everything?" Alexi reasoned.

"None of us can. That's why community is so important," said Edith.

Edwin explained, "In the same way as he missed this, he was able to study Augustine at a high level and, I believe, missed some of the life-changing power of it all.[308] To be honest, he captures some responses that Christians have genuinely had to the 'problem of evil'—as if documenting historical vignettes. It's almost painful how accurate some of it is. But I don't think it's a good example of how one can actually engage the gospel of Jesus Christ in addressing the problem of evil. The sermons are so unsatisfying, right? It's just sad that, as you say, there isn't a third sermon that is able to reveal a progression to a truly powerful Christian response."

"All the priest really does is justify evil and suffering!" Alexi exclaimed.

"True!" Edwin replied.

"I think it shows that Camus somehow missed in Christianity the very thing that it seems he was still looking for," Edith said.

"Oh?" Alexi asked. "What do you think he was after?"

---

307. Bellos, "Introduction," in Camus, *Plague*, xxii.

308. Chapter four of Camus's dissertation, *Christian Metaphysics and Neoplatonism*, entitled "Augustine," centrally addressed this doctor of the church. Camus does mention *privatio boni* on pages 118–21. However, he quickly moves to narrow in upon the topic of free will. In the introduction, written by the translator of the English edition, Ronald D. Srigley explains that Camus was deeply impacted by Augustine, circling back later in life to this topic in *Notebooks*. Why? Because to outgrow nihilism, Camus saw some reason to go back to Christianity, but then he suggested going back further to the Greeks. Augustine is pivotal here because Camus considered Augustine as standing at the nexus between Greek and modern thought, having forged, in Camus's view, a powerful coherence between faith and Greek "reason," which he considered nothing less than "miraculous"! However, given Camus's reading of Nietzsche, he may have forced himself into a false dichotomy. For example, Camus's ultimate identification of Augustine with the moderns over the Greeks may have led to him to miss the full depth and vitality of Augustine's thought. See Srigley, "Introduction." I therefore argue that Camus may have missed, as previously discussed, Chenu's "Augustinian Sap," and further material, to help him engage the irrationality of evil. Perhaps, to address nihilism, there is a good reason to avoid retreating to the Greeks and lodging into absurdism. Some have been briefly discussed.

"Camus's voice comes through in Dr. Rieux. What he's wanting isn't justification but an engaged humanity brave enough to look death in the face and, given his profession, a certain healing. Jesus, the divine physician, does this powerfully. It's a rogue idea, but I think Dr. Rieux—"

"—and therefore Camus—"

"—gets closer to the radical nature of the gospel than Father Paneleaux does. But in doing so,

I think he stops short in appreciating the full radicality of its position."

"Which is?"

Here Edwin jumped back in: "Not justifying evil. Death isn't sidestepped. Instead, the gospel is a defiance of death—in whatever form it comes—and an invitation to life, and life to the full, rooted in a heart that finds its home in him: healing. Jesus goes to the crux of the matter, this power of love in a world where the love of power holds dominion, and deals with it head on." Alexi nodded, so Edwin continued: "I don't see God sitting there justifying all the pain and suffering. I see him moved."

"But in Camus's defense," Edith admitted, "I used to think I needed to justify it all, as if that was being a good Christian."

"What made you stop?"

I think I realized two things. One: God doesn't need me to defend him. And two: while I think that God can be moved by love to justice, and sometimes this has needed to mean judgment to stop the chaotic rule of evil, I am not convinced that most of what we are talking about is his will or anything he is okay with. Instead, Jesus is the clearest representation of God that we have, and what I see is Jesus interrupting the reign of evil and death."

"Interrupting?" Alexi rolled that idea around in her mind. "So, like a way to stop it before it gets that far?"

"I think so. The goal would be to interrupt that trajectory, or those downwards spirals of vengeance and violence."

"How?"

"By interjecting that closed system with something new: his life and his love. Pouring it out—"

"As a response to our call or cries?"

"Right." Alexi saw in her mind's eye the "love me" art, the version with blood dripping down it.

"Honestly, Alexi, this seeing our pain, engaging with it, giving weight to it, and dealing with it—all of that captivates me. I think it is even more interesting when you think about trauma."

"Oh, why?" Alexi asked, reaching for some snacks of her own, already cradling a small glass of red wine.

"Well, if we define trauma as interrupting our flow of life—our understanding of the world so completely that its severing introduces not just a fear of death, but the disorienting experience of death in life—even as we live on—then Jesus is a game changer."

"Why?"

"Because what else does God do but interrupt death with his life? Resurrection life."

"Oh, that's interesting." Alexi wanted to talk more about this. But the main issue was still bothering her: the fact that there was evil and suffering in the first place. Yes, Jesus engaged this problem head on with his death on the cross, but why is evil and suffering even possible? "If God is the creator, why did he create evil?"

"What a fantastic question," Edith said. "To which one must answer: did he?"

Alexi looked confused.

Edith explained, "The distinction I make is between reason and justification. I think that there are some reasonable things to think about regarding causality, but this is different than saying that something should be this way. After all, when we cry out at injustice, isn't it because we protest '*It should not be like this*'? The pain lies in the horrendous gap between what we experience, the "is," and what we feel we should expect, a moral 'ought.'"

"But how do we know it *should* be a certain way," Alexi reasoned.

"That's a great question," Edith replied. "I think as humans, regardless of culture or background, we seem to have a shared intuition that the world should be different; our cries testify to this every day. I think it is because of a shared history and experience—the fall—the ripping of the world at the seams; things are not as they are meant to be. But note that this speaks to causal reasons but not a justification of the results."

"Reason but not justification? You said that before, but what do you mean?"

"In the sense that God doesn't say suffering is okay. Indeed, Jesus wept. Jesus addresses injustice wherever he finds it. Jesus died to turn the world upside down because he did not think it was the right way up.

"Huh," Alexi said, curious as to how this would unfold. "What would atheists say?"

"There are different perspectives, of course, but I find that popular neo-atheism doesn't have a leg to stand on in this respect. There's no real 'is/ought' distinction. After all, in that naturalistic worldview, the world is simply how it is, with humans having evolved in a certain way. There is no objective way that reality or relationships should be. As a result, suffering simply is. Thus, the problem of evil dissolves. In fact, suffering might even be seen as necessary, accompanying the mechanism of the survival of the fittest."

"Oh, wow," Alexi said.

"It was my dissatisfaction with this very Western enlightenment approach, and its answers, that led me to explore the different ways in which people and cultures have attempted to understand the shock of death, the pain of suffering, and the pursuit of peace. That's what first took me to India," Edith admitted. "My parents are still atheists."

"I didn't realize," Alexi replied.

"I must say that I've always found that the mid-twentieth century atheist existentialist philosophers, like Sartre and Camus, describe the human condition in a much more satisfying way than the neo-atheists. Now this is over-simplistic, but in part that's a legacy from Husserl's phenomenological method that suspended certain presumptions about things like God to prioritize the description of phenomena, of the lived experience, as we found it. Evil and suffering is a complicated topic, and I could say much, much more, but I have to tell you about a stream of Christian thought that goes way back to the church fathers and connects these threads.

"Which is?"

"The central thought is that of lack, or more profoundly, a nothingness. Regarding lack or disordered reality, counterfeit money is a good analogy in that it is best identified by it lacking the qualities of the genuine kind. This idea of lack translates to how, for example, relationships should function and how abuse can include an absence of care or support. Now, some have even gone further to suggest that evil as a nothingness, a black hole in reality: an erosion or falling away from the substance and goodness of the world itself.[309] Here, evil is a privation or absence of good, the Latin term being *privatio boni*."

---

309. Such as contemporary theologian John Milbank.

"I've got a good quote to explain that," Edwin said. He couldn't help but jump in. He brought his phone over to the table. "You see," he said, "while St. Augustine thought that the dynamic of sin was a deviation from the created order, like a counterfeit, evil itself wasn't part of creation. John Milbank, a contemporary theologian, argues that 'because evil is uncaused, there is indeed a sense in which it possesses us like an anti-cause proceeding from a Satanic black hole.'"[310]

"Well, Milbank's not messing around!" Alexi said. "But how would something uncaused or uncreated be possible within creation?"

"A fantastic question," Edwin said. "I can't do it complete justice now, but the logic goes along these lines: humanity is made in the image of God with free will. Adam is able to imagine a false alternative to the actual: 'a false simulacrum within the repleteness of reality.'"[311]

Edith translated that for Alexi: "A simulacrum is a fancy word for a representation disconnected from actual reality, often attempting to create or replace it with its own version of truth."

"So, they reject the real for an illusion?"

"Right," Edwin explained. "It's an irrational choice because it has no real foundation or justification, but it is still a choice that has real consequences."

"Why?"

Edwin replied, "It's a rejection of 'being' where this distance might be experienced as nonbeing."

"But what would that mean?" Alexi asked.

"I find Christos Yannaras really insightful here," Edwin said. "Through his Orthodox lens, he saw this choice as a 'refusal of God's call to realize life as a living communion with Him,'[312] resulting in an 'organic amputation from the mode of life.' He argued that this relational distance allowed for a consciousness of nothingness which he thought Heidegger described well as estrangement (*Entfremdung*)."[313]

"So back to evil?"

Edith jumped in again, "Ah yes. This is hotly debated, but after the Boxing Day Tsunami, David Bentley Hart wrote a fascinating book also arguing that evil should be understood as *privatio boni*. He made it clear that (until the choice) 'this is not to say that evil is then somehow illusory;

---

310. Milbank, *Being Reconciled*, 18.

311. Milbank, *Being Reconciled*, 8.

312. Yannaras, *On the Absence*, 89.

313. Yannaras, *On the Absence*, 90.

it is only to say that evil, rather than being a discrete substance, is instead a kind of ontological wasting disease.'"[314]

Edwin continued, "This all helps us understand, in part, why humanity might have become ungrounded, untethered. Why we struggle to feel alive!"

"That's so interesting. And the solution?" Alexi asked.

"A grounding of our being, or participation, back in the One who is Life," Edwin said.

"A rooting; finding our home in him," Edith echoed.

Edwin extrapolated, "Yannaras is really interesting in how he unpacks the impact of Jesus as the second Adam on the human person. He explains the possibility of a 'complete reversal' because in Jesus 'a human person hypostatizes (brings into existential reality) a new mode of existence for human nature.' This mode is a re-creating an 'existential unity' between God and humankind."[315] It's not a mode defined by autonomy, as Sartre may have it, but exceeds and overflows what is possible in human nature alone and disconnected."

"You both agree with defining evil as a privation of good?" Alexi asked.

"I certainly think it has some merit," Edith responded. "This is theoretical, of course, and as I said, hotly debated, but I also think it helps resource our understanding to see a greater complexity to the problem instead of artificially or tritely 'solving' it."

"Huh. So, Solving the problem of evil would be bad?" Alexi said.

Edith replied: "Some, like the German theologian Jürgen Moltmann, have asked whether to do so from one's armchair wouldn't be entirely immoral."

"Well," Edwin interjected, "it's like how Jean Améry, who lived through the horrors of Auschwitz said, 'I do not have [clarity] today and I hope that I never will. Clarification would amount to disposal, settlement . . .'"[316]

Edith concluded, "At some level, morality demands evil stay unintelligible, even if populated by all manner of ineffable horrors."

"I can see that," said Alexi, never having encountered this family of thoughts before. They felt uncomfortable but perhaps in a good way.

<hr>

314. Hart, *Doors of the Sea*, 73.

315. Yannaras, *On the Absence*, 92.

316. Améry, *Mind's Limits*, xi.

Edwin added, "Obviously, humans still bear some responsibility, and we could debate over what God allows and what he doesn't. But I've found knowing of this possibility certainly deepens my understanding of what is at stake and who or what might be to blame for evil."

"Because it's then not as simple as saying, 'God created everything, so he created evil,'" Edith finished.

"Absolutely."

Edwin wanted to connect this back to what really mattered—the heart. "You know those houses we talked about? The new builds in Amsterdam after the war, like false teeth amongst the old? Well, that's not unique to Amsterdam; it happened all over the continent. The description of World War Two that truly stopped me in my tracks was from Samuel Puterman. Upon returning home to Warsaw in 1945, he wrote, 'I thought you'd be there waiting for me . . . What greeted me instead was the lingering stench of the ashes and the empty sockets of our ruined home.'[317] While the ashes practically explained what had befallen Puterman's hometown, I find the emptiness, the lack, the privation of his once flourishing home—saturated in the goodness hindsight expects—most descriptive."

Edith corroborated, "Puterman's account is powerful as it brings together that concept of evil as *privatio boni*, a privation of good, and evil as a lack of a home for the human heart or life—that feeling of ungrounding or suspension."

Edwin elaborated: "The concepts of 'good' and 'home' that Edith picked up on are not strangers. Saint Augustine, who engaged most influentially with *privatio boni* among patristic theologians, often returns to the theme of finding home in God: 'My soul is like a house . . . It is in ruins, but I ask you to remake it.'[318] By inviting God into the midst of his turmoil, Augustine finds Jesus' words faithful: 'We will come to them and make our home with them,'[319] asserting like doxology, "our heart is restless until it finds its rest in thee."[320]

That talk of lack and home resonated deeply with Alexi even though she refused to show how much. How she had longed to close the front door of her childhood house that had emptied out the last vestiges of love and invited in vultures. She hated it. It felt cheesy, but she couldn't deny

317. Quote by Samuel Puterman, recorded in Grynberg, *Words to Outlive Us*, 440.

318. Augustine, *Confessions*, 6.

319. John 14:23.

320. Augustine, *Confessions*, 3.

it. She resolved that some crystal-clear reason might prevent her from dwelling in these thoughts. "So, if you had to distill it down, what do Christians really believe about evil and suffering?"

Edith obliged, seeing that Alexi wasn't ready to release those emotions just beneath the surface. "Well, there is some variation, absolutely. But if I had to distill it down most faithfully at this point in my journey, then I would summarize my position in, say, five points:"

"I love how you're a painter but you're also so linear," Alexi laughed.

"He doesn't!" It was a running joke that Edwin would always find his next task on a checklist on the fridge. Alexi quickly grabbed a pen and a scrap of paper. The five points, more or less, could be:

1. Suffering is not "okay" or just something that "happens to happen," as in neo-atheism.

2. There may be some causal reasons, but we don't have to justify it all. Reason without justification.

3. God is moved by his love to be present in our suffering, which can hugely affect our position in and through these storms.

4. God offers us future hope. In short, a future world where this isn't the case. A new heaven and earth, united without tears and death.[321]

5. And in the meantime, we can join with Jesus to bring change, bringing pockets of heaven to earth.

Edwin jumped in, "The philosopher Susan Nieman has recognized that suffering and evil such as in Auschwitz destroyed the hope of the enlightenment narrative of perpetual progress of humanity: 'the conditions in Germany should have led to genuine civilization, not barbarity.'[322] However, that doesn't not destroy all hope. As the theologian Charles T. Mathewes has argued, 'Hope does not demand belief in progress'[323] but instead that we are not 'abandoned' in our tragedy."[324]

"But that doesn't mean there can't be change," Edith clarified.

321. Rev 21:4.

322. Neiman, *Evil in Modern Thought*, 254.

323. Mathewes, *Augustinian Tradition*, 56. Original quote from Lasch, *True and Only Heaven*, 80.

324. Paraphrase of argument, Mathewes, *Augustinian Tradition*, 56–57.

"Right," Edwin said, "it just means hope for change is not wedded to humans thinking that they have civilized beyond barbarity. Only Jesus can change hearts and minds, bringing real, sustainable change."

55

Peter

The Revolution

HEAVEN AND HELL

Saturday, September 3rd, 1994. Les Vosges.

> "Celebrate the revolution that happened once and for all when
> the power of love overcame the love of power." ~ N. T. Wright,
> *The Day the Revolution Began*, 416.

Peter wanted to spend as much time as he could with Father Michael before he left for Yugoslavia.

"You really like Camus, hey?" Father Michael said as he folded his clothes.

"I resonate with so much. He captures something."

"Tell me, what did you find?" Father Michael said as he was packing.

"Here," Peter said, reading, "'the protest against evil, which is at the very core of metaphysical revolt, is significant . . . It is not the suffering of a child which is repugnant in itself but the fact that the suffering is not justified.'"[325]

"I agree," Father Michael said. "The fact there is no justification—the irrationality—makes it so

---

325. Camus, *Rebel*, 101.

much worse. You know, the German theologian Jürgen Moltmann called Camus and Horkheimer's atheism of 'metaphysical rebellion' the only 'serious atheism.'"[326]

"Who's Moltmann?"

"As a young man, he'd originally planned to study physics, but World War Two got in the way. He was in Hamburg during those apocalyptic bombings. At only sixteen years old, he and his schoolmates were made anti-aircraft gunners."

"Caught on the wrong side of history," Peter said. "So, he doesn't speak about suffering abstractly?"

"Not at all. It was in the midst of profound, disorientating suffering that he met Jesus. The bombings created a firestorm that consumed whole communities, including many of his friends. It was then he said he called out to God for the first time."

Father Michael stopped packing to find and split open *The Crucified God* to a passage he frequently revisited. They sat on the side of his bed as they read:

> The problem of modern man is no longer so much how he can live with gods and demons, but how he can survive with the bomb, revolution and the destruction of the balance of nature ... The vital question for him, therefore, is how this world which he has usurped can be humanized.[327]

"So powerful," Peter said, as the light filtered on to them through the old lace curtains. "He thought there was hope for a more humanized world?"

"Right. After all, hope had found him in a personal, humanizing way: Jesus found him, able to meet him through the barbed wire of the prisoner-of-war camp, as a brother in suffering."

"So why did he call Camus and Horkheimer's atheism 'serious'?"

"Because he felt it hit on something profoundly true about the nature of reality: the irrationality that presents itself as inhumane absurdity."

"That didn't undermine his faith?"

"Like Moltmann, I think that Camus's metaphysical atheism, also present in Dostoyevsky and others, is actually helpful in revealing what Jesus did on the cross."

"I don't get it," Peter admitted.

326. Moltmann, *Crucified God*, 223, 252.
327. Moltmann, *Crucified God*, 92.

"It's because we find in Jesus a serious, profound response. Jesus launches a unique protest: an effective rebellion against sin and death that humanity could not have done alone. By taking on flesh and giving his life rather than taking it, Jesus interrupts the downward, inhuman trajectory of human life. Since he is the definition of heaven—the presence of God—on earth, his engagement also addresses and begins to heal the rupture—the metaphysical wound—between heaven and earth."

"Which changes what?"

"The inhumane and the irrational: the human heart and the structure of the world."

"But how?" Peter pressed him.

Impassioned, Father Michael explained, "For a start, the nature of humanity changes. Jesus is the New Adam. He offers a way to life, and, as a result, a new paradigm for living this out connected to the one who is Life. Remember how Camus implored humanity 'to learn to live and to die, and in order to be a man, refuse to be god'? Well, if we learn to accept our own finitude, then we are finally free to partner in this different mode of life."

"And the structure of the world?"

"Right. Moltmann sees Jesus as a metaphysical rebel because his compassion provokes him to confront the reality of death—coming face-to-face with it. Jesus engages the problem on a spiritual but also metaphysical level. If the origin of evil is related to a metaphysical wasting disease, then addressing this disease or rupture is powerful in God taking evil and suffering seriously. For some this includes the power of death that's taken on a life of its own."

"So, you're saying God takes the unjust, irrational nature of suffering seriously?"

"I am," Father Michael replied, resolute. "And there's more: we're looking forward to a new heaven and new earth where there is complete healing. But this rupture starts to heal wherever Jesus is, for in Jesus, heaven—the presence of God—and earth overlap. Jesus then invites his people in a dignifying call to walk out their humanity by hosting and sharing God's loving presence in a relational way. Ministering the healing love of Jesus (heaven on earth) to the world around them."

"But Camus was astute. If it's true, why didn't he see the full radicality of it?" Peter asked.

"He studied theology and wrote on Augustine, so he gets close. He wrote that Christ came 'to solve two major problems—'"

"'—evil and death, which are precisely the problems that preoccupy the rebel.' Yeah, I liked that part too,"[328] Peter said, finishing the passage.

"Camus also understood that 'divinity abandoned its traditional privileges and drank to the last drop, despair included, the agony of death.'"[329]

"Then, what did he miss?"

Father Michael opened the book partway. "Moltmann thought that Camus missed the unique power of Jesus' humanizing rebellion because while he could see that 'the crucified God renounces' the 'privileges of an [unbreakable] idol,'[330] and truly suffers, he still 'saw Christ too much in terms of . . . traditional passion mysticism and too little as the protesting God involved in human sorrow and suffering . . . He saw God vanish on the cross, but he did not see Christ's death on the cross taken up into God.'[331] Peter, this aspect of Moltmann's work is controversial, but without needing to fully embrace it, I think it speaks to there being further dynamics at play."[332]

"Like what?"

"Camus sees the suffering and emptying but not the metaphysical rebellion that only Jesus as Life—being itself—could do, reweaving the ruptured tapestry of being."

"The heaven and earth thing?"

"Right. Heaven—God's spiritual presence—reunited with earth so that God can dwell with his people and his people with their God.[333] Some might say it's a sort of holy, creative anarchy that erodes the structures that have been parasitic on the wounds of the world: dysfunctional, dehumanizing, despotic kingdoms welcoming hell on earth."

Ah, hell on earth. "I always thought what Jesus did was so passive," Peter admitted, "but this costly, passionate knitting back together of the world and humanity, all this life and death, it makes so much more sense to me."

---

328. Camus, *Rebel*, 32.

329. Camus, *Rebel*, 32.

330. Moltmann, *Crucified God*, 303.

331. Moltmann, *Crucified God*, 226.

332. Moltmann images Jesus' protest against death or "metaphysical rebellion . . . in the cross of Christ [as] a rebellion in metaphysics or better, a rebellion in God himself." Moltmann, *Crucified God*, 227.

333. Moltmann, *Crucified God*, 227.

"Powerful but love; he's a paradox. You know, the British theologian N. T. Wright talks about the crucifixion as 'the day the revolution began'! A revolution, he argues, 'happened once and for all when the power of love overcame the love of power.'[334] The result shouldn't be more blood. Instead, those following the way of Jesus are invited into a 'genuine humanness' that equips us 'to bear and reflect his image,' to love."

Peter jumped up and pulled back the curtains. The light streamed, unfiltered on his face. He reasoned out loud: "Christianity doesn't deny the irrationality of suffering. Jesus breaks the power of sin and death and invites us into life: to break its hold over ourselves and others!" Peter felt like he wanted to scream this from the rooftops. He felt it! He felt this fire in his heart, pressing this truth deep within. Affirming it. Truth resonated with his soul, having found its precise frequency. Tension rose, amplified like an opera singer singing to a splendid wine glass.

If only the moment could have existed eternally, unbroken. He'd have liked it better that way. Peter had to ask something, knowing it might break him. He returned, sitting beside Father Michael. He'd avoided bringing it up, fearful of the answer. "We're empowered to create gardens of Eden, not hell on earth, right?" Peter said. "So, tell me this," Peter asked, his anger peaking, "In Yugoslavia, why are there priests praying for the soldiers before they commit horrendous crimes?"

Heinously, just as Hitler had attempted to leverage religion as a tool for an ungodly agenda, Milošević had no qualms about using the ancient traditions of the Eastern Orthodox Church to bless his nationalist forces before he sent them to kill and destroy.

"I know Peter, I hear you," said Father Michael, grieved to the core. "As to why? In part, it's historic and cultural—you pray for someone before they go into battle and might die. But, of course, I agree with you: that's entirely different from justifying what's been happening. I think there's two things to hold onto here. The first is this: a knowledge of where Jesus would be. Which is where?"

---

334. Wright, *Revolution*, 416. Note that N. T. Wright is clear to say that this approach does *not* play different "theories of atonement against each other" in what he calls a "false either/or" (416). Wright does not reject "Penal Substitutionary Atonement" in favor of "Christus Victor." Instead, through his study of the Pauline Epistles, Wright makes a case that to reduce what happens at the cross to this concept alone does not fully capture the radicality of what Jesus accomplished in what Paul is communicating. He asserts, "To suggest, as many have done, that we have to choose between "victory" and "substitution" is to miss the point . . . The New Testament *affirms both and indicates . . . the relationship between them*" (358, italics original).

Peter answered correctly, "With the people."

He nodded. "And the second regards something important to remember. While the world is not our final home, we are called to change and transform it. It matters so deeply. This is the reason why—when Christianity has failed to live up to this calling—critique has often arisen from within."

"Can you give me an example?"

"William Wilberforce leading the abolition of the slave trade."

"Another?"

"Alcuin of York. He confronted Charlemagne, the Frankish king of the early Middle Ages that became the Roman Emperor of Europe."

Peter remembered a little about how Charlemagne had hunted in the Vosges. "Wasn't he brutal?"

"He was, and he lived in a very brutal time," Michael continued. "Charlemagne loved the Virgilian, Greco-Roman virtues, especially the valorization of battle. But his ungodly behavior grated on Alcuin of York, the scholar and clergyman. So, he wrote to confront his powerful friend."

"Surely questioning Charlemagne was the same as signing your own death warrant?" Peter asked.

"Without a doubt. Yet he seems to have listened to Alcuin's arguments about how faith could not be forced, promptly repealing the heinous laws that had once made being pagan a capital crime. There's also the example of Saint Francis of Assisi—who bravely met with the Muslim leader Sultan Malik al-Kamil during the Crusades—and even Nathan the prophet confronting King David."

"Evidence of Christianity critiquing itself. Interesting," Peter said in quiet thought.

"Holding itself to its own standards: to see others as fully human. The Roman Empire had no problem with its lust for death and glory before Christianity transformed it. The followers of Jesus had changed the world. It was only based on this change—this recognition of dignity and worth of all—that Alcuin and others could found their challenge. Their critique was a resistance against allowing the world to fall back into its old patterns—the same cycles of violence."

"Calling it to be better."

"Right. Calling it to bear the image of Christ and not themselves," Father Michael said as he placed his Bible squarely on top of his folded shirt. He'd finished packing for now.

"To forge outposts of heaven, not hell," Peter concluded.

Father Michael's flight was in just a couple of days' time. Peter thought it was noble, right even, but was nevertheless overwhelmed by the magnitude of his loss. Seeing this, Father Michael encouraged him: "Peter, you need to promise me you will focus on your healing! You need to learn to walk with this truth, to see it woven—folded—into your own life first." Peter agreed in a lackluster fashion as Father Michael closed his suitcase, the latches clicking into place.

56

WW2

Gibraltar

THE IN BETWEEN

Wednesday, 8th November 1943. Western Europe.

After Henry had thoroughly assessed the information from Ophélie, he, Yves, and a man whose name would never know, radioed London quickly from a bell tower. The responsibility was now firmly across the Channel.

Henry's trip over the Pyrenees was far from easy, but if you'd asked him, the real heroes were the *Résistance* members who stayed on the ground. During his escape, wherever the chain of *La Résistance* had been broken, loyal men and women had risen to take their place, causing the path to shift organically.

Thankfully, Henry's Spanish was much better than his French. His new cover—that his injury was from the Spanish Civil War—seemed to work quite well. However, at one checkpoint, the remaining suspicion was only assuaged after a complete search of his person. They didn't find anything immediately incriminating but got ever-so-close to finding the compass that London had insisted they hide in a coat button. It had been a lifesaver in the catacombs. But the Reich had become savvy to that hiding place: discovering one now meant instant identification as a spy— and death. Yet, after the checkpoint guards had wrenched on each of his buttons, they gave up. His fellow *Résistant* saw Henry give the faintest of smirks as they turned away.

A few days later, they arrived in Gibraltar. *How apt*, Henry thought, given that his journey had begun with 161 Squadron at "Gibraltar Farm." It turned out that they were just in time for mandarin season. After everything, these orange jewels couldn't have tasted sweeter.

Twelve days later, a ship carrying this crop was waiting in the harbor with Henry's place paid for by a bribe. He would still need to be hidden among the cargo, but it was something. At least the plan came with inbuilt snacks, Henry had joked.

As their travel was coming to an end, the Spanish *Résistant* asked about the smirk. Relaxed in the relative heat, and with their conversation covered by the bustle of honest lives shuttling modest goods, Henry replied, "Well, they were just tightening it."

"Sorry?"

"London reversed the thread. They never think of twisting it the other way!"[335]

Accosted for a crumb by a curious little macaque monkey and throwing a chunk of bread to send him away, the two men laughed that something so simple could foil those who dared to establish an empire that tried to bend the world to their own image. Perhaps the war could end in their favor after all.

---

335. Lovell, *Of Spies & Stratagems*, 64–65.

57

Peter

Bitter Residue

THE IN BETWEEN

Monday, September 5th, 1994. Les Vosges.

Peter hated goodbyes; they reminded him of boarding school. He couldn't watch Father Michael's car drive away as he had with Nana's.

Where can I go? Peter found himself at the café.

Still disoriented, he was taken aback to find that there was something waiting for him when he arrived. After waiting and pressing for weeks, *now* someone knew something?

"I saw her," a crusty old man said somewhat nonchalantly, stirring his café.

"You did?"

"She didn't look back. She could be anywhere now," he said. "Plenty more fish in the sea . . ."

"What did you see?" Peter pressed him further.

"Weeks ago, getting on the train. A Monday, I think." He kept stirring.

Peter was wide-eyed. The man wasn't wrong; in hours she could have connected to anywhere in the country. Maybe she went back to Russia?

Men gathered to encourage him. Valiantly, they tried their best.

387

He bent forward, hands clutching his head, his face buried between his knees. He fought back tears. *Of course she left. Of course she did.* Just having it confirmed like that made it worse. Perhaps he should also go, maybe even to the monastery in Italy as Father Michael had suggested?

Just then, Pink Floyd came on the radio. This was the first time that he had heard "A Great Day for Freedom." He resonated with the optimism after fall of the Berlin Wall, and the frustration that followed. But the solution of turning to a loved one, seeing all but the "bitter residue" slipping away?[336] It was brutally honest but also agitated him. Was that the best we could do? Besides, Hélène wasn't even there to turn to . . . Then he remembered what Camus had said: "What the world expects of Christians, is that Christians should speak out loud and clear . . . and confront the blood-stained face that history has taken on today."[337]

It wasn't about a grand gesture or being a savior; it was about living in a different way.

That was it: there was nothing here anymore. Peter left without looking back; the men still sat around their drinks. He ran back to *presbytère*. Father Michael had already left.

He continued running to the edge of town; there were only two exits.

Just then, he saw it: a friend driving Father Michael to the airstrip. Peter ran at top speed, his legs pumping. Then, for fear they would not see him or stop, he launched himself right in front of it. The car did brake in time, but he still collided, thrown a foot or two in the air.

He hit the ground and rolled. *I'm okay*, he thought. He picked himself up and moved to the door. A sharp pain. *Oh, there was a limp.*

The driver was fearful. *Was he really okay?*

"I'm coming too," Peter said, pushing Father Michael's meticulously packed bags out of the way, jumping in the back, heart pounding.

"What a foolish thing! I suspected that it wouldn't be long before you joined me, but this rather exceeded my expectation," Father Michael teased with a straight face.

336. Gilmour, "Great Day for Freedom."
337. Camus, "Unbeliever and Christians," 71.

58

<hr>

Alexi

The Wreckage

THE IN BETWEEN

Sunday, July 17th, 2016. Southern France.

"That's beautiful," Edith said as she sat next to Alexi on a blue and white beach towel. The sun beat down, unfiltered. Alexi had drawn a remarkable sketch of Lili throwing a ball with her dad in the ocean. Never had there been a more pasty-white chest; Edwin was unquestionably a sun-deprived academic of the old order. But rarely had there also been anything more beautiful than their relationship. Strong, genuine, and full of fun, it intrigued Alexi and drew her in.

"I wanted to capture it for you," Alexi replied.

Edith beamed, thanking her. "Do you want to join them?"

"Maybe later."

Seeing more pictures, Edith asked, "What's this one about?" Alexi explained it was just her playing around with the idea of the directionality of love. Alexi hadn't planned to, but this quickly led to her baring her soul: "You said with Jesus, we're not alone in our pain. I've finally let myself feel love, I promise. But how do I make it go deeper? To the heart of it? It all hurts so badly." Her voice cracked, barely getting out the last few words: "Can Jesus really change things?"

"I know, I know," Edith said, rubbing her back as Alexi burrowed her head into her chest.

"I just want the hurt to stop," Alexi sobbed. She felt silly, breaking down in the midst of paradise, but still felt it vividly.

Edith held her until enough pain had edged out the way for Alexi to raise her head, her eyes red and puffy. Then, a welcome moment slid in. Alexi caught a glimpse of a funny sight: a group of young and middle-aged men attempting to get beyond the breaking waves to where they hoped to catch a wave that could bring them heroically to shore. But they were doing it all wrong. They were running up against the waves as if brute strength would get them through. One by one, the men were getting struck down only to come back up, spluttering. One had already given up, returning to shore, his wetsuit boot flopping half off.

After laughing a little with Alexi, Edith offered, "You know what I've found? The deepest cracks of my heart have allowed me to feel love most deeply."

"But how?" Alexi had hoped to start shading her sketch again, but her hand felt rigid, her pencil frozen above the page. Poised.

"Jesus exchanges sorrow for joy. Life for death," Edith said.

"What about trauma?" Alexi interrupted, wanting to get right to it. She moved the sketch pad entirely off her lap.

Edith hadn't expected this but valued directness. "It's helpful to think about what this means. Trauma disorientates so completely that it causes a rupture in our understanding of the world.[338] An example might help. I have a friend, Hannah, who used to be a fighter pilot. She told me one time about how much they really need to trust in their dials because—after going through whatever they've had to face—it can become incredibly disorientating. If you can't see the horizon, say it's dark or cloudy, then it's possible to think you're flying level but could actually be nose-diving or upside down!"

"Oh, wow," Alexi said.

"There's even this illusion where you can feel you're leaning in one direction but you're not. So, the overcorrection can cause you to spiral and crash."

"So, losing the horizon is like trauma?" Alexi asked, astutely.

---

338. Shelly Rambo's *Spirit and Trauma* is a foundational text for the nascent field of trauma theology. Rambo makes a lucid distinction: "Suffering is what, in time, can be integrated into one's understanding of the world." While "trauma is what is not integrated in time, it is the difference between a closed and open wound." Rambo, *Spirit and Trauma*, 7.

"That's it," Edith encouraged. "Whether one event or cumulative experience, trauma ruptures our ability to see the lay of the land: what is up or down, light or dark. Losing sight of the horizon is like shattering our worldview. It can be incredibly disorientating, lonely, and disconnecting. More acute than suffering, trauma is a rupture so complete that it can feel like death invades life. [339] Even if we lived on through the event, the brush with death profoundly impacts us."

"Death invading life . . ." Alexi echoed. "That connects with what you said about the fall," Alexi reasoned.

"Isn't that interesting? That would make the fall a primary, global-scale trauma where death rips into the tapestry of the world."

"But there's hope?" Alexi asked.

"The gospel speaks directly in terms of life and death: what else does God do but end the reign of death with his Life?"

"But what about practically, like with our minds?" Alexi pushed.

"Right. Our minds want reasons. That's why, after experiencing trauma, you can search over and over for a reason you never find because it was never there. This leaves us condemned to replaying the event in search of reason, only to exhume the pain again and again."

"So, is there an answer, really?" Alexi's question felt perilously taught like a tightrope ready to break.

"I wish it were as easy as saying 'add rationality where there is irrationality,'" Edith admitted.

"Then what are we left with?" Alexi said, despairing. "Life has to mean something, doesn't it?"

"You're right. To start, we're left with the rest of the internal fabric of our lives, torn but beautiful. I like to think of the inside world as a landscape full of stunning vistas and hidden foggy mountains, and, after experiencing trauma, landslides and bottomless crevasses. Sometimes, it can feel like there is little left, like the cities of Amsterdam and Hamburg after they were bombed." Edith paused for a second, "What did the people do next?"

"I guess, survey the wreckage? Like in the Blitz?"

---

339. Rambo also elucidates the connection between trauma, life, and death: "For those who survive trauma, the experience . . . can be likened to a death. But the reality is that death has no end; instead, it persists," Rambo, *Spirit and Trauma*, 7. Rambo calls this open wound, where death persists in the midst of one's physiological life, the middle, or after Derrida, the "intermezzo." Rambo, *Spirit and Trauma*, 28.

"Right. Presence and witness are so important. It takes time. To process, to lament. To find solid ground, even before you feel comfortable enough to reorientate. After and through this process, I believe there can be hope for healing; to learn to navigate and rebuild. To traverse the landscape again and call it home."

"But if reasons don't help, how can we rebuild?"

"Sometimes we try to find a scapegoat—manufacture a reason and dehumanize an 'enemy.' But then we build something uglier and less conducive to life. To heal in a healthy way—for ourselves and our communities—we need a different approach. Recent breakthroughs in traumatology speak to this really well."

"Like what?"

"Healing needs to be holistic: it needs to understand that the landscape of the mind is not only affected by trauma but also the body. Van der Kolk's *The Body Keeps the Score* has been so valuable in equipping us to understand how the body can store trauma. And so even if trauma is understood as a wound to the soul—"

"—or a rupture in understanding—"

"—then the body has to be taken seriously as we approach healing. Engaging body, soul, and, arguably, spirituality, is also incredibly valuable in this holistic approach."

"Which is such a huge pivot," Alexi recognized.

"Right, because the West after the Enlightenment practically ignored the body," Edith said, "reducing it to an obstacle, impediment, or tool. And yet, Jesus taking on flesh and becoming embodied has always been central to the biblical narrative."

"So, you're saying we've overlooked some of the genius of an incarnate God?"

"Without doubt!" Edith said, thrilled at seeing Alexi make these connections.

"Okay, the body's important. But what do we do with that knowledge?" Alexi didn't want the kid's version. She loved talking to Edith because she honored her heart *and* mind by giving it to her straight.

"The secular world's helpful to look at again. It's awakened to how embodied rhythms might help the body deal with stored trauma."[340]

"Like tapping and stuff?"

"Right," Edith replied.

---

340. Van der Kolk, *Body Keeps the Score*; Korn, *Rhythms of Recovery*.

"But isn't that New Age?"

"Some practices, perhaps. But we shouldn't be so quick to throw out the core insight. The idea of rhythm and body has a rich heritage that even anchors into scripture, which is laced with music, even songs of praise repeated in the heavens. Rhythm has a very interesting heritage in philosophy, involving central figures like Nietzsche, Heidegger, and Henri Bergson, as well as in theology through Luther, Hans Urs von Balthasar, Erich Przywara, and others."

"So, don't write it off too soon?"

"I think there's real merit to seeing rhythm as a theological category.[341] If we allow ourselves to do so, then we can start to engage with cutting-edge research about trauma."

"Like?"

"The work of the psychologist and philosopher Thomas Fuchs. He connects the ideas of rhythm and synchronization. Essentially, traumatic ruptures cause desynchronization."[342]

"Oh, that's interesting."

"I think so. If desynchronization looks like the experience of a fall out of time and connectivity with others in the world, then what might help?"

"Rhythms of resynchronization?" Alexi replied.

"And where might we find these embodied rhythms?"

"I'm going out on a limb here, but I'm guessing Jesus?" Alexi said playfully. Her eyes were much less red and puffy now. Instead, they almost sparkled.

Edith laughed, encouraged that Alexi could joke a little. "Right. We have a savior who values the whole person—body, soul and flesh—and calls us into a life that embraces it all. Think of it this way. This *is* good news: even if we've completely found ourselves completely disconnected from other people, we are never alone. If we let him, Jesus can still find us and resynchronize our hearts—not just to human communal rhythms but to Life itself."

Alexi affirming, "It's all connected."

"And vital," Edith said. "It makes perfect sense that the body is important in navigating and moving through trauma when you see the Son

341. Eikelboom, *Rhythm: A Theological Category.*

342. Fuchs, "Melancholia as a Desynchronization."

of God choosing this holistic, body-engaged mode for healing the world. A mode that connects body and soul, heaven and earth."

"But what does it actually look like?" Alexi asked, still raw.

"Sometimes I've found deep healing in a worship service, but more often than not, it's been about consistent rhythms of taking the resurrection pathway, of death to life, where we can revisit those deep wells that we've talked about."

"Like what?

"The practice of communion has really helped."[343]

"But isn't it just about remembering what happened to Jesus?"

"On the night before his death, Jesus explained that to remember him, his followers should take communion, but he didn't mean a passive recalling. Instead, it was an invitation to attune our lives to the contours and rhythm of the death and resurrection of Jesus in a practical, embodied way. Remembering our baptism: where we died with Christ to also rise with him, changed. It's an active participation here and now in these defining events."

"Active embodied remembering," Alexi said as she thought.

"It's a practice that holds space to witnessing suffering but also gently orients us to weave our story with his hope, his Life. The philosopher Paul Ricoeur talked about how vital storytelling is for the construction of meaning.[344] He even saw that the contours of the resurrection story of Jesus might help reconfigure the horizon of expectation so that past pain may be integrated into a coherent life story with hope for redemption."[345]

"But is it just a story?" Alexi's eyes widened as she searched for truth inside Edith's eyes.

343. Cockayne et al. offer both a firsthand and nuanced theoretical account of this. See, especially, Cockayne et al., *Dawn of Sunday*, 83–84, which includes this assertion: "The structure of embodied practice in liturgies offers a powerful antidote to survivors who have come to expect chaos and unpredictable violence in their exhausted and hypervigilant bodies."

344. Ricoeur, *Time and Narrative*; Ricœur, *Figuring the Sacred*, especially 203–62. On "rupture" and the merits of thinking of this interruption in the motion of our lives as akin to interruptions in poetry, see Ricœur, *Figuring the Sacred*, 45. This poetic approach to thinking rupture is also explored in Eikelboom, *Rhythm*.

345. "We are readers and writers of our own lives, subjects and authors of our own biographies, and our solace is in being able to weave, with freedom and imagination, our fragmented selves into the wider cloth of the biblical tapestry," Ricœur, *Figuring the Sacred*, 32.

"Narrative power does not necessarily equate to fiction. Instead, something powerful happens when symbolic and narrative aspects of human experience align with objective reality."[346]

"Explain that."

"A true story is like a horizon. We need it to find ourselves within the bigger picture: up, down, life, death, good, and evil. Hence why story is key to healing."

"Like the horizon for fighter pilots."

"Exactly."

"But," Alexi protested, "all this depends on Life conquering death. If Jesus, Life, won, then why is there still this tension?"

"Ah, the 'now and the not yet'?" Edith offered.

"Yes! That's what Edwin called it."

"That's a great question. And I promise I'll give you a short answer . . . Tell you what, we're on a French beach, right? During the war, the Allies landed on the beaches of Normandy."

"D-Day," Alexi said. "*I am* British!"

"Right! Well, was that the end of the war?"

"Well, no, but the beginning of the end."

"Exactly. There was almost a whole year before they pushed back the Third Reich to Berlin and ended the war. A year when the tide had turned, the direction of the war was entirely different, but it was not over yet. A year where countless more lives were lost."[347]

"Like in Amsterdam?"

"Exactly." She paused. "The liberation of Paris began in the August of 1944. In September, by the time Paris was rejoicing in the fresh scent of freedom, Anne Frank and her family in Amsterdam were being sent on the last train to Auschwitz." Edith's eyes started to tear up. She'd tried to control it. Alexi felt selfish; she suddenly realized that she'd been so obsessed about her family history that she hadn't heard anything about theirs. Edith's family had not been unlike Anne's. As the Allies advanced, Anne's father, Otto, had plotted it on a small map pinned to the wall to give them hope. If only the liberation of Amsterdam hadn't needed to wait until spring the following year.

---

346. See for example Peterson, *We Who Wrestle with God.*

347. The D-Day analogy is used in the *Alpha Course.* See Gumbel, "How Can I Resist Evil?"

59

WW2

The Liberation

THE IN BETWEEN

Summer 1944. Paris, France.

After sending Henry back to England via the Comete line, Violet and Matthias were called on by the Oberführer Schultz's operatives from time to time, but they mainly worked in Paris within the Combat network. They witnessed firsthand Camus's sweat as editor-in-chief of *Combat*, the main Paris-based publication now informing the *Résistance*. They also helped distribute it. How it reminded them of those early days with the Musée de l'Homme group. Only there were fewer of them now.

The camaraderie was genuine, though laced with fear, lest anyone become complacent and too familiar with life under occupation. Camus had urged Simone de Beauvoir and Jean-Paul Sartre, who had recently become more involved, to get out of Paris after a member of *Combat* had been arrested and had shared names, possibly including theirs.[348] Making things even worse, one lady in particular was still making life difficult for Violet. Her jealousy over Jérôme was still alive, even though both of their husbands had died in the same public way. She'd even tried to discredit Violet in front of Camus, but he was more insightful than to fall for that.

---

348. Beauvoir, *Prime of Life*, 590.

396

Members of the French *Résistance* all over the country *and world* were itching to take their country back. In London, on the evening of June 5th, 1944, Marie-Madeleine Fourcade, leader of the Alliance Intelligence Circuit, was getting ready to return to her life undercover in France. Having heard an odd hum while packing her bags, she was taken aback to discover something plucked right from her dreams, no longer quixotic fantasy, but valiant reality:

> I opened the window and the noise became deafening, but not a single searchlight swept the sky nor had the air raid warning gone. It was impossible to see the aircraft flying in massed formation above the sleeping capital. They flew over in a never-ending stream. Holding my breath and looking steadily in the direction of Nazi-Germany, I could see, beyond the barbed wire sealing the frontiers, beyond the prisons, the dawn that was bringing to our enslaved friends the first glimmer of their victory.[349]

D-Day had arrived. Operation Overlord unleashed, uncoiling like a tight, indignant spring. Five Normandy beaches—Utah, Omaha, Gold, Juno and Sword—would receive one hundred fifty thousand men landing by sea vessel or parachute, with American paratroopers and men on gliders dropped further inland. Some gave up their blood on these foreign beaches, an offering to the lives of others. Others got through. A mixed multitude of colors and countries side-by-side rallied to emancipate brothers crushed in a fascist vice.

The D-Day armada appearing at Normandy out of the morning mist was absolutely shocking given the false intelligence that had encouraged Hitler to defend his northern sea borders. Likewise, closer to the date, Operation Bodyguard had led them to believe that Calais could be a landing target. Heightened radio traffic reinforced these layers of deception, and they had even ingeniously crafted a Phantom Army Group—a fake army made up of inflatable and wooden equipment—designed to look like a US army unit, to fool reconnaissance aircraft flying over Kent.

While Hitler had just woken up, struggling to comprehend the immensity of what had happened, news spread like a shockwave through the countryside, resuscitating those on their last legs. In no time at all, Paris heard. But this was no surprise to many *Résistants*—this was what they had been planning for! The BBC had fired off two hundred "personal

349. Fourcade, *Noah's Ark*, 308–9.

messages" the night before, triggering action on a grand scale. The national sabotage plans—Vert, Violet, Blue, and Bibendum—were a-go, targeting railways, telecommunications, electricity, and troop transport.

The coordinated effect was phenomenal. Since 90 percent of German troop transport was still achieved using rail or horses, destroying bridges and halting train transport gave vital time to Allied troops fighting for their lives in Normandy without a flood of fresh Axis forces, especially the tanks that Hitler had kept in reserve. Frustrated at waiting, many of these tanks took their anger out on small villages.

In the next months, millions more troops would land through Normandy, and, in August, the Mediterranean coast, liberating from the south. The gamble of attacking first in Western Europe had worked.

Once unleashed, the *Résistance*, still living behind enemy lines in Paris and across the country, became bolder. De Gaulle's warning of a 'premature insurrection' on the eve of D-Day didn't stop many. But this was incredibly dangerous, with youngsters gunned down by patrols.

Armbands emblazoned with FFI, *Forces Françaises de l'Intérieur*, started appearing on hundreds of thousands of men and women, many of whom had watched the decline of their country but had yet to join the *Résistance*. Latecomers were called "*Résistants du Mois de Septembre*" or, in the case of those who had laid down weapons back in June 1940, the "mothballed"! Sartre was often rolled into this category; more of a "writer who resisted rather than a *Résistant* who wrote."[350]

On August 11th, the radio announced that the Americans were just outside Chartres.[351] The fight to take Paris back was about to kick off. De Beauvoir and Sartre immediately set to their bikes, leaving the small town of Neuilly-sous-Clermont, just north of Paris where they had been staying. They took back roads to avoid the Germans, many of whom were retreating, only to jump on a train and have it peppered by with machine-gun fire from an RAF plane just a few miles down the track.[352] But it was worth it; they couldn't miss history being made in their dear Paris.

The liberation of Paris began on the 19th of August and ended on the 25th, though the *Résistance* had started an attempt earlier on the 15th. The Allies wished to avoid a long, drawn-out siege, but de Gaulle would have none of it. Despite his earlier warning, he was unwilling to leave these brave men and women alone as had happened in Warsaw.

---

350. Aronson, *Camus and Sartre*, 31.
351. Beauvoir, *Prime of Life*, 590.
352. Beauvoir, *Prime of Life*, 591.

With his dogged decisiveness, he even threatened to detach and send in the French 2nd Armored Division if Eisenhower kept delaying.

Simone and Sartre arrived back in Paris to find Albert Camus and friends on the Café de Flore terrace, planning.[353] Camus gave them the opportunity that they had been thirsting for: to live history and write about the liberation.[354]

FFI posters were plastered around Paris, calling for mobilization. De Gaulle was, after all, insistent that it had to be the French liberating the French! Fighting in the streets escalated. As de Beauvoir worked on her article, she was narrowly missed by a bullet.

Matthias found himself busy, feeding intelligence to the *Résistance* about the movements of the occupying forces—which bunkers, where, and, possibly more importantly, who. Nearby, Violet helped with anything she could, including shuttling food and supplies to civilians.

At one point, de Beauvoir and Sartre turned up at the *Combat* office, at 100 Rue Réaumur, to be met by locked doors guarded with Tommy guns. Camus and colleagues had become accustomed to working with guns at the ready, anticipating that "at any moment German soldiers could come and it would have been a bad mess."[355] However, de Beauvoir now observed amid this hive of activity a "tremendous gaiety" from top to bottom.[356]

During one meeting, Sartre was given the task of keeping the iconic Comédie-Française theater safe during the confusion of a half-liberated Paris. News came in sporadic, sometimes contradictory bursts, often via jubilant heralds atop bicycles. Sartre made his way across the eerie city—in some ways never more alive—electrified, while cobbles bore the red silhouettes of bodies in their last moments of being. But within moments of arriving, Sartre fell asleep in an orchestral seat.

That's when Camus found his friend, joking, "You've placed your seat in the direction of history!"[357] Of course, at the time, Camus had no idea how time would twist these lighthearted words.

The first open issue of *Combat* shared the news, even if slightly premature: "Today, August 21, as this newspaper hits the streets, the liberation of Paris is nearing an end. After fifty months of occupation, of

353. Beauvoir, *Prime of Life*, 591.
354. Beauvoir, *Prime of Life*, 595.
355. Aronson, *Camus and Sartre*, 25.
356. Beauvoir, *Prime of Life*, 595.
357. Aronson, *Camus and Sartre*, 145.

struggle and sacrifice, Paris is rediscovering the feeling of freedom, even as bursts of gunfire erupt at street corners around the city."[358] As Camus read it on the radio, Violet and Matthias and the whole team listened, full of pride. The team cheered, hugged, and kissed. *Perhaps all the sacrifice had been worth it? It might actually amount to something?*

The Parisian Liberation Committee called on all citizens to "cut down trees, dig anti-tank ditches, barricade the roads. A people victorious shall greet the Allies." After significant delays, on August 24th, General Leclerc of the Free French disobeyed his superior, American Major General Gerow, and sent a vanguard from his 2nd Armored Division into Paris.

The very next day, the German military governor of Paris, General von Choltitz, surrendered. He signed over his garrison to Leclerc at the Gare Montparnasse, the site of the 1895 locomotive derailment that had captured Peter's imagination. Here it was: another grand enterprise of man undercut and humiliated despite its hubris.

On August 25th, 1944, the very same day that von Choltitz surrendered, de Gaulle moved back into the War Ministry on the Rue Saint-Dominique as if it were his eternal right. Allied command—who had always been suspicious of de Gaulle—had wanted to bring different leadership to France, but it was abundantly clear that the only voice the French wanted to follow was de Gaulle's. That day, he broadcast for the first time within the capital, concluding, "Paris! Paris outraged! Paris broken! Paris martyred! But Paris liberated!"[359]

358. Camus, *Camus at Combat*, 11.
359. Gaulle, *Discours et Messages*, 476.

60

Alexi

Typhoons & Sap

THE IN BETWEEN

Sunday, July 17th, 2016. Southern France.

Lili didn't want a break from the water, but Edwin needed a quick rest. He toweled off and sat with Alexi and Edith, a cool carbonated drink in hand. His hair stuck up—funny in places—but they didn't say anything.

Alexi asked Edith, "So you're saying that because of Jesus' death and resurrection, the direction of things *has* changed, but it's not yet over, like the difference between D-Day and the end of the war?"

"Right! We are in the age of the church, and Jesus is coming back," Edith replied.

"What do we do in the waiting?" Alexi asked, eager to hear her answer.

"We won't settle for a world enslaved by sin and death. We'll want to join with heaven in seeing pockets of heaven break out—the unity of heaven and earth rather than the unraveling," Edith offered.

Just then, a small honeybee flew past. Alexi first thought it was a wasp but melted when she saw its round fuzzy body. "What are you doing here, little one?" she asked before it flew away.

"You know," Edwin said, "we've talked a lot about Camus. In *The Rebel* he said something that has continued to resonate with me over the years."

"What's that?" Alexi asked, curious.

"That 'there are two sorts of efficacity: that of typhoons and that of sap.'[360] What if the resurrection was the typhoon and participation with Jesus allows for the flow of sap? Love and relationship!"

"I think I get you: access to a different type of power and life even as we wait for the end of the war," Alexi said.

"Right," Edwin confirmed.

Edith added, "The 'now and not yet' after D-Day looks, for us, like resynchronizing to the rhythm of heaven. Drilling wells of wonder so that the 'efficacity' of God's life can transform us from the inside out. Why settle for an unraveling world when you can help usher in its transformation?"

Edwin offered, "Like the *Résistance* networks at work after D-Day—but instead of blowing up bridges, perhaps it looks like building them?"

360. Camus, *Rebel*, 292.

61

Peter

Bread

THE IN BETWEEN

Thursday, July 6th, 1995. Yugoslavia.

> "All of our humanity is dependent upon recognizing the humanity in others." ~ Archbishop Desmond Tutu

> "God became man that dehumanized men might become true men. We become true men in the community of the incarnate, the suffering and loving, the human God." ~ Jürgen Moltmann, *The Crucified God.*

Working with the Red Cross was preeminently meaningful but utterly exhausting. The days were long, but the months felt short. Peter regretted not explaining to Edwin and Edith why he'd written on the postcard that they would be "proud" of him. At first, he thought he should wait until he'd truly earned it, but now so much time had passed that reaching out felt awkward. Besides, there was nothing to boast about. This was war; everyone was doing their all. He was embarrassed that he'd written it.

Each morning, while Father Michael offered spiritual care, Peter taught mathematics to groups of displaced youth, helping them find normal rhythms and think of the future. In the afternoon, they worked together on the first-aid stations or delivering supplies. The need was overwhelming. Father Michael had to force Peter to take breaks. "You have to rest and commune with heaven if you have any chance of ministering heavenly peace and hope," Father Michael encouraged him.

Peter's feet were hot and sore. Funny, they were working for the Red Cross, and yet he couldn't find a Band-Aid when he needed one. His clothes desperately needed a wash. His jeans felt oddly stiff.

Often, at the end of the day, they found themselves silent, thinking of a different place and another time. Reading Camus and Sartre had opened up a whole new world of philosophy and theology that Peter had been completely unaware of. Sometimes, it felt good to dip into a book and come out the other side in the cafés of 1930s France, or a classroom in Germany, watching Heidegger, the "Magician of Messkirch," in his element.

This connected with what Edwin and Edith had shared in Amsterdam. Even if he wasn't writing, it was a comfort to Peter to feel connected in some way. He remembered that meal together fondly. Peter didn't want to think what would have become of him if he hadn't visited them at that time. While he'd been resistant, both the love they showed and the message they had shared meant something to him. Even more so now. Marcel's critique of Sartre's vision of human reality rang often in Peter's ears. Marcel had thought that Sartre's vision was tragically atrophied because Sartre thought it impossible for one to "be open to the other to welcome him in the deepest sense of the word, and to become at the same time more accessible to oneself."[361]

Peter also fondly remembered how Bernard had confided in him about the impact of Marcel's contemporary—the Jewish Lithuanian philosopher, Emmanuel Levinas—upon his life and thought. Levinas's concept of radical hospitality intrigued Peter, even more so in the midst of so much pain and hatred.[362]

One evening among the many, Father Michael explained to Peter that, in the seventies, Levinas was identified as being part of a movement among French intellectuals first called, albeit pejoratively by the atheist philosopher Dominique Janicaud, "the theological turn of phenomenology."[363] With rigor, these philosophers, each in their own

361. Marcel, *Mystery*, 102.

362. Note that Jean Luc Marion, for example, has developed some of Levinas's insights in a Christian direction during his critique of traditional metaphysics. Marion argues that God is absolutely other and pure gift. See Marion, *Idol and Distance*.

363. Janicaud and Coutine, *Theological Turn*.

way, mapped the felt contours of the relationship between humanity and God in a world all too aware of war.

Peter was also surprised to learn that Levinas's *The Theory of Intuition in Husserl's Phenomenology* was the first book on phenomenology that Sartre ever read, having run to the nearest bookstore on the Boulevard Saint-Michel immediately after those apricot cocktails. Rather than wait for a paperknife to cut open the book leaves, a critical step in those days, de Beauvoir remembered that Sartre had torn it open with ravenous anticipation, devouring it as they walked.[364]

Levinas's religiously suffused philosophy became more radical over time. The trauma of living through the savage ripping apart of the continent—the sheer disregard for human life—informed a philosophy indignant about what mattered most. It did not start with the self-obsessed individual of Descartes, Kant, or even Heidegger, but instead with ethics. The posture of the human heart and life towards the "other," another who isn't me yet whose very presence demands something of me: my care, my life. An unshakeable value confirmed by the almost spectral presence of the Judeo-Christian God in and behind the human person.

It was just a couple of days later that Peter would feel this demand upon his heart. This came in the form of a man Peter later found out was called Davud. He first met this man when busy at an aid station, irrigating wounds. Simple but necessary care. A woman approached Peter—toddler perched on her hip—asking for his help. After finding someone to man his station, Peter approached the man she'd led him to. He was crumpled where old concrete walls came together. Peter's presence spooked him. The man reacted, making a guttural noise, he threw himself into motion. He fled, picking up speed. His humanity seemed to drip off from the ragged ends of his war-torn clothes.

The erasure of humanity might be entirely active or glaringly passive. Active, like the harrowing sadism Jean Améry encountered in Auschwitz, intent "to nullify the world."[365] He wrote that the torturer could "turn the other—along with his head, in which are perhaps stored Kant and Hegel, and all nine symphonies . . . into a shrill squealing piglet at slaughter."[366] Or passive, like the Jewish philosopher Hannah Arendt identified when she observed Adolf Eichmann during his trial in Jerusalem. Arendt settled on the term "the banality of evil" to describe how

364. Beauvoir, *Prime of Life*, 135–36.

365. Améry, *Mind's Limits*, 35

366. Améry, *Mind's Limits*, 35

this active nullification of the humanity of others was made possible by many, many others like Eichmann, who were not moved by compassion to act beyond their bureaucratic bounds.[367] In doing so, one might ask whether they abdicated their own humanity to become cogs in a machine of death.

No aspect of thought felt more pressing to Peter than how to resist dehumanization: this rancid tendency that plagued the world. Resonating with Marcel, he found in Levinas the conviction that we become human when we see the other as human. In *Ethics and Infinity*, Levinas explains that when I rise to ethical responsibility, recognizing the other's humanity by saying "here I am," I also constitute or instantiate myself as truly human: an ethical human actor.[368] Father Michael had paraphrased Levinas's radical ethic as an arresting hospitality—not unlike that described by Jesus' Sermon on the Mount—calling one to give "the bread from my own mouth."[369] Peter wrestled with what this meant in practice, though he needn't have worried.

The man looked hungry. Scorned by others, he cowered as Peter, again, gently approached. He looked every part the pariah, an outcast, a leper. Peter gave what little money he had with him to a boy who, like a number of others, had gathered to watch. This man had lost many whom he loved, onlookers explained; he screamed all night and wandered as a ghost all day. The man's face could tell his story a thousand times better than words. He couldn't have been more than forty, but his skin looked aged, loose, and almost scaled: a pale yellow falling into gray—dirt tracing each wrinkle. Everyone was struggling and doing their best to keep some semblance of normality and dignity to avoid falling into the abyss, but to Peter, this man seemed like a vision from the other side.

Just minutes later, as Peter was questioning his decision not to fetch something himself, the boy returned. It was bread, and just enough. Peter received it and quickly gave it over to the man. His dirty, long fingernails clasped the bread. As his dry, sticky saliva met the first taste, Peter offered his water bottle also. "Thanks" could wait. But what confused Peter was how the shame, the pain, and the nothingness that had captured his face kept hold. The mam seemed just as frozen despite this admittedly small act of love and care.

---

367. Arendt, *Eichmann in Jerusalem*.

368. Levinas, *Ethics and Infinity*, 11, 109.

369. The original quote is from Levinas, *Otherwise Than Being*, 79.

The minutes seemed long, the onlookers restless as the sun beat down. Peter didn't know what to do. Maybe pray for him and try to sort out better accommodation? He needn't have worried: the man did something unexpected, instinctual, and brave. He reached out to Peter as if receiving alone was not enough. To complete his humanity, he needed to invite Peter in: he needed to share, to give. Invited, first by his eyes alone, and then by the raising of the man's right knuckle towards him, bread in fist, Peter was beckoned closer.

A yes rose up in Peter. A bare, gut-wrenching yes. He had no need for the bread, having eaten in the barrack kitchens that morning, and this man probably knew that. He wasn't meeting a need in Peter for food—but for connection.

Dirt clung to the fluffy holes in the bread, but Peter didn't flinch. The man put it in his cupped hand. At that moment, Peter had one choice. He acted quickly before his better reason could kick in and placed it in his mouth. In doing so, the man somehow connected Peter to something more real than he had ever conjured from within himself. A circuit was completed. A powerful, surging ebb, as if the Creator himself had eagerly awaited this consummation of design.

Though another level from Marje's harmless cooking, Peter didn't even squirm. In the moment, it didn't matter because nothing mattered more. The man began to cry, the powder of the dirt first mixing into a stubborn mud. But then more came, carving a trail down his face. His frozen expression, a nothingness unimpressed by both horror and heaven, slowly melted into a softness.

The tears kept coming. Peter received more bread. Together they ate. The crowd watched, transfixed. Then his eyes creased as he looked at Peter deeply: how funny they were, even laughing as a honeybee buzzed around his face. Here was a pocket of heaven. No one rushed to leave. Love turned out towards each other, strangers but brothers.

> 'You can give without loving; but you cannot love without giving,' ~ Amy Carmichael

62

WW2

Humiliation

THE IN BETWEEN

Saturday, August 26th, 1944. Paris, France.

After rekindling the eternal flame at the Arc de Triomphe, on the 26th of August, de Gaulle marched down the Champs-Élysées ahead of Leclerc's French 2nd Armored Division before jubilant crowds.

Simone de Beauvoir said of the liberation, "Seldom indeed does one achieve a long-awaited pleasure and find it all one could have hoped for."[370] "All that day, Sartre and I walked the flag-draped streets of Paris. I saw women in their best clothes clinging around soldiers' necks; the tricolor shone resplendent from the summit of the Eiffel Tower. What a tumult of emotions surged through my heart!"[371]

The underbelly of liberation was, however, vengeance. It was now that this viper struck Violet and that fateful picture taken. She had lost track of her friends among the jubilant chaos but, like many others, had been relaxed, joyfully trading her gun with American soldiers who wanted them as souvenirs. Out of nowhere, a group of vigilantes, high on the fumes of liberation but not having had their fill of violence, publicly confronted her. Acting upon a rumor, this gang of both men and

370. Beauvoir, *Prime of Life*, 597.
371. Beauvoir, *Prime of Life*, 597.

women accused her of *collaboration horizontale* as if she'd had romantic and physical relations with the enemy, betraying her nation. There was no trial or jury. One of the GIs tried to intervene, but he was pushed away, rebuked firmly, and told that this had nothing to do with them; "the French" had to deal with this alone.

They forced Violet to come with them. Short of starting a gunfight, she had no other choice. Violet became, like far too many other women, a scapegoat upon which to excise the humiliation of occupation.

Betrayal—especially such a public humiliation as this—wounds deeply. She did what she could to hold her head high, but the worst of it was the lie of it all. They cut her hair. She saw it float down in front of her. Then, they paraded her through the streets. Men and women leered at her as if they were morally superior. If only her scars could have testified to her story.

Violet couldn't defend herself: her operations remained confidential. Nor could she reveal the role of the Oberführer, for the war raged on elsewhere. She looked desperately in the crowd for Matthias. He was miles away, celebrating, jovial. He wouldn't forgive himself when he found out, spiraling downwards, curving in upon himself.

When they finally left Violet alone, she recovered her things. She presumed that the necklace from Henry would be gone forever. But it was still there. A reminder to herself that she hadn't lived a lie. She *was* a hero.

It wasn't until Violet was alone that she cried deeply and hard. The only way that she was able to keep her head about her was that—like the original bearer of her communion name taken from St. Felicity—she knew who she really was, and how to "suffer with." A world that can crucify the Son of God, calling him dangerous, blasphemous, and all manner of things, was more than capable of betraying others.

But this is not the end of the story. While the Son of God descends, he also raises to new life the misunderstood, the betrayed, and the underappreciated. The human. Inviting all into the fullness of their identity as sons and daughters of God; into peace, into flourishing, into home. Bearers of this privilege are not guaranteed an easy life, money, or power. Instead, they are tasked with establishing an upside-down kingdom that makes those values pale in significance: where the first is last and the last, first.

63

Alexi

Resynchronization

THE IN BETWEEN

Sunday, July 17th, 2016. Southern France.

Having worked up an appetite, Edwin had gone to scope out the spread of sea-adjacent snacks raised on a plastic table to keep them out of the sand. Alexi took the opportunity to ask Edith a burning question: "I get the vision: to flourish even if we find ourselves embedded in an outwardly hostile, dehumanizing land. But to share that hope I need to know it first, right? So how do I get there? How do I break through?"

"It's all connected. What Jesus does," Edith said, "is open up a way—so that those feeling stuck—held fast by death—might enter into a new mode of life with the one who is Life."

"Like a pathway through the waves?" Alexi said, seeing the wall of water still standing in the way of the aspiring group of surfers. The number of original members rapidly dwindled, but there was a steady stream of others to replace them.

"Sort of, but in a very specific way. Do you know what technique they could use so that it isn't so—"

"—defeating?"

"I was going for painful, but that works too," Edith chuckled.

"Duck diving?" Alexi asked, drawn forth from some distant place in her mind.

"Exactly. Going under the water, ducking down under the wave, and then up on the other side."

"They dive with the board, right?" Alexi asked.

Edith gestured, "Look." They watched as a group of three in the distance disappeared under a large wave. Edith tried to explain the technique, which Alexi found pretty amusing.

"They come out the other side, positioned differently. What does that remind you of? Going down under the water and back out again?"

"Baptism? But I've never really understood it."

"Duck diving is a pretty good metaphor for it on a number of levels. The waves are like the onslaught of everything keeping us under siege. The hurt and memories of the past that just won't stop coming. The weight and consequences of sin—hurting ourselves and others as we've tried to keep our heads above water. And even the law: an impenetrable wall of water showing that we cannot match up to the standard of love: doing what is true, good, and just. All of us have fallen short, and more often than not, we're kicking ourselves for it."

"So, Jesus allows us to duck dive to the other side?" Alexi asked as she traced this swooping path on a fresh page with her pencil.

"In a funny way, yes. Diving down is like a death to this old way of life. We can't sidestep this death. But we can go through—under—it." Edith continued, "See that guy?" as another young man returned defeated to shore, beat up, with a rapidly growing bruise to the face where the surfboard had hit him. "We can keep trying to match up to the law, prove we're good enough, and defeat anyone and anything that stands in our way."

"Clothed in pain and vengeance," Alexi offered.

"Right. In service to saving our egos or own gods, we become stuck—the living dead."

"Or?" Alexi asked.

"We can let that vision die to make way for another. We can allow the wave, the law, to teach us. The law reveals our need for grace. It invites us to live in a different way. It encourages us to join our lives to the one who opens a path through death, to resurrect with him."

"So, we don't stay dead?"

"Right. He invites us into a new space where we are positioned differently: in him, the one who is being, who is love. This is a mode of life defined by grace. Grace for others. Grace for ourselves. Grace for healing. You know what's also interesting? Once on the other side, the waves—like the just and loving law of God—become the source of the surfer's joy." That was well timed, as a surfer from a different group had just caught a spectacular wave. He fist-pumped the air with delight as his friends cheered. Edith continued, "If we let God be God, we're released to be sons and daughters. Instead of anxiously wearing masks to keep up the show, we can be fully supported—grounded in Christ—to feel, live, *and heal.*"

"Grace instead of the crushing pain of falling short," Alexi tested to see how that sat in her heart. "But surely this doesn't make everything magically okay?"

"You're right. This repositions us for resilience and healing, but it doesn't suddenly erase the past."

"Then, we need something more?"

"No, not more. We need to rest and revisit this, to resynchronize our lives to this resurrection rhythm so that our hearts genuinely live rooted in this place. Some people call this spiritual breathing. I think what was helpful for me to understand was that after giving my whole life to Jesus in baptism, in one sense, yes, everything immediately changed. But, in another, there was still more to come. Jesus had opened this pathway; he'd broken the siege and invited me to a new mode of life, but I had to live this out with him to see the change echo through me."

"Which is where those rhythms come in?" Alexi said, appreciating the rhythmic lap of the waves breaking on the beach.

"Exactly," Edith said. "It's about a consistent posture of life: a practice of humility that leads to joy. The rhythm of coming to the cross. Embracing spiritual practices like communion where we can bring our sin, pain, and shame, and leave them there to resurrect anew, re-attuning our hearts to the rhythm of heaven and the concerns of its King."

"So, revisiting and retracing the path of resurrection?" Alexi said, sketching the basic shapes of the man victorious, surfing the wave.

"Right. Think of it this way: who, in a dry, desert land, would learn the pathway to a deep well and only visit it once?"

"You'd visit all the time."

"Right, likely every day. These spiritual practices are like touchpoints that should change us so that we're sent out more alive: resynchronized and recalibrated to the one who is life: 'For in him we live and move and have our being.'[372] Edwin loves how Christos Yannaras explained it as being 'attuned existentially' to the 'mode of existence revealed in Christ.'"[373]

"Now I get it: our story is marked by his story, resynchronized so that we live differently."

"So that we can live," Edith concluded. "Connecting back to trauma, the resurrection rhythm might also reweave us back into our time and space after experiencing trauma in a way that helps us put our feet back under ourselves as men and women with a hope and a future.

"You're saying Jesus can bring hope now?"

"His presence has changed the landscape of my heart. I imagine inviting Jesus to come, lantern in hand, to explore the scary, torn parts of the landscape of my heart. I've found him faithful to bring his peaceful presence into dark ruptured valleys, reattuning it as a place where heaven can reign, where the songs of heaven ring out: 'Holy holy holy, is the Lord God almighty . . .'[374] Fear disappears when I spend time there, as if having a picnic. Then it doesn't seem as scary anymore, and the related memories can be woven back into my story; the deepest ruptures and valleys backfilled with overflowing love."

"I like that picture."

"Some of my academic work has engaged the theologian Lexi Eikelboom," Edith shared. "I really like her concept of eschatological weaving."[375]

"What's that?" Alexi asked, her interest piqued.

"There's much more to it, but it speaks to how the future hope of the fullness (and rhythms) of heaven might enter earth and transform our lives right now: 'The eschatological weaving of the end into time changes the form by which time moves forward.'[376] I wonder if this rhythmic weaving can't be understood as the rhythms of heaven helping suture traumatic ruptures—or wounds—in time and understanding."[377]

---

372. Acts 17:28.

373. Yannaras, *On the Absence*, 92.

374. Rev 4:8.

375. Eikelboom, "Rhythmic Eschatology," 209.

376. Eikelboom, "Rhythmic Eschatology," 209.

377. Note that this application is original to the present author and not asserted at the current time by Eikelboom.

64

Peter

The Medics

THE IN BETWEEN

Saturday, July 8th, 1995. Yugoslavia.

When the other volunteers came to ask him for help, Peter had already long surrendered his life. He was not perfect—nor did he need to be—but was making these pockets of heaven wherever he could, defiant against the reign of hell on earth.

Sometimes, he failed at it spectacularly; other times, it felt like this was exactly what he was made for. In those moments, it felt like someone else, Love, was talking with and through him, offering much more compassion than he could muster alone. He had nothing but also everything at the same time. He now delighted in the little things. Things before he'd been too turned inwards to notice. Like the little girl with big brown eyes and a messy blue teddy. Her smile—despite it all—lit up his inner world like a flare. Everything had once seemed so meaningless to him. But now everything was so saturated with value. He wasn't going to stand by and let that be extinguished.

The group of volunteers and medics had come to ask Peter to come with them with a couple of practical things to the UN safe area of Srebrenica. Bosnian Muslims had been flocking to the area, and the Red Cross needed more support there. Peter's math brain came into its own when it came to organization and flow.

"I'll be back in a couple of days," Peter told Father Michael.

"It will go quickly," he replied, assuring Peter as he leapt into the back of the mud-dusted medic van.

65

***

Alexi

The Message

THE IN BETWEEN

Sunday, July 17th, 2016. Southern France.

Having realized that Edwin was serious about needing a quick rest, Lili reluctantly entered dry land. She nestled close to Alexi on the beach towel, dripping. Alexi opened her bag to put away her sketchbooks to avoid them getting wet. At that moment, Lili saw a necklace in her bag.

"It's just a junky old thing," Alexi said, pulling it out. "I just can't bring myself to get rid of it."

"It's beautiful!" Lili said, opening it up. It had a picture of a lady inside. "She's really pretty."

Alexi smiled. "I guess she is." Lili looked at it much more closely than Alexi ever had, having considered it as tainted by association with her mother.

Suddenly the hinge pin came out; the only thing that had held it all together. Alexi said it was old, and it was waiting to happen, but Lili left, embarrassed and apologetic.

"It's okay," Edith said, who had been visiting with a church friend close by. She followed Lili, reassuring Alexi as she left, "I'll chat to her."

The truth was that Alexi may never know that the necklace had once belonged to Mrs. Disraeli, wife to the prime minister of England and confidant of Queen Victoria. Though, she apparently had hated it, disregarding it as a gaudy, politically motivated gift. Nor might Alexi ever know that Henry had brought it over to France in the RAF plane, it being with him as he jumped out . . . or it laying around Violet's neck. But what she was about to find out was something no one else had seen in over half a century. As she fiddled to get the pin back in place, she saw something reflect in the sharp summer rays. There was paper inside the pin. Just a small piece, wound up.

It was simple but bold: "*Je t'aime.*" She was struck. *Why now?* Alexi knew it wasn't meant for her, and yet it felt as if God wanted her to see it. She had somehow carted this necklace around this whole time, feeling unloved, thinking it was trash when it had this treasure inside.

Alexi smiled deeply as she looked back out upon the reliable crash of the waves. Lili had found Edwin. He had been biding his time: knowing that being pulled back into the water was inevitable. But he didn't mind, not really; he counted it a privilege.

Edwin and Lili re-entered the swimming area where many other families were playing, protected from the waves because of the stone walls jutting out into the sea. Beyond them, clusters of surfers bobbed up and down waiting for a wave to catch—those who had realized their limits and, instead of standing up to the waves, had "duck dived" under them to the other side.

However, Alexi still saw a steady stream of little boys and girls, men and women, closer to shore, puffing out their chests as if they could take on the waves themselves. As she watched, she felt convicted that she'd done the very same thing. Trying to steamroll her way through—to match up to the waves like expectations or some legal perfection, trying to say she wasn't that bad really and prove why she should be loved. Each time, getting pushed back, more and more exhausted, bruised, and battered. The last thing she used to think she needed was a God to add to this.

But now it dawned on Alexi that she had it wrong. What if she already was loved? And what if God wanted to free her from living under constant condemnation? "For God did not send his Son into the world to condemn the world, but to save the world through him."[378]

Alexi recalled that the death or "going under" of baptism was like duck diving: it broke the siege—the pattern of being pummeled by the waves—condemned by them. It would mean coming out the other side

378. John 3:17.

free. Here, her heart could be released from the fickle, parasitic demands of humans. While the good laws of God would remain the same, like the constant sets of waves coming in, she was now on the other side of them, ready to catch a wave. The same wave that before would have crashed down upon her now became something more fun, a life-giving wave she could catch, excited and energized: almost walking on water!

A smile came over her as she watched the surfers, clinging tight to the small note. In this new life, sure, she could fall off the wave, but she would still be positioned and empowered differently. Love would live inside of her. And love? Love, if you let it, will perfectly fulfill the law. She got it: the Christian life wasn't about going against her nature but about an internal change through the Holy Spirit that just starts to shine through—a transformation that you can't force but that you live.

Alexi ran, tripping over the wave-like ridges of sand, to find Edith. "You don't need to do this for us," Edith said sincerely after Alexi told her that she wanted to be baptized.

"I've never wanted anything more," Alexi said, buzzing.

66

Peter

The Siege

THE IN BETWEEN

Saturday, July 8th, 1995. Yugoslavia.

What Peter and Father Michael hadn't fully realized was that while the United Nations Security Council Resolution 819 had declared Srebrenica and Žepa "safe areas," they were anything but. They were never demilitarized; in fact, the Serbian forces still had a stranglehold on the area.

Peter and the ICRC medics went there just as the siege of Srebrenica was about to end. It was chaotic, but there was no way to predict things that were going to escalate right then. They made a choice. They didn't want to abandon the people by turning back.

67

Alexi

No Turning Back

THE IN BETWEEN

Sunday, July 17th, 2016. Southern France.

> "He sank down absolutely. But then rose up again from the abyss, lighter" [able to] "tread as in a dance…[whereas] finitude's apprentices lose wit and courage." ~ Søren Kierkegaard, *The Concept of Anxiety*, 195.

"Your presence is my home," Alexi whispered to God, as Edwin and another dad readied her in the water. They baptized her in the name of "the Father, the Son, and the Holy Spirit."

Edith watched, her arms and a towel wrapped around Lili. They weren't alone. The church had gathered on the beach to support Alexi, many having played a role in welcoming to the community and making space for her to flourish.

The water closed in upon her. The world as she knew it was swallowed up. She closed her eyes. Darkness.

Then? Her heart took a beat. She felt it clearly in her body. Reset.

Light. Her body rose out of the water. She took a sharp breath.

It felt less like a rough defibrillator shock than a sudden relaxing into—like when a safe lock is finally orientated to its home setting and the door flies open. *Home.* Alexi knew it.

She threw her fists in the air with a joyous cry, her arms raised in victory. She didn't care who saw.

A chorus joined in the celebration, so diverse and raw that it reflected heaven. She had no plan other than be. Her body and soul united; heaven and earth. A holy moment.

The beach spontaneously rang with an oddly familiar song: "I have decided to follow Jesus. No turning back. No turning back."

§

While Alexi had breathed these new breaths, she still did not know how or why Peter had breathed his last. Perhaps she never would.

68

Peter

Your Brother's Blood

THE IN BETWEEN

Friday, July 14th, 1995. Yugoslavia.

It would be a couple of days before even Father Michael knew he was missing. As the "safe area" fell, the town of Tuzla, thirty miles northwest of Srebrenica, started receiving displaced people. But humanitarian and aid workers soon came to the shocking realization that the men and boys were absent.[379]

In his inner world, Peter didn't turn in upon himself. To the last, he poured out his life. It was simply the next step in the life of surrender that he had chosen in his baptism.

He died among strangers who he knew were brothers.

How? He was caught up in the chaos and the evil, predictably indiscriminate after its release. Genocide.

At Srebrenica, over eight thousand Bosniak Muslim men and boys were killed by units of the Bosnian Serb Army.

Among those dead were nine ICRC workers.[380]

Many victims are still being identified, though the number decreases every year.

379. See, for example, United States Holocaust Memorial Museum, "Srebrenica."
380. International Committee of the Red Cross, "Remembering."

§

The Lord said, "What have you done? Listen! Your brother's blood cries out to me from the ground ~ Genesis 4:10.

§

Didn't we say "never again"? Must Dionysus continue to laugh as blood is split, or Wotan ride upon the clouds with glee? Must the question posed by Wagner's ring cycle forever be unsettled, boring ever deeper: which is more powerful—the love of power or the power of love?

> "Believing in the resurrection does not just mean assenting to a dogma and noting a historical fact. It means participating in this creative act of God's . . . Resurrection is not a consoling opium, soothing us with the promise of a better world in the hereafter. It is the energy for a rebirth of this life. The hope doesn't point to another world. It is focused on the redemption of this one." ~ Jürgen Moltmann, *Jesus Christ for Today's World*, 81.

Epilogue

Over the last two thousand years, there have been millions from different times, tribes, nations, and tongues, who—like the fictional character of Peter—have seen their lives change course because of encountering and listening to the call of Jesus. Many of them counting the cost. Each, in their own profound and imperfect way, have brought heaven to earth as ones who have refused to frame the world in such a way so as to say that evil and suffering simply are to be expected, or worse, embraced à la Nietzsche. From the Christian martyrs at the Colosseum to contemporary nursery workers, teachers, and carers—what unites them is the choice to orientate outward and live in the pattern of Christ—embracing an integrally humanizing gospel.

Peter started his journey seeing the world bleeding out, shot through with pain. That makes sense in a world ripped at the seams and is the reason why this hurts, why it makes us so furious. It is precisely because of this, not in spite of it, that he ends it changed and empowered to make pockets of heaven, like when he shares bread with the man in the former Yugoslavia. This reflects those quiet, holy moments that I have seen in the lives of others, often in unglamorous places, too precious and profound to share. These dark moments are where the gospel really shines.

Presently, there is a very real tension in "the now and not yet." But in Jesus, we don't grieve without hope or live without purpose. This is not an ignorant rejection of reality but an intimately connected, radical defiance acquainted with both death and life.

We all know the brush of death. But do you know life?

Jesus came for the life of the world.

THE END

Bibliography

Améry, Jean. *At the Mind's Limits*. New York: Schocken, 1986.

Aragon, Louis. "Les Lilas et Les Roses," *The Poem Itself: 150 of the Finest Modern Poets in the Original Languages*, edited by Stanley Burnshaw et al., 98–101. Fayetteville, North Carolina: University of Arkansas Press, 1995.

Arendt, Hannah. *Eichmann in Jerusalem: A Report on the Banality of Evil*. New York: Penguin Classics, 2006.

Aron, Raymond. *The Opium of the Intellectuals*. New Brunswick, New Jersey: Transaction, 2001.

Aronson, Ronald. *Camus and Sartre: The Story of a Friendship and the Quarrel That Ended It*. Chicago: University of Chicago Press, 2004.

Athanasius, St. *On the Incarnation*, trans. Penelope Lawson. Crestwood, New York: St. Vladimir's Seminary Press, 1998.

Augustine. *Confessions*. Translated by Henry Chadwick. Oxford: Oxford University Press, 2008.

Baumgardt, Carola, and Jamie Callan. *Johannes Kepler: Life and Letters*. London: Victor Gollancz, 1952.

Beauvoir, Simone de. *The Blood of Others*. Translated by Yvonne Moyse and Roger Senhouse. New York: Knopf, 1948.

———. "Manifesto of the 343." *Nouvel Observateur*, Apr. 5, 1971.

———. *The Prime of Life*. Translated by Peter Green. London: Penguin, 1965.

Bellos, David. "Introduction." In Albert Camus, *The Plague, The Fall, Exile and the Kingdom, and Selected Essays*, ix–xxvi. Everyman's Library. New York: Knopf, 2004.

Bernier, Olivier. *Fireworks at Dusk: Paris in the Thirties*. Boston: Little Brown & Co., 1993.

Blamires, Cyprian. *World Fascism: A Historical Encyclopedia*. New York: Bloomsbury USA, 2006.

Brother Andrew. *God's Smuggler*. Translated by John Sherrill and Elizabeth Sherrill. Grand Rapids: Revell, 1967.

Brouwer, L. E. J. *Collected Works, Volume 1: Philosophy and Foundations of Mathematics*. Edited by A. Heyting. Amsterdam: North Holland, 2014.

Budiansky, Stephen. *Journey to the Edge of Reason: The Life of Kurt Gödel*. New York: Norton, 2022.

Camus, Albert. *Camus at Combat: Writing 1944–1947*. Edited by Jacqueline Lévi-Valensi. Translated by Arthur Goldhammer. Princeton, NJ: Princeton University Press, 2007.

———. *Christian Metaphysics and Neoplatonism*. Translated by Ronald D. Srigley. Columbia: University of Missouri Press, 2007.

———. *The Fall*. Translated by Justin O'Brien. New York: Knopf, 1958.

———. *The Myth of Sisyphus*. Translated by Justin O'Brien. New York: Vintage, 1955.

———. *Notebooks 1942–1951*. Translated by Justin O'Brien. New York: Marlowe, 1998.

———. *The Plague*. Translated by Stuart Gilbert. In *The Plague, The Fall, Exile and the Kingdom, and Selected Essays*, 1–272. Everyman's Library. New York: Knopf, 2004.

———. *The Rebel: An Essay on Man in Revolt*. Translated by Anthony Bower. New York, New York: Vintage Books, 1991.

———. "The Unbeliever and Christians." In *Resistance, Rebellion, and Death: Essays*, 67–74. New York: Vintage, 1995.

Churchill, Winston. "We Shall Fight on the Beaches." *Hansard*, Jun. 4, 1940.

———. *The Second World War, Vol. 3: Their Finest Hour*. Boston: Houghton Mifflin, 1949.

Cockayne, Joshua, et al. *Dawn of Sunday: The Trinity and Trauma-Safe Churches*. Eugene, Oregon: Wipf and Stock, 2022.

Cocteau, Jean, dir. *La Belle et la Bête*. Paris: DisCina, 1946.

Cook, John Granger. *Empty Tomb, Resurrection, Apotheosis*. Wissenschaftliche Untersuchungen zum Neuen Testament 410. Tübingen: Mohr Siebeck, 2018.

Correll, John T. "The Moon Squadrons." *Air & Space Forces Magazine*, Jul. 1, 2012. https://www.airandspaceforces.com/article/0712moon/.

Craig, William Lane. "Religious Epistemology." Bethinking. https://www.bethinking.org/truth/religious-epistemology.

———. "William Lane Craig on Logical Positivism." YouTube video, Jul. 10, 2009. https://www.youtube.com/watch?v=URknwFd2n7g.

Dalton, Hugh. *The Second World War Diary of Hugh Dalton, 1940-45*. London: Jonathan Cape, 1986.

Dante Alighieri. *The Divine Comedy*. Translated by Mark Musa. In *The Portable Dante*, edited by Mark Musa, 1–586. New York: Penguin, 1995.

De Lubac, Henri. *The Drama of Atheist Humanism*. Translated by Mark Sebanc. Revised ed. San Francisco: Ignatius, 1995.

Deleuze, Gilles. *Difference and Repetition*. Translated by Paul Patton. New York: Columbia University Press, 1995.

———. *Nietzsche and Philosophy*. Translated by Hugh Tomlinson. New York: Columbia University Press, 1983.

———. *Pure Immanence: Essays on a Life*. Translated by Anne Boyman. Brooklyn: Zone Books, 2001.

———., and Claire Parnet. *Dialogues II*. Translated by Hugh Tomlinson, Barbara Habberjam, and Eliot Ross Albert. London: Continuum, 2006.

———., and Félix Guattari. *What is Philosophy?* Translated by Janis Tomlinson and Graham Burchell III. New York: Columbia University Press, 1996.

Derrida, Jacques. *Specters of Marx: The State of the Debt, the Work of Mourning, and the New International*. Translated by Peggy Kamuf. New York: Routledge, 1994.

Descartes, René. *Meditations, Objections, and Replies*. Edited by Roger Ariew. Translated by Donald A. Cress. Indianapolis: Hackett, 2006.

Desmond, Edward W. "Interview with Mother Teresa: A Pencil in the Hand of God." *Time*, Dec. 4, 1989. https://time.com/archive/6703981/interview-with-mother-teresa-a-pencil-in-the-hand-of-god/.

Dirckx, Sharon. *Am I Just My Brain?* Epsom, UK: Good Book Company, 2019.

Dodgson, Charles L. *Euclid and His Modern Rivals.* London: Macmillan and Co., 1879.

Dosse, François. *Gilles Deleuze/Félix Guattari: Biographie croisée.* Paris: Découverte, 2007.

Duffy, Carol Ann. "Mrs. Icarus." In *The World's Wife*, 54. Reprint ed. London: Faber & Faber, 2001.

Eikelboom, Lexi. *Rhythm: A Theological Category.* Oxford: Oxford University Press, 2018.

————. "Rhythmic Eschatology." In *Game Over?*, edited by Christophe Chalamet, et al. Berlin: de Gruyter, 2017.

Evans, Craig A. "Mark's Incipit and the Priene Calendar Inscription: From Jewish Gospel to Greco-Roman Gospel." *Journal of Greco-Roman Christianity and Judaism* 1 (2000) 69–81.

Fackler, Guido. "Music in Concentration Camps 1933–1945." Translated by Peter Logan. *Music and Politics* 1 (Jun. 1, 2007) 1–86. https://doi.org/10.3998/mp.9460 447.0001.102.

Fanon, Frantz. *Black Skin, White Masks.* London: Pluto Press, 1967.

Feferman, Solomon. "Provenly Unprovable." *London Review of Books*, Feb. 9, 2006.

Feuerbach, Ludwig. *The Essence of Christianity.* Translated by Marian Evans [George Eliot]. Cambridge: Cambridge University Press, 2011.

Fondation Anne de Gaulle. "Paris Anne de Gaulle." YouTube vídeo, Jun. 23, 2023. https://www.youtube.com/watch?v=PAfFlMA-Q7E.

Fondazione Monte Verità. "History of Monte Verità Ascona." https://www.monteverita. org/en/monte-verita/history.

Fosl, Peter S., and Julian Baggini. *The Philosopher's Toolkit.* 3rd ed. Hoboken, : Wiley, 2020.

Foucault, Michel. "Interview with Michel Foucault." Interview conducted by D. Trombadori, 1978. In *Michel Foucault. Essential Works of Foucault 1954–1984, Vol. 3: Power*, edited by James D. Faubion, translated by Robert Hurley and others, 239–98. New York: New Press, 2000. Series edited by Paul Rabinow.

————. "On the Genealogy of Ethics: An Overview of Work in Progress." In *Essential Works of Foucault 1954–1984, Vol. 1: Ethics: Subjectivity and Truth*, edited by Paul Rabinow, translated by Robert Hurley et al., 253–80. New York: The New Press, 1997.

————. *The Order of Things: An Archaeology of the Human Sciences.* Routledge, 2002.

Fourcade, Marie-Madeleine. *Noah's Ark.* Translated by Kenneth Morgan. New York: Dutton & Company, 1974.

Frege, Gottlob. *Grundgesetze der Arithmetik, vol. 2.* Jena, Germany: Hermann Pohle, 1903. Appendix.

Fuchs, Thomas. "Melancholia as a Desynchronization." *Psychopathology* 4 (2001) 179–86.

Fukuyama, Francis. *The End of History and the Last Man.* New York: Free Press, 1992.

Gandhi, M. K. *An Autobiography: The Story of My Experiments with Truth*, translated by Mahadev Desai, series edited by Shriman Narayan, 16–20. Ahmedabad, India: Navajivan, n.d. https://www.mkgandhi.org/ebks/An-Autobiography.pdf.

Gaulle, Charles de. *Discours et Messages, 1940–1946*. Paris: Berger–Levrault, 1946.

———. *The Complete War Memoirs of Charles de Gaulle: The Call to Honour 1940–1942*. Translated by Jonathan Griffin. Vol. 1. New York: Simon and Schuster, 1968.

Gilmour, David Jon. "A Great Day for Freedom." Track 5 on *The Division Bell*. Pink Floyd Music. EMI Records, 1994. CD.

Goodrick-Clarke, Nicholas. *The Occult Roots of Nazism: Secret Aryan Cults and Their Influence on Nazi Ideology*. New York: New York University Press, 1992.

Gödel, Kurt. "The Modern Development of the Foundations of Mathematics in the Light of Philosophy." In *Kurt Gödel: Collected Works: Volume III: Unpublished Essays and Lectures*, edited by Solomon Feferman et al., 375–87. New York: Oxford University Press, 1995.

———. "Some Basic Theorems on the Foundations of Mathematics and Their Implications." In *Kurt Gödel: Collected Works: Volume III: Unpublished Essays and Lectures*, edited by Solomon Feferman et al., 304–23. New York: Oxford University Press, 1995.

Grayling, A. C. *Descartes: The Life and Times of a Genius*. New York: Walker & Co., 2006.

Green, Martin. *Mountain of Truth: The Counterculture Begins, Ascona, 1900–1920*. Hanover, NH: University Press of New England, 1986.

Grynberg, Michal, ed. *Words to Outlive Us: Voices from the Warsaw Ghetto*. London: Granta, 2003.

Gumbel, Nicky. "How Can I Resist Evil?" *Alpha Course*, Episode 8. Holy Trinity Brompton and Alpha International, 2016.

Gutting, Gary. *Thinking the Impossible: French Philosophy Since 1960*. Oxford: Oxford University Press, 2013.

Harriman, K. R. "Early Christian Responses to Purported Miracles." June 23, 2024. https://krharriman.substack.com/p/early-christian-responses-to-purported.

Hart, David Bentley. *The Doors of the Sea: Where Was God in the Tsunami?* Grand Rapids: Eerdmans, 2011.

Hawking, Stephen. "Gödel and the End of Physics." Lecture presented at the Dirac Centennial, University of Cambridge, Oct. 3, 2003. https://www.damtp.cam.ac.uk/events/strings02/dirac/hawking.html.

———. *The Theory of Everything: The Origin and Fate of the Universe*. Beverly Hills, CA: New Millennium, 2002.

Hawkins, Ann. *The Early Novels of Benjamin Disraeli*. New York: Taylor & Francis, 2024.

Heidegger, Martin. *Being and Time*. Translated by Joan Stambaugh. Albany, NY: State University of New York Press, 1996.

Herman, Judith Lewis. *Trauma and Recovery: The Aftermath of Violence—From Domestic Abuse to Political Terror*. New York: Basic Books, 2015.

Henry, Michel. *Barbarism*. London: Bloomsbury, 2012.

Hilbert, David. "Address to the Mathematical Society of Westphalia." Münster, Germany, Jun. 4, 1925.

———. "Naturerkennen und Logik." Translated by James T. Smith. https://old.maa.org/press/periodicals/convergence/david-hilberts-radio-address-english-translation.

Hoinski, David, and Ronald Polansky. "The Modern Aristotle." In *Contemporary Encounters with Ancient Metaphysics*, edited by Abraham Jacob Greenstine, 180–201. Edinburgh: Edinburgh University Press, 2017.

Horkheimer, Max, and Theodor W. Adorno. *The Dialectic of Enlightenment*. Stanford, California: Stanford University Press, 2002.

Hughes, Virginia. "The Tragic Story of How Einstein's Brain Was Stolen and Wasn't Even Special." *National Geographic*, Apr. 21, 2014. https://www.nationalgeographic.com/premium/article/the-tragic-story-of-how-einsteins-brain-was-stolen-and-wasnt-even-special.

Humbert, Agnès. *Résistance: A Woman's Journal of Struggle and Defiance in Occupied France*. New York: Bloomsbury, 2008.

International Committee of the Red Cross. "Remembering Nine ICRC Employees Killed 20 Years Ago in Srebrenica." Jul. 9, 2015. https://www.icrc.org/en/document/remembering-nine-icrc-employees-killed-20-years-ago-srebrenica

Jackson, Julian. *A Certain Idea of France: The Life of Charles de Gaulle*. London: Penguin, 2018.

Janicaud, Dominique, and Jean Francois Coutine. *Phenomenology and the Theological Turn: The French Debate*. New York: Fordham University Press, 2001.

Joyce, James. *Finnegans Wake*. London: Faber and Faber, 1939.

Kerr, Fergus. "A Different World: Neoscholasticism and its Discontents." *International Journal of Systematic Theology* 2 (2006).

Kierkegaard, Søren. *The Concept of Anxiety: A Simple Psychologically Oriented Deliberation in View of the Dogmatic Problem of Hereditary Sin*. Translated and edited by Alastair Hannay. New York: Norton, 2014.

———. *Eighteen Upbuilding Discourses*. Translated and edited by Howard Hong and Edna Hong. Princeton, NJ: Princeton University Press, 1990.

———. *The Sickness unto Death*. Translated by Alastair Hannay. London: Penguin, 2004.

Kirkpatrick, Kate. *Sartre and Theology*. London: T&T Clark. 2017.

Koestler, Arthur. *Scum of the Earth*. London: Jonathan Cape, 1941.

Korn, Leslie E. *Rhythms of Recovery: Trauma, Nature, and the Body*. New York: Routledge, 2021.

Kremer, William. "The Strange Afterlife of Einstein's Brain." BBC World Service, Apr. 17, 2015. https://www.bbc.com/news/magazine-32354300.

Lacouture, Jean. *De Gaulle: The Rebel 1890-1944*. Translated by Alan Sheridan. New York: Norton, 1993.

Lasch, Christopher. *The True and Only Heaven: Progress and Its Critics*. New York: Norton, 1991.

Lennox, John. *Can Science Explain Everything?* Epsom, UK: Good Book Company, 2019.

Levi, Primo. *If This Is a Man*. Translated by S. J. Woolf. London: Folio Society, 2000.

Levinas, Emmanuel. *Otherwise than Being or Beyond Essence*. Translated by Alphonso Lingis. Pittsburgh: Duquesne University Press, 1998.

Levinas, Emmanuel, and Philippe Nemo. *Ethics and Infinity*. Translated by Richard A. Cohen. Pittsburgh: Duquesne University Press, 1985.

Levy, Bernard-Henri. *Sartre: The Philosopher of the Twentieth Century*. 1st ed. Cambridge, UK: Polity, 2003.

Levy, Steven. "My Search for Einstein's Brain." *New Jersey Monthly*, Aug. 1978. https://njmonthly.com/articles/historic-jersey/the-search-for-einsteins-brain.

Lewis, C. S. *A Grief Observed*. London: Faber & Faber, 1961.

————. "Myth Became Fact." In *God in the Dock: Essays on Theology and Ethics*, edited by Walter Hooper, 63–67. Grand Rapids, Michigan: Eerdmans, 1970.

Lincoln, Bruce. *Theorizing Myth: Narrative, Ideology, and Scholarship*. Chicago: University of Chicago Press, 1999.

Lokhorst, Gert-Jan. "Descartes and the Pineal Gland." In *The Stanford Encyclopedia of Philosophy*, edited by Edward N. Zalta. Published Apr. 25, 2005; substantive revision Sep. 18, 2013. https://plato.stanford.edu/archives/win2021/entries/pineal-gland/.

Lovell, Stanley P. *Of Spies & Stratagems*. Englewood Cliffs, New Jersey: Prentice-Hall, 1963.

Lucas, J. R. "Minds, Machines and Gödel." *Philosophy* 137 (Apr. 1961) 112–27.

Lunacharsky, Anatoly. *On Education*. Translated by Ruth English. Moscow: Progress, 1981.

————. *Religion and Socialism*. 2 vols. St. Petersburg: Spovnik, 1908–11.

Luther, Martin. *Lectures on Romans*. Edited by Hilton C. Oswald. Translated by Walter G. Tillmanns and Jacob A. O. Preus. Vol. 25. Luther's Works: The American Edition. St. Louis: Concordia Publishing House, 1972.

Lyotard, Jean-François. *The Postmodern Condition: A Report on Knowledge*. Translated by Geoff Bennington and Brian Massumi. Minneapolis: University of Minnesota Press, 1984.

MacIntyre, Alasdair. *After Virtue: A Study in Moral Theory*. London: Gerald Duckworth & Co., 1981.

Marcel, Gabriel. *Homo Viator: Introduction to a Metaphysic of Hope*. London: Victor Gollancz, 1951.

————. *Metaphysical Journal*. Chicago: H. Regnery, 1952.

————. *The Mystery of Being, Volume II: Faith and Reality*. South Bend, Indiana: St. Augustine's, 2001.

————. *The Philosophy of Existentialism*. Translated by Manya Harari. New York: Citadel, 1991.

Marion, Jean-Luc. *The Idol and Distance: Five Studies*. Translated by Thomas A. Carlson. New York: Fordham University Press, 2001.

Marling, William. "Coca-colonization." *American Quarterly* 4 (1996) 731-39.

Malraux, André. *Le Triangle Noir*. Paris: Gallimard, 1970.

Marx, Karl. *Critique of Hegel's Philosophy of Right*. Translated by Joseph O'Malley. Wiltshire, UK: Cambridge University Press, 1970.

Mathewes, Charles T. *Evil and the Augustinian Tradition*. Cambridge: Cambridge University Press, 2001.

Megill, Jason. "Lucas-Penrose Argument About Gödel's Theorem." *Internet Encyclopedia of Philosophy*. https://iep.utm.edu/lp-argue/.

Merleau-Ponty, Maurice. *Adventures of the Dialectic*. Translated by Joseph Bien. Evanston, IL: Northwestern University Press, 1973.

————. *Humanisme et terreur: Essai sur le problème communiste*. Paris: Gallimard, 1947.

Mettinger, Tryggve N. D. "The 'Dying and Rising God': A Survey of Research from Frazer to the Present Day." In *David and Zion: Biblical Studies in Honor of J. J. M. Roberts*, edited by Bernardo F. Bato and Kathryn L. Roberts, 373–86. Winona Lake, Indiana: Eisenbrauns, 2004.

Michelangelo. *The Complete Poems of Michelangelo*. Translated by John Frederick. Chicago: University of Chicago Press, 1998.

Michon, Pascal. *Marcel Mauss Retrouvé: Origines de l'Anthropologie du Rythme*. Paris: Rhuthmos, 2015.

Milbank, John. *Being Reconciled: Ontology and Pardon*. London: Taylor & Francis, 2003.

———. *Theology and Social Theory: Beyond Secular Reason*. Oxford: Blackwell, 1993.

Milbank, John, and Slavoj Žižek. *The Monstrosity of Christ: Paradox or Dialectic?* Edited by Creston Davis. Cambridge, Massachusetts: MIT Press, 2011.

Moltmann, Jürgen. *The Crucified God*. London: SCM, 1974.

———. *Jesus Christ for Today's World*. Translated by Margaret Kohl. Minneapolis: Fortress, 1995.

Murdoch, Iris. *Sartre: Romantic Rationalist*. New Haven: Yale University Press, 1965.

Music and the Holocaust. "Natzweiler." https://holocaustmusic.ort.org/places/camps/central-europe/natzweiler/.

Musurillo, Herbert Anthony. "The Martyrdom of Perpetua and Felicitas," in The Acts of the Christian Martyrs, edited and translated by Herbert Anthony Musurillo, 106–31. Oxford: Clarendon Press, 1972.

Neiman, Susan. *Evil in Modern Thought: An Alternative History of Philosophy*. 1st Princeton Classic edition. Princeton, New Jersey: Princeton University Press, 2015.

Nietzsche, Friedrich. *Beyond Good and Evil*. Translated by Walter Kaufmann. New York: Vintage, 1966.

———. *The Birth of Tragedy*. Translated by Walter Kaufmann. New York: Vintage, 1967.

———. *Ecce Homo*. Translated by Anthony M. Ludovici. New York: Dover, 2012.

———. *The Gay Science*. Translated by Walter Kaufman. New York: Random House, 1974.

———. *Thus Spoke Zarathustra*. In *The Portable Nietzsche*, translated by Walter Kaufmann. New York: Penguin Classics, 1977.

Ortlund, Gavin. "A Baptist Case for Real Presence in the Eucharist." YouTube, Jan. 16, 2023. https://www.youtube.com/watch?v=qGIRjz5qSpA.

Pacini, David S. *Through Narcissus' Glass Darkly: The Modern Religion of Conscience*. New York: Fordham University Press, 2008.

Pascal, Blaise. *Pensées*. Translated by A.J. Krailsheimer. Reading, UK: Penguin, 1966.

Patel, Rahil. *Found by Love: A Hindu Priest Encounters Jesus Christ*. London: Instant Apostle, 2016.

Penrose, Roger. *The Emperor's New Mind: Concerning Computers, Minds, and the Laws of Physics*. Oxford: Oxford University Press, 1989.

———. *Shadows of the Mind: A Search for the Missing Science of Consciousness*. Oxford: Oxford University Press, 1994.

Peterson, Jordan B. *We Who Wrestle with God: Perceptions of the Divine*. New York: Random House, 2023.

Polanyi, Michael. *Beyond Nihilism*. Cambridge: Cambridge University Press, 1960.

———. "Why Did We Destroy Europe?" In *Society, Economics & Philosophy: Selected Papers*, edited by R. T. Allen, 107–15. New Brunswick, New Jersey: Transaction, 1997.

Polanyi, Michael, and Harry Prosch. *Meaning.* Chicago: University of Chicago Press, 1975.

Pursell, Brennan. *Benedict of Bavaria: An Intimate Portrait of the Pope and His Homeland.* North Haven, Connecticut: Circle, 2008.

Rambo, Shelley. *Spirit and Trauma.* Louisville: Westminster John Knox, 2010.

———. *Resurrecting Wounds: Living in the Afterlife of Trauma.* Waco, Texas: Baylor University Press, 2017.

Reid, Constance. *Hilbert.* New York: Copernicus, 1996.

Ricœur, Paul. *Figuring the Sacred: Religion, Narrative, and Imagination.* Translated by David Pellauer and Mark I. Wallace. Minneapolis: Fortress, 1995.

———. *Freud and Philosophy: An Essay on Interpretation.* Translated by Denis Savage. The Terry Lectures. New Haven: Yale University Press, 1970.

———. *Time and Narrative, Volume 3.* Translated by Kathleen Blamey and David Pellauer. Chicago: University of Chicago Press, 1990.

Robinson, Marilynne. *Absence of Mind.* New Haven: Yale University Press, 2011.

Rousso, Henry, and Stanley Hoffmann. *The Vichy Syndrome: History and Memory in France Since 1944.* Translated by Arthur Goldhammer. Revised ed. Cambridge, MA: Harvard University Press, 1994.

Russell, Bertrand. "Am I an Atheist or an Agnostic?: A Plea for Tolerance in the Face of New Dogmas." http://www.positiveatheism.org/hist/russell8.htm.

———. *The Autobiography of Bertrand Russell.* London: Routledge, 1998.

———. *History of Western Philosophy.* London: Routledge, 2004.

———. *My Philosophical Development.* London: Routledge, 1995.

Sartre, Jean-Paul. *Being and Nothingness.* Translated by Hazel Barnes. London: Routledge, 2003.

———. *Colonialism and Neocolonialism.* Abingdon, UK: Routledge, 2006.

———. *Existentialism Is a Humanism.* Edited by John Kulka. Translated by Carol Macomber. New Haven: Yale University Press, 2007.

———. *No Exit.* New York: Vintage, 1955.

———. *Politique et autobiographie, Situations, X.* Paris: Gallimard, 1976.

———. *War Diaries of Jean-Paul Sartre: November 1939–March 1940.* Translated by Quintin Hoare. New York: Pantheon, 1984.

Schaeffer, Francis. *The God Who Is There.* Downers Grove, IL: InterVarsity Press, 1968.

Scheips, Charlie. *Elsie de Wolfe's Paris: Frivolity Before the Storm.* New York: Abrams, 2014.

Schnitker, Harry. "The French Catholic Church from 1940 to 1945." Catholic News Agency. https://www.catholicnewsagency.com/column/51668/the-french-catholic-church-from-1940-to-1945.

Schulz, Eric, and Claus Wischmann, dir. *Max Lorenz: Wagner's Mastersinger—Hitler's Siegfried.* Documentary. EuroArts, 2009. https://www.youtube.com/watch?v=oQKmK9EUAjc.

Scrivener, Glen. "What Christians Believe . . . in 90 Seconds!" Premier On Demand. YouTube video, Dec. 6, 2017. https://www.youtube.com/watch?v=uOjTFQd8hl4.

Searle, John R. "Minds, Brains, and Programs." *Behavioral and Brain Sciences* 3 (Sep. 1980) 417–24.

Shorto, Russell. *Descartes' Bones: A Skeletal History of the Conflict Between Faith and Reason.* New York: Knopf Doubleday, 2008.

Simpson, Christopher Ben. *Deleuze and Theology*. London: Bloomsbury T&T Clark, 2012.

Snapper, Ernst. "The Three Crises in Mathematics: Logicism, Intuitionism, and Formalism." *Mathematics Magazine* 4 (1979) 207–16.

Solzhenitsyn, Aleksandr. *The Gulag Archipelago, Volume 1*. Translated by Thomas P. Whitney. New York: Harper Collins, 2020.

———. *One Day in the Life of Ivan Denisovich*. London: Vintage, 2003.

Spears, Edward. *Assignment to Catastrophe*. London: Heinemann, 1954.

Spotts, Frederic. *Hitler and the Power of Aesthetics*. London: Pimlico, 2003.

Spurgeon, Charles H. "Communion with Christ and His People." https://www.spurgeongems.org/sermon/chs3295.pdf.

Srigley, Ronald D. "Introduction." In *Christian Metaphysics and Neoplatonism* by Albert Camus, 1–35. Translated by Ronald D. Srigley. Columbia: University of Missouri Press, 2007.

Steiger, Andrew W. "A Critical Exploration and Theological Critique of Michael Polanyi's Structured Ontology." PhD diss., University of Aberdeen, 2021.

Suttel, René. *Catacombes et carrières de Paris: Promenade sous la capitale*. Paris: Sehdacs, 1986.

Tannery, Claude. *Malraux, The Absolute Agnostic; Or, Metamorphosis as Universal Law*. Chicago: University of Chicago Press, 1991.

Teresa, Mother. *A Simple Path*. New York: Ballantine, 1995.

Tillich, Paul. *The Courage to Be*. New Haven: Yale University Press, 1952.

———. *Systematic Theology, Volume 1: Reason and Revelation; Being and God*. Chicago: University of Chicago Press, 1951.

Tolstoy, Leo. *The Kingdom of God Is Within You*. Translated by Constance Garnett. London: Cassell, 1894.

Trueman, Carl R. *The Rise and Triumph of the Modern Self: Cultural Amnesia, Expressive Individualism, and the Road to Sexual Revolution*. Wheaton, IL: Crossway, 2020.

United States Holocaust Memorial Museum. "Books Burn as Goebbels Speaks." Holocaust Encyclopedia. https://encyclopedia.ushmm.org/content/en/film/books-burn-as-goebbels-speaks.

———. "Srebrenica 1993–1995." https://www.ushmm.org/genocide-prevention/countries/bosnia-herzegovina/srebrenica-1993.

University of Michigan. "Die schönste Zeit des Lebens: Rare Music Manuscript from Auschwitz." 2018. https://www.youtube.com/watch?v=ok6UI472B1I.

Van Dalen, Dirk. *L. E. J. Brouwer—Topologist, Intuitionist, Philosopher: How Mathematics Is Rooted in Life*. London: Springer-Verlag, 2013.

Van der Kolk, Bessel. *The Body Keeps the Score: Brain, Mind, and Body in the Healing of Trauma*. New York: Viking, 2014.

Van Heijenoort, Jean. *From Frege to Gödel: A Source Book in Mathematical Logic, 1879–1931*. Cambridge, MA: Harvard University Press, 1967.

Vian, Boris. *Froth on the Daydream*. Translated by Stanley Chapman. Harmondsworth, UK: Penguin, 1970.

Volf, Miroslav. *Exclusion and Embrace: A Theological Exploration of Identity, Otherness, and Reconciliation*. Nashville: Abingdon, 1996.

Wang, Hao. *Reflections on Kurt Gödel*. Revised ed. Cambridge, MA: Bradford, 1990.

Watson, Peter. *The Age of Atheists: How We Have Sought to Live Since the Death of God.* New York: Simon & Schuster, 2014.

Weikart, Richard. *Hitler's Religion: The Twisted Beliefs That Drove the Third Reich.* Washington, D.C.: Regnery History, 2016.

Whitehead, Alfred North. *Nature and Life.* London: Cambridge University Press, 1934.

Wittgenstein, Ludwig. *On Certainty.* Edited by G. E. M. Anscombe and G. H. von Wright. Translated by Denis Paul. New York: Harper & Row, 1972.

Wojtyła, Karol. "Participation or Alienation?" *Analecta Husserliana* 6 (1977) 61–73.

Wright, N. T. *The Day the Revolution Began: Reconsidering the Meaning of Jesus's Crucifixion.* New York: HarperOne, 2018.

———. *Simply Jesus.* New York: HarperOne, 2011.

———. *The Resurrection of the Son of God.* Vol. 3 of *Christian Origins and the Question of God.* Minneapolis, Minnesota: Fortress, 2003.

———. "What Is the Gospel?" N. T. Wright Online. YouTube video, Dec. 2, 2022. https://www.youtube.com/watch?v=jioXgjPumVI.

Yannaras, Christos. *On the Absence and Unknowability of God: Heidegger and the Areopagite.* Edited by Andrew Louth. Translated by Haralambos Ventis. 2nd ed. London: Bloomsbury T&T Clark, 2007.

Yourgrau, Palle. *A World Without Time: The Forgotten Legacy of Gödel and Einstein.* New York: Basic, 2009.

Zizioulas, John D. *Being as Communion.* Crestwood, New York: St. Vladimir's Seminary Press, 1985.

Index

www.ingramcontent.com/pod-product-compliance
Lightning Source LLC
Chambersburg PA
CBHW060303100726
47907CB00002B/261